GO TO HELL

THE TAMSYN WEBB CHRONICLES #2

JASON FISCHER

aRgOnautica
pRess

Argonautica Press
PO Box 481
Ashburton, VIC 3147
Australia
www.argonauticapress.com

Cover by Powdermonkey Design
First edition 2021

ISBN:
978-0-6484787-6-8 (paperback)
978-0-6484787-7-5 (ebook)

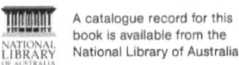 A catalogue record for this book is available from the National Library of Australia

Copyright © 2021 by Jason Fischer

All rights reserved.

No part of this book may be reproduced in any form or by any electronic or mechanical means, including information storage and retrieval systems, without written permission from the author, except for the use of brief quotations in a book review.

GO TO HELL

For Kate, Logan and Lottie, my everything

CONTENTS

Chapter 1	1
Chapter 2	17
Chapter 3	31
Chapter 4	41
Chapter 5	53
Chapter 6	65
Chapter 7	79
Chapter 8	87
Chapter 9	101
Chapter 10	119
Chapter 11	139
Chapter 12	151
Chapter 13	163
Chapter 14	173
Chapter 15	185
Chapter 16	197
Chapter 17	209
Chapter 18	227
Chapter 19	245
Chapter 20	265
Chapter 21	277
Chapter 22	289
Chapter 23	305
Chapter 24	319
Chapter 25	333
Chapter 26	347
Chapter 27	361
Chapter 28	377
Chapter 29	391
Chapter 30	405
Chapter 31	419
Chapter 32	433

Coming Soon	451
Excerpt From The Tamsyn Webb Chronicles #3 - Dead Last	453
About the Author	469
Other Books By Jason Fischer	471
Acknowledgments	473

1

"Who here has killed someone?"

Tamsyn was dressed in a black vest and fatigue pants, hair pulled back into a severe pony-tail. Dozens of soldiers and sailors stood before her, at ease, and she recognised the quiet contempt. She was the civilian "expert" brought in to tell the military how to do their job.

A lifetime ago, she'd worn a uniform too. She'd killed her share of people too, far too many to bear thinking about. Tamsyn Webb was not quite twenty-one years old, and she carried her past like a sack full of rocks.

"I asked a question. Who here has ended the life of a human being by force?"

Half a dozen people raised their hands. She pointed to the nearest, a commando twice her size. He was a tough looking customer, face marked by a jagged scar. The man was all muscles and when he looked at her, his lip curled up slightly.

"You. Tell me who you killed, and why."

"I shot five Taliban when they hit our convoy near Logar.

A roadside bomb took out our vehicle, killed the driver. I was the only one able to return fire."

"How did you kill them?" Tamsyn said, and she got right into his personal space.

"Machine gun mounted up top. Sent twenty of those bastards running for their lives. Five confirmed kills."

"Machine gun. Hmm," Tamsyn said, not breaking eye contact. "So, Mr. Afghanistan, have you fought any zombies?"

"No," the man said, the sneer visibly falling from his face. Tamsyn stepped back, looking over the group.

"Anyone? Anyone here fight a zombie? No?"

She let the group chew on that for a moment, and then continued.

"You are the luckiest bastards on the face of the planet," she said. "Out there? It all went to hell. 99% of the human race, wiped out. Not just killed either. Attacked by people who were dead. Corpses, moving and trying to eat you alive. It is bloody scary."

She saw it then, washing across their faces. Survivor guilt, writ large. These leftovers of the Royal Navy had seen out the entire outbreak at the Cayman Islands, turning boats away at gunpoint. Three years in hiding, never once in danger.

"You haven't seen them. You're all soft. If a zombie came at you, all your training, your tough guy bullshit? It's all useless. You will panic, and you will die."

She gestured behind her at the training ground. The Royal Cayman Police Force had a paramilitary arm, and they'd set up an urban assault course for the British military, the type where people could kick in doors and rescue hostages.

"I have fought a lot of zombies. So, I'm here to give you

my expertise in surviving an attack. I want you six to come forward, the ones who put their hands up earlier. Everyone, muffs on please, this is a live fire exercise."

The marines and commandos stood at the spray-painted line, readying their assault rifles. In the distance was a bullet-pocked shopfront, glassless windows facing the group.

"You know how this goes. Kill the bad guys, spare the hostages. Okay Paul, hit the switch please."

Cardboard targets started to appear in the doorways and windows, rapidly appearing and disappearing. The six shooters peppered the targets with ease, shooting cartoon zombies that lurched out, hands stretched into claws, mouths open. Expert shots, tight groupings on the head like they'd been told, and they spared the token "survivor" who leapt out.

Tamsyn waited until the all clear, and then gave a slow, sarcastic clap.

"Yep, you nailed 'em. Alright killers, we're going onto the next part of the course. This one is where you meatheads get to boot the doors in, and clear a building like you're playing Call of Duty. Except I'm going to raise the difficulty level."

She handed out a bunch of random pistols, in various states of disrepair. The veteran she'd mocked before checked the clip, eyebrows raised when he noticed it was half-empty.

"Leave the big guns here. Out there in the real world, you dropped them days ago. You're hungry and scared, and you're down to a handful of bullets, your combat knives, and then your bare hands. Now, imagine that you have a horde of walking corpses closing in on you. I'm talking tens of thousands, maybe a hundred thousand zombies, and they've cut you off. The only way you are going to live is if you get through this building."

Tamsyn gave a signal to the control tower, and a recording started playing through the loudspeakers. A low moaning, rising from thousands of rotten throats, cribbed from every horror movie Tamsyn could get her hands on. It started off low, but grew in volume until Tamsyn had to shout to be heard. All the swagger from her volunteers was gone now, and they stood with their pistols in hand, trying not to look rattled.

"All you have to do is get through that building in one piece," she said. "In fact, don't even bother engaging with the targets. Go!"

They set off at a slow advance, approaching the assault course by rote. Tamsyn started screaming at them through a megaphone.

"You don't have time for this fancy bullshit! Ten thousand zombies are right behind you! Enter the building now!"

The first marine kicked in the front door, and they poured in, yelling as they cleared the first room, and then they started crying out, all discipline gone. Tamsyn heard a pistol shot, and then someone screaming. In no time flat the group had broken through the back door, and one marine fell to his knees, retching onto the ground. The big veteran from Afghanistan came storming over to Tamsyn, red with fury.

"Goddamn sicko," he screamed into her face. "I should kill you."

"You need to wake up, mate," she said, perfectly calm. "What's in there is your world now. If you can't deal with that, then yes, you are going to die."

Something in her eyes broke through the man's anger, and he backed away, shaking his head.

It had taken a little doing, but Tamsyn had gotten approval from the island's Coroner to exhume several fresh corpses from the town cemetery. The bodies were strapped into remote-control dollies. The moment anyone entered that part of the course, actual dead meat came at them, stinking and awful. Death, up close and personal.

"Next six volunteers, you are up," she shouted, tipping out a big bag of pistols. "No-one goes home till you all go through that door."

Over the loudspeakers, the undead horde cried out for living flesh, and the men and women in uniform turned pale.

A BUS CAME for the marines, who slunk up the steps, robbed of all bravado. Tamsyn watched them leave the training compound, giving them a cheery wave that nobody returned.

"What are we going to do with the bodies, miss?" the Sergeant she only knew as Paul asked. He looked at her as if she was unhinged, and Tamsyn supposed that on some level she actually was.

"Leave them hooked up to the dollies. I'm training another group on Wednesday, and I want those corpses to really stink."

"There is something wrong with you, lady," the policeman grumbled, hitching up his belt. He whistled through his teeth, and a trio of constables set to fixing the course. They swept up the bullet casings, handkerchiefs over their faces to ward off the stink.

"Hey, don't blame me for making it realistic," Tamsyn said.

The skin between her shoulder blades itched suddenly, and she turned, certain she was being watched. A young woman was lurking near the edge of the training course, staring intently at Tamsyn. She seemed familiar, with long wavy hair and, but Tamsyn couldn't quite place her. One of the police officer's girlfriends?

"Jog on, love," she said, flipping her the bird. "You're not meant to be here."

By the Tamsyn fetched her bicycle from where it leaned on the fence, the young woman was gone. She rode away from the training grounds, ringing the little bell.

Tamsyn Webb was important these days. She was on the Privy Council, a special advisor to no less than Prince Harry himself. Even though fuel supplies were getting low on Grand Cayman, she still rated a vehicle with a driver, which she almost never used. She simply preferred to cycle home, alone with her thoughts, soaking up the endless sunshine.

Times were tough in the post-zombie Cayman Islands. Fuel rationing meant that few drove, and on an island that used to import almost everything, most things were now in short supply. As she rode through George Town, she passed dozens of empty banks, now just a reminder that the Caymans were a tax haven in the old world.

Turning onto her street, Tamsyn rode into her front yard, dumping the bicycle on the front lawn. It was a modest home, but it suited her needs, and there was enough laughter inside to forgive the peeling paint. She threw open the front door, her face splitting into an instant smile.

The excited cries, the patter of tiny feet slapping against the tiles, and then Tamsyn caught a flying toddler, who was all giggles and smiles.

"Malcolm, you little monkey," she laughed, and tickled her son mercilessly. They lay in the hallway, laughing themselves stupid. They were still that way when Olivena found them. The heavy-set Jamaican woman wore rubber gloves, and looked exhausted.

"He has been drawing on the walls again," she scolded. "I have to scrub every wall in this house. If he were my child, I would use the wooden spoon. So naughty!"

Tamsyn tried to keep a straight face. Olivena made out that she was strict, but she had a soft spot where Malcolm was concerned. Tamsyn's son was running rings around his nanny, and Olivena secretly loved it.

"I'm very sorry, Olivena. I'll try to keep the markers locked in a drawer." The nanny grizzled in response, her complaints following her up the hallway and to the kitchen. Tamsyn and Malcolm broke into laughter again.

They made peace over tea, enjoying fish stew. Olivena had a good hand with the spice, and Malcolm rarely refused anything that she put in front of him. Malcolm sat in his high chair, face and bib covered with food, babbling about his favourite toys.

Tamsyn smiled sadly. Her little man was growing by the day, and some days she could see her father in his profile. Malcolm Webb, the boy's namesake, who died trying to get her to safety. Then she saw Eddie Jacobs in his face, the way little Malcolm was quick to smile and laugh, and she felt a dark bubble rise up from her chest.

Eddie. God, how she missed that man. He'd been a meat-head from the start, but he'd been *her* meat-head. They'd finally found love, he'd given her Malcolm, and now he was gone. Just like everyone else in her life, their lives ending in her wake. It was like she'd sucked up their opportunities, all of their remaining days like some sort of vampire, continuing on when everyone else simply stopped...

Malcolm flicked a spoonful of food at her forehead, and she snapped out of her melancholy. Olivena clambered out of her chair, grumbling and already reaching for a dishcloth, but Tamsyn saw the suggestion of a smile in the corners of her mouth.

"Good shot, mate," she whispered to Malcolm.

A STORM HIT Grand Cayman that night, rolling in from the west. Once Malcolm settled down in his cot, Tamsyn sat on her porch to watch it. Drink in hand, she marvelled at the storm's power, the driving wind and rain. The lightning show was spectacular, and it suited her somber mood.

The power flickered, and then it finally cut out around 9pm. Navy engineers had hooked up the reactors from two of the nuclear subs to the George Town power grid, but it was patchwork at best. Tamsyn happily sat there in the dark, drinking rum and watching nature scour the world.

She drank most of the bottle, and sang pop songs to herself, crying drunkenly when she realised that all of these people were now dead. After her service in the Texan Republican Army, Tamsyn could sleep almost anywhere, and she fell asleep on the porch decking, the warm rain tickling at her toes.

The nightmare came almost instantly. In the dream she opened her eyes, and her house was surrounded by the dead. Not the slavering corpses tearing up the world, these were *her* dead, and they were packed up against the edge of the porch, staring at her. Their faces were pale and bruised, eyes sunken, beady, drinking her in as they crowded around her. They stretched across her front yard, and down the road, as far as she could see.

She could not move in this dream, and it was like their attention had her pinned to the wall. Tamsyn was a butterfly flush with life, and it frustrated these dead, a parade of familiar faces who'd made a special trip just to see her.

Tamsyn recognised many from Gravesend, everyone she'd doomed. It was her fault the zombies got through the town barricade. Her one stupid mistake had killed hundreds, had led to the massacre on the docks. She saw Ali, her best friend from school, and he stared at her, nothing human left in his eyes. She'd left him behind. Watched him die.

"You're not safe," he said.

Others pressed forward. She saw people who'd died on that awful voyage from England to Texas. Ones who'd died in the war, others who died in nuclear bombing of Corpus Christi. Again, her fault. She saw Baxter, poor doomed Baxter, and her loyal soldier shook his head, not unkindly.

"You're not safe," and he tried to say more, but his mouth worked uselessly, and he gave up with a shrug. Naomi and old Clem Murray tried then, and pleaded with her earnestly, assuring Tamsyn that she was not safe.

Then her father stepped forward, and Tamsyn cried out. His lips were still stitched up with black thread, the same as she'd last dreamt of him, and he held little Milly in his arms, her foster daughter who'd died in a mushroom cloud. Her little face took Tamsyn in, and she mouthed the words "not safe."

"I bloody get it, okay!" Tamsyn cried out. "What am I meant to do?"

The ghosts parted then, and Tamsyn's heart skipped. Eddie stepped onto the porch, wincing as if the effort cost him dearly. He was arm in arm with her mother, who looked angry.

"Tam, you gotta go love," he said. "Please. It's the boy."

Behind the crowd there was a soft glow, like a sun rising, but the light was all wrong, unnatural. The storm began to fail, and Tamsyn's personal crowd of ghosts fell aside, wailing, unable to look upon the approaching light.

"Go!" her mother screamed, and then Tamsyn woke up with a start. She was still sitting on her porch, but it was dawn, the storm long since passed. Heart still racing, she climbed to her feet, back and legs aching from the awkward way she'd slept.

Always with the dreams. She'd had vivid nightmares for years now, even before the zombies came, but they were getting worse. Sometimes a good drink kept them at bay, but this was happening almost every night. Too often she woke screaming, setting off the neighbourhood dogs, and little Malcolm would join in from his cot, confused and crying. Olivena would hustle in, warm milk already in hand, soothing them both back to sleep with old Jamaican lullabies.

If she had too many bad nights in a row, Tamsyn drank on the porch, or hid in the toolshed while she worked through a bottle. Olivena did not approve of Tamsyn self-medicating, and kept trying to drag her to her church, to meet a selection of her friends' sons. Tamsyn could think of nothing she wanted less. Her heart still ached for Eddie, and she turned away anyone who looked like a gentleman caller.

If it wasn't for her work and for her son, Tamsyn had the feeling that she just might fall off the face of the earth.

"I've gotta get my shit together," she muttered, stretching her back. Then she saw the jeep turning into her driveway, and swore. The driver was a young ensign in Navy whites, which only ever meant one thing. She threw open the front door, and ran into her kitchen in a panic.

"Olivena. Olivena! Where did you put my skirt?"

Olivena was sat next to Malcolm's high-chair, spooning goop into his face. The boy squealed with delight when he saw her, and the sight made her feel like the worst mother on the face of the earth. Too drunk to get up and feed her own son...

"I ironed your skirt this morning. It is hanging up behind your bedroom door," Olivena said pointedly. Tamsyn hit the bathroom at a run, splashing water on her face and attacking her boozy mouth with a toothbrush. She scrubbed at her armpits with a wet cloth, wishing she had time to wake up under the shower.

"Privy Council isn't meant to be till tomorrow," she mumbled. In under two minutes she had her hair up in a bun, and wriggled into the smart skirt and blouse that Olivena had picked out for her. Jamming her toes into her flats, she whirled through the house like a dervish, snatching up papers and folders.

"I'll be home later," she shouted, planting a big kiss on Malcolm's face, and even giving one to Olivena for good measure. The Jamaican pushed her away, waving at her face.

"You smell like rum. Drink this," the portly woman said, pushing her own coffee into Tamsyn's hands. Smiling gratefully, she drank it as fast as she could.

Opening the door, Tamsyn held herself high, trying not to look like the wretched drunk who'd run inside bare minutes ago. The ensign looked at her with barely veiled amusement as he opened the passenger door for her.

He drove her through George Town, the town streets empty except for some children on bicycles, and palm branches knocked down in the storm. Tamsyn tried to go over her papers for the day, fighting off the urge to vomit whenever the ensign took a corner.

"Big day today," he began, and Tamsyn held up her hand.

"Look mate, I know you're being polite. I'm trying really hard not to throw up right now. Please, can we just have a quiet ride today?"

"Yes, ma'am," the random ensign said with a frown. She wasn't winning many friends in the armed forces. With a sigh, she returned to her items for the Privy Council.

Resources, dwindling. Almost no diesel left on the island. Bankers and hedge fund managers were being pressed into farm-work, with work crews clearing away the rainforests and jungle for more farmland. A report on her own efforts at training the Royal Navy in zombie combat, and another raft of motions and reasons why the government-in-exile were too scared to leave the Cayman islands.

All she wanted to do was take this fragment of civilisation and go home. Tamsyn remembered the horrors of Gravesend, the knowledge that no-one was left to help, to reclaim the island from the zombie hordes. All along, the leftover government had been here, hiding with the coconuts and all the world's money.

She gripped her files and papers, anger bubbling in her gut. She had no doubt that today's meeting would be just as pointless as the last one. When the jeep pulled up outside of the Government Administration Building, her hangover was replaced by the will to fight, to knock some heads together.

The driver opened the door, and Tamsyn bustled out, gritting her teeth when the ensign didn't salute her. Her whole existence on the Privy Council was due to Prince Harry's goodwill, and even the rank and file of the Navy knew it. Part of her relished the battles over the Council table, the way the pompous old shits resisted any of her ideas.

One of the few things that keeps me going, she thought. She worked her way into the building, past the complicated ballet of assistants with more paper, guards on every door, and then finally into the Council chamber itself, various talking heads and military brass now finding their seats.

Sliding into her own chair, Tamsyn looked to Prince Harry, her one champion. She stopped cold. Sat to his right were a trio of strangers, men in uniforms she'd never hoped to see again.

Americans. One was a five-star General, the other an Admiral with acres of fruit salad and medals hanging from his chest. The third was a man in suit and tie, and Tamsyn recognised him from the TV, back in the old world when her dad forced her to watch the news before her homework.

Vice-President Wycliffe. He'd spent the last few years hiding out on Hawaii with the remainders of the US government. When a zombie ripped out President Palin's throat, he got the top job.

The man looked too perfect. He had a strong jaw, and when he spoke his teeth were white and straight, a clashing wall built just for photographs. Wycliffe kept his hair neatly combed over a precise part, with just a touch of white at the temples. Tamsyn had heard stories of the man's religious convictions, and when the Texans brought life back to the zombies, he'd come for them with guns blazing.

Only Jesus was meant to come back, right? she thought, worrying at her nails.

"We'll be blunt, your Highness," Wycliffe said. "We need your boats, and we need your men."

Tamsyn saw Prince Harry share a look with Terry Fallot, his Prime Minister, who gave a slight shake of his head. The other members of the Privy Council looked guarded, almost terrified. As always, the Governor of the Caymans sat self-importantly in his chair, but today even he had the rare sense to keep his mouth shut.

Secret Service agents hovered around the edges of the meeting room, watching everybody. Tamsyn sat very still, and hoped that nobody noticed her. That none of these Americans realised who she was.

"We are getting slaughtered over there," Wycliffe said. "Damn zombies are clumping together, hordes that are millions strong. We've got the Cubans nipping at us wherever we try to set up shop, it's – it's a damn mess."

"Vice-President, we lost our country too," Prince Harry said. "We'd like nothing more than to go home, but it's just not safe yet."

"We are allies!" Wycliffe suddenly shouted, banging on the table with the flats of his hands. "Are you just going to sit on this island while we all die?"

"We have to look at the safety of our personnel, the protection of our remaining assets," the Prime Minister began, but Wycliffe waved off the excuses.

"I've heard enough of this. You're a bunch of damn cowards." He stood, even as the General lay an impressive sheaf of papers on the table. An agreement, complete with empty signature page.

"We'll give you one week to come to your senses. If you will not participate in our joint survival, I will dissolve all alliances between our countries."

Prince Harry stood, followed a heartbeat later by the rest of the table. He shook the Vice-President's hand, face a thundercloud. Tamsyn knew how much it galled him to wait on this island, to let the undead stink up England while he sat here in safety. Tamsyn guessed that he alone wanted to help the Americans, and badly.

The Americans started to leave the Privy Council chamber when the five-star General stopped in front of Tamsyn, recognition washing across his face.

"You're Tamsyn Webb," he said, and drew his sidearm. The room erupted into pandemonium. Secret Service agents leapt into action, guns already drawn, and the British Marines posted by the door responded in kind, rifles up and tracking. Everybody was shouting, and Tamsyn was frozen, staring into the black mouth of the pistol pointed at her chest.

"Captain Webb," the General shouted, "For your war crimes, I am placing you under arrest."

2

"It's all true," Tamsyn told Prince Harry. "I did everything they say I did."

They were holed up in a small office, just her and the Prince. Had he not been there, Tamsyn had no doubt that the Council may well have just handed her over. The Americans had left without Tamsyn, the Secret Service hustling the Vice-President back to his helicopter, guns still drawn.

"When I was an officer in the Republican Texas Army, I had command of a company of the re-humans. The zombies we brought back to 'life' with the salt treatment," she explained.

"We were losing the war. Our superiors had bloody betrayed us. So yes, I put live weapons in the arms of the undead, and I ordered them to attack the American soldiers."

"Jesus," Harry said, rubbing at the bridge of his nose.

"It was war. That bastard who just ran out to his helicopter nuked our city because of what I did." A tear ran down Tamsyn's cheek. "He pushed the red button, and my stepdaughter died."

"He *nuked* a city?" Harry said, eyes wide.

"Please, your Highness," Tamsyn said. "You cannot work with these people. They've lost their way."

"We might not have any choice," Harry said. "Do you – do you still know how to do it? To bring the dead ones back?"

"As God is my witness, I will never bring another one of those poor bastards back over," Tamsyn said. "They are better off with a bullet between the eyes."

"Good," Harry said. "If we're going to keep you here, best you're not breaking the laws of nature."

"Keep me here?"

"You are one of my loyal subjects. I am not going to turn you over to some politician with his knickers in a twist."

Tamsyn smiled, and the Prince responded with his own crooked grin. He let her out of the small office, and immediately they were bombarded by the other members of the Privy Council, all of whom were waiting for a private audience with the last remaining Royal.

"Your Highness, we cannot harbour a war criminal!" Terry Fallot shouted. The Prime Minister was livid.

"It's only their say so," Harry responded.

"We have extradition agreements with the Americans. We've got secret agreements and promises binding us together. We absolutely must hand her over for trial."

"Wake up," Tamsyn shouted. "There's no countries left. They'll shoot me, and then they'll just take all your bullets and fuel anyway."

All of the politicians began to rage at her, and Harry raised his own voice, ordering the Marines to clear a path for himself and Tamsyn. They held the talking heads back with rifle stocks and implacable faces, giving Prince Harry enough time to hustle Tamsyn outside.

"This isn't good news for you," Harry admitted on the door step. "After that mess, Fallot will probably force me to drop you from the Privy Council."

"Hang on, aren't you the future King or something? What's the bloody point if you don't get your own way?"

"Sadly, it hasn't worked that way since the Magna Carta," Harry scoffed. "Go home and lay low. Let me sort this out."

Once more she climbed into a car driven by an ensign. This boy was even younger than her, and he tried at least three times to make a pass at her on the way back to her house. Nothing could have been further from her mind, and he kept it up until she threatened to break his nose.

"It's about to be World War 3, and here you are trying to get lucky. Kid, I will absolutely destroy you," she said. "God, just drop me off here."

She slammed the door shut and he hit the gas, spraying her with dust and small stones. Tamsyn walked through George Town in a poisonous funk, eventually shedding her shoes and walking the rest of the way home barefoot.

A few minutes later, the same ensign drove back towards her, and Tamsyn balled up her fists. She kept a fold-back knife in her purse, and as the car approached she stepped through the motions in her mind. When he pulled over, he would try to snatch at her. She would respond with a knee to the crotch, a fist to the nose, and then the knife if that wasn't enough to dissuade him.

Holding herself up high, she blinked with surprise as the jeep blasted past her. She saw that the seats were full with military brass, and the young ensign looked terrified. A few seconds later a troop transport came around the corner at full pelt, packed to the rafters with royal marines and sailors.

Across the road, she saw the same girl from the training course, staring at her, grim face framed by that long wavy hair. Spine tingling with terror, Tamsyn walked away faster.

"Fuck off!" she yelled at the figure. "Just leave me alone, you weirdo!"

When the next vehicle came out of the Navy base, Tamsyn started to run home, and when she heard the distant call of a klaxon, she ran at a flat sprint. Something was terribly wrong. The alarm wailed over and over, echoing across the beautiful island.

That was when she heard the growing roar of a jet engine, and then another one. A second later she saw an entire squadron of fighter jets screaming overhead, flying low. Then the rolling whump of explosions, deafeningly close.

A moment later, the jets were gone, and the klaxon had fallen silent. Smoke rolled across the town. Tamsyn thought she heard a distant scream, and somewhere near the Navy base, an old fire alarm trilled.

Tears running down her face, she turned into her street at a flat run, her bare feet already stripped raw from the stones. Most of her neighbours were out on their porches and in the street, pointing at the smoke, terrified. Olivena was on the front doorstep, a crying Malcolm on her hip.

"Tamsyn, what is happening?" the older woman cried. "Who bombs us?"

"Americans," Tamsyn gasped, and reached for her son. Little Malcolm clutched at her blouse, sobbing and afraid. Throwing the door open, Tamsyn ran inside.

She'd learnt many lessons since the world ended. No house was ever truly a home, and any place that Tamsyn slept, she was prepared to abandon at a moment's notice. When she managed to peel the terrified toddler from her blouse, she stripped loose from her good clothes. It felt like she was shedding a personality for the last time, and in a way Tamsyn supposed that she was.

Before Malcolm came along, Tamsyn thought nothing of leaving her weapons and gear lying all over the place, but now she kept everything dangerous locked in a cupboard next to her bed. She grabbed the padlock, and then her mind went blank. She shook with panic.

"Olivena!" she cried out. "Where did I put the key?"

"What key?" the older woman said, appearing in the bedroom door.

"This key, the key to the....to all my bug-out stuff."

"I do not know, Tamsyn. You never tell me where you put the key for that."

"Goddamnit!" Tamsyn cried out. There was another explosion, this one close enough to rattle all the windows. Tamsyn raced around in the room in her underwear, trying to tune out the wails of her toddler, the panicked gabble of Olivena. Rummaging through stacks of dirty clothes and dog-eared paperbacks, Tamsyn finally emerged with a toolbox. She spilled pliers and screwdrivers everywhere, until she held up a claw-hammer.

"Come on," she said, fitting the claws of the hammer under the hasp. She'd screwed it in deep, worried about Malcolm getting inside, and cursed herself as she struggled to bust it open.

"They're getting closer!" Olivena said, fretting over the explosions. Malcolm sobbed hysterically, and cried out for her over and over. Against the explosions, Tamsyn could now hear gunfire, coming from the naval base. She could hear the beating sound of helicopters, and a lone anti-aircraft gun pounding away in the distance.

"Open, damnit!" Tamsyn grunted. Putting all of her weight into it, the hasp finally snapped open, taking a large chunk of the wardrobe with it. In moments she was wriggling into a set of motorcycle leathers, and she strapped on a gun-belt. A compound bow, nothing as good as the rig she'd lost in Cuba, but good enough to do the job. A quiver of hunting arrows, and a bug-out bag with clothes and some food for herself and Malcolm.

"Where are we meant to go?" Olivena cried. Ignoring her, Tamsyn snatched up Malcolm, and ran out to the side of the house. Her bicycle, complete with child seat. She strapped the toddler in, hands shaking a little. She'd spent all of her adult life running from danger, and in her experience, survival was myopic. It came down to her, her kid, and throwing everyone else to the wolves.

Olivena came hustling around the corner, the large lady struggling to keep up. When she saw Tamsyn raise the kickstand, she stood in her way, already huffing from the short jog.

"Please Tamsyn, you have to help me."

"You're going to be okay. The Americans are only here to seize weapons and soldiers. They won't touch you."

"How can you know that?" Olivena said, anger spotting her cheeks. "You are just going to leave me here! How do you know I will be safe?"

"Look, I don't know if you will be safe," Tamsyn admitted. "Take whatever food is left in the house, and hide in the jungle. They'll be gone soon."

"Hide in the jungle," Olivena scoffed. "I am fifty-eight years old. I have diabetes. Do you think I will last one night in the jungle?"

"Please Olivena," Tamsyn said, voice level. "Move out of my way."

"No. I have raised that child for you!" Olivena yelled. "You are a very bad girl! Very selfish!"

Gunfire now, and closer. Tamsyn drew the pistol from her hip, and held it level at the large Jamaican woman. Olivena's mouth fell open in a frightened O, and tears leaked down her round jolly face.

"Damn you to hell," Olivena said, slumping against the weatherboard of the house. "I will call on every Loa. I will put pins in a doll with a lock of your hair. I will spill the blood of a chicken and curse your every step on this earth."

"I don't care, lady," Tamsyn said. "I'm already cursed. Knock yourself out." With more dark words on her lips, Olivena suddenly froze in place, gasping, and then she was on the ground, clutching at her chest, her overweight body finally betraying her in this moment of extreme stress.

Tamsyn knew CPR.

Tamsyn rode past.

For one moment she wondered what sort of monster she was now, and then she was surviving, escaping, an animal on the run, a she-wolf guarding her cub. She did not look back.

"Mummy! Mummy! I scared!"

"I know, mate," Tamsyn huffed. She poured all of her energy into the bicycle, and when she hit the downhill stretch into George Town itself, she kept pedalling. She had the bike in top gear, and her arms fought the speed wobbles as she whizzed towards a war-zone.

Then the wavy-haired girl appeared out of nowhere, stepping in front of her bicycle.

"Oh my god, just piss off!" Tamsyn screamed, narrowly dodging the girl. Was she hoping to steal her bicycle? If she made another appearance today, Tamsyn decided she would give her a blood-nose, even right in front of her own son.

It fell into place then, where she'd seen the girl before. Tamsyn had overseen the installation of the corpses into the training course, and there was the corpse of a young girl in the mix, same wavy hair. Choked to death on a chicken bone. There'd been complaints about the exhumations, of course, and so Tamsyn supposed she was the dead girl's sister, perhaps a cousin, pissed off at the insane woman who'd disrespected her family's dead.

You're all bloody dead now! Focus on the bigger picture, lady!

Tamsyn had a view of the bay now, and it was an absolute disaster. The Yanks had caught the remainder of the Royal Navy with its pants down. Helicopters danced around the British warships, discharging US soldiers on rappel lines. On the horizon was an American battleship, a big one, and an aircraft carrier that spewed planes and fusillades at any ship that hadn't struck the flag.

A British cruiser lay broken and burning, lifeboats and sailors in preservers spreading out from the sinking ship like a dusting of sugar. American patrol boats weaved through the smoking wreckage, hauling in anyone still drawing breath.

Vice-President Wycliffe had given the Privy Council one week to honour its commitments. But once Harry had refused to hand Tamsyn over, the Americans had come at them like a sledgehammer, within the hour.

Mighty convenient, she thought. *They had this raid all teed up and ready to go. If it wasn't me, it would have been something else. Someone giving Wycliffe the stink-eye. The coffee too cold.*

She could rationalise it all she liked, but the dark little cynic in her soul knew that all of this was on her. No matter what she did, she was a black thread running through this broken world. Tamsyn Webb brought destruction wherever she went, and she'd lost count of how many deaths she'd caused just by being somewhere. Olivena's threat of a curse felt like nothing at all.

The Navy base was gone, which only left one option. Tamsyn headed over to the main wharves, once home to cruise liners and luxury yachts. Now, the two remaining nuclear subs were drawn up to the docks, a fat tangle of insulated wire sprawling out of each conning tower. Navy technicians were all over the submarines, working fast to separate them from George Town's power grid.

Cars littered the docks, abandoned with the doors open, and in some cases the engines still running. Tamsyn saw some of the useless talking heads from the Privy Council making for the gangways. Prime Minister Fallot was boarding, followed by a trio of assistants, arms laden with bags and cases.

"Wait," she shouted, pedalling towards the submarines. The nearest submarine was free of the power-lines, and the last figures were already climbing through the hatch, the gangway rolled away and clear. Tamsyn swore, and headed towards the second nuclear sub, flinching as a bomb exploded nearby.

The two vessels were HMS Vengeance and HMS Victorious, and with a wry smile Tamsyn chose Vengeance. She supposed that was all she knew, and no-one in the human race could hope for a victory today.

A line of Royal Marines were guarding HMS Vengeance,

holding off the pleading locals who wept and begged for safe passage. The power-lines were cut loose, but still the submarine didn't cast off. The Marines scanned the crowd restlessly, in a visible panic.

Tamsyn pulled up at the rear of the growing crowd, pulling Malcolm and all of her gear off the bike. She strapped her son to her back, cursing under her breath as he wriggled around in the harness. Laden down like a packhorse, she shoved her way through the crowd, stepping on toes and using the tip of her compound bow as a spear. Malcolm fretted and wailed, daunted by the screaming people, the bombs getting closer. Soon she was at the edge of the dock, screaming at the Marines.

"You have to let me on!"

"Lady, I don't have to do jack shit," a Marine with heavy acne scarring yelled. He looked rattled, inches away from losing control. "Step back or I will drop you."

"I'm a British citizen. I'm on the Privy Council, moron!"

"Bullshit. All of you, get back!" The Marine fired his assault rifle into the air, a short burst. The crowd panicked, and dashed in all directions. An old man fell into the water, where he bobbed and wailed, beating on the sides of the huge submarine. A young man took a running jump at the submarine, but slid down the curve, scrabbling for purchase the whole way down.

The Marines were drawing beads on people now, and Tamsyn realised it was that final beat before the thunder of gunfire, when fear turned into bullets and good sense went right out the window. She got right up into the young Marine's face, arrow nocked to her compound bow. Before he could bring his gun to bear on her, Tamsyn had the point of a barbed arrow held bare inches from the Marine's eye.

"All of you, hold your fire!" Tamsyn screamed. She still

had the steel of command in her voice, and the Marines paused. Tamsyn slowly lowered her bow, drawing the tension out of the pull. When the arrow was gone, the Marine finally drew a deep shuddering breath, a scared young man in a uniform.

"Alright then?" Tamsyn asked, and the boy nodded. Tamsyn turned, eyeing off the ugly crowd.

"Now you lot, bugger off!" Tamsyn shouted. "There's no room on this boat for you. Get your own ride."

Tamsyn felt a strange moment of vertigo then, and she saw her at the edge of the crowd. Olivena, grim-faced and staring at her.

What the hell? Had the portly woman recovered from her heart attack, flagged down a ride to the port? Tamsyn felt a flush of shame for leaving this kind woman to keel over and die in her driveway.

"Just go away!" she cried out. Head bowed, Olivena turned away, and then was simply not there.

Oh no, Tam. You are losing your freaking mind. That did not just happen.

At that moment, one of the locals made a rush for the gangway, and Tamsyn was pulled from her grim reverie, rapping the man on the head with the carbon stock of her bow. Another man produced a cricket bat from somewhere, but she rapped him across the knuckles, and again, until his fingers lost their grip and the weapon fell underfoot.

Then one last car pulled up on the dock, and the last few people scattered, and then a pack of Marines came crashing through the stragglers, rifle butts swinging. Tamsyn saw the familiar glimpse of red hair, and then a moment later she was caught up in the tide, the kid with acne scarring hauling her up by the straps of her bags and getting her onto the gangway. Then she was swept along the gangway with everyone else, and hands helped her through the hatchway, into the choked interior of the submarine.

Tamsyn felt the press of bodies, and fought away the claustrophobia of the close corridor. She was swept along as they jammed more and more people into the submarine, and then finally she heard the loud clang, felt the pressure in her ears change. They were sealed inside.

"Keep moving," someone said, and then Tamsyn staggered as the submarine powered up, surging forward. The crew were running them flat out from the docks, and then her ears popped again as the submarine sank into the water, going for maximum depth and speed.

"Mummy!" Malcolm sobbed in her ear. She couldn't even reach up an arm to comfort her boy, strapped to her back like another piece of baggage.

"It's okay darling, we're safe now," she said. The people in the corridor began to move, and she pushed up through the centre of the craft, past tiny workstations, past compact machinery and sensors. Sailors were helping the new arrivals through to the crew quarters, and in a few moments she was climbing into a spare bunk with Malcolm and all their gear. She gladly slid the little curtain shut, grateful for even the illusion of privacy.

"Hush darling," Tamsyn said, holding her boy close. "We're okay. Please, you don't need to cry."

Little Malcolm was inconsolable, and wailed, over and over, tears spilling down his face and onto Tamsyn's. He bunched his fists into her jacket and sobbed, over and over.

"Shut that kid up!" someone snarled. "We're meant to be running silent!"

"You'll get us all killed, lady!"

Tamsyn held Malcolm close to her chest, trying to squeeze

the panic out of the boy. A morbid part of her mind wandered to that old war story, where the Viet Cong were coming, and a mother smothered her own crying child to keep it silent.

He kept this up for a long time, until somebody swept the curtain aside. A huge commando, the one with the jagged scar across his face. Tamsyn had not seen him since the day she'd humiliated him at the training exercise, and she swallowed nervously. She took note of his name tag now, saw that his surname was LEYLAND.

"Hey mate," he said softly, looking into Malcolm's eyes. Malcolm drew in a shivering breath, about to let loose with a fresh wail, and then he stopped. The man held up a finger, face twinkling with a smile, and then with a magician's flourish was suddenly holding a toy. A plastic horse, complete with moving legs, head and tail.

"My little girl gave this to me," the commando told Malcolm. "A present when I went to Afghanistan, to keep me safe. I want you to have this horse. I need you to keep it safe for me."

"Horse," Malcolm said, sniffling, but he reached out for the toy horse, tears forgotten. *Thank you,* Tamsyn mouthed to the commando, and he threw her a friendly wink before drawing the curtain shut.

SOMEWHERE IN THAT nightmare journey through the depths of the ocean, Tamsyn finally nursed Malcolm to sleep. The submarine ran in near silence, and jammed into the tiny bunk, she couldn't shake the feeling that she was in a mausoleum, shelved in with hundreds of other bodies. She lay there in a panic for a long time, convinced that the air was running out, that the walls would fail under the press of the ocean.

Malcolm drooled against her cheek, still clutching the toy horse in his grubby little fist, and then sleep reached for her. She walked through the fog of dream, and Tamsyn was once more on the *Paraclete*, the beaten up cargo ship that first took her away from England. She walked the deck, watching the icebergs in the Atlantic, and to her surprise she was arm in arm with Eddie, her sweet Eddie, as if he hadn't ended as a zombie slave with her arrow in his head. He tried to say something, but the words seemed to fail him. She was content to wander with his ghost, blissfully unaware of the awful waking world, but he held her at arm's length, his mouth working silently, an engine of tongue and teeth that couldn't quite turn over.

"His crown is black," ghost Eddie finally managed to tell her. "You beware of that black crown boy."

3

She might have slept for a few hours but when someone drew back the bunk curtain Tamsyn's brain told her it had only been five minutes at best.

"Oh, piss off," Tamsyn grunted, and then she cracked an eye open. It was Prince Harry. He looked like hell, with a blood-stain on his shirt, eyes lined with dark bags. He was so pale in the fluorescent light that his ruddy cheeks were almost washed away.

"Sorry, Your Highness," she mumbled. Malcolm snored quietly, and she didn't know if she could move him.

"No, stay there," Harry whispered. "Let him rest."

"Thank you," she replied. For a moment he grinned at her, but it fell away, and he was all responsibility, carrying the weight of the dead and those who survived.

"What happens now?" she asked.

"We're going to hold a special meeting of the Privy Council. In the mess."

"Oh goody. Any of those oxygen thieves still alive?"

He glared then. She'd gone too far.

"The Prime Minister, the Archbishop of Canterbury, a

couple of Lords and Ladies. Some others over on Victorious."

"Rule Britannia, bitches."

Harry laughed, despite himself. Malcolm stirred at the sound, and then the boy shifted, settling back into sleep.

"Tamsyn, I don't think we're getting out of this mess."

"I don't think so either."

"I can't say what the Council is going to do. About you."

Tamsyn felt a tight hand twisting around her stomach then. He'd always protected her, fought for her place at his side. She was no longer sure that her patron would or even could defend her now, not after that disaster.

"I only want one thing," she said. "Keep my Malcolm safe. Put him with good people."

"It won't come to that."

"We both know it will."

"It might," Prince Harry conceded. "Don't think any of it matters much now."

"Yep. At this point, we're all just different flavours of fucked."

Malcolm stirred into bleary-eyed wakefulness, right on the swear word, and let out an almighty wail.

"Tamsyn, you are either the best or the worst parent ever."

SHE SWAPPED her motorcycle leathers for a smart shirt and jeans, the neatest clothes she could find in her bug-out bag. Cursing herself for only packing one shoe of her pair of sneakers, she was forced to put her smelly old Doc Martins back on.

Leyland offered to watch Malcolm while she went to

face the music. She took one final look at the boy, wondering if this was the last she'd ever see of him, and saw him chuckling over a silly song the commando was singing.

God, Buddha, whoever is out there, please, please watch over my boy, she thought. Leyland threw her a quick wink, and she nodded, grateful for even a scrap of kindness.

The Vengeance was low and cramped, and Tamsyn felt like the low-hanging pipes and conduits were pressing in on her, tried not to think about the incredible pressure of the ocean pushing in on the hull.

An escort arrived for her, a big Marine with a pistol on his belt. No-one else on the submarine was going about armed, and the significance wasn't lost on her. She wasn't in handcuffs yet, but she wasn't going to face the Privy Council as an equal, or even as a citizen.

In their eyes, she'd as good as destroyed the United Kingdom, and perhaps she had.

The Vengeance was big for a submarine, but it only took a minute or so to get to the mess hall. Tamsyn thought back to the Paraclete, and the Petty Cash, the boat she'd taken to Cuba with Eddie and Clem. The little dinghy she'd taken to the ocean, near death and terrified, when what was left of Britain found her.

It felt like she'd spent years on the water, sliding around the world, leaving death and terror behind her, washing up on some new shore where it all started again. What would happen at the end of this boat ride? Extradition? Jail?

Perhaps they should just leave me on the nearest rock and run for their lives, she thought.

Two more Marines stood on guard outside the hatch, and Tamsyn saw them stare right through her, their discipline barely hiding the contempt, even hatred. Her escort span the wheel, wrenching open the hatch.

The mess hall was packed with furious Tories. There was the Prime Minister, the Leader of the Opposition, First Sea Lord McKenzie, Baroness Patience Clair-Wisdom, the Earl of Huntingdon, and then the names and titles started to fail Tamsyn. There were more Marines, the Captain of the submarine and his aides, and in the centre of all this hostility was Prince Harry, who looked at Tamsyn firmly, lips clenched in a tight white line.

A court martial then. Tamsyn stood at ease, even as the adrenaline started pumping, her heart racing. She could feel the weight of the ocean around them, crushing in, and she wondered if they'd still be glaring at her when the hull finally gave, when the salt-water swept the life out of them all...

"Miss Webb," Prime Minister Fallot began in his strident tone. Tamsyn struggled through her dark thoughts, grabbed for the tiny bit of self-control left to her.

"Perhaps we should be calling you Captain Webb now."

"I don't hold a commission anymore. The woman who gave it to me is dead. That whole sorry country is extinct. The bastards who did that to the Republic of Texas just stomped all over the Cayman islands, if you weren't paying attention."

"Tamsyn, enough," Prince Harry said, and Tamsyn winced, nodding. She'd come out swinging straight away. Fallot just looked at her as if she was a dog crap on his shoe. After a lengthy pause, he continued.

"Because we sheltered you, our armed forces have been decimated. We have lost our safe haven, and most of the Privy Council. We were safeguarding the machinery of the United Kingdom, and yesterday you snuffed out our final hope. Do you accept responsibility for this?"

"Sure, why not?" she said. She felt the intake of breath in

the room, the moment before every man and his dog would come at her with further accusations. *Time to press on.*

"I did what they said I did. I armed the undead, and turned them on the living. Because of that, the United States nuked an entire city of innocent civilians. But that attack on the Caymans? They were just looking for any excuse to take your toys."

"Nonsense!" Baroness Clair-Wisdom cried. "We had an alliance with the United States, right up until your provocation!"

"We should have handed you over!"

"War criminal!"

The room started to go nuts, and Tamsyn felt her hands curl into fists. Once more she was back in survivor mode, surrounded by a dangerous horde, and in an instant she weighed her options. Attack that Marine, take his handgun, and shoot her way clear to the door. Or go straight for Fallot, using that moment of surprise to take him hostage.

Or take a swing at the nearest man with a gun, and go for a pyrrhic victory, forcing them to gun her down right in front of the nice lords and ladies. Tamsyn was inches away from making this play when Harry slowly stood up, arms folded.

"That's enough," he said, and gradually the room fell silent. The Prince once more took his seat. Fallot licked his lips nervously, and at a nod from the Prince he continued.

"The Right Honourable Lord Hood has advised that we convene the Judicial Committee of the Privy Council," Fallot said, indicating a drowsy old geriatric in a neat suit. "It is the highest remaining court in the land. We have a Justice of the Supreme Court and enough Councillors to form a committee quorum. Today, we will make a judgement on your war crimes."

Tamsyn cracked up laughing. Fallot smacked his palm on the table-top, shouting for order.

"By all means, let's have a jolly good hearing," Tamsyn said. "Are we going through the Geneva Conventions first? If you can find the bit about arming resurrected zombies, I'm all ears."

"You will be silent!" the ancient judge to Fallot's right shouted. "We may issue an Order In Council on any matter."

"Your Highness, we have put before you the draft Order," Baroness Clair-Wisdom said, sliding a document across the table to Prince Harry. "It prohibits the use of the undead as a weapon in any way, and is retrospective. We agree with the Americans that it is a grave crime against humanity. In Captain Webb's case, we deem this to be a war crime."

"We are now at war with the Americans, but we are confident a diplomatic approach will be heard," Fallot said to the Prince. "In this Order you will see that we have decided upon immediate extradition of Captain Webb into the custody of the United States."

Now that she was hearing the words, Tamsyn felt herself relax. They had all of their cards on the table, and now that she knew what she faced, she could act. Even though she was fighting for her life now, she felt herself shift into the usual combative mode that she took to every Privy Council meeting.

Listen to their nonsense, and then tell these cowards exactly what she thought of them. Just another day at work, really.

"I will not sign this," Prince Harry said after a long moment, and pushed the document away.

"We expected this," Prime Minister Fallot said. "Your fondness for Captain Webb is admirable, but short-sighted.

We have also drafted an Order *Of* Council, which does not require the acting head-of-state's signature. We will go around you if we must, Your Highness, regrettable as this is."

"Hey," Tamsyn called out. "Just sign it, Your Highness!"

"You - you want me to sign it?"

"Absolutely. We learnt about these Orders in high school Legal Studies. Fascinating stuff, really."

"You'll go to the Americans. They'll - they'll shoot you."

"I'm happy to roll those dice."

Eyebrows raised, Prince Harry took the proffered pen, and put his elaborate signature to the Order. Tamsyn clapped her hands.

"Yay. You just made a law. A piece of primary legislation, am I correct?"

"Be silent," Fallot called out. "Take Captain Webb and place her in the brig."

"So I guess all that's left now is to get this ratified by both Houses of Parliament. Then it becomes a law. Am I right?"

An ensign had her by the upper arm now, but as she spoke the realisation sank in. Prince Harry was on his feet, as were the leftover bits of the Privy Council. Voices were raised, and then someone shouted.

"Last I checked, it was pretty quiet at Westminster!" Tamsyn hollered. "Those overpaid twits haven't done a day of work since 2012."

"Your Highness, these are extraordinary times," Fallot protested.

"I understand you need a quorum of twenty members to conduct business in the House of Commons?" Tamsyn shouted over the hubbub, in her best parade ground voice. "I count the Prime Minister there, the Honourable Leader of the Opposition, and a couple of random parasites."

"I said put her in the brig, sailor!"

"Oh yes, let's not forget the House of Lords. We're going to need a majority of the Lords to hold a sitting. How many of the 826 members of the House of Lords are in this submarine right now?"

She was thankful then for every moment that her father had filled her head with politics and civics lessons. He'd taught her civil disobedience back in Gravesend, so of course it was time to take it up a level. Tamsyn smiled broadly, and slowly raised her hand, extending her middle finger, while she mouthed the words *fuck you.*

"Order!" Lord Hood cried out, clapping his hands together. Everyone ignored the geriatric law-maker, on their feet and arguing between the chairs and tables in the mess room.

Prince Harry climbed on top of the table, clutching the pipes on the ceiling, and with his free hand he whistled loudly through his teeth.

"Get control of yourselves!" he shouted. "Sit down and shut up, right now!"

Chastened, the Prime Minister and all of the other people took their seats. Harry swung down from the ceiling, for all the world like a swashbuckler, and Tamsyn definitely fell in love with him, just a little bit.

"Your Highness, I've heard what the Honourable Privy Council has to say," Tamsyn said. "I request a right of reply."

"Speak."

"I am a citizen of the United Kingdom. You cannot arrest me or confine me if I have broken no law."

"Correct."

"Now that we've got that out of the way, I've got a few things to tell these other twits. May I have the floor?"

"Tamsyn, you can take your time. Marines, if anyone

interrupts her, I want them sent back to their bunks with a nice cup of tea. Am I clear?"

The Marine released Tamsyn's upper arm, and saluted the Prince. Around her, the crusty elite of the United Kingdom squirmed, and it tickled the darkest corner of Tamsyn's heart.

"I did some questionable things in the war. So did the other guys. But I'm looking at the biggest group of criminals on the face of the earth. You had the means to save anything up to sixty-six million lives, but you packed up the liquor cabinet and you ran. There were people starving, and scared, and you left them all to die."

She paused for a moment, and let the words sink in. Other times she'd told them this in more polite terms, and the Privy Council had rationalised this behaviour, offered excuses, but now they had to hear her. It was *glorious*.

"They were torn apart by the living dead, and their government wasn't there to help them. You should have stayed. You should have fought back, like the rest of us. You cowards. You shameful pieces of shit."

The Prime Minister drew in a breath, opened his mouth. He saw the look on Prince Harry's face, and closed his mouth again.

"I have asked you, I have begged, I have drawn up plans and schedules for re-colonisation, I have met with everyone I could, and every time you offered me excuses. Lies. Now you've got no choice. I say we go home, right now. We save the colonies and the outposts that are still standing. Because it is the right thing to do. Because a bandit nation has taken away your safe little hidey-hole. Because I will personally head-butt the next person who tells me we're not doing it."

"You heard the lady," Prince Harry said, looking at the Captain of the *HMS Vengeance*. "Set a course for home."

4

"We knew of three remaining colonies when we left Gravesend," Tamsyn said. "The prison island of Sheppey. The leftovers from Gravesend holed up in the Tilbury fort on the Thames. And there was a group up in Manchester, but they were doing badly."

She was addressing a small group in the submarine's command centre. Prince Harry, Captain Grant who ran the *Vengeance*, Prime Minister Fallot, and, to her surprise, Leyland.

"Any others?" the scarred warrior said. Leyland was a Regimental Sergeant Major, and the highest-ranking survivor from the 43 Commando Fleet Protection Group Royal Marines. Anyone who wasn't a submariner answered to him.

"Our radio guy heard from lots of groups in that first year, but they weren't organised. Usually a family, or a group of neighbours with a ham radio. They couldn't get to us, and we couldn't help them. We just stopped hearing from them, one after the other."

"Were there any groups on the Isle of Man?" Fallot asked. "Privy Council wants the Isle cleared of undead, and our first settlement to start there."

"It's not the worst idea," Tamsyn admitted. "But there were no survivors there. Our records put their population at 85,000 before the outbreak. That's a lot of zombies packed into a small place."

"Well, fire one of the nuclear missiles at it!" Fallot said. "Clear it out, and get it ready for the living."

"Your Highness, I promised to play nice with the PM, but... that's just a special level of dumb," Tamsyn said.

"We're not wasting the Trident missiles on the undead," Prince Harry said. "Radiation isn't likely to harm them, and the land will take years to recover. We need to be able to farm, to live in a place where our kids won't be born with two heads."

He glanced at Tamsyn as he said this, and she felt a thrill flush through her stomach. *What was that?* she thought. For a moment her brain threatened to shut down, but she found the power to continue.

"The best bet is to head straight to the Isle of Sheppey," she said. "Governor Bridgely was running a tight ship there. She knocked the causeway down to keep the undead out, and had the prisoners reclaiming marshland for farming. Absolute rotten bitch, but the place might still be going."

"You said you went into London, to find help," Prince Harry said. "The photos, and your sketches. Do you think...?"

"There is no-one left alive in that mess," Tamsyn said, and wished she could take the words back. His freckled face fell, and he wasn't a Prince then, just a young man who'd lost his entire family. She noticed the tension in his shoulders, the tight set of his jaw. She only had herself and her son to worry about - the pressure on Prince Harry must be phenomenal. To hear that on top of that there was no hope for any of his family was reality finally hitting home.

"I want to find all of them," Harry finally said. "All of those hidden people, the ones we left behind. Give them back their country."

"Me too," Tamsyn said. "But don't expect much. It was really bad when I left. Plus, the zombies will just be thawing out from winter now. Any survivors are about to get hit hard."

The Prime Minister looked pale in the fluorescent light.

"Hey, at least you don't have to worry about pleasing the voters anymore," Tamsyn told Fallot. "There's fuck all of them left."

AT DOVER, the dead crawled all over the port, little more than mummified skeletons. Their clothes were tattered rags, and the past few winters had left these undead badly damaged. *Freeze, thaw, shuffle, repeat.* They shuffled aimlessly, up and down the piers, along the frozen slush of the beach, only flinching when the salt spray got too close.

Tamsyn slowly panned the periscope across the town, and what she saw wasn't promising. There were thousands of the undead visible, a sick promenade of walking corpses from the marina through to the ferry terminal, and behind that they were packing the streets, shuffling past the broken windows of restaurants and tourist traps. Along the high street, a fire had burnt unchecked, and there were gaps in the shopfronts like missing teeth, all ruined lumber and snow and even more undead, stumbling pointlessly through the wreckage.

She kept panning until she reached the white cliffs, clean and cheerful, and her heart twinged at the sight. It felt like a thousand years since she'd last seen these, sailing a doomed ship in the opposite direction.

"Welcome home, Your Highness," Tamsyn said, handing over the periscope to Prince Harry. She watched his face as he took in the devastation, and for a moment he let his soldier face slip, mouth trembling. After a few long moments he gave it over to Captain Grant, who could not conceal his shock. The other officers in command all took a turn, and were speechless from what they saw.

Tamsyn tried to be charitable towards these others, but they'd avoided most of this mess. Everything she'd learnt about tactics and logic told her that the Navy had done the right thing, evacuating the government, but it rubbed her raw. These were professional warriors, and they'd avoided the place for *years*.

Leyland was a cool customer as he took in the carnage.

"All of the ports like this?"

"They will be," Tamsyn said. "Apart from mega-hordes, the coffin-dodgers don't travel far. Any population centre will still be crawling with those things."

"Coffin dodgers!" Harry barked with laughter, and the tension in the command room eased a little.

"We had heaps of names made up for them," Tamsyn said. "Maggot sacks. Gut shufflers. Stinky Stevens. I could go on."

"We should call them Zulu Charlies," Leyland offered. "It can stand for 'zombie corpses'."

"That's not bad."

Harry took Captain Grant to one side, conferring with him, a hint of a smirk on his face. The captain of the submarine nodded once, and barked out a string of commands.

Once more they were on a war footing, and the submariners took to their battle stations. Grant patched the periscope feed into one of the main screens, and Tamsyn watched as many of the ensigns and the rank and file saw the zombie threat for the first time.

"Listen up," Harry said. "William the Conqueror landed down the coast from here, about a thousand years ago. Worked out well for him. And now it's our turn. We're back for our birthrights and all that stuff."

He nodded to Grant, who gave the order. Tamsyn heard the dull thud as a rocket fired from the Vengeance, and then the periscope feed caught it streaking out from the depths, leaving the English channel for a brief moment, before punching into a knot of hundreds of the undead. Zombies, dock, everything vanished in the explosion.

The whole submarine clapped and cheered.

ABOUT A MILE OFFSHORE from the mouth of the Thames, the two Trident submarines rose to the surface. The sea water poured from the *Victorious* and the *Vengeance*, as they finally emerged from the depths.

Tamsyn was still worried about the Americans, and as awesome as it was to blow up part of Dover for kicks, she wondered if the Yanks had seen any of that on their satellites. She wondered how much they still wanted to take her back, force her to face whatever passed for justice now.

"All of the satellites are starting to fail," Leyland told her when she voiced her fears. "They need people monitoring their orbits and writing software patches, just to keep them up in the sky. GPS barely works now. So no, I doubt they saw that."

"You folks ready?" Prince Harry said, already hustling up the metal steps. Above, the deck hatch opened, and Tamsyn relished the daylight, the fresh air.

"Mummy?" she heard, even as the grubby hands tugged at her pants. Smiling, she lifted her son up, clasped his little arms around her neck.

"You hold on tight mate. We're going back outside."

"Outside," he repeated, a note of worry in his voice.

"Don't worry, Malcolm," she said. "We've come back home."

"Vena?" he said, his pet name for Olivena. Tamsyn felt her heart twinge, wondered if her housekeeper was okay. Had anyone survived the Americans' hit on the island?

"We had to say goodbye to Vena," Tamsyn managed. "This is Mummy's old home. Do you remember me telling you about England?"

"Inland," he said.

Hustling Malcolm on her hip, Tamsyn followed the flow of people up to the deck. The seasoned submariners were doing fine, but after a week of hiding beneath the surface, the peers and the politicians were pushing past each other to get to daylight and fresh air.

When Tamsyn stepped out onto the deck, the brisk air washed over her, and after so many months in the Caribbean sunlight she really noticed the chill of the English spring. Waves crashed against the sides of the *Vengeance*, sending up spray and Tamsyn breathed it all in.

"There it is," Harry said at her elbow. "The Isle of Sheppey."

He handed her a pair of binoculars, which she juggled in her free hand. She panned across the mouth of the Thames, and once more she looked on that lonely beach, the barricades, the gritty sand where her father had breathed his last.

She tried to push the memory from her mind, and looked beyond the dunes, up to the town behind it. Sheerness, where they'd given her a lonely room to grieve in, offered her a place to live that she didn't want.

"Does not look promising," Harry said, and Tamsyn grunted in agreement. The barricades and the razor wire was still there, but no armed guards, no-one moving along the row of shops and beach-houses. The appearance of two enormous submarines should have sent half the island running towards them.

"No zombies at least," Tamsyn said, handing the binoculars back. "Perhaps they've pulled back from the shore. The Governor had the farms and everything planned around the prison."

An ensign came running, and delivered a report to Captain Grant. He addressed those gathered.

"I've had the radio room trying to raise someone. We've tried the emergency band, even the civilian band. There's no-one on the air-waves, no-one at all."

"Well, that might not mean anything," Tamsyn said. "You need power to run radios and transmitters. If the Islanders lost the power station over at Grain, they'd have run out of fuel pretty quickly."

"Your Highness," the Prime Minister said. "Your zombie expert has clearly misremembered the situation. We must regroup at the Isle of Man."

"Now hold on, you-" Tamsyn said, looking at Malcolm and holding in a swear. "There was an entire community here. The towns, all three prisons. Thousands of survivors. Why would I make that up?"

"We only have the evidence in front of us," Fallot said. "It does not seem safe, so we must move on."

"This submarine is not going to be safe if you don't pull your head in," Tamsyn said icily. "You abandoned these people to die, so perhaps it might be polite to make contact with them?"

"Tamsyn, Terry, stop it," Harry said, and she bit down on the next insult, settling for glaring at the Prime Minister. Malcolm started fussing on her hip, and began to sniffle at the raised voices.

"I want a team on the ground," Harry said. "Sergeant Major, handpick a group and take a launch over. I want you back here before dusk with a full report."

"Yes, Your Highness," Leyland said with a crisp salute.

"Here, I'll watch Malcolm," Harry said, taking the boy from Tamsyn. "I want my zombie expert going too."

WHEN THE LAUNCH HIT LAND, Tamsyn piled out with all the others, hauling on a handle and dragging the boat out of the surf. In moments Leyland's handpicked crew were on the sand and moving, assault rifles at the ready, scanning the dunes for any sign of movement. This was their bread and butter, and Tamsyn was glad to have these men and women around her.

Two Marines, a female Gurkha, a SAS trooper in black fatigues, Leyland, and her. She approved of the small number, knew that throwing a big group at this mission could get people killed. For a moment she felt the same thrill she had back in Texas, being out on a patrol, knowing the people around you had your back. Willingly entering into danger, but being ready for it.

Wish we'd had you fellas here last time, Tamsyn thought.

She had her bow ready, arrow nocked, pistol bouncing around on her hip. She'd never found the focus with firearms that she had with the bow, but it would be mighty handy if some rotten bugger came up close and personal.

The Marines were named Martins and Poulsen, and they kept watch while the Gurkha worked at the tiger-wire barricade with wire-cutters. She'd introduced herself as Corporal Sushma Thapa, a tough woman with jagged scars running from her temple down to her chin. She moved fast and sure, rolling back a section of the barricade, gun at the ready as she stole into the dunes, head high as if sniffing out prey.

Can't believe I ever thought I was a tough customer, Tamsyn thought. *Sushma looks like a stone carving in a uniform.*

Sushma gave the all-clear sign, and they followed her, slipping from dune to dune, guns tracking in all directions. Tamsyn was slightly out of step but her basic training came back to her, and at least she didn't embarrass herself as she tagged along with the professionals.

She fought against the tension of her bow, a rig set at a higher pull than she liked. It worked well enough back on Grand Cayman, back on the target range, but she missed her old bow, lost the day she lost her man -

"Which way?" Sushma whispered in her ear, and Tamsyn jumped. She hadn't even seen her slide up next to her. If the Gurkha had wanted to drop her, she'd already be dead.

"Police station is that way," Tamsyn said, pointing up the street. "Accommodation's down that street."

The Gurkha flashed up a series of field signals to the rest of the group, and then they were moving into Sheerness itself, past the ice-cream stands and empty pubs. Governor Bridgely had set up the Tesco as a makeshift ration centre, but the carpark was empty of queues, trestle tables knocked over, tents flapping in a light breeze.

No people, but there were no undead either. If there had been an outbreak on the island, the zombies should have been swarming all over the place, bumping into things and generally stinking up the joint. Tamsyn thought back to the mystery of the Marie Celeste, a ship abandoned with no explanation, and wondered what had gone wrong here in the last three years.

Leyland's crew flowed up the main street, crouched behind post-boxes and rubbish bins, watching the rooflines, peering beneath abandoned vehicles. Tamsyn almost relaxed then - these folks had everything under control.

The SAS trooper looked her way, flashing a series of hand signals. They were different to the ones she'd learnt in Texas, and she shook her head, not understanding what he was trying to tell her. He came back to her position in a crab walk, rifle tracking to windows, alleys, bins, all over the place. He was overdoing things, showing off to her, and she rolled her eyes.

She'd heard Leyland refer to him as Reynolds. He looked like a video game character, all garbed in black, complete with green-tinted goggles, headset and enough gear to start a one-man war. She'd met 'operators' before, elite special force types, and they generally rubbed her up the wrong way. She'd gone through a war as a grunt, and had seen enough of their condescending bullshit to last one lifetime.

"Stay next to me, Miss," Reynolds whispered, and rested a hand on her upper arm. "I'll keep you safe."

"I keep myself safe," she scoffed, shaking herself loose from the man's grip. His lips turned downwards, and just like that he went from would-be-saviour to nasty.

"Whatever, bitch. Don't come crying to me."

"Promise I won't."

The man in black left her for dust, returning to his position. Sushma had led them all to a bus shelter opposite the police station. Reynolds had a sighting glass out, and peered out at the window.

More field signals. Tamsyn shook her head, and Sushma crept closer, whispered.

"No movement inside. Nothing on infra. Door ajar."

"Listen, the undead don't give off heat. Be bloody careful!"

The group crossed the street to the police station at angles, forming up alongside the small store-front compound. Sushma crept up to the door, nudging it open with the barrel of her rifle. She crab-walked over the threshold, and was lost to the gloom of the interior.

The others were still scanning for threats, but Tamsyn relaxed the draw on her bow, eased out the tension from her muscles. She guessed the whole town was abandoned, and when Sushma reappeared, she was also in a relaxed attitude, rifle slung across her shoulder. The Gurkha had a ledger in her hands, opened to the last entry.

"The station log," she said. "Last entry was over nine months ago. One man arrested for hoarding supplies. Then nothing."

The ration lines at Tesco. The policeman who'd offered her comfort the day her father was shot, gone with no explanation. As Tamsyn scanned the buildings around them, she noticed no evidence of violence. For some reason, the whole place had simply stopped one day.

"We're not going to find anything here," Tamsyn said, standing up and cricking her neck. "If there's anyone left, they're at the prison. Let's go."

5

Leyland found a tourist map of the island in an empty ice-cream parlour. It was a little over seven miles to the main prison, HMP Swaleside. This was where Governor Bridgely had set up her headquarters all those years ago, and where she'd set out crews of prisoners to reclaim the marshlands.

"Sir, we've been ordered to return by dusk," Reynolds protested to Leyland.

"I'm going to pretend I didn't hear that, trooper," Leyland said, fixing the man with the full force of his Regimental Sergeant Major glare. The man in black deflated almost instantly, and pretended to fiddle with a piece of his equipment instead.

"Fourteen miles, there and back," Leyland said. "Most folks could run that distance in three hours. I'm going to give you boys and girls two and a half. Am I clear?"

"Sir," the professional warriors said.

"Oh god no," Tamsyn groaned.

They ate a quick lunch over the map.

"Quickest route appears to be the coastal road," Leyland

said, pointing at the map with a yellowed thumbnail. "We'll go through Minster, and then turn inland towards the prison."

"Suggestion," Tamsyn chimed in. "Yes, the coast road is quicker. However, there is a country club if we go through to Halfway Houses. They'll have golf buggies, bikes, all sorts of stuff we can use."

Not to mention the cemetery where my Dad is buried, she added to herself.

"Says there's a bicycle shop here," Reynolds said, indicating a spot on the map a half mile down High Street. "We can kit up there, and ride along the coast. Get there and back before dusk."

"What is your problem?" Tamsyn said, staring up at the tall trooper. "They're not going to leave without us."

"Girl, we know what we're doing. You don't."

"I beg your fucking pardon?"

"Our job is to get you there and back in one piece. We're not traipsing over the meadows on your say so."

"Oh, I get it. You're scared. Might just keep you alive out here."

"You two, stow it," Leyland interrupted. "New plan. We source bicycles or a working vehicle. We take the back roads to the prison, observe, and get the hell back to the sub. Understood?"

"Sir."

Once more they patrolled through those empty, creepy streets. They checked all the vehicles they passed, only to find flat tyres, dead batteries, dry fuel tanks. The bicycle shop was stripped of everything, even down to kids' scooters and skateboards.

"Makes sense," Leyland said. "If they're out of fuel,

everyone's riding on bikes. Okay people, we'll try the country club. Eyes open, and double time."

They set off at a jog, and within half a mile Tamsyn realised how far she'd let her fitness slip. The other soldiers tromped down the road effortlessly, while she huffed away, heart hammering.

"Too much rum and pork," she managed, struggling to keep up. Sushma snorted with laughter. The Gurkha loped along with no issue, and Tamsyn was pretty sure she could throw her over her shoulders without missing a beat.

"Hey, I've been meaning to ask, how did you get those scars?" Tamsyn said, indicating the ragged marks across the Gurkha's face and chin. "Knife fight?"

"No. Was from our farm, back in Nepal."

"Oh," Tamsyn puffed, disappointed. She'd been hoping for a gory tale to take her mind off this sudden exercise.

"A wolf was killing our goats. I tracked it and killed it with this," she said, pulling out a blade from a sheath in the small of her back. It was the curved kukri, the signature weapon of the Gurkhas.

"Wow. You're a bad-arse. Were you already enlisted?"

"Was my ninth birthday."

"You killed a wolf when you were nine?"

"It was eating the goats."

They left Sheerness for the countryside, and still did not see a single soul. The main road took them past a holiday village, and this showed the same signs of sudden abandonment. Tamsyn saw clothes pegged on clotheslines, footballs and dolls dropped to the ground, the cabins left with doors and windows opened to the elements.

No signs of violence, just a sudden and unexplained evacuation. Leyland ordered his team through the cabins, and most things were left untouched, with one notable exception.

Every crumb of food was missing from the place. There was a cannery set up in the common area, lids and jars coated with dust. Every spare bit of lawn and dirt had been given over to a victory garden, now a feral tangle of bean-plants and cabbage gone to seed.

Huffing like a racehorse, Tamsyn poked through a communal store in the recreation room, looking for safe drinking water. Someone had built a bunch of ramshackle shelves, with only a handful of jars and tins remaining. A ledger behind a desk, with a complete record of all of the park residents, and how much food went to which family. The last date matched to the police station log.

"Where the hell have they all gone?" Leyland said.

Past the holiday camp was an outlying suburb, newly built when the world stopped. What Tamsyn saw then made the hair prickle up on her arms. Every house for streets around had been carefully demolished, stripped to the ground. There were still stacks of bricks and roof tiles, lumber in neat piles, and hundreds of footprints tracking through the destroyed front gardens.

All around them, the houses had been pulled apart by hand. One house was partially demolished, but the attempt was abandoned, the house a mess of pipes and masonry, dry-wall and bits of the kitchen trodden into the front-yard beneath hundreds of feet.

"This is not right," Tamsyn began.

"You reckon?" Reynolds interrupted.

"Governor Bridgely said they had a massive housing shortage here," she continued, ignoring the black-clad arse-hole. "They barely had enough houses for the people living here before they blew up the bridge. So why abandon their homes, and knock down half of a suburb?"

The group pondered this for a long moment. Sushma considered the direction of the tracks, and consulted the map of the island.

"They're making something at the prison," the Gurkha said.

"These weirdos have scavenged enough material to build a palace," Leyland said. "Let's pay them a visit."

THE COUNTRY CLUB looked like it had been hit by locusts. Every brick, every piece of timber and steel, stripped down to the foundations. The overgrown greens and fairways were scarred and torn, with pieces of timber and tin scattered all over a trail that led straight towards the prison.

"No bicycles here, Sir," Reynolds called out, kicking through the rubble. When Leyland looked away, the black-clad trooper flipped Tamsyn the bird. At this point in their cross-country run, Tamsyn barely had enough energy to shake her head at the man. Sneaking a peek over Leyland's shoulder, Tamsyn looked at the tourist map of the island, and decided now was as good as ever.

"Got a confession to make," she said. "I'm very unfit."

"No kidding," Leyland said.

"Another confession. I suggested this route for selfish reasons. My dad is buried less than a mile from here. I'm going to visit him."

"Out of the question," Leyland said, wearing the officer's expression that was ten times as scary as someone raging and screaming at her. There were a thousand ways an officer could make your life hard, and if you drew that focus with a stupid plan, and doubled down with insubordination...

Fuck it.

"These bastards murdered my dad the moment we stepped ashore. I saw them put him in the ground, and heard all of their lies and excuses. So no offense, but I owe this one to the old man. I'm going."

Leyland looked at her for a long, heavy beat, and then he put his fingers between his teeth, let out of a short whistle.

"Everyone, take five. The zombie expert wants to take a break from our vital mission. For personal reasons."

Poulsen and Martins muttered to each other, even as Reynolds clapped sarcastically.

"Thanks everyone," Tamsyn said. "You're a great bunch."

She walked away from Leyland as fast as her wobbly legs would allow, still huffing away. Everything ached as she staggered across the ruined rows of townhouses, beating a shortcut towards the cemetery. It was embarrassing how far she'd let her conditioning slip. *A few bike rides and drinking on your porch does not make you fit.*

Behind her, the shift of brick against brick, and the animal part of her brain kicked in, flipping her straight into killer survival mode. She went down on one knee, arrow nocked, bow up and tracking. One long breath, a swear word, and then she let out the tension from the string, let the pulleys wind back to rest.

It was Sushma following her, kicking her way through the wreckage. Tamsyn had been a heartbeat away from putting a feathered shaft in the Gurkha's throat.

"You would not have hit me," Sushma called out. "Your arms were wobbling."

"Bullshit. I was on the Commonwealth Games archery team. I am as steady as a rock."

"Was just a little wobble," Sushma said. "Try it again."

"I won't draw on you. That's just weird. Weirdo."

Sushma pulled a ridiculous face, tongue wagging. Slinging her rifle over her shoulder, she waved her arms around, pretending to be a zombie.

"I am coming to kill you. Your arrows will never stop me."

Tamsyn barked with laughter. She sought and found her focus, and drew suddenly, aiming for a spot just before the Gurkha's front foot. A flash as the arrow crossed the distance in a heartbeat, and in the same moment Sushma slid gracefully to one side, an economical movement. The shot missed her by a mile.

"I see now. You can hit a still target or a walking corpse. A warrior, not so much."

"I was trying *not* to hit you," Tamsyn laughed, and then launched another surprise arrow, this time to a spot within a hand's breadth of Sushma's waist. This time Sushma's feet were rooted still, but her right hand moved with gunslinger speed, pulling the kukri knife out of its sheath and in the same movement batting away the arrow. Tamsyn stared in shock as two parts of the arrow fell to the ground, neatly sliced down the shaft.

"How in the living blue fuck did you just do that?" Tamsyn said, awed.

"Mongolians taught me," she said, casually sheathing the blade. "They can shoot their bows from horseback."

"Yeah, yeah. Stop wrecking my arrows."

The Gurkha followed Tamsyn all the way to the cemetery, a tiny ball of murder in a uniform. Tamsyn found herself remembering the bronze statue of Pocahontas she'd been obsessed with, drawing the exotic figure over and over, and wondered why she'd ever thought the Native American had been bad-ass. For the first time in ages, she wished she had a pad and pencils to hand, to sketch this amazing warrior.

"Can you do any other cool tricks?"

"I tried to do this once," Sushma said, and mimed driving her palm up into Tamsyn's nose. "It is all made up. You cannot push the nose bones up into a brain."

"I killed two zombies at once. I stapled their heads together with an arrow."

"Tamsyn, you are telling lies."

"I've got heaps better lies than that."

They reached the cemetery then, and Tamsyn was sad to see the state of the place. When the islanders had buried her father here, they'd kept the grounds tidy, the grass mowed flat, the weeds at bay. Going by the dates in the records they'd found, no-one had touched this place in nine months.

"Dangerous?" Sushma asked, rifle pointed towards the nearest grave. Tamsyn scoffed and nudged her barrel aside.

"That only happens in the movies. Everyone buried here had a clean death."

That answer seemed to satisfy Sushma on some philosophical level. Tamsyn scanned the weathered markers, and felt ashamed that she couldn't remember exactly where her father was buried. She remembered the ceremony, the empty homilies of the priest, that awful moment where she'd once more seen Simon Dawes face to face, but she could not place the grave in her mind's eye.

"Shit, shit, shit," she muttered. "Clock's ticking."

They checked row after row of headstones and markers, and she took in the names of the lucky dead, the bland inscriptions offering rest and peace, the names of those they left behind. Faded plastic flowers and knick-knacks still adorned some of the headstones, now barely visible through the tangles of weeds and long grass.

Another year or two, and you'd barely know this place was here at all.

"Damnit," Tamsyn muttered. "It was a white marker, a wooden cross thing. His name was Malcolm Webb."

"Malcolm Webb," Sushma repeated. She poked her rifle barrel through the undergrowth, while Tamsyn was straight out on her hands and knees, ripping fistfuls of grass out and hoping to find the grave. She felt the clock ticking, and knew she'd never get this chance again. She had until the moment Leyland ended this break, and not a second sooner.

Tamsyn wanted to cry with the frustration of it all. She remembered life with her mother and father, the innocent years before the outbreak. He should have lived to be grumpy and old, to walk her down the aisle, to meet his grandchildren, but here Malcolm had ended, his body forgotten, with no one to mourn this brilliant, funny man.

Now she couldn't even find the spot. Feeling like the worst daughter in the world, Tamsyn raced up and down each row, ignoring the ornate headstones and markers, looking for a blank spot in between them, the little lump of earth that was his pauper's grave.

"Tamsyn, look," Sushma said at her elbow, voice low. Instinct had her nock an arrow before she raised her eyes to look, and then she had to refrain from laughing. Less than thirty feet away, a rabbit emerged from a tangle of long grass, plump and fearless, nose and ears twitching.

Grinning, the Gurkha placed her hand on Tamsyn's bow, and shook it slightly, mocking the wobble she supposedly had on the draw. Pushing her aside with a friendly elbow, Tamsyn found her focus, the magic moment between woman and bow, where she was in perfect commune with the physics of this act.

Inhale from the diaphragm. Draw. Slow exhale. Release.

Her arrow streaked across the graveyard, and snagged the rabbit through the throat. It leapt upwards, kicking once, and then it was still, the life already leaving it. Tamsyn looked triumphantly to the Gurkha, who clapped politely.

"Very nice," she said. "Me, I catch them with my hands. But you shoot okay."

Tamsyn knelt by the rabbit, extracting her arrow. The animal looked healthy, and would go towards feeding someone today. Then she sat back with a start, falling on her arse with an undignified squawk as another rabbit appeared, racing out from under her feet.

"Well, go on!" she called out to the laughing Gurkha. "Catch that one with your hands if you're so good."

"Catch what?"

"Very funny," Tamsyn said, leaping to her feet and taking off after the rabbit. The thrill of the hunt had taken some of the sting out of her failed mission to find her dad's grave. She dashed through the headstones, kicking through the grass, and she saw the flick of ears and tail, the second rabbit weaving and running for its life. She put the bloody arrow back on the string, drawing, trying to keep her arms steady, knowing that it was damn hard to shoot accurately on the move.

The rabbit suddenly stopped, breathing rapidly, staring at a spot in front of it. With a hoot of triumph, Tamsyn let fly, string and pulleys and carbon fibre launching death at two hundred and seventy feet per second.

The arrow passed through the rabbit, and then it simply blinked out of sight.

"What the hell?" Tamsyn breathed. Walking all around

the spot where she'd seen the rabbit, she could see wet earth and grass, damp enough to pick up the details on the bottom of her boots, but no rabbit tracks. Extracting her arrow from the clay, Tamsyn wondered if she was losing her mind.

Clay on her arrow. She thought of the clay that spattered the gravedigger's pants, the sticky mud she'd tossed down onto her dad's coffin. With a start of recognition, Tamsyn knelt down, pulling away weeds, and there it was. A wooden marker, fallen to the ground now, paint flaking, but there were the words. MALCOLM WEBB, 1962-2013.

"It was the rabbit. The rabbit brought me here," Tamsyn said to Sushma, who'd arrived moments later.

"You shot that rabbit."

"No. The second one. It was right near the first one."

"Only one rabbit."

"I saw it! I followed a bloody rabbit here, okay?"

Then she saw it again, looking at her from the edge of the woods. Staring straight at her. Tamsyn lifted her arm silently, pointing at the animal, but after a moment of looking, Sushma shook her head.

"Ghost rabbit?" the Gurkha said after a long moment, and then touched the limp corpse hanging from Tamsyn's belt. "I wouldn't eat that."

"Too right," Tamsyn said. She left the furry body lying on her father's grave, and pushed an arrow into the clay, the best marker she could give him at a moment's notice.

"I miss you Dad," she said, and then the words fell out. "I can't come back here, and I'm sorry about that. I wish you could meet your grandson. He's beautiful, he looks a bit like you. He looks like Eddie too. Eddie Jacobs! You'd never have believed we'd get together. I lost him in Cuba, him and Clem. We went to America too! I wish you could have seen it Dad, seen all the things you've missed out on!"

A rough bark of laughter, and Tamsyn looked up. There was Reynolds, pissing on someone's headstone a few rows away.

"You finished yet?" he said. "I'll help you dig the old man up if you want him to come along."

Rising, Tamsyn gripped her bow in a white-knuckle rage. It took everything she had not to launch an arrow at the smug bastard, standing there and mocking her final goodbye. Her moment, long dreamt of, and he'd ruined it.

"No," Sushma said. "Do not."

The Gurkha drew her kukri, and sharpened its edge on the nearest headstone, all the while staring at the black-clad trooper. He stared back at her for a long minute, even lighting up a cigarette. Eventually, he lost the staring contest, and stubbed out his half-finished smoke on his palm, pocketing the rest. He withdrew from the graveyard with an unfriendly grin.

"Is he going to give you trouble?" Tamsyn said, looking at her new ally with admiration. *Such a bad-arse.*

"I killed a wolf when I was a girl," Sushma said, snorting with laughter. "Now that I am a woman, imagine what I could do to a dog."

6

Leyland led the small group away from the dismantled suburb, leaving the churned up golf course and entering the island's marshland. The mystery house dismantlers had completely ignored the roads and taken their building supplies straight into the mud and the muck. A straight line of footprints and destruction, aimed right at the prison.

"Do your zombies break apart houses?" Leyland asked Tamsyn.

They're not my zombies, she wanted to say, but he'd been giving her a frosty treatment since her admission about the graveyard. *Behave yourself, Tamsyn.*

"Re-Humans are strong enough to do this," she said. "They're the ones who were brought back into themselves with a salt treatment. The Cubans had another kind, the Muñecas. It means doll. They put embalming fluid and salt into a zombie's brain. Made them into slaves, fighters, whatever."

Oh Eddie, she thought, remembering the moment he came at her, all the goodness cooked out of him with that poison. She put an arrow through her beloved's skull, and in nightmares she'd relived that awful moment over and over...

"Living zombies? Embalming fluid? She's having a bloody lend of us!" Reynolds said. Martins and Poulsen scoffed.

"Enough. Behave yourselves," Leyland said.

"I don't give a shit if you believe me," Tamsyn said, seething at Reynolds. "How else would you explain this?"

"Maybe they're doing a boot-camp?" Poulsen offered cheekily.

"If I lived in this shit-hole, I'd tear it down too," Reynolds laughed.

"I said enough!" Leyland roared, and that shut them down instantly. He turned back to Tamsyn, two bright red spots on his cheeks.

"You said the Governor here was reclaiming this marsh for farming, building up around the prison," Leyland said.

"Perhaps," Tamsyn said. "Maybe they're making a fortification, more walls. We used all sorts of junk to barricade Gravesend."

"That makes no sense," Sushma said. "They already have an island. Then fences. Then prison walls."

"Yes. It's a lot of effort for a barricade they don't really need," Leyland said. "Something's off here."

They continued following the track of bricks and churned up mud, a thick scar blazed right across the national park. Tamsyn saw the marsh-birds at play, living a life largely undisturbed by the end of humanity. A family of bunnies emerged from a tuft of grasses, and Tamsyn thought again about the weirdness at the cemetery. A rabbit who was dead and then wasn't dead.

A vision? A ghost? Tamsyn had seen a lot of weird stuff in the past few years, and who was to know what the rules were for death now? Perhaps there *were* ghosts. Or perhaps she had seen one messed-up thing too many, and was simply losing her mind.

There was one other possibility - she'd never have found Mal's overgrown grave without supernatural help. After ending hundreds, even thousands of lives, Tamsyn Webb had finally received a favour from Death.

"Watch out," Sushma said, a moment before Tamsyn's boots hit a slick piece of mud and flew out from beneath her. She landed flat on her arse in the mud, her bow flying off to sink in a stretch of manky water. Leyland's group set about to laughing.

"Walk with your eyes, not your feet," the Gurkha said.

"What does that even mean?" Tamsyn muttered. She got up, slid around a little bit more, and dug around in the water, finally finding her bow. She eyed the pulleys and actions with a weary eye - if she didn't strip, oil and dry this bow soon, it would be ruined.

Tamsyn didn't care too much about the random arseholes in her group, but she felt sad when Leyland let a touch of disappointment wash across his face. Since her display at the training course, he must have been expecting some kind of zombie-killing bad-arse, and here she was basically getting in the way.

Trying not to explore her daddy issues too deeply, Tamsyn walked forward extra carefully, and wondered how much she resembled an awkward duck. She was making extra noise, legs splayed stiffly, while the professional warriors made it through the last of the muck with no issue. The group climbed out of the last of the marshlands, and Leyland signalled a forward crawl up a steep rise.

More hand signals, and Tamsyn sighed internally. She had no idea what they were saying to each other. They crawled forwarded through the long grass until they were on the verge of the main road, a ribbon of asphalt now cracked after years of neglect.

Beyond that, the prisons, three fortresses of razor wire and brick. Her Majesty's Prisons Swaleside, Emley and Stanford Hill, a cluster of justice from that old world, the one where they still had laws and council meetings and terrible television.

But surrounding the whole complex was a new structure, a towering mass of brick walls and towers, with patches of tin and roof tiles. Makeshift scaffolding reached up to unsafe levels, and even from here she could see the shapes of people moving around the outside of the structure, hauling building materials. Others ferried up new material from great stacks formed around the structure - entire suburbs worth of bricks and lumber, heaped in piles higher than houses.

What they'd built so far made her eyes swim - the shapes of the building were all wrong. There were no right angles, nothing but an outer shell that stretched up and out, bulging out and full of hollows in other places, and above everything was a mad crown of towers, fingers of material stretching up into the sky, promising to be far taller than the tallest watchtowers of the prison.

Through gaps in the outer shell Tamsyn could see more building work, honeycombing out from the prison walls themselves. It looked like nothing that made sense, a sinuous structure that was equal parts bee-hive and ants-nest.

"What the ever-living hell is that?" she whispered, awed. The others were looking through rifle scopes and binoculars, and eventually she talked Sushma into unclipping her scope and lending it to her.

Tamsyn got a closer look at the builders of this immense, insane structure. They weren't moving with the stiff gait of the undead, and did not have the waxy horror-show skin of the Re-humans or the Muneca. They were normal people, working together, cooperating on the most insane working bee she'd ever witnessed.

"Well?" Leyland asked her.

"They're not undead," she said. "But something's definitely off about this."

"You reckon?" Reynolds scoffed.

Leyland muttered into the radio, their lifeline back to the submarines. The crackle of milquetoast from the talking heads offered these helpful suggestions - *observe, gather intel, report back*.

Apart from the tools that the Islanders were using to fasten the bizarre building together, Tamsyn couldn't spot anything even resembling a weapon. When she'd last visited this island it definitely had a paramilitary feel, so to see the people so relaxed and unguarded was another mark in the "weird" column.

"Is it a watch tower?" Leyland muttered.

"Stupid design," Sushma said. "All weak points. Even the archer could destroy it with no trouble."

"Gee, thanks."

"If they are so worried about the undead, why no guards?" Leyland said. "We should have been spotted already."

Tamsyn kept scanning over the crowd of workers. They were definitely moving like people, but she saw a few things that seemed strange. Their hair was a little unkempt, as were the beards she saw. Their clothing was filthy, as you could expect from a building site, but there were other things. There was a person wearing only one shoe. Another with a scrape on her arm, bleeding unchecked, the woman uncaring. The people worked together on their tasks, but not once did she say any of them talk, pause to rest, or even slack off once.

These people were definitely alive, but that was where the resemblance ended. They seemed like a hive of insects, smart enough to build an insanely enormous structure, and intently focused upon the endeavour.

"What are we even looking at here?" Leyland finally said.

"Something new," Tamsyn replied. Still scanning across the hundreds of builders, she paused, instantly recognising the figure of Governor Bridgely. The steel-spined warden was out there with everybody else, lugging a stack of roof tiles. She looked a little dishevelled but otherwise alive.

"There's the boss. Right there. Woman with black uniform, white hair up in a bun."

"Bridgely?" Leyland asked.

"Yep."

As one, the workers stopped work. Tools fell from limp hands, and they scrambled down the scaffolds, away from the stacks of brick and lumber. The people walked in a lockstep, not quite moving in ranks but still marching to some unheard beat.

"Look at this spooky North Korean shit," Reynolds said.

From the other side of the building site came an entire parade of people. Some held tins of food, others sacks of rice, while others ported entire water coolers from offices. It seemed like a village had been looted of anything that could be remotely identified as food.

Much like with the building supplies, they deposited a small mountain of food and drink in one spot, and promptly turned around to fetch more. The behaviour was exactly like ants porting food.

"Well, that's weird," Tamsyn said.

That was when a pack of thirty people hauled forward a dead cow on ropes and rollers. It was dumped with the rest of the food.

Tamsyn and the soldiers could only watch in shock as the builders tore into the stack of food. A cluster of people descended upon the cow, tearing into its flesh with their hands and teeth.

"Surely that makes them zombies," Poulsen said. The eaters were pulling out organs now, great ropes of gut and gizzard, and disassembling the animal over a broad area. From a distance it seemed like an effective way to feed a large group of people. Within a few minutes the food was all but gone, with nothing left of the pile but tins, packets, bones and bottles.

Next they fell upon the nearby field, digging holes with their bare hands. As one the workers squatted, voiding their bowels and bladders, neatly burying the refuse before rising, and staggering back towards their twisted building project.

Food and toilet break for hundreds of workers, completed in less than 10 minutes. It was like some alien mind had the broadest idea of what a human body needed, and each person was granted this and no more.

"Fetch that one. Assume hostility," Leyland barked, and Reynolds and Martins were off and moving towards the latrine field, keeping low. Governor Bridgely was at the edge of the group, stuffing her bodily waste into a hole in the ground.

The capture was a thing of beauty. As much as she hated the man, she had to admire Reynolds' skill. He emerged from a tuft of grass, the black-clad figure visible for only a split second as he snatched at the Governor, hauling her back into the grass and out of sight.

Less than a minute later, Reynolds and Martins had Governor Bridgely back to their position, her head covered with a silk hood, hands bound behind her back with zipties. Leyland flashed a few hand signals, and the two Marines and Reynolds set up a tight perimeter, watching the building site for any sign of movement.

So far, it had been a clean extraction. None of the strange Islanders were coming after them, and were all resuming their strange task. Once more, Tamsyn looked upon the woman who had offered her safety, a home in exchange for her murdered father.

Going by what she'd seen today, Tamsyn was very glad to have turned her down.

"We have to assume she is infected," Leyland said. "You and you, fireman's lift. We'll take her back to the eastern shore, and we can get a full team out from the Vengeance to interrogate her."

"No," Tamsyn interrupted. "We can't move her."

"What? What the hell do you mean?"

"They're totally like ants. Whatever these people have become. They set trails, with pheromones or something we don't understand. Then these other 'ants' follow, hoping to find food. If we bring her back to the submarines, all of these weirdos there? They'll follow us, hoping to find another dead cow or something."

"Well, what do you suggest?" Leyland said, at a loss.

"Let me talk to her," Tamsyn said. "I know her, or I knew her. I'll find out what's going on here."

Leyland nodded, and Sushma pulled back the hood. Governor Bridgely peered at their group, more curious than upset. The woman looked like hell, her face a smear of make-up and old food, and the smell wafting up from her was overpowering.

"Governor Bridgely, I-"

"You are Tamsyn Lottie Webb," the Governor said, revealing teeth half-rotted. She curved her face up into a smile, but the expression was a tortured grimace, a facsimile at best. She gave this up, her face settling back into neutrality.

"You remember me?"

"We all know who you are, Tamsyn," she crooned.

"What the hell happened here? What are you building?"

The Governor worked her mouth for a moment, as if searching for a word that would suit, then gave up with a shrug and another grin. This time she stretched her grin as far as it would go, teeth bared, cheeks high and pinched, and then relaxed back to her nothingness.

"You've gotta stop doing that. You're creeping me out. Look, when I left you here, you were going to reclaim this marshland, build more houses, plant crops-"

"You were in the United Kingdom," the Governor interrupted, eyes fixed on some distant point. "You were in America. You were in Cuba. You were in the Cayman Islands. You are back here."

"How can you know all that?" Tamsyn whispered.

"You caused death in Gravesend, London and the Isle of Sheppey. You caused death in the Atlantic Ocean. You caused death on Corpus Christi, Maryland, New York, Texas, South Carolina, Florida. You caused death in Cuba. You caused death in Grand Cayman. You caused death on the Isle of Sheppey."

"You - you shut up!" Tamsyn said, anger flooding her cheeks. Worse than the litany of death that had followed her around the world was the matter-of-fact way that the Governor was laying her sins out in front of the group.

It had to be the Americans. All of this stuff was on her personnel records from Texas, in the records of her sessions with the shrink the Republican Army had found for her. Any other explanation just made her brain *twitchy*.

"We've been looking for you, Tamsyn Lottie Webb," Bridgely continued.

"It's time for you cut this shit out. Governor Bridgely, if you don't start giving me some straight answers, I will slap the stupid out of you."

"Governor Bridgely. You know this one," Bridgely said.

"Of course I know you, Governor Bridgely. You're the stupid bitch who killed my father, and we just caught you shitting in a field with a cult!"

Tamsyn slapped the woman, hard. The Governor barely reacted to the insult, and seemed enthralled with the experience.

"Violence," she said. "You reach for violence so quickly."

"I'll give you bloody violence, lady. Why are you building that stupid thing over the hill? Is someone making you do all this?"

"The Vanguard," Bridgely said simply.

"Now we're getting somewhere. Who is the Vanguard?"

"We are the Vanguard."

Tamsyn reached for another insult, for some way of breaking this idiot, but then she found her tongue stilled. With some panic she realised that her muscles were shutting down, her knees locking in place, and with the last movement left to her neck, she saw that her colleagues were the same, frozen where they stood. Martins, Poulsen and Reynolds were stone still, their rifles held low as hundreds of the Islanders approached, a swarm of filthy clothes and unnatural smiles, unhurried as they walked to meet the intruders.

Oh shit, oh shit, oh SHIT.

Leyland was frozen in place, hunched over notebook and pen, fingers struggling to continue writing. Sushma stood in the middle of an equipment check, visibly struggling to move, face clenched in silent fury. Then Tamsyn felt her head moved *against* her control, her gaze redirected towards Governor Bridgely. Hands still bound, the older woman rose to her feet, lips moving, and her face was the entire centre of Tamsyn's universe.

"We will make you Vanguard," she continued. "Builders needed. Food makers needed. A lot of work to do still."

Tamsyn struggled, fighting the bizarre paralysis with everything she had. Zombie were one thing, but this went beyond all logic, went into a place her mind wasn't prepared to go. Was this a gas, some kind of drug? Was she being hypnotised now? Was this part of the infection somehow?

This is total bullshit. She felt the fingers around her bow twitch, squeezing the grip a little tighter. The barest movement, but enough to encourage her. She could beat this thing.

"Tamsyn Lottie Webb, you are a great prize. Your essence shall be dealt with harshly, down in the low place."

She could hear the low murmur of the approaching crowd, not words exactly but many excited sounds, gasps, baby-babble, multiplied by thousands of throats. Somehow this was even creepier than the sound of an oncoming zombie horde. In a few more moments they would be surrounded, consumed.

The fingers on her bow-string trembled, just a small tremor. Tamsyn resisted the urge to move her eyes downward, not wanting to give away her resistance to the paralysis.

"We have found all of your Guides, your Psychopomps and Reapers. You were the last one left, Tamsyn Lottie Webb. The last one with the power over Death."

What the hell?

"Now you are Vanguard."

Governor Bridgely came for her then, eyes wide, teeth gnashing, seeking to bear her down. With one last effort of will Tamsyn freed herself from the invisible bond holding her still. Letting out a cry of defiance, she drew back on the bowstring, ready to sink an arrow straight into the Governor's heart.

TWANG. Still fouled up from the dunking in the mud and from months of wear and ill maintenance, the bowstring completely derailed from the cams, whipping loose, lashing Tamsyn across the face and hands. The arrow flew off sideways, the bow-arm snapped in half, and then Tamsyn was on her back in the grass, with only a broken bow between her and the mad gnashing of an insane woman.

"Sushma! Leyland! Help me!" Tamsyn cried out. Even with her hands bound behind her back, the Governor was strong, and much heavier than her. Struggling to push those teeth back with a length of fibreglass, Tamsyn finally saw the scar on the side of the woman's neck. A circle of teeth, but the wound had healed, silvered over with time.

The infection wasn't killing people any more. It had gotten far worse.

Thrashing around, wishing she could reach the pistol on her belt, she saw as the smiling crowd reached Martins and Poulsen, embracing them, nipping at their exposed necks, their hands and faces. Reynolds was struggling now, his rifle twitching slightly, tears streaming down his face. Leyland frowned at his note-pad, as if trying to remember something important.

"Sushma! Snap out of it!" Tamsyn cried. Her arms trembled, and the gnashing teeth came closer and closer to her.

Tamsyn tried very hard to think of good things in her final moments. She tried to remember Malcolm, both her father and son. She tried to think of her mother in happier days. She tried to conjure up the memories of Eddie's kisses, of the aching love and loss he'd given her in two short years.

But in the end, it all came down to animal survival. She screamed defiance as an insane person tried to bite her in the face. All of her higher functions fell away as she scrabbled around in the dirt with a predator. Her face and hands bled from the whipping of the broken bow-string, and it was falling in her eyes, stinging, mixing with the fear sweat and her own tears.

Then Governor Bridgely's head was simply gone. Above her spurting neck stump stood Sushma, bloody kukri held in one fist. Tamsyn finally managed to wriggle loose from the twitching corpse, coughing, a distant part of her mind hoping that none of that spurting blood had fallen into her mouth, nose or eyes.

"Get up," Sushma said. "Trouble."

A classic understatement, as thousands of smiling assassins were amongst them. *The Vanguard*. Tamsyn staggered over towards Reynolds and the fallen Marines, hauling out her pistol. She sent a few shots into that feeding frenzy, satisfied as her wild shots struck into limbs and torsos, eliciting cries of pain. She did not have marksman accuracy with pistols, and didn't need it today. Sushma joined her with assault rifle blazing, emptying a clip into the group, professional groupings that cleared a path to their fallen comrades.

Martins was completely gone, his throat severed by an enthusiastic biter, but Poulsen still lived, shrieking and bleeding as Sushma hauled him to his feet. Tamsyn slapped Reynolds with some satisfaction, and a moment later he broke free of the paralysis.

"Do you need me now?" he said to her. She slapped him again, harder. Sushma and the wounded Poulsen came past them, shouting to Leyland, the nearest Vanguard freaks less than a few steps behind them.

Tamsyn shook Leyland until he stirred, and then he was up on his feet, roaring, ordering everyone to *move, move, move!* The crowd of Vanguard crossing the fields broke into a jog, and then a run, still smiling as they closed in on them.

7

Leyland and his routed expedition were forced to escape back through the marshes, sliding around in the muck. Hundreds of Vanguard came at them by the most direct route, heedless of the treacherous bog around them. Tamsyn saw more than one of them fall into the mud, trod underfoot by dozens of its companions.

Even more of the Vanguard were running around the marshes, taking to the main highways and running at an impressive speed. This was different to the old undead, who came at you in a straight line, regardless of what was in the way. These freaks were planning ahead, working to get them in a pincer. She tried not to think about how they'd all been paralysed by the thing hiding in the Governor, and wondered if it was a spore, a bizarre frequency, something like hypnotism.

The ghost rabbit. All of the things this Vanguard knew about her, and where she'd been. Zombie bites that didn't kill. Weird stuff about "reapers" and "guides". Tamsyn was in uncharted territory here, and shitting her pants. She had three bullets left in her clip, one in the chamber. If those things caught her, turned her into a grinning slave...

Tamsyn settled on a worst-case scenario as she huffed through the muck. She would take three of these things with her, and then send herself into hell. This plan helped to calm her down, knowing that she had the final power over how she would go out.

"Lift up your knees," Sushma said, barely out of breath. Tamsyn was huffing like an asthmatic donkey, and just as graceful. A Vanguard girl came lurching forward, mouth flapping around in a *ha-ha-hee!*

Tamsyn felt her foot catch in a root, and lifted her gun in a panic, sending a bullet far over the monster's head. The next round found the teenager's chest, and she sank backwards into the brackish water, still smiling at the sky.

Two bullets left.

"Get out of there!" Reynolds said, lifting her by the armpit and wrenching hard. Tamsyn felt her feet slide free, and then she realised that her left boot was still stuck in the bottom of the swamp.

"Oh that's just excellent, you idiot," she snapped at the man. Scowling at her, Reynolds sprayed another short burst into their pursuit till the gun clicked dry, and he fumbled in one more precious clip.

Poulsen was leaning heavily on Leyland's shoulder, who dragged him through the marsh. The Regimental Sergeant Major fired his sidearm at a middle-aged man, the freak laughing, arms pin-wheeling, dying with a splash and an almighty fart in a swamp. Any qualms any of them had at shooting unarmed civilians seemed to have vanished the moment that Martins died underneath their gnashing teeth.

Tamsyn felt the strain of their cross-island hustle, and

now to run back with one boot on seemed like the cruellest way to cark it. As fit as Leyland and the others were, she could see the strain on their faces, mixed with the fear of this freaky situation.

She regretted every day she'd spent on her fat arse, drinking instead of staying fit, ignoring her kid, marking time in paradise when she could have been doing cross-fit or eating a salad or something.

"I thought zombies were meant to be slow," Sushma said, separating a Vanguard's hand from his wrist, and then his smiling head from his shoulders. She seemed calm as she hacked away at this enemy, bloody kukri weaving elegantly through the press of reaching arms.

The laughter was close now, and she could hear them breathing right behind her, their own splashing advance scarily close. Staring behind her in panic, Tamsyn fought to increase the distance from the horde, but she felt her eyes drawn towards the smiling face of a happy young woman. She felt her limbs stilling, her will weakening, the overwhelming urge to *stop*, to *wait*. Tamsyn turned away while she still could, and the paralysis instantly ended.

"Don't look in their bloody eyes!" she screamed out.

Finally they reached the edge of the marshlands, climbing through the reeds and scaring away flights of wild birds. Leyland and the others were out on dry land and running through the overgrown golf-course, and already the other Vanguard freaks were on the edges of the fairways, converging on their position.

Tamsyn climbed out of the muck, white-faced and huffing away, with more smiling killers mere feet behind her. She hobbled awkwardly after Leyland and the others, and frantically fought to tear off her remaining boot.

"Here," Sushma said, her kukri parting through laces and leather with surgical skill, not even nicking Tamsyn's skin. Without even turning the Gurkha flicked the wicked knife backwards, carving a cackling old woman from temple to temple, and then the pair were free and running through the waist deep grass.

"Hurry!" Leyland called. The horde running after them were running at a sprint, every movement seemingly amped to the limit of human ability. Their own group had a small lead over the infected emerging from the swamp, but the Vanguard would close this gap in seconds.

Reynolds and Leyland were firing single rounds from their rifles at the crazed people emerging from the reeds, the shots winging past Tamsyn and Sushma. Winding up like a baseball pitcher, the Gurkha tossed a grenade into the edge of the marsh, and it erupted with a WHUMPH, sending a cluster of the infected screaming and falling back into the waters.

Then they were running through the ruins of the country club and back towards the highway, death and insanity mere metres behind them. Reynolds and Leyland had Poulsen now, and his head was hung low, a high keen of pain falling out of his lips. Tamsyn scooped up a brick as she ran, pausing only to smash it straight into the face of a man grasping at her jacket. She winged the bloody brick into the forehead of a teenage boy, and sent him into a coma or a smiling death or both.

Screaming, running, and all the laughing, and Tamsyn felt like she was running a marathon through a Hieronymous Bosch painting. Leyland was on the radio to the *Vengeance*, hollering for support, for rockets, for any damn thing. Poulsen was somewhere beyond pain, and he was crying, screaming hysterically. Sushma ran her own assault rifle dry, and then tossed it aside with a philosophical smile, once more unsheathing the bloody kukri, ready to carve her way through the approaching human jungle.

WHUMPH. WHUMPH. Reynolds was firing grenades from his barrel-mounted launcher in all directions, dropping clusters of the Vanguard, but it still wasn't enough. Then he had his pistol out and barking, quick sputters that spoke of dwindling ammunition.

Her whole body shaking as lactic acid destroyed her muscles, Tamsyn joined Leyland and the others at the top of the hill. Everyone had stopped. From here they were overlooking the towns, the sleek shapes of the two submarines out in the estuary.

Then, the ultimate horror. There were more Vanguard in front of them, several small groups converging the block the main road ahead. Reinforcements from some other part of the Isle, crossing through the fields and the levelled suburbs. The pincer movement was complete, and their hill was completely surrounded.

"Do something!" Leyland screamed into the radio. The group from the *Vengeance* were drawn up in a small circle, Poulsen in their centre. The warriors sent out every bullet, every bomb, every nasty little trick they'd brought with them, and it still wasn't enough.

Tamsyn gut-shot a man wearing a butcher's apron, and the smile on his face was gone, replaced with a bewildered howling. *One bullet left*, she thought, and steeled herself to put it through her own brain.

"We are Vanguard!" Poulsen suddenly cried, reaching out and clamping onto Reynolds. Without hesitation, Tamsyn put her last bullet through the man's head, a moment before his teeth could sink into the black-clad Trooper's throat.

Her feet were cut to shreds from the bricks and rubble, and she was exhausted, her limbs and chest in red hot agony. The coast and safety was still miles away, and a horde of crazy bastards moving in on them from all directions.

"What a stupid way to die," Tamsyn said, and slumped down onto the road, facing the oncoming horde. She let the useless pistol fall from her fingers, and looked at the butcher, wishing she had her old drawing gear, and enough time to make one final sketch of this mad scene.

She saw the butcher, looking down on his own body. Tamsyn frowned at the impossible sight. There were others too, lost little figures falling behind the advancing group, and the realisation finally sunk in, pushing past the last rational part of her mind. A veil lifted from her mind, a veil of her own making, and she finally believed what her eyes were telling her.

Olivena. The girl with the wavy hair. Her morbid dreams. The spooky things that the Governor tried to tell her. People dying in stupid ways, wherever she went.

She, Tamsyn Webb, could see ghosts.

Climbing to her feet, crying and trembling, Tamsyn looked at the advancing Vanguard, and could see something more bizarre. Each of these people had a shadow, a mirror-image of themselves, not quite in sync with their smiling flesh body. Their spirits, trapped just outside of their bodies, and someone else was behind the wheel.

"Go away!" she screamed, as the first rank of the Vanguard came reaching for her. The hands came closer, smiles drawn into wide, creepy rictuses, and Tamsyn felt her will slipping, her poor battered body seizing up.

"Be still," she said, calmly and clearly. The words didn't feel like her own, and they had a weight to them, a command.

The front rank of the people coming for her stopped, confused, the smiles vanishing from their faces. The paralysis gripping her ended. Beside her, she saw Sushma, Leyland and Reynolds freed from their own hypnosis, and they lashed out with boots, kukri, and combat knives. More bodies fell, more ghosts stepping clear of their stolen bodies.

There is something else in there with them, Tamsyn realised. *And it is not human.*

"Be still!" she said again, and this time froze dozens of the Vanguard into place, pushed and shoved around by the smiling ranks behind them. Sushma and the others looked at her, stunned at the effect of her words.

"Be gone. Leave here," she said. With her strange new vision she saw the trapped ghosts struggling, pulling away from their bodies, and whatever was in the body of each person staggered visibly, unable to resist the movement, pulled along with it. Tamsyn whispered to each person, stilling the reaching hands and chomping teeth, sent them reeling away with fear in their eyes. These people pushed back, retreating from her, pushing back against the advancing horde, slowing the inexorable advance.

"Whatever you are doing, girl, do not stop!" Leyland said. He was barking more words into the radio, and someone chattered back excitedly.

"Give the order, or we are all dead!" he ordered the person on the submarine. A second later, both the *Vengeance* and the *Victorious* lit up the dusk with flight upon flight of rockets, arcing up and then down, falling upon the Isle of Sheppey like thunderous hammers.

They were clearing a path to the coast, breaking apart the horde with fire and fury. Tamsyn stepped forward with a triumphant cry, her exhaustion and pain all but forgotten.

"Be still! Be gone!" she cried out, turning away those monsters wearing human skins. As the four survivors ran through the smoking, sizzling carnage, over hundreds of the dead and dying, the Vanguard finally fled in terror, melting back into the landscape.

8

"You said they were alive!" Prime Minister Fallot argued. "We could not fire upon living people!"

"I also said they were infected!" Leyland said, furious to the point of insubordination. They were back in the command centre of the *Vengeance*, linked to the *Victorious* by CCTV. Tamsyn was far from impressed by the milquetoast hand-wringing that both the Prime Minister and the Opposition Leader were offering up, and just about everyone else was shouting and talking over each other. It turned out that Prince Harry had nearly ordered the arrests of all the remaining politicians when they would not allow the submarine crews to use deadly force against the infected civilians.

Going by the carry-on, they were painting it as Cromwell versus the Crown all over again.

"Your little failed expedition has left us with more questions than answers," the Opposition Leader piped in from the screen above the table, surrounded by various Lords and nitwits. "Strange buildings, some woman with an obvious mental illness. You have far exceeded your mission parameters, Regimental Sergeant Major! You have murdered unarmed civilians!"

"Oh please!" Tamsyn scoffed. "You saw the body-cam footage, the photos we took. They were tearing us apart, you nonce!"

"It is fitting that a war criminal defends war crimes!" the man continued from the closed circuit feed.

"What's more, you haven't given us sufficient explanation, Miss Webb," Prime Minister Fallot continued. "One minute they are 'tearing you apart', the next those poor people are turning aside meekly and running off, all on your say so! Not to mention your murdering of Corporal Paulsen."

"He was infected, you prat!"

"Given how you killed those innocent civilians, who were no doubt protecting themselves and their property, are you surprised that Corporal Paulsen tried to defend himself? You have blood on your hands, Miss Webb."

"You are unbelievable! You saw what they did!"

"She said she knew that Governor, the one that went crazy," the Opposition Leader chimed in. "She spent time on the Isle of Sheppey and met with these people. What's to say she didn't know about this mad cult? Maybe she is a part of it!"

"She wanted to put us all in danger!"

"Someone throw her off the damn boat! She's a menace!"

Tamsyn threw up her hands in disgust. Prince Harry looked on the whole scene, unimpressed by his advisors and loyal servants.

"If you are quite finished, Terry," he said.

"I am not finished," the Prime Minister said. "And you have once again exceeded your authority, Your Highness!

We are the rightly appointed leaders of the United Kingdom armed forces, and it answers to us, not to your little lackey, not to officers who should know better. These little favours and preferences stop, and they stop today, good sir!"

"I am your bloody Prince!" Harry shouted.

"And when we want someone to cut a ribbon, we shall let you know," Fallot cried back, face reddened.

Everyone went berserk at that comment. Prince Harry was perhaps moments away from giving the Prime Minister a bloody nose, and he wisely left the command centre, a handful of the officers following. With a satisfied grin, Fallot took over the meeting.

"When our justice system is restored, you will have your reckoning, Miss Webb. Two good Marines and countless civilians have died today, and all because of your 'heroics'."

Tamsyn kept silent, ignoring the triumphant grins of the collected political twits. All she could think of was what that *thing* inside Governor Bridgely had said. That list of who she had killed, and then the final part where it said she was going to cause more death on the Isle of Sheppey.

It had seemed like mad nonsense at the time, but it had been prophetic. Once more, the awful black thread that followed her through life had struck again.

This lot are right, I am bad news, she thought, but she would never admit it. And she certainly wasn't going to tell anyone about ghosts, possessions, or the whole bucket of crazy they'd uncovered on the Isle of Sheppey.

"I have redirected the fleet to approach the Isle of Man," Fallot continued. "We are going to seize the island, assist any survivors as best we can, and contain any who cannot be helped. The United Kingdom will be reborn there, and ensure its own safety until all of its institutions are restored."

From the look the room gave her, those institutions were going to include a nice little gilded cage for Prince Harry, and a much plainer variety to lock away Tamsyn Webb for good.

HARRY HAD TAKEN over a section of bunks at the rear of the *Vengeance*, holding a council of war with the people he could trust. The number was depressingly small, and consisted of the four survivors from the trip to Sheppey, Harry himself, Chief Petty Officer Vassily, Lieutenant Commander Gilbert and Midshipman Fraser.

This was the core group that had sided with Prince Harry, disobeying their superiors to fire the rockets onto the Isle of Sheppey. Captain Grant was a stickler for the rules, and had sided with the Prime Minister and his leadership group, despite the evidence that their own people were being ripped apart by monsters onshore.

Vassily, Gilbert and Fraser had been relieved of their duties and confined to their bunks, pending a court-martial in the coming days. They were being given three days to prepare a legal defence, and had been disarmed and locked out of any and all operating systems.

There was a similar group over on the *Victorious* who'd also ignored the orders of their Captain, firing the rockets that saved Leyland's people. Harry had spoken to this group briefly in the radio room on the *Vengeance*, but Fallot and Captain Grant were at his elbow, listening to every word.

"Those bastards have cut me out of everything," Harry fumed to the group. "They're being very polite about it, but I'm not stupid."

"Can't you just take over?" Tamsyn suggested.

"It came very close to that," Harry admitted. "If I try, if I really try to seize power from Fallot, they will very politely put me in the brig. And they would be right to do it."

"Why does any of this matter anymore?" Tamsyn said. "This 'nation' is down to just over five hundred people. You should be in charge!"

"These are good men and woman in the crew, and I don't want to put them in that position again," Harry said. "They received their orders, right or wrong."

"What's done is done," Lieutenant Commander Gilbert said. Everything about the woman was crisp and precise, creases and polish from top to toe, and not even a flyaway hair coming from her perfect bun. She'd been Grant's number two on the *Vengeance*, and according to ship gossip her recent disobedience was the first black mark on a record as pure as the driven snow.

"Any word about this stupid mission, Chief?" Leyland asked Vassily.

The Chief Petty Officer was the real boss of any ship, and Vassily was no exception. Up until the thwarted rebellion, the broad Greek man had been responsible for every nut and bolt, every rocket, every sailor without a commission. Tamsyn guessed that being made to sit on his hands was killing the man.

"When they get to the Isle of Man, the *Vengeance* will take the southern half, the *Victorious* the north," Vassily said. "They want to use all the non-nuke rockets to clear out concentrations of the undead."

"I heard the PM say we were wasting them rockets, helping you lot," Midshipman Fraser said. He was a skinny little nerd who seemed to swim around in his uniform, eyes darting around with a touch of anxiety, and had been instrumental in unlocking the rocket racks from the bridge. His defiance had effectively killed his career, and rumour had it that Grant wanted his commission to boot.

"Save it," Leyland told Tamsyn, a second before she exploded. "Resources are thin. Sometimes in a war, you don't get the air support you need."

"They were gonna kill us!"

"Here are the facts," Reynolds said, talking over her and making her hackles rise. "The mission went south. Even with the rockets we were lucky to get out. We take our lumps and we move on."

"You'll definitely get your lumps," Harry said, face drawn. "Unless we nuke the place, we don't have enough rockets to clear the undead from the Isle of Man. Everyone without a Peerage is going onshore with a rifle and a prayer."

"I'm sure the PM will put us in the thick of things," Tamsyn said. "Easy way to get rid of the troublemakers, right?"

"That's why I'm going with you," Harry said. "If they put you in harm's way, they'll put me there too."

"You idiot! That's exactly what they want!"

"Control yourself," Gilbert told Tamsyn, who seethed and ground her teeth and counted to ten. Swearing at princes wasn't a good life choice, especially one willing to risk his life for her.

My god, he is a handsome idiot, she thought, and then the anger passed.

"I will keep fighting for you all," Harry told the disgraced officers. "Right now I'm ceremonial at best, but I won't give up."

Vassily, Fraser and Gilbert turned out with a smart salute, and returned to their bunks to contemplate their fate. Harry put a hand on Leyland's arm as he made to leave.

"Leyland, a moment. I want to speak with everyone who went ashore."

The Prince looked at Tamsyn, Sushma, Reynolds and Leyland, waiting until Gilbert and the others were out of earshot. Some of the off-shift sailors were sleeping, so he pitched his voice low.

"I watched the body-cam feeds, heard everything on the radio," he said. "It went bad very quickly. By rights, you lot shouldn't have made it back alive."

He stood close to Tamsyn.

"And you simply told those freaks to go away and leave you alone? I'm not buying it. You haven't told us everything, have you?"

"You're not going to believe me."

"We live in a world where the dead have come back to life. I think we're past that."

"Okay," Tamsyn said, taking a breath. "Something happened to me on the Isle. I will paraphrase the Sixth Sense and tell you that I can now see dead people. And rabbits."

She glossed over the events from the rabbit ghost in the graveyard, her conversation with Governor Bridgely, and what she was finally able to see as the Vanguard surrounded them.

"Right," Reynolds scoffed. "I suppose you can see auras and stuff too."

"I don't know how any of this works, dickhead," Tamsyn said. "But you saw what I saw. We were paralysed by people who weren't people anymore. And I was able to make some of these people leave us alone. Just go with that if that's all your little brain can handle."

"No worries, Spooky," he said, but Tamsyn saw through the bravado. This cocksure man had just encountered something he couldn't browbeat or outfight. Sarcasm was probably the last line of defence his mind had to hold off the impossible.

"I believe you," Sushma said. "What you say is only logical."

"Thank you?" Tamsyn said.

"They still walk because their souls are trapped in the flesh. They cannot reincarnate."

"Unbelievable," Reynolds laughed.

"It is an awful fate," Sushma told the Trooper. "Stuck in rotting meat. Unable to move on. Would you leave your parents and friends trapped like that?"

"It's just nature being weird. Like that fungus that turns the ants into zombies. When your brain is dead, you just stop."

"So if you are bitten and you die, you do not want -" and here the Gurkha mimed a pistol to the head.

"Well, I don't want to stink up the place," Reynolds said quickly. "Plus, you need to curb the infection."

"Enough with the theology," Leyland said. "Now Tamsyn, I don't want you breathing a word of this to anyone else. We're already in enough trouble here."

"Understood."

"Next time we see any of those things, we need to find out more. About what you can do with these spirits or visions or whatever they are. So keep your head down, and we'll do some research on the Isle of Man."

"I'll research the shit out of this, don't you worry," Tamsyn said, looking down to see a grubby pair of hands yanking on her pants. She clapped her hands to her mouth, moments after the swear word had left. It was her Malcolm, and he looked a little distressed.

"The lady," he said. "Mummy, I scared!"

She'd left him with Baroness Constance St. Clair, one of the Peers who wasn't openly hostile towards her. Tamsyn felt like murdering the upper-class twit for letting her toddler wander around in a busy nuclear submarine.

"Malcolm darling, where is your Auntie Constance?"

He pointed down the corridor, past the long line of bunks. The Baroness was leaning against her bunk, head bowed, back tense. Swallowing up Malcolm's little hand in her own, Tamsyn walked towards the woman, trying to find her moment of calm.

There's not many babysitters to call upon, she tried to remind herself, knowing that losing her shit at the Baroness wouldn't help anyone in the current crisis.

"Lady St. Clair?" Tamsyn asked gently. "Is everything okay?"

The Baroness slowly turned towards her voice, her face a mask of shock.

"I need help," she finally managed.

"Look, I know he can be a handful, but I just need a few more minutes," Tamsyn said. "I really appreciate you helping."

"Please," she said, and slowly twitched open the curtain to her bunk, just a fraction. There laying on the bunk, her eyes open and staring at nothing, was the body of Baroness Constance St. Clair.

"Oh shit. Oh man," Tamsyn whimpered, and tried to shield Malcolm's eyes from the sight. He was clutching her pants, looking at the bunk with confusion, but not once had he stared in the direction of the woman leaning against the bunk.

"What is happening to me?"

"Lady St. Clair, I - I think you just died."

Woman and ghost stood together in the corridor, bound

by that awful realisation. One of the sailors hustled back from the showers, whistling at nothing and wandering past the scene towards his own bunk. Without missing a beat, he moved aside just enough to avoid the ghost, even as he studiously avoided looking at the spirit of the Baroness, and he did not seem to realise he was doing it.

Tamsyn thought about her own life, before the moment the veil had lifted from her eyes. She too had moved through a world of ghosts and spirits, unaware.

"You have to help me. I don't know what I'm meant to do," Lady St. Clair pleaded, hysterical and loud. She laid her hand on Tamsyn's forearm, and instantly a flood of cold ran up and down her skin, sinking right down into her bones.

"Please don't do that," Tamsyn said, teeth gritted. "Don't touch me."

She withdrew her ghostly hand, and the cold feeling receded. By Tamsyn's feet, Malcolm began to fidget and sniffle, and was perhaps moments away from a fire-siren wailing. Kneeling, she drew her son in close, and twitched the curtain closed on the corpse.

"Am I stuck here forever? On this submarine?"

"I honestly don't know."

"No-one else can see me."

Tamsyn nodded slowly. She was still staring at the bunk curtain, at the impossible moment.

"Am I going to come back as one of those things?"

"No. You died a clean death. You're going to be okay."

The spirit seemed to ease a little, the worry easing from her face. She was less *there*, the colour of her spectral flesh and clothing dulling, fading like smoke. Just like that, she was moving on.

"Wait," Tamsyn said "I need your help before you go."

"Anything," the spirit said.

"I need you to give me a secret. Something about Prime Minister Fallot."

"Secret?"

"Something awful about the man, something only you might know. He's going to put us all in great danger. Prince Harry too. Please, give me some ammunition. I won't misuse it."

Lady St. Clair looked down at Tamsyn, her eyes set in an impossible stare that made the living woman shiver. Finally she spoke.

"When Terry Fallot was Deputy PM, he had a hooker overdose in his flat. A male hooker. Some very important people made the problem go away. I - I helped the problem go away. There's no evidence, not even a rumour outside of a very small circle of people. Whisper that into his ear, and also this - Constance loved you very much, you silly Eton poofter."

"I can't say that!"

"He will know it's from me."

"Okay."

The ghost smiled, her features washing together, and then she was gone.

HUDDLED in her bunk with Malcolm under the crook of her arm, Tamsyn dreamt again that night. It was the old dream, the one where the dead visited her, but now she knew it for what it was. Not the nightmares of some damaged girl, not clues from her subconscious, but an honest to god visitation from the afterlife. They were all here, sad-eyed yet welcoming. She saw them all, the folks from Gravesend, everyone she met in America, the young doctors from Cuba who'd helped bring Malcolm into the world. All of her personal dead, and at this stage in her misadventures it was quite the large gathering.

There were a few new arrivals. Martins, Olivena, Poulsen, and Constance St. Clair. In the logic of the dream she understood that they were here to bear witness; that a protocol had to be followed.

There was something else beyond this, a presence that was terrifying and huge, but it was not paying attention to her. It would be very good to keep it that way.

Language was hard in her dreams, and everything was a surreal jumble of images and locations, but for the first time ever she understood that the people here were real, were spirits checking in on her.

Then she saw her mother, her father with his stitched mouth. Clem. Eddie. The smallest circle around her heart, and they crushed in around her, smiles and sparkling ghost tears. Eddie held her hands tightly, so tightly, and this felt real, the crush of her fingers in his big hands.

"We are watched," Eddie said, struggling to say more. Tamsyn saw that the witnesses to this dream were conferring, and looked scared. Behind the dream version of their stolen house in the Florida Keys, the setting sun pulsed an angry red. The ghosts began to withdraw, vanishing into shadows, slipping underneath the sea that wasn't water. Soon it was just Eddie, her mother, her father and Clem.

"You must not die," Clem said. "It is not safe for you here!"

He wasn't the leathery Re-Human from his final days, but was a younger version of himself, years before the booze ruined him utterly.

"I will try really hard not to die, you dickhead," she replied.

Her father struggled to speak, the stitches on his mouth frustrating him. Her mother could only flail around, once more telling her to "be quick about it", her final words to her before the car crash that ended her life.

"The Black Crown Boy knows about you," Eddie managed with a gasp. The setting sun flared, reversing direction, rising in the sky, going from red to blazing white heat.

"Watch our little man, love," Eddie said. "He's important."

"Go the Red Devils!" Eddie crowed to the sky, and Tamsyn frowned. Not the best time to talk about football. Clem and her parents were shaking, but as the sun approached its zenith they fled with a panic, scattering in all directions.

Then everything was searing light and terror, and Tamsyn sat up with a cry, banging her head on the bunk above her. Little Malcolm stirred a little, but he settled back into sleep, blissfully unaware of the dead family watching over him.

9

The fire teams from the *Victorious* and the *Vengeance* made a beachhead just south-west of Castletown. Tamsyn hustled out of yet another launch, but this time they had serious numbers on their side, with a little over two hundred shooters getting ready to advance. Only skeleton crews were left to run the nuclear subs, and even the off-shifts had been given guns and pushed out the door.

"I've never been to the Isle of Man," Tamsyn said. Once more she was teamed up with Sushma and Reynolds, but this time Chief Petty Officer Vassily and Midshipman Fraser were in their six, armed for bear. Gilbert was back on the ship, scrubbing toilets and hoping her replacement didn't break anything.

"It was lovely here once," Prince Harry said, doing a final check on his equipment. He was in their fire-team, and was carrying just as much gear as anyone else. Some of the talking heads had also joined the ground force, which worried Tamsyn more than the cowards hiding back on the subs. There was an excited air amongst those gathered on the beach; the sailors and marines had been cooped up, kept away from any action, and the politicians and lords were treating the whole thing like a fox hunt.

"These idiots are one-hundred percent going to get killed," Tamsyn said, eyeing off her new gun warily. During her fit-out she'd confessed to being an awful shot with a rifle, so Reynolds swapped out some of his gear for standard Marine issue, giving her his SPAS-12 riot control shotgun and a bandolier of extra shell clips.

"You don't have to be able to aim," he told her. "See this hook on the stock? Just sit that under your elbow. Get right up close, and you'll punch a hole through anything."

"I feel weird without a bow," she said.

"It is not bad that you are an archer," Sushma said. "But that does not make you a complete warrior. You should know all the tools of war."

"I've tried," she said, hating the whining note that escaped her mouth. "Went through basic and I sucked. Turns out silent bow skills were handy with the undead, so they just, er, they just let me through."

"I *could* fight with only this," Sushma continued, flourishing her kukri. "Would make for good action movie, yes?"

"Well, of course, because you're a bad-arse bitch."

"It would make me stupid. I would die. I do not want to be stupid and die."

"We're going to see a lot of that today," Tamsyn said glumly. The Isle of Man was crawling with undead, clustered around the coastal population centres. As the head of the Marines, Leyland had been part of the mission planning session. He tried his best to control the cluster-fuck that was about to unfold, and it was his plan to take Castletown first.

It was a picturesque village, neat little terraces and old pubs hugging the coast and the docks. Above the town squatted the ancient, grey stone of Castle Rushen. Tamsyn tried to remember what her Dad had said about the place, and remembered something about Robert the Bruce capturing it a few times.

"All right, listen up," the Regimental Sergeant Major roared through a bullhorn, and the fire teams gathered around. "We need a base of operations, and it's going to be that castle there. Team leaders, you all have your whistles?"

A chorus of merry tweeting. Harry whistled through his own whistle, waggling his eyebrows at Tamsyn. She cracked up laughing, making a few people stare at her. *Whatever. You probably all think I'm unhinged at this point.*

"Everyone follow the plan and we'll get out of this alive. No heroics. Even teams, get to your position. Odd teams, you're with me. Let's go."

He turned off the megaphone with a squeal, and gave a whirling signal over his head. Lurking a few hundred metres offshore, the *Vengeance* set off its klaxons, an unholy wail that washed across the island.

It went against all of Tamsyn's instincts to engage the undead by making as much noise as possible. Already small crowds of the coffin-dodgers were emerging from the town proper, shuffling towards them in little groups. For a moment she was worried that these were more Vanguard, more people stuck on puppet strings, but using a rifle scope she saw the lurching walk, the rotten leathery flesh, the flies and dragging entrails. These were just the good old-fashioned walking corpses that came at you, stinking at hungry.

Tamsyn wondered about the souls or the spirits of the zombies - she'd seen firsthand the resurrection of the undead with the salt treatment, the moment when a dead thing opened its eyes and had a living soul inside of it. Since her misadventure on the Isle of Sheppey, Tamsyn could sometimes look at people and they just seemed... brighter, for want of a better word. People like Prince Harry seemed to pulse with light, while the Prime Minister seemed to have a dimmer light around his shape, with a dark wiggle on the edges, like the beginning of a migraine.

Auras are so bloody stupid, Tamsyn thought. When she tried to bring on her visions she gave herself a headache more often than not, and it only told her stuff she knew anyway. She'd hit on the trick a few days ago - stare at someone, really stare at them and through them, like you're trying to figure out a bastard Magic Eye picture, and *voila*! Mystical second sight.

But now she focused on the nearest undead, a wasted corpse in rags, at least four years dead and near mummified. Almost straight away she saw it. A thin black line, shooting straight up from the top of the zombie's head, stretching up and into the sky. As she focused and her head began to pulse with pain, she could see more black threads, big handfuls of them pulled up taut, black lines between the ground and the heavens. Thousands of the undead, pushing through the township, and more little lines in the distance, clusters of the wandering dead being drawn down from the hills by the klaxons.

Sushma slapped her on the back, and instantly the vision was lost. All she could see were shuffling corpses, walking towards too many idiots with guns.

"Are they Vanguard?" the Gurkha asked.

"No. Just plain old monsters."

They were hustling along the road into town, the team-leaders blowing on their whistles for all they were worth, and then they were running over the foreshore and down onto the beach. Everyone else hooted and hollered, and some of the volunteer shooters were firing off rounds into the air in their excitement. Reynolds looked genuinely pained at the waste of ammunition.

Then the fire-teams split. The even teams spread out and formed a wide line, with at least three metres between each shooter and their neighbours. They had their backs to the surf.

Their instructions were to make a racket, and shoot any zombies that walked onto the beach. If at any time they looked to be overrun, they were to walk backwards and into the safety of the salt water, and wait for collection.

The odds teams had the toughest part of the mission. During the ruckus they were to move fast and quiet, through the foreshore and esplanade area of the town, and infiltrate Castle Rushen. They needed to secure the gates, clear the interior of all undead, and snipe zombies from the castle walls. While they were up there they were to act as spotters for the *Vengeance*, directing rocket strikes towards concentrations of the undead.

Tamsyn understood that in the ideal world this was a great plan to lure out the undead and save most of the town's infrastructure. In the real world, they were going to get their faces eaten off.

The people placed in the odds team were those best equipped to go toe-to-toe with the undead. Leyland's Marine teams were front and centre, and the older sailors who'd seen action in the Middle East made the bulk of the force. Leftovers from other branches of the defence forces like Reynolds and Sushma peppered the group.

Tamsyn would have preferred these squads to have body armour and hand-to-hand weapons, to keep silent and light, but Leyland had disagreed. It was going to be noisy and fast. Shock and awe tactics.

That only works if the enemy can be scared of you. Zombies just don't give a shit, Tamsyn thought, and then there was no time for anything but the world's worst fun run. She was still a little sore from the run across the Isle of Sheppey, and already she could feel the weight of the shotgun and the extra ammunition.

"You are puffing a lot," Sushma said. "Back in Nepal, we would make you run up the mountain with a bag of rocks on your back. This is just a beach. It's flat."

"It's sandy, shut up," Tamsyn said. Vassilly and Fraser were struggling a little too, both of them more used to poking around the gizzards of a submarine. Reynolds flowed across the sand like a video game character with an entire armoury, who was ready to run a marathon with no problem. She hated him a little bit more just for that fact.

Harry was fine. He seemed positively alive, like one of the Pevensey kids from the Narnia books, a secret King ready for the thrill of battle. Tamsyn was grateful for his presence, and he'd effectively put himself near Tamsyn as a human shield.

It didn't mean that Fallot wouldn't put Tamsyn in harm's way, but Harry was making things a lot more difficult. Before they left the boat, Tamsyn had whispered a few words in Fallot's ear, and enjoyed watching him turn white at Constance St. Clair's words from beyond the grave.

"Back off, or I'll tell everyone what I know," she'd threatened, and then she spent the whole boat ride with her stomach in knots. Blackmail didn't sit easily with her, but she needed to protect herself, and little Malcolm, who was back on the boat with the handful of other VIP children evacuated from Grand Cayman.

Going after Fallot was either insurance, or dangerously stupid.

Behind them came the first crackle of gunfire, with every

damn idiot opening up their guns all at once. The sound spurred her on, and she kept pace with her fire-team. Harry signalled to move up onto the foreshore, and then they were finally off the damned sand and onto turf, and then up and onto the esplanade. The other teams ahead of them were moving low, keeping to the shelter of old stone walls and shopfronts.

"Oh shit, oh no," Fraser whimpered behind her. There were still pockets of the undead in the town, moving towards the racket of the klaxons and the gunfire on the beach. A handful of zombies noticed their team moving along the front of some terraces, and came for them with mindless hunger, dark mouths hung open, moaning.

Tamsyn got the head to toe shivers then, same as she had since the early days, since Gravesend, and right through the stupid Second Civil War. No-one ever became a zombie expert, not when faced with something so unnatural, so dead and deadly all at once.

"Be still!" she said, but the creatures didn't notice her, their spirits buried too deeply in these rotting shells. They were still inside somewhere, but only salt or a bullet to the head would free them. Reynolds raised his rifle but Sushma pushed it down with the palm of her hand, and stalked forward, kukri flashing.

Down went a reaching hand, fingernails black and sharp. A leg, severed at the knee. She broke through neck and neck vertebrae with ease, dropping their withered heads like bad fruit.

"Good," Tamsyn said. "Silent is very good."

Ahead of them, the other Odd teams were hitting resistance on their way to the castle. Screams of terror, and the cracking of gunfire, shouting and confusion. These sheltered men and women were having their first taste of the undead, and it was all going to custard very quickly.

"Keep moving," Harry ordered. "We've got to secure that castle."

They were through the seaside streets and into the historic town centre, and then everything around them was going to hell, very quickly. Hundreds of undead were stumbling through alleyways and streets, drawn by the sight of the living. The zombies moaned as if in ecstasy, the sound reaching above the klaxon, the gunfire.

The beach diversion wasn't working.

Leyland's hand-picked teams were panic-firing in all directions, drawing more undead into the town square, and they were very nearly boxed in. A handful of sailors were climbing up onto a wrecked milk lorry, trying to get above the oncoming horde, and the team leaders were shouting each other, some of them blowing on their whistles for some godforsaken reason.

Tamsyn felt her head swim for a second, and then she got a quick glimpse of the black strings above the zombies heading their way, and saw that some unseen force was pulling them, the black threads bunched together like a kid with fat fists around a bunch of balloons. This invisible puppet master was moving the undead away from the beach and towards the castle.

"We've got to go!" she screamed out. "They're coming! They're all coming!"

"This way, fall back!" Leyland yelled through his megaphone, and this mostly worked. The marines led a fighting withdrawal, firing careful bursts at the zombies who had very quickly filled the lanes and alleyways, packed in shoulder to shoulder.

Behind Tamsyn, a shop window crashed open, and the

undead came out through the shards and broken framing, all windmilling arms and gnashing teeth. She had her shotgun up and tracking, and with an almighty BANG she vaporised a rotten head into mist.

Her next shot went wide, punching a hole into the shop's awning. Her team-mates were replying with their own rifle-shots, dropping the dead across the window sill, but still they came, dozens and dozens more, packing the abandoned shop to the brim. She could see the daylight through the rear of the building, the doors and windows ripped from their hinges. That was way too smart for a standard rotting corpse, or even a group of them.

Without a doubt they had all been drawn in to her exact location.

She got off one more thunderous round from the shotgun when she felt something yanking on her combat harness. It was Reynolds, and he was shouting something, hauling her away from the writhing wall of dead flesh, of reaching hands and snapping teeth.

"We've gotta go!" he said again, and this time Tamsyn registered just how screwed they all were. The undead had now surrounded the milk lorry, beating on the panels and reaching up to the terrified sailors up on the roof of the cab. One last unfortunate woman was scrabbling up to join them, but two and then three hands wrapped around her lower legs, hauling her down to the ground and to her miserable death.

There were others cut off, screaming and shooting, and the last she saw of one Marine was of a wild-eyed man, swinging a fixed bayonet, carving away dead flesh to no effect before being dragged down.

In seconds the entire attack force was completely routed, fleeing the town square in all directions. The zombies were slow but they moved with precision, encircling the living, cutting them off from each other, and then moving in for the kill.

Whoever was pulling those black strings had a good eye for tactics.

Tamsyn still felt Reynolds grip on her harness, yanking her forward. The shotgun was forgotten in her hands. Breaking glass above them, and then the undead were falling amongst them from a second story flat, teeth snapping and arms pin wheeling. They fell down upon the living, biting and tearing, and Tamsyn narrowly avoided what was left of a woman with thin strands of black hair, who hit the cobblestones with a meaty smack.

Sushma was back to hacking away with the kukri, but everyone else was panic firing in all directions. With every pull of the trigger Tamsyn winced, arms wobbling and eyes closing, and she did little but pepper the zombies with shot. Next to her Vassily screamed out in pain, fresh blood pulsing out from a gunshot through his left bicep.

"You bloody idiot!" he screamed.

"I'm sorry! I'm sorry, Chief!" Fraser cried, fighting to free his pistol from the clutch of a zombie with shattered legs. Tamsyn stepped in, clubbing the ravenous corpse with the butt of her shotgun, and the Midshipman freed himself.

"Fire on the town square. Fire, damnit!" Leyland screamed into the radio, face white with panic. Tamsyn had seen this moment too many times, when that primal and supernatural fear took away sense and reason from even the most capable of men and women. RSM Leyland wanted to run, and run, and run some more.

"Call it off, there's people still back there!" Reynolds cried out.

Leyland was trapped behind the opaque filters of terror,

and only as he sent some laggard on with a boot to the arse did he turn back and see the sailors trapped up on the lorry, abandoned by their own people as the living dead reached up for them.

"No!" was all he managed to say.

BOOM. Righteous fire from the heavens, and the concussive force sent Tamsyn sprawling, winded and terrified. A car door winged just overhead, burying itself into a brick wall. Rotten meat fell like rain, as if God had just smashed the shit out of an offal piñata.

When the ringing in her ears died down, Tamsyn still heard the settling of masonry, the screaming of the wounded, and that endless moaning, the hum of thousands of rotten throats, hungering for human flesh.

Before landing, the mission planners had guessed the local population to be perhaps two to three thousand zombies. There were enough zombies still pouring up the streets and out through the broken buildings to fill a couple of Led Zeppelin concerts.

Why had the entire zombie population of the Isle of Man converged on this quiet town? She'd seen devices during the war that caused mega hordes, but one look to the skies with her mystical kung-fu bullshit vision showed more and more zombies, coming through the fields, moving around like pieces on a big war map.

But there were already thousands here, and they'd moved here as slow as the oldies in a buffet line. Whoever, whatever was controlling these zombies, it had known they were going to land on this spot, to try and take this castle.

If their plans were known in advance, there was nothing they could do, nowhere they could go. They would either starve on the subs, or on some unpopulated rock. Underneath the panic and the survival mode, the intellectual part of Tamsyn knew it was game over.

Her body did not. She joined the press of panicked survivors, a perverse running of the bulls as they pushed at each other, trying to get through to safety. Dimly Tamsyn knew that she should be helping the wounded, should be checking on her friends, but she had reverted to pure selfish survival. Time for the guilts and an alcoholic blackout later, if she got out in one piece.

Nice. You're rationalising this as you go, you cold-hearted bitch, she thought. More zombies were stepping from the rooftops now, a kamikaze squad of death from above, falling into the packed press of humanity, and causing complete mad panic.

You poor bastards. First zombie fight and you fall into a meat-grinder full of clown arseholes and glitter.

Tamsyn had snuck into a couple of concerts underage, back in the old world, and she remembered the press of bodies, the loss of control as every mug pushed up against you. It had been exciting then. Now it was a nightmare. Barely three people away, a zombie child was tearing viciously into a big soldier's face, his colleagues turning rifle butts against both man and monster.

An awful moment where everyone was both frantically moving and going nowhere, and then they were through the bottleneck of slaughter, out on the foreshore and running for their lives. Tamsyn felt the shiver as her unnatural vision came on strong. The sky was thick with black lines, all bent in her direction, as if she was drawing them in like a magnet.

No wonder death seems to follow me, she thought, a hysterical bubble of laughter escaping from her lips. *It really does.*

"Get into the water!" someone cried out next to her, and

she realised it was Reynolds. They were on the sand now, the zombies already crossing the foreshore behind them.

Then the impossible. The zombies were moving from a shuffle to a quick walk, from a quick walk to a lurching run, breaking their stiff bodies apart to move in one final rush against the living. Tamsyn remembered Clem after the salt treatment brought his spirit back into his zombie body. Every movement brought his dead muscles one step closer to complete failure, and the Re-humans had planned ahead for the moments their bodies would fail them, had spoken of prosthetics and mobility aids. In the wild, zombies had always moved slow, as if instinctually aware of the need for self-preservation.

Now, the coffin-dodgers were running like the bloody clappers.

Salt was the only thing that would save the living now. The crashing foam ahead of them was a lifeline, and the surviving shooters ran for it like they were stuck in Dunkirk. Already the distraction teams were waist-deep in the sea, yelling and waving the others towards them.

Ahead of them, *Vengeance* set up rocket after rocket, pounding the town and the foreshore back into the Stone Age, but still the undead came on, a tide of greens and browns and open mouths, running and climbing over the stacks of dead meat, unafraid of the explosions hammering their ranks.

Then, the *Vengeance* finally ran dry. No rockets left, unless they wanted to launch a nuke at this situation. Tamsyn struggled through the seaweed and the grit and then finally she was sloshing through the foam, giddy with relief. Around her the mixed group of shooters set up a ragged cheer, but most of the survivors were huddled together, shaken and numb-looking. Within the hour, they'd lost a full third of the people who'd set foot on the shore.

On the very edge of the water the undead were bunching up, a horde thousands strong. They were reaching for the living, moaning in frustration, jostling to get as close to the sea as possible but unable to go any further.

The submarine finally killed off the klaxon, and Tamsyn thanked God for small mercies. She pushed out against the waves, shotgun held above her head like they'd shown her in basic, and watched as the first set of inflatable launches returned to the submarine, overloaded with survivors. In the group still awaiting pickup she could see Reynolds and Fraser, fastening a tourniquet to Vassily's wounded arm, and a moment later Sushma appeared, splattered with gore from head to toe.

"That went badly," Sushma said.

A terrified scream from the rear of the wading survivors, and Tamsyn saw the impossible. The zombies were wading into the shallows, howling with pain, and moving towards the survivors en-masse. Harry was back there, carrying a wounded man over his shoulder, stress written across his face.

"Just leave him!" she screamed out to the Prince. *God, what have I become?*

"Everyone, swim to the sub," Leyland hollered, his megaphone lost or soaked. It was a good half-mile out to the *Vengeance*, and everyone had just finished a panicked run of two or three miles, while the dead Manx tried to eat them.

"I won't be able to swim," Vassily called out, gesturing to his wounded arm.

"Grab my belt," Reynolds said. "Fraser, this is your damn fault so you help too."

"I'm sorry," the lanky midshipman said. "I'm not leaving."

He raised his hands, blood pouring from several bite-marks. He looked to the others, eyes wide with the realisation of his own mortality.

"I'll draw them off," he said firmly. "Hurry, they're getting closer!"

"Kid, you are a damn hero, but that's no way to go," Tamsyn said, but hefted her shotgun. "Do you want me to?"

He looked down to the gun, and looked up with a different pair of eyes.

"We are Vanguard," he said, and lunged at Tamsyn. She flinched, her shot flying past Fraser's head, and then he was on top of her, teeth snapping, pushing her down into the water and gnashing away.

She was down on the bottom, the grit scouring at her hair. Fraser pushed down on her with all of his weight, and all the air left her lungs in one panicked bubble. Her eyes flew wide open, and she could see that smiling face down in the water with her, descending towards her throat, teeth spreading. She snagged her fingers through his hair, holding him at arm's length, but he was bearing down on her, surprisingly strong for such a skinny kid.

She clenched her own teeth tight, fighting the burning urge to draw in a breath, and made herself stare at Fraser's face. As her body burnt through the last bit of oxygen, her unnatural vision returned, and she saw a double image of Fraser, one the smiling killer, the other a horrified kid, waiting just behind his shoulder.

Be still! she thought, and to her surprise it worked. The smile vanished, and Fraser froze in place. Her vision was starting to cloud over, and she was seconds away from a lungful of salt water.

Be gone! she thought, and Fraser rose, legs churning up the grit as he ran. Tamsyn thrashed around before finding her feet and she stood in the waist deep water, drawing in a long shuddering breath.

Reynolds already had Fraser in a headlock, driving his combat knife into the boy's chest, bleeding the life out of him. Tamsyn met his eyes, and nodded. It sucked, but the big man had done the right thing.

"Vanguard?" Fraser whispered, and then he stared at nothing, bleeding out into the waves. The ghost of Midshipman Fraser stepped free of his dying body, and stood to one side, watching sorrowfully as the survivors escaped. Tamsyn wondered if he would always be here, stuck in the waters around the Isle of Man, or if he'd move on to some other place. Would he come back in her dreams, haunt her like the others?

All around Tamsyn saw people dumping guns and gear, swimming ferociously towards the submarine, and then she saw why. The undead were almost waist deep into the water, crying their agony to the heavens, and then they launched forward and swam, rotten arms and legs carving through the water with Olympic precision. Surely the brine was breaking apart their tendons and eating through mummified muscles, but the undead were giving it everything they had, one final burst to infect these living invaders.

Tamsyn wasn't sure she could manage the swim out to the submarine on a good day. Leyland was helping Reynolds tow Vassilly through the water, a practised manoeuvre that would get them all to safety if they had the time.

They were out of time. They were out of everything. Thousands of murderers, churning up the water like a horde of incoming piranhas, screeching with fury and agony.

So of course, Sushma was swimming straight towards the horde.

"You crazy woman!" Tamsyn said in amazement. Then she saw Prince Harry, struggling with the man he'd been carrying. Some of the others at the rear of the human pack were tugging on the infected man, trying to draw him away, and one man hefted up a rifle butt, almost too scared to hit the beast for fear of striking the Prince.

Even in the face of certain defeat, the Gurkha wasn't giving up, and she pushed aside the other people, calmly slitting the infected man's throat and pulling him away, setting him down to die in the foam. She pointed Harry towards the submarine, and then set herself in the waist-deep water like a stone, kukri raised as the horde drew closer.

A stupid last stand, but Tamsyn decided that she liked Sushma's style. If she could sell her own strange life to get Harry free, it was worth it.

This certainly beats dying while swimming, she thought, and slogged back to stand next to Sushma, shotgun at the ready. The Gurkha smiled at her.

"Now you are a warrior," she said, and then braced herself with that impossibly sharp blade, watching calmly as the frothing mass of undead closed in.

Tamsyn saw the black lines above the swimming monsters, all converging and stretching towards the single point where she stood. She realised then this was all for her, all to wipe her off the planet. If she had stayed behind on the beach, the others might have gotten away.

If only I had a blade like Sushma's, something to cut those puppet strings, she thought, and mused that the supernatural display looked like a weird harp, taut strings ready to pluck. She imagined running her fingers across the strings like an angel, and to her surprise a handful of these control lines wavered, the zombies underneath collapsing in a twitching convulsion, no longer swimming forward.

"I'll see you in the next life, Tamsyn," Sushma said, kukri held level. Tamsyn tried again, imagining that she was gripping a whole bunch of the lines, tying them in knots, shaking them around. She was able to affect dozens of the undead, but it was nowhere near enough. Thousands of swimmers, metres away now, and Sushma was tensing up, ready to make her first slice.

Slice, Tamsyn thought. Instead of thinking of her new gift as a set of fingers, she thought of it as a knife, a sharp blade like the kukri. This time she ran through the black lines with a thought, and they parted, falling aside, drawn back to their invisible controller.

The first ranks of the undead were in a visible panic now, screeching in absolute agony. All they wanted now was to leave the salt water, and they fought against the oncoming swimmers to escape.

"What did you do?" Sushma whispered.

Tamsyn struck again and again with her mind-blade, slicing away the strings, until there was nothing before her but a fleeing horde, wailing and thrashing and retreating to the shore.

10

The atmosphere on the *Vengeance* was grim. When they'd escaped from the Caymans the submarine had been packed to the rafters, but now there were empty bunks dotted throughout the boat, each one like a coffin with a draw-curtain.

They'd lost close to one-third of the merry shooters who'd landed on the Isle of Man. Perhaps some of them were still there, carrying the Vanguard around in their bodies, treading over the shattered bodies of their friends. If they returned to the Isle in a year, would there be more weird structures along the shore?

They didn't have that year. Chief Vassilly had let slip to her that the food supplies onboard the *Vengeance* were already low when they'd left the Caymans. The Navy had tried to buy goodwill from the islanders, sharing rations while the farms got up and running.

"In less than a week, we will all be on half-rations," Vassilly said. "A month after that, we're done."

Both the submarines had enough nuclear fuel to circumnavigate the globe, endless fresh water from the desal plant room, and with enough supplies for the personnel they could see out years, wait until the undead rotted away before seeking landfall. And whatever this Vanguard were, these new living zombies were little better than locusts. They would smile, build, eat everything and then starve.

At least they would die smiling. Tamsyn looked around the submarine to see anger and fear on every face, with the open knowledge that the best efforts of the Royal Navy had ended in a bloody rout. The shifts went on in the boat as they always did, but the sailors were getting slapdash, sly drinking during their shifts, obeying their orders in the most passive-aggressive of ways. The brig was constantly full of brawlers and drunks.

"Look around," she said to the Chief, cradling a drowsy Malcolm in her arms. "Do you think we'll even last the full month?"

An electronic blat from the speakers, signalling the change of shifts. Still awaiting his court martial, Chief Vassilly scrubbed every inch of the boat, cleaned the latrines, mopped up the sick and blood. Lieutenant Commander Gilbert appeared, handing over her own cleaning gear to Vassilly, and Tamsyn noticed that her uniform was wrinkled, stray hairs escaping from her tight bun. Gilbert grunted at Tamsyn, and crawled straight into her bunk, snoring within seconds.

If this stick-in-the-arse woman was losing the fight against entropy, everything was officially over.

Malcolm started with more anxious mewling, and Tamsyn shushed the boy, trying to rock him into sleep. He had been bedwetting most nights, and every morning when she took up a spot in the laundry queue, others muttered darkly at her, caring only about their own dirty underwear.

Whenever the boy cried out with the night terrors, others bunking further down the ship simply screamed at him to shut up. She was terrified of what might happen to them both the next time someone ran out of patience with her kid.

"Please stop crying mate," she whispered, hugging him close. He clutched his toy horse tightly in his fist, shuddering and sniffling. Finally he was still, but he was miles from sleep, staring dark-eyed at his little horse, catatonic and limp in her arms.

We've gotta get out of here, Tamsyn realised. Every waking moment she spent in a mild state of panic, remembering her own whispered threats to the Prime Minister. She had almost no friends here now. What if someone arranged an "accident" for her? What if this whole stupid submarine went Lord of the Flies on each other, and she was trapped amongst it?

She'd heard stories from Harry about the blame games the Privy Council was playing now. It wasn't their fault all of the zombies were in Castletown. The "zombie expert" hadn't given them sufficient warnings or training. Regimental Sergeant Major Leyland had botched the raid, and even ordered supporting fire on his own people. Leyland's plan had wasted rockets, weapons, even lives.

Going by Fallot's latest rantings, it had been a solid plan in the eyes of Privy Council, and the little people had found a way to ruin it, perhaps even sabotaged it. The lords and ladies met at all hours now in the command centre, trying to scramble up an alternative plan, a place to settle this dwindling fragment of humanity. Operation Final Home. Harry told her that the PM and the Opposition Leader were barely on speaking terms now, and in one heated argument had even suggested the *Victorious* and the *Vengeance* go their separate ways, to form two colonies.

One day they wanted to take the Shetland islands, the next they were going to nuke the Isle of Wight and wait five years to reclaim the land from the undead. It was dumb idea after dumb idea, and worst of all was the realisation that Tamsyn couldn't come up with anything better.

Shift change that day brought both Sushma by the bunk for a visit. Both she and Reynolds were taking turns as brig guards and security in the mess hall, and Sushma shared today's story about the assistant cook, whom she'd dragged to the captain's quarters when he was caught hoarding supplies.

"Slap on the wrist," the Gurkha explained. "In my village, you steal and hand comes off at wrist."

Little Malcolm had a hero worship for Sushma, and her silly faces and tickles brought a hard-won grin from the boy. As the formidable warrior made the toddler squeal with delight, Tamsyn's own smile faded at the corners. What kind of mum couldn't make her kid happy, or keep him safe?

All Tamsyn hoped for now was a castle to hole up in, or a lighthouse on some tiny spit of land. Perhaps a friend or two for drinking company, a veggie patch and a fishing rod. Bucket loads of booze, just to help her forget the horrors she'd seen, and the new horrors that were peeling away the edges of her sanity.

Even the most picturesque lighthouse wouldn't fix anything. She was Death now, and she knew it. Tamsyn felt the dark electricity dancing around in the submariners' souls, the same frantic fatalism she'd felt on the *Paraclete* when it died in the middle of the ocean.

She knew from experience that things were going to get nasty on this submarine, very soon.

Tamsyn needed to get fighting fit, and fast.

Eddie's dad had spent more than one turn behind bars, and he'd passed on the finest of prison fitness tips onto his boy, which he'd passed on to Tamsyn, back when they were going through basic in Texas. When space was at a premium, you got inventive with sit-ups and weight resistance, and he used to do push-ups with her sitting on his back. She made do with Malcolm, figuring he was a plump little fellow and she was getting back into shape.

He thought it was hilarious, and kept trying to turn her pushups into a game of ride-the-horsey. Whenever he slept, she would try and go into beast-mode to make up for lost time. Barefoot running up and down the corridors, trying not to wake the off-shift, and then she learnt that the sailors were allowed to run around the perimeter of the guided missile launch tube compartment. There was an exercise bike or two hidden around the submarine, but competition for these was fierce, and she didn't want to piss off any more of her enlisted neighbours.

She was running past the radio room right when she noticed some sort of commotion. The acting Lieutenant Commander was pacing around behind the radio operators, who were working in a mad panic.

"Clear up the mess on that audio," the officer commanded. "This is a multi-billion dollar submarine, not a walkie-talkie."

One of the operators turned on a loudspeaker for the officer's benefit, and Tamsyn heard a squelchy murmur, rhythmic, cutting in and out. She paused by the door as if stretching, but no-one was noticing her for now.

"Is there something wrong with the surface antenna?"

"No sir," an operator said. "The signal is very weak."

"Well, boost the signal! Give it more power!"

"Sir - it - it doesn't work like that, sir."

"We've got an option," another operator said. "We've got an X-Sub buoy down in the launch tube compartment. Very powerful. We should get a clear signal then."

"Well, launch it!"

"It's single use only. We need the Captain's permission to launch it."

"He's off shift. I'm acting in his authority. Launch the buoy."

One of them made the call to the torpedo room, and then she heard a distant *whoomph* as the buoy shot out into the deep. Seconds later, the squelch was replaced by a female voice, crystal clear.

"--anyone listening, please respond. This is One Angel Square, is anyone out there?"

"Sir?" one of the operators said, offering the officer a handset. After a moment, he took it.

"One Angel Square, this is Brevet Lieutenant Commander Willard of the *HMS Vengeance*. Please advise your location."

A long moment, and then the woman transmitting the SOS squealed into her microphone, the sensitive equipment responding with a squeal.

"Oh my god, someone's answering. Daniel, go get the boss!"

"Who are you?" Willard demanded.

"I'm Quinn," the woman said in a thick northern accent. "Are you guys on a boat or something?"

"Submarine, ma'am," Willard said. "Again, please advise your location."

"One Angel Square. Um, in the middle of Manchester. Great big building that looks like a sliced egg."

"How many are in your group?" Willard asked.

"We've got almost three hundred in the building."

Tamsyn nearly fell over. There were still survivors out there! Gravesend had lost contact with the Manchester communities early in the outbreak, and had written the whole city off as overrun.

"How many of the infected are around your location?"

"Millions, mate. Millions of the damn things. We're stuck in here."

"Willard, switch that off," a voice said behind Tamsyn, and she jumped.

It was Captain Grant and he was pissed. The man was all bad breath and messed up hair, still wearing his pyjamas. Grabbing her by both shoulders, he pushed her against the wall, and leaned in close, looming over her.

"Speak a word of this, and I will end you," he snarled at her. He was a man with a secret, and his aura jangled with barely suppressed violence. Tamsyn absolutely believed him.

Tamsyn joined a poker game that wasn't a poker game in the senior ratings' mess hall that night. It was just matchsticks in the kitty, and sour faces around the table. The grand conspiracy, held in plain sight, and even as they bid and bluffed, they updated each other on the plan.

"I'll raise you," Leyland said, and quietly added, "How are we looking for supplies?"

"I'm in," Chief Vassilly said, sliding more matches into

the kitty, and as he leant forward he muttered, "Got a guy on the armoury during the day-shift."

"I'm out," Harry said with a cheeky grin, showing his awful hand. "I've got a few more of the officers on side, good folks that I trust."

"I've got the senior ratings from communications and the back-afties ready to go," Lieutenant Commander Gilbert said, adding more matches to the pile. A huge relief - they could shut down the radio and the engines on the *Vengeance* if it came to that.

"Reynolds says that the security detail is about fifty-fifty. Did you even shuffle that deck?" Tamsyn asked, tipping over her terrible cards. Little Malcolm was on her knee, slobbering into his fist and humming some tuneless drone. This deep voyage to nowhere was having a profound psychological effect on her boy - in the old world she'd have to find an expensive psychologist for him ASAP. In this world, he'd get his own gun one day, if he was lucky.

Outside of this small group, she couldn't even find a babysitter anymore.

When Tamsyn had whispered to Harry about the transmission from Manchester she'd started this whole thing, but there was nothing else for her to do but wait. She wasn't welcome in the wardroom or the officer's mess, as an untrained "oxygen-thief" the sailors viewed her as little more than a nuisance, and she'd already pissed off the two most powerful people on board.

Gilbert won that hand, and they dealt out again. It was ten minutes until the shift changeover, and then six hours until the next shift and go-time. Once Captain Grant went to bed, the whole nasty mess was going to kick off.

Prince Harry was planning a mutiny.

"No turning back from this," Harry said quietly. "If anyone wants out, I'll understand."

"It's not even a choice," Tamsyn said. "It's the right thing to do."

One of the weapons techs asked to join the game, and they were forced through three excruciating hands before the shift klaxon, unable to discuss the plan. Tamsyn tried to fight down the paranoia that danced around in her head, and tried not to watch the door for armed marines, come to arrest them - or worse.

"Get some sleep," Harry told her kindly, and she shook her head at the impossibility of that statement. She felt like her heart was running on three swift espressos, and felt that way until she climbed into her bunk with her broken little kid, and her head sank into the pillow and a dozy sleep.

A DREAM of the mansion in Florida, and it was just her and Eddie on the beach. The ocean was completely still, and they were ankle deep in the water. Over Eddie's shoulder, the sun was close to the horizon, but it was red, angry, pulsing with fury. He had her by the shoulders and was shaking her.

"WAKE UP TAMSYN, WAKE UP!" he screamed into her face, even as blurry hands reached for him, sealing up his mouth, dragging him down into the water, before reaching for her...

SHE WOKE UP WITH A START, just as a man tore aside the curtain on her bunk. In that fraction of a second she realised it was the protective officer assigned to Prime Minister Fallot, a bullet-headed cop whose name she couldn't remember.

His eyes widened when he realised she was awake, but then he leapt forward, pressing a pillow down on her and Malcolm, trying to smother them both. She screamed and fought, punching and kicking at the man, scratching at his arms. The man was stronger than her, pushing down with all of his weight.

She felt Malcolm squirming around on top of her, his own little lungs struggling to fill, and then she fought back with a fury. Finally she slammed her knee up between his legs, and the man fell away with a gasp, losing just enough grip on the pillow for her to tear her way free.

All around, she could hear shouting and screaming. Barely five feet away, two other men were rolling around on the corridor floor, a brutal fight that was all dirty tricks and disabling blows.

That was all the chaos she could take in as the killer cop came for her again, eyes watering and fists swinging. She took a blow to the cheek that left her reeling, and then the man's hands were around her throat, squeezing tight, even as Malcolm wailed and screamed in fear…

Then a blur of steel, and the man was without a head, blood pumping all over her. The hands relaxed and slid away from her throat, and the man toppled to the floor, neck still pumping out his life-blood. Sushma stood over his body, kukri clenched in her fist.

"Everything has gone wrong," she said calmly. "Come with me."

With a screaming toddler on her hip, Tamsyn followed the Gurkha through the corridor, witnessing horrors at every turn. Sailors had been murdered in their bunks, and others were fighting to the death with tools and kitchen knives. Unable to tell who was friend or foe, Sushma barrelled forward, brutally clearing a path forward with fists and elbows. Tamsyn stuck close to the frenzied warrior, feeling useless and scared at the sudden violence on the boat.

"We need to take the armoury," Sushma yelled over her shoulder. A full phalanx of men in riot gear came tromping down the corridor, so Sushma led them down the stairs to the next deck, weaving past brawling submariners and leaping over the bodies of the dead and dying.

How did things get so bad so fast? Tamsyn wondered, trying to shield Malcolm's eyes. They'd planned a bloodless coup, and meant to give full information to everyone about the survivors in Manchester, put things to a vote. This mess had kicked off mere hours before the planned mutiny, which told her that this was someone else's plan.

"Fallot," she gasped.

This crackdown was dark and awful, even for the conniving Prime Minister and his twits. Just days ago they'd been all about the rules, waving around court martials and brig-time, and now everyone was flipping into murder and insanity.

Tamsyn felt claustrophobic at the best of times, and now the tin-can world of the submarine pressed in around her. Up above, even if it all went to hell, there was somewhere you could run, somewhere you could hide. Down here it was the length of a football pitch on four cramped decks, full of murder and betrayal, and no escape for anyone.

A gun-shot, and then another. A huge no-no on a submarine, where a stray bullet could punch a hole through the hull. Screams up ahead, so of course Sushma was heading straight towards the violence, kukri ready for blood.

They were all around her now, fists and batons flying. She caught a blow to the rear of her skull that left her reeling, and she clutched Malcolm closer, instinctively shielding her child from the violence pressing in on all angles. Then they were packed in by bodies, arms and legs flailing in all directions.

This is how we die, Tamsyn thought, and tried to find peace, to be grateful that it wasn't zombies doing her in. Here at the end though, she was simply shitting herself, and crying out in panic, and there was no dignity for her or poor Malcolm. She barely noticed the jagged red and black lines around everyone - these highly trained men and women had reverted back to cave-men. *Kill or be killed*.

Sushma gave a guttural growl and shouted a word in her own language, over and over, and then finally she fell into carving her way through the blockage like a human blender. Finally they were through, and Tamsyn followed Sushma over the screaming mass of the injured, slipping over blood and spilled entrails, deeper into the heart of madness.

Another gun-shot, close now. Sushma and Tamsyn raced around the last corner to see Vassilly slumped against the front door of the armoury, a red smear following him down to where he sat on the deck. A chef's cleaver was embedded in his shoulder, the blade buried deep past the clavicle. He held a pistol in his left hand, the right one still bound up in a sling. Three dead men lay slumped on the floor before him, one still twitching as his dying nerves fired from the legs down.

"Mummy, I scared!" Malcolm cried. A warm patch ran down Tamsyn's side as his bladder failed him.

"I had to do it," Vassilly said, weeping as he looked up at the pair. "They're killing everyone."

He was struggling to reload his clip with one good hand. Sushma knelt down and helped him.

"What the hell happened?" Tamsyn asked.

"We don't know," he gasped. "We still had two hours until go-time when - when -"

He gestured at the dead bodies, unable to frame that thought.

"Did Fallot do this? Captain Grant?" Tamsyn asked.

"No-one planned this!" Vassilly sobbed. "They all just went crazy!"

A rattle on the deck plating, and Vassilly tried to fix one bleary eye on the sound. He raised his pistol, arm wobbling, and then lowered it to the deck,

"It's you," he said. Leyland and Reynolds were walking up the corridor, the big marine splattered with blood, a length of piping clenched in one hand. Beside him Reynolds brandished his combat knife, his entire forearm drenched red.

"Leyland, Reynolds, what the hell is going on?" Tamsyn asked. "Wait, what are you doing?"

They said nothing, but kept walking towards them. No, they were stalking. Then they ran towards them, makeshift weapons raised, eyes dead and empty, like they were lizards stuffed into human skins.

Then they smiled.

"Mummy!" Malcolm cried.

"Stop!" she cried, and then her vision swam, showing her the black strings tugging on their heads, stretching up through the roof of the submarine, and jerking them forward. *Slice!* She parted the string with her strange new talent, and the two men staggered to a halt, looking around in confusion.

"Oh. Oh god," Leyland said, and dropped the bloody pipe. "What the hell have I done?"

Reynolds looked at his own combat knife with a grimace of distaste, wiping the blade on his pants leg before sheathing it. A moment of silence as the group looked at each other distrustfully.

"That wasn't me doing those things," Reynolds finally said, tapping his head. "Sure, I was there. I remember - everything. But something else was *up here*, driving me."

"I believe you," Tamsyn said. "It's like the Vanguard again. Or something like it."

Then she thought back to Fallot's goon trying to murder her. There was nothing supernatural about that – it was pure human evil, a stupid murder caught up in this larger madness.

"How did you-" Leyland asked. "That was you who stopped it?"

Tamsyn nodded.

"If we go back to - to being that way, could you break us loose?"

"Yes."

The big marine was shaken for a long moment. This was something no-one could even hope to understand. Tamsyn saw the moment when he pushed all that nasty stuff down into his gut, and she wondered who was collecting the most demons today.

Reynolds and Sushma were kneeling down by Vassilly, applying pressure and working to free the cleaver. The stout Chief was howling in agony, and their efforts were causing the blood to spurt out of him even faster.

"Just leave it alone!" Vassilly screamed. "Don't touch it."

"Chief, we need these guns," Leyland said, and Vassilly nodded in understanding, his face flushed and running with tears. The three of them took a moment to move the stricken Chief to one side, as gently as they could. When they set the man down, he'd leaked more of his life out across the floor.

More screams, and the thunder of footsteps against the deck, getting closer. Sushma took the key to the armoury from Vassilly's belt, and then they were snatching up rifles and extra clips. Reynolds snagged a tac-vest in one hand, and tossed Tamsyn a riot shotgun with the other.

"Let's go!" Leyland shouted, locking the hatch and pocketing the key. It sounded like a herd of elephants storming down the deck. Tamsyn didn't like her chances of severing these people from the madness infecting the ship - what if there were just too many? Her weird gift was too unreliable.

"Get to communications," Vassilly yelled, face pinched with pain. "Gilbert went there to shut down all the radios."

Leyland bent to pick the man up, but the Chief swore.

"Don't be stupid! Go!"

It made sense, but it was awful. They left him there, perhaps moments away from bleeding out, his arm shaking as he raised his pistol to cover the corridor. Then it was all running and Malcolm crying and the panicked *pop-pop-pop* of Vassilly emptying his clip, and the sounds of a mob beating a man to death.

Was Harry one of those killers now? Was he smiling, blood-spattered, fury dangling on a black string? If he'd fallen tonight, Tamsyn thought she might just lose all hope.

Leyland dropped one smiling killer with the butt of his rifle, but then there were more, swinging coffeepots and kitchen knives, and one man swung his belt like a whip, the thick buckle crashing into Tamsyn's head and making her see stars.

Slice, damnit! she thought, but she couldn't focus on the

dark lines, couldn't see anything but the violence around her. There was no way for her to sever these people from the madness driving them to kill.

One man reached for Malcolm then, and she didn't even have the time to aim the gun. Her own rage kicked in, the rage of a mother on the defensive, and with one swift motion she stoved in his face with the butt of the gun. She stomped on the downed man with a primal cry, and then someone had her by the collar, dragging her away. She lashed out again, and a moment later she realised it was Reynolds, nose bloody from her glancing blow with the gun stock.

"Easy killer, we're here," he said. Leyland closed a hatch behind them, throwing over the locks. The monsters hammered on the other side, but could not get through. It was a reprieve, but they found themselves faced with a different kind of insanity.

The command centre of the *Vengeance* was like a butcher's nightmare. Dead submariners were slumped in their desks, some still wearing their headsets. Captain Grant still lay tangled in death with one of his officers, his face completely buried in the ruins of the other man's throat.

Prime Minister Fallot had Lieutenant Commander Gilbert backed up to one of the walls, a pistol held to her forehead. Behind them was a console in ruins, wiring and parts strewn everywhere. Another officer was madly working to fix the damage.

"Ah, your confederates are here," he said, face fixed into a nasty grimace. "All of you, put down your weapons. Do it!"

"Don't," Gilbert began, and then Fallot pistol-whipped her across the face.

"Your murderous little coup ends now!"

"Prime Minister, you are making a big mistake," Tamsyn

said. "This isn't what you think."

"We know you were planning a mutiny, you lying little bitch," Fallot said. "We didn't know you were going to murder half the boat to do it."

"This wasn't us! It's the infection."

"More fairy stories! You have lied to the Prince, you have lied to the Council, and I am done with your lies," Fallot said. "Your guns. Now!"

Gilbert was terrified. Tamsyn knelt, placing her shotgun on the deck, and a moment later the others did the same.

"Step back from the guns. Up against that wall. No tricks!"

Tamsyn and the others pressed themselves against the far wall. There were consoles and other gear between them and Fallot. Tamsyn hoped that one of the trained killers next to her would find a way to end this before anyone else died.

Oh for my old bow, she thought. *I could put an arrow through his eye as easy as breathing.*

"Sir, I -" the officer fixing the radio began.

"Did I tell you to stop? Fix the damn radio!"

"The nukes, he-" Gilbert began, and then Fallot pressed the gun into the meat of her shoulder and pulled the trigger. The noise was deafening this close, and then everyone was screaming and shouting. Leyland and Reynolds made to take down the PM, but he waved the gun in their direction, a dangerous look in his eyes.

"What the hell are you doing, Fallot?" Tamsyn said.

"It wasn't meant to be this way!" Fallot said. "We didn't want this butchery, this mad violence."

"Sir, put down your gun and let the Lieutenant Commander go," Leyland barked. "This is wrong."

"You gave us the idea, Miss Webb," Fallot said. "You, with

your grim little story about your boat ride to America. We're only making the same decision."

"No, you can't do this," Tamsyn said, realisation washing over her. It was that awful moment on the *Paraclete* all over again, when people got scared and made dark plans.

"What is he talking about?" Reynolds asked.

"They want to sink the sub. Mass suicide."

"One quick flash and it's all over," Fallot said. "We have eight 500 kiloton missiles onboard. No-one will feel pain."

"There has to be a better way," Tamsyn said.

"There's nowhere we can go!" Fallot cried. "There is nowhere safe left on this planet! Now, Lieutenant Commander. What are the codes for the missiles?"

"They change every day," she said, snuffling through a bloody nose. "You can ask the Captain over there. Or Willard, I saw him running around clutching a bloody chair leg. I haven't had the code in weeks."

"You're lying," he said, but his face fell.

"We need to get to land," Tamsyn implored Fallot. "Not everyone has gone crazy. We might be able to save some lives."

"There's only one way to save these people. My way," Fallot said. Through the throbbing of her pained head, Tamsyn could see the squiggle around him, a dark migraine aura that seemed to weigh the man down. As much as she despised the man, she could sense how much he was suffering. He thought he was doing the right thing, and that made him doubly dangerous.

"Sir, I've got a connection," the officer kneeling by the sabotaged equipment said. "I can raise the *Victorious*."

"Put me through," Fallot said. "Captain Bleckly, this is Prime Minister Terry Fallot on the *Vengeance*."

Leyland tensed up, ready to rush for the guns on the

floor. Fallot twitched the pistol his way, flashing a dark smile. The radio squealed.

"Prime Minister, this is Sub Lieutenant Crake. Captain Bleckly is dead, sir. The men have gone mad sir, they're killing each other."

How far has this rage gone? Tamsyn thought. *What if the Manchester survivors have this too? What if it's everywhere now?*

"Listen. We are locked out of the nuclear option. I'm ordering you to fire half your warheads at the *Vengeance*."

"No!" Tamsyn cried. "You bloody idiot!"

"I can't do that, Prime Minister."

"You will do as you are ordered, Sub Lieutenant! Complete the plan."

"There's no-one left alive with the nuke codes. We're locked out as well."

"Well thank God for that," Tamsyn said. "End this madness, Fallot."

"Crake, launch all remaining torpedoes at the Vengeance. That is an order!"

At that moment, a silver flash launched across the command room, and Sushma's kukri buried itself in the Prime Minister's eye. He fell to the floor with a surprised whimper, dragging Gilbert down with him.

Reynolds moved like a panther, taking out Fallot's pet officer with a blow to the throat. Tamsyn ran to the microphone the man had cobbled together, nearly falling over and dropping Malcolm in her haste.

"*Victorious*, please stop!" Tamsyn cried out. "Do not fire upon us!"

"Go to hell," the voice on the radio said. Then their entire universe shook, as torpedo after torpedo struck the *HMS Vengeance.*

11

Malcolm was howling, clutching at her tightly. At some point she'd fallen to the deck, scraping her knees. Warning alarms screamed from the decks of dead men, a red strobe-light flashed across the ceiling, and water was leaking into the command centre, six inches deep and freezing cold.

The hull groaned and creaked, the sheets of steel buckling and shrieking in protest. Then the deck shook again, tossing her back down into the water.

An entire bank of equipment had sheared free of the wall, falling on top of Leyland and pinning him to the floor. Reynolds and Sushma were struggling to lift the weighty console, even as Leyland cursed and fought to keep his head above the rising water.

"Mummy! Mummy!" Malcolm cried. Tamsyn thought of that scene in the *Titanic* movie, where the mother serenely gathers her children back into bed, even as the waters lap in.

"I am not that kind of mum, kid," she said shakily. Sloshing through the water, she reached down to Gilbert, wrenching her above the water with her free arm. Coughing and choking, the wounded officer shook off the death grip of the dead Prime Minister.

"Focus," Tamsyn told the woman. "We are not dying today. You can drive this boat, correct?"

The Lieutenant Commander looked around at the screaming equipment, the flooding deck, at Reynolds and Sushma fighting the weight of an ocean to free their friend. She fought for composure and found it like a pro.

"Yes. But we have three hull breaches, we'll need to be bloody quick."

"Show me what to do," Tamsyn said. Gilbert slid a dead man out of his station, and handed Tamsyn the headset. Still clutching Malcolm in the crook of one arm, she sat down behind a confusing array of controls and screens. Gilbert sat in the captain's seat, with ten times the chaos in front of her.

"Oy, come and bloody help us!" Reynolds shouted. "Leyland's gonna drown, you stupid bint!"

"We'll all drown if we don't raise this submarine," Gilbert said frostily. "Keep your composure, Trooper."

"Yes Ma'am," he said.

Just then there was a mad banging on the sealed hatch, and the muffled shouting of the people on the other side. They sounded furious.

"Tamsyn, ignore that," Gilbert said. "You have a control in front of you marked Rear Hydroplane Angle. What is the setting?"

"This says ninety degrees."

"Use the buttons to set it to 25 degrees."

Tamsyn tapped away at the control, and the display changed to show the new setting. A nearby workstation spat sparks and went dark, and Tamsyn looked to Gilbert, hoping for some sage advice before the whole place went dark.

"Shit on a biscuit," the officer said. "One of the breaches is to the aft ballast tank."

"Leyland has only a few inches left," Sushma called out calmly.

"Tamsyn, you have the auxiliary tank control on your module. Can you see it?"

"What am I looking for? What the hell was it called again?"

"Orange keypad to the right of the buoyancy readouts. No, the other one. Now this is the most important part. You will have to purge the auxiliary tanks with compressed oxygen at the same moment I purge the remaining ballast tanks. We will count down from 3."

"What? How the hell do I do that? Where's the purge button?"

"There's no button. It's on the screen in front of you, use the orange keys to scroll down."

"I can't do this!" Tamsyn cried out, setting off a fresh wave of wailing from her terrified kid.

"Captain Tamsyn Webb," Gilbert said frostily. "If you can use an iPhone, you can perform this one, simple operation. You will purge your tanks on my count."

"Dad never got me an iPhone," Tamsyn muttered. She tapped away until she found the appropriate menu item.

"Ladies, please hurry it up!" Leyland spluttered as the water began to rise up his face.

"Three. Two. One. Go."

Tamsyn hit the purge command at the same time that Gilbert did. For a long moment, nothing happened.

"Did – did I do it wrong?" Tamsyn asked, and then the

submarine shot upwards at great speed. It felt like the giddiest part of a roller-coaster ride. Moments later the ascent stopped abruptly, and Tamsyn's ears popped like a bitch. Malcolm found one new thing to scream about as he clutched his own young ears, howling from the change of pressure.

"We've surfaced," Gilbert said matter-of-factly.

"We did it!" Tamsyn whooped.

"We're still taking on too much water. We need to get to the lifeboats. Now."

"A little help?" Reynolds called out. With a look to Gilbert's still bleeding shoulder, Tamsyn put Malcolm in the crook of the officer's still good arm. Sloshing through the water, she squeezed through the straining figures of Sushma and Reynolds, trying to get a grip on the console. Leyland was lifting his head as high as he could, his nostrils barely clearing the rising flood.

More banging from outside the door. They were furious, beating and shouting through the thick plate. The hull gave another groan, the metal vibrating, and then the whole boat tipped forwards, completely covering Leyland with water.

"For god sake's, Tamsyn, lift the bloody thing!" Reynolds shouted.

"I'm trying!" she said. She heaved and pushed until she was red in the face, but she just wasn't strong enough to get a grip on the big steel box. She felt hopeless and realised this beautiful man was about to drown right before her eyes.

She took in a huge gulp of air, and ducked her head underwater, latching her lips onto Leyland's and breathing into his mouth. His eyes opened wide in surprise, but he took the breath. She surfaced and repeated the process, passing life to the trapped man.

"Get a lever or something," she gasped. "We're not strong enough."

Next to the sealed hatch, the intercom began to squeal, before finally dying with a loud *pop* and a spray of sparks. The water rose inches in seconds.

"We have to leave him," Gilberts called out. "It's time to go."

"Are you mad? We can't just let him drown!"

"We're all going to drown."

"She's right," Reynolds puffed. "We can't save him."

More banging on the hatch, but this time it wasn't a mad beating. It was the ever British and ever polite *shave-and-a-haircut, two bob*.

"There's someone alive back there!" Tamsyn shouted. "You know, alive but not insane!"

Wading against the rising waters, Tamsyn threw open the hatch. There was a whole squad of sailors and marines wearing riot gear, and at their head was Prince Harry, face shield splattered with a spray of blood. Tamsyn felt foolish for having run from what was obviously safety during the madness.

"Get in here!" she shouted. "Leyland is trapped under the water."

"It's good to see you too," he said. His group hustled in, and strong hands joined Reynolds and Sushma, until they heaved the console up just enough to slide Leyland free. There was no time for assessing his spine, and he snatched at the nearest hand, rising to his feet. He winced with the movement.

"Cracked every damn rib," he said. "Well, don't just stand around, get to the boats!"

Grabbing Malcolm from Gilbert, Tamsyn followed the riot squad through the flooding boat. More and more systems were going dark, and the faint red of the emergency lighting kicked in, lending everything a nightmare tinge.

Corpses were floating in the corridors, savaged to death, while mad men and women were still frothing from where they knelt in the water, beaten bloody and zip-tied to pipes and fixtures. It seemed like Harry's handiwork, and she approved of the tactic. Very easy to kill in self-defence, and noble to save someone who couldn't control their actions.

Slice, Tamsyn thought, severing each of the afflicted from their black thread, and understanding returned to their eyes, quickly followed by terror when they realised they were trapped.

"Sushma! Cut them loose!" Tamsyn cried. With a nod of understanding she nicked at the zip-ties, freeing the people that Tamsyn was able to release from their unseen master. Her control over the strange sight cut in and out, and soon she found she was unable to free anyone at all, a migraine effectively shutting her "powers" down. She wept as she brushed past the gnashing teeth and kicking legs of the afflicted, fighting to keep up with the others.

"I'm so sorry, I can't help you!" she cried, trying not to look at the doomed men and women, still raging and murderous even as the waters rose. Then she was stumbling through an open hatch, into fresh air and driving rain. On the upper deck, Harry's group were working by torch-light, inflating a fifty-seat launch and getting ready to cast off.

Tamsyn held the fussing Malcolm close to her chest, eyeing off the water that was licking the base of the conning tower. The deck beneath her gave a lurch, and people cried out in panic.

"Come on," Reynolds muttered, watching impatiently as the chemical agents inflated the hull of the big launch. It was inflating quickly, but they had perhaps a minute or two at best.

Then, Tamsyn felt a wave of dizziness, the overwhelming urge to turn her face towards a random stretch of the ocean, perhaps a mile in the distance. She felt the cold chill of Death run up her spine, and knew she was looking upon the final location of the *HMS Victorious*. She watched with sickening realisation as an enormous plume of water erupted into the heavens.

The noise of the nuclear explosion was overwhelming, and she felt it down to her bone-marrow, to the bottom of her sour little soul. Then a blinding flash, a mushroom cloud that seemed equal parts steam and smoke, and a wall of water shot out, a tsunami perhaps fifty metres high. It was rolling towards them, and fast.

"Everyone get in!" someone yelled, and dozens of people fought to get into the half-inflated boat, struggling with oars and life-jackets. The mushroom cloud was growing, the plume of steam growing thicker until it looked like a deadly cauliflower, looming far overhead. The roar seemed to go on and on, so loud that it dwarfed the panicked shouting all around her. Someone stuffed a life-jacket in her hands, and even as she clambered over the half-inflated rubber she tried to stuff Malcolm into it.

My god, the radiation, Tamsyn thought, and then there was only time to try and grab onto a handle, to hold onto her little boy as hard as she could. Then the first wave caught them, and there was nothing to do but hang on, the tremendous force lifting both life-raft and submarine and tossing them around like bath toys.

Everything shook, and Tamsyn screamed in terror. The life-raft was caught on the edge of the huge wave like a surf-board. At one stage the raft tipped slightly, and Tamsyn could see all the way down, the bottom of the ocean more than fifty metres below. If they fell now, the drop would kill everyone on board.

The monster wave started to lose its force, and it set down the raft, only dropping the last few metres onto a rolling swell. Perhaps a dozen people had fallen out of the life-raft, bobbing around in life-jackets or struggling to stay afloat, while others clutched to the handles, shaken but alive.

There were people missing, who'd fallen out of the life-raft, or never boarded it to begin with. Tamsyn could not see Lieutenant Commander Gilbert in the survivors, and she mourned the brave woman for a long moment - if not for her, they'd all be drowning, sucking at the last of the air...

"Mummy!" Malcolm wailed, gesturing back the way they came with outstretched fingers. "My horsey!"

"Your horsey's gone mate," she said, hugging the boy tight. "No more horsey."

THE LIFEBOAT WAS the picture of misery - thirty-nine survivors shivering, huddled together for warmth as the drizzle turned into a full downpour. The survival kit was missing some of the rations, pilfered by poor old Chief Vassilly when the supplies drew tight. Tamsyn shared a chocolate bar with Malcolm and then she showed him how to hold his mouth open, swallowing the raindrops that fell past his lips.

"They'll be waiting a while to get that working," she told her boy. A solar water-still danced behind the life-raft, eking out next to nothing from the ocean in the poor daylight.

As the highest-ranking officer, Leyland took command of the life-raft. He brought order to the panic-stricken survivors, and gave out jobs to everybody, keeping his people focused on busy-work. The life raft was an unwieldy lozenge, intended for people to wait in until the help arrived, and it rowed like a bouncy castle full of rocks.

Everyone took a turn on the oars, fighting to make headway against the thunderous waves of the Irish Sea. Others worked to tend injuries, some tended the fishing lines cast off the stern, and some wags started a singalong, working through the Beatles songbook.

These people are wonderful, Tamsyn realised. *They saw almost everybody die today, were almost killed by their own. We are lost at sea, possibly radioactive, and now they are singing Yellow Submarine.*

Tamsyn was relieved that most of her friends had survived today's slaughter. Sushma sat uncaring in the rain, sharing smiles and jokes with her boy. Reynolds was catching a doze, despite the rain and the cold, using Harry's leg as a pillow.

Oh, Harry. To these stranded men and women he was somewhere between a mascot and a good luck charm, and Tamsyn could feel the goodness radiating from him, could even see his golden aura whenever her migraine eased up. Someone had turned up with a deck of cards, and the world's soggiest game of gin-rummy was underway.

"Your attention, ladies and gents," Leyland said, parade ground voice drowning out both chatter and wild weather. He held up a laminated map from the supply locker.

"Near as we can calculate, we're perhaps fifty nautical miles from the nearest shoreline, somewhere between the Isle of Man and Blackpool. Our fine vessel floats like a pregnant sea-cow, so we will be lucky to make twenty nautical miles in a day."

His words were met with a chorus of good-natured booing, which he met with a face like a sea-wall.

"We have learnt of trapped civilians in Manchester. They

require our assistance. Once we make shore, we are then duty bound as members of Her Majesty's Navy to undertake their rescue. Any questions?"

"Before we start rowing, can you just shoot me now?" Harry quipped.

"I would, Your Highness, but there are only three guns on this vessel, and to be frank we will require all of the bullets."

"Someone hand me an oar then," the Prince said. "The sooner I get bitten by a zombie, the happier I'll be."

Prince Harry was like the hero in a POW escape movie, the one who lifts the spirits of the broken and makes the dangerous possible. The survivors were reinvigorated, and people cursed good-naturedly as they rowed to a distant shore.

The drifting choir moved onto *Hard Day's Night*, and Tamsyn shivered and rowed to keep warm and wondered why it felt so good to be in such a miserable situation.

EXHAUSTION FOUND HER, and she slipped into the dream almost as soon as she closed her eyes. Once more she walked along the beach in the Florida Keys, but this time there was no Eddie, no Mum and Dad, no crowd of dead friends. Just her, and an ocean that stretched out forever, and a dark red sun, sliding down and down and growing, dominating the sky.

"TAMSYN LOTTIE WEBB," it said to her, the edges of the disc vibrating with each booming word. "I HAVE SEEN YOU."

"No shit," she said, shaking voice betraying her. Her teeth were vibrating painfully, and then the strange sun reversed direction, climbing back towards noon, driving her to her knees in the sand, pouring unnatural energies down on her.

"I HAVE DRIVEN YOUR ALLIES FROM THIS PLACE," it said, indicating everything in the dream world with a sudden flash, brighter than the nuclear explosion, and she could see her finger bones through the hand she threw up to protect herself. Behind her, the mini-mansions shook into splinters.

"YOU ARE THE LAST ONE. SEEK DEATH, AND I WILL RENDER MERCY TO YOUR COMPANIONS."

"Was that mercy? What you did on the boat?"

The red sun dipped suddenly towards the horizon, and it rose back up, trailing millions of black lines that stretched out to some infinite point.

"WE HAVE THIS WORLD. SURRENDER, LAST OF THE GUIDES, AND WE CAN OFFER SETTLEMENT."

"Girl Guides is a bunch of old sexist bullshit. I was a Cub Scout."

The sun drew low until it filled her entire universe, and it drew the black lines in tight, millions upon millions of monsters upon leashes, and she knew they were all suddenly aware of her.

"SEEK YOUR DEATH," it demanded. "OR THERE WILL BE MADNESS FOR YOUR COMPANIONS. PAIN FOR YOUR CHILD."

Somehow, Tamsyn found the strength to get to her feet, to stand up tall and face that terrifying vision. She bunched her hands in fists, and threw her head back.

"You leave him alone, you big red motherfucker!"

"YOUR LIFE FOR HIS."

She wished she had a weapon of some sort, as futile as that was. The sun pulsed again, bearing down on her, and then she reached out, imagining the shape just as she'd imagined a sword of the mind, back on Sheppey. Then she felt it in her hands, that old familiar weight. Her bow, as fresh as the day she'd picked it up in the store. Nocked on the string was an arrow of deepest shadow, ending in a point so sharp it hurt her to look upon it.

Grinning, she drew the string back, aiming her arrow towards the centre of that twisted orb. Another bright flash, and a roar that was equal parts anger and frustration. Quick as thought the false sun retreated across the sky, booming and shaking and shuddering around the edges, and she sent arrow after arrow into it, wounding it gravely as it sank behind the horizon.

Then there was nothing but a sky of pure black, without stars or moon. The ocean was still, slightly luminescent. Tamsyn willed herself awake, but she felt pinned to the dream island, unable to return to her body.

Slowly, a boy emerged from the glowing water. A normal looking kid, perhaps fifteen, dressed in a school uniform. A prefect, or a school captain. He strode towards her with purpose, smiling broadly, eyes dancing with a mad light.

Around his brow, a crown forged from utter darkness.

Tamsyn sank an arrow deep into his breast, and she awoke.

12

A driving rain came in from the west during the small hours, and Tamsyn fell into the numb rhythm of rowing, bailing, trying to warm her frozen child, and doing her best not to lose her mind. Half of the sailors around her had woken during the attack, and were still in vests and boxer shorts, and a few poor souls wore only their underwear.

She bundled up Malcolm underneath her damp windbreaker, letting him shiver directly against her skin. She thanked the stars for her long habit of sleeping clothed, something she'd done since the earliest days of the outbreak in Gravesend.

Never know when you might need to run for your life, am I right?

By torchlight, Leyland and the other sailors argued over the map. The GPS in the survival kit had no satellite to connect to, and without the stars to guide them they were relying on guesswork and a compass.

For every foot they rowed forward, the wind caught the

cumbersome raft and blew it three foot in some random direction.

No-one was singing Beatles songs anymore.

By noon of the next day, a storm hit them hard, and it was pointless to even row. The survivors of the *Vengeance* were a huddle of human misery, and some of the sailors were showing signs of exposure. There were two survival blankets in the supply locker, shared around between the people suspected of passing over into hypothermia.

That night, three sailors and one of the marines died. Tamsyn felt each of them go, stepping clear of their failed bodies with confused expressions, still packed in by the warm and the living. She sent them on with a kind word and a sad smile, and they ran across the surface of the waves towards the east, free of all care.

Dawn brought them to a lonely bay, a marshland overlooked by acres of abandoned farms, and the survivors spilled out as one, sobbing and broken. Thirty six living souls, all that remained of Her Majesty's Navy. Those with the presence of mind remembered to drag the life-raft clear of the waves, and they brought their meagre supplies out and onto the land.

They lined up the three dead bodies on the mud, and could not even spare the blankets to offer them dignity. Only half of the survivors even had adequate clothing, and still the rain came in, miserable and cold.

There were no buildings visible from the shore, nothing but the marsh, and then wheat and canola crops in the good soil above them, the fences surrounding the fields sagging and fallen in places. In some ways Tamsyn thought they were lucky not to have washed up in Blackpool or near Liverpool - even a small pack of zombies would easily wipe them out now.

Squinting into the rain, she reached for her strange second sense, trying to scan for the undead, and saw nothing. A headache pinched around her head like an iron band, and she left off, unconvinced that her "powers" had even worked.

Under her windbreaker, little Malcolm shook and whimpered. What heat she had to share she was rapidly losing, and if his little body was to join the three laying on the sand, Tamsyn swore she would walk out into the ocean there and then.

Men and women lay slumped on the grit, or huddled together and coughing. They'd all been awfully close to a nuclear explosion, had breathed in the steam and the spray of the waves it sent out. Tamsyn tried to cast her mind back to her dad's history lessons, of the people who'd died in the fallout of Hiroshima and Nagasaki. Would her hair and nails start falling out?

Had she survived everything just to die in this awful, lingering way?

"Alright, that's enough," Leyland boomed out, a hand to his shattered rib-cage. "You're in Her Majesty's Navy, not the Girl Guides. Stop moping around and get to work. We paid good money to train you in survival skills, so get over this little boat ride and SURVIVE!"

"Yes Sir!"

Reynolds and Sushma led a group who carved apart the rubber life-raft, cutting out sections for shelter and bedding. As they set to it with their flashing knives, they looked all the world like they were dissecting a beached whale, and not a scrap would go to waste.

Others set about kicking over rotten fence posts, and gathering sheaves of wheat for kindling and to strew on the ground. In under an hour they had a series of crude structures erected above the beach, and most of the shelters held a campfire, belching out smoke and a little warmth.

"Are you alright?" Harry said, checking in on Tamsyn and Malcolm. Her boy was sleeping in a sleeve of raft rubber, his little clothes drying on sticks in front of the fire. The colour was returning to his face, but his sleep was light, and he twitched and whimpered, caught someplace bad in his little mind.

"This is all I wanted once, to come home," Tamsyn said. "Be careful what you wish for."

Tamsyn slipped into an exhausted doze, arms wrapped around her son. Almost immediately she was brought into the strange dream space, but this time she was back in Gravesend, sat at the bench in front of the Pocahontas statue.

Something was awfully wrong. She couldn't move, could only look upon the statue, and it was changing shape, twisting until it was once more the boy with the black crown, realised in brass. Then he was descending from the plinth, moving slowly towards her.

"TAMSYN," he said in a voice that was the rush of a windstorm, the clanging of bells. "I CAN SEE YOU. I CAN SEE THEM AROUND YOU, ALL THEIR WARMTH AND LIFE."

She tried to imagine the bow in her hands, but she was fixed in place by the statue's empty eye sockets, and she could not repeat that trick. Her fingers twitched in frustration, but still her hands lay folded in her lap.

The statue-boy flowed across the lawn, a single step that

brought him within arm's reach of Tamsyn, and now it was his turn to be frustrated. He could proceed no further.

"YOU SEE, I CANNOT HARM YOU HERE. THERE ARE RULES THAT MUST BE OBSERVED."

He paced around in front of her, each step a sickening slide that mocked the movement of the human leg. He snapped his fingers as close to her face as he could, each click the striking of a great gong.

"BUT I WILL BRING MADNESS TO THOSE YOU LOVE."

Tamsyn knew that he could.

"I CAN REACH ANYONE WHO WALKS BY YOUR SIDE."

The black crown boy had reached down into the depths of the ocean, planting the seeds of madness amongst the sleeping. In the logic of the dream he showed her how he'd done it, an ancient secret she couldn't take from this dream place. She was a beacon that drew his wrath, and those around her would always be in danger.

"I WILL GIVE YOUR BOY A MONSTER'S SMILE. YOU WILL BE FORCED TO SMOTHER HIS LITTLE FACE."

"Noooo!"

Finally she broke free of the trance, and she was on her feet, her bow singing fury, and shaft after shaft entered the bronze body, driving it back, pinning it to the base of the plinth.

The bronze statue looked up with the face of her mother, her body as mangled as she'd been the day a drunk driver destroyed her with his car. She lost her form, sliding around the arrows until a bronze puddle lay on the ground, and the boy climbed up, booming with laughter.

"BE QUICK ABOUT IT," the black crown boy said,

echoing her mother's last words, and with one final click of the fingers he released her from the dream.

TAMSYN AWOKE IN HER SHELTER, alone and with a smoking fire. Little Malcolm was gone from her arms, clothes and all.

"Malcolm. Malcolm!" she screamed, and then she was on her feet and running out of the shelter, screaming like a mad woman. She scanned the little cluster of shelters, looking frantically for her child, screaming at everyone, her panicked mind refusing to turn their responses into words.

Finally someone took her gently by the shoulders and turned her around. Down on the beach below she saw her little man, walking hand in hand with Sushma. He had found a little stick somewhere, and was dragging it behind him through the grit, making a long wiggly line to join his footprints.

The fight fell out of her, and she was on her knees then, crying. Then Sushma was there, lifting her up, and Malcolm was in her arms and crying too.

"I thought they got you," was all she could manage, which only made the boy howl even more.

When they finally subsided into snuffles, Sushma patted her awkwardly on the shoulder.

"He was awake. I thought you could use the rest."

"You scared me," Tamsyn replied.

"Fear is useful," Sushma said. "Now you have adrenaline, and can run or fight. Fear becomes power."

"That sounds like a slogan for a self-defence place. You sound like Yoda."

"I like the Star Wars."

Tamsyn heard a faint sound, a distant shouting, and

turned to see Reynolds running through the wheat fields, waving his arms. He had a big smile on his face. When he eventually returned to camp, he spoke of shelter, and more.

Tamsyn joined the group following Reynolds away from the shore, climbing up into the hills. This isolated stretch of coast was nothing but miles of farmland, fields grown out into seed, a smudge of grey highway running right on the horizon. The marsh underneath them was the outlet of an estuary, with a brown worm of river working inland. There would be plenty of fish here, Tamsyn realised, her father once more lecturing to her from the past.

Reynolds led them to a cluster of farm buildings, and off to one side was a squat building, halfway between fortress and temple. The roof was crenelated, a castle realised in miniature, and the ancient stone blocks were dotted with lichen and moss. It held a commanding view of the coastline and the marsh. It felt sacred here, the perfect place for a timeless building. The end of the world had come and gone and left no impact on this place.

"Cockersand Abbey," Reynolds said, pointing to a sign. "It was built in 1184."

"Yes, we can read, thank you," Tamsyn scoffed. There were other signs dotted about the grounds, and the ruin of a much larger church, little more than a stone outline now. The rain had eased up, but this Abbey would be a welcome shelter, big enough to fit their whole group.

Inside the building, a restoration was underway. The ornate walls were braced in places, with new stone blocks laid out, and masonry tools stored in a neat pile, with no sign of violence or fear. Over their heads, the ceiling curved up into a grand vault of carved stone, as solid as anything Tamsyn had ever slept under. There were niches for the plaques and statuary long since looted by Henry VIII, and an empty slab where the altar had once been.

Downhill, a winding footpath led to an imposing farmhouse, complete with dozens of outbuildings and barns, but Leyland held the group back, urging caution.

"Anything there?" he asked Tamsyn, who scanned the site, looking for black threads, weird spirits, for anything at all. She shrugged. *Most useless super-power ever.*

"Okay. Sushma, Reynolds, and you three blokes with the guns, I want you to clear that place out. Carefully."

They crept and hid and entered the building like one organism, through windows and the flapping back door, while the rest of the group huddled together, hefting oars and rocks, watching nervously. Malcolm wanted to play in the farm shed, and whimpered when Tamsyn told him no.

An eternity, and then the group reappeared, working their way through the barn and the outbuildings. Then they reappeared, all stealth gone, and everyone relaxed.

"Empty?" Leyland asked.

"No," Sushma said, sheathing her dry kukri. "Husband and wife, wife got the bite so husband shot her. Then...he shoot his own brains on roof."

They'd hit the post-apocalyptic jackpot. The farmhouse had enough rooms and bedding for them all, and clothes for those who needed them. There was preserved food in the cellar, and big bunches of smoked salmon hanging from the ceiling beams.

One shotgun, prised from the cold dead hands of a grieving husband. A rifle in parts, more rust than iron, but Reynolds was sure he could repair it. Tamsyn unearthed an old hanky filled with a mixture of shells and bullets.

The barn was another treasure trove, with a new harvester and a kitted-out workshop, but the real find was in the fields behind the barn. A family of horses, grazing freely. Chickens roamed throughout the farm complex, ignoring the newest visitors, and a trio of pigs wandered through the vegetable garden and compost piles, eating themselves stupid. Sheep with overgrown coats were out in the canola, surrounded by more food than they could possibly eat.

Every gate and stall was wide open. The dead farmer had turned out all the animals before enacting the awful tableau inside, giving them freedom in his final minutes. They'd been creatures of habit though, and hadn't wandered far from what they knew.

The farmer had old-style fishing nets in a locker, with several pairs of waders hung on hooks. There was a small processing plant in a shed, with racks for gutting and scaling fish, and a smoker. Under a tin lean-to the farmer had kept a big fishing boat, still hooked up to a tractor.

Best of all, the dead farmer had sheds full of old junk, inherited from his father's father and beyond that. Old ploughs, scythes, the coils of a copper still, many things a clever person could put a use to.

Leyland put the group to work, and by dusk they had the animals rounded up and re-housed, everyone clothed and fed, and fires crackling in every hearth in the house. There was a small cemetery near the Abbey, with the dead from around the district, and here they buried the three dead sailors, as well as the farmer and his wife. Harry read out the rite from the Common Book of Prayer, but the atmosphere was more grateful than mournful, and Tamsyn recognised the feeling.

Better them than me, she realised, and knew many there shared this thought.

The half-starved group scoffed down a dinner of smoked fish and preserves, and worked through the farmer's whiskey stash, toasting him at every turn. Tamsyn got herself two-thirds of the way to pickled and then stopped. Even here, with the camaraderie and relief around her, she did not feel safe. They got lucky, but there were zombies everywhere, and even now the black crown boy could be leading them to her.

Or worse, these people could awaken as puppets, turning on each other, and this sad little adventure would end in this farmhouse.

Scooping up Malcolm from where he slept by the fireplace, Tamsyn snagged some extra blankets and a flashlight, and left the cheery little party. Nodding to the half-sober guards by the door, she took her son out to the ancient abbey, and made a nest of blankets on the floor.

She took a moment to hammer in pegs around the stout door, jamming it closed. Deciding it should keep out anything short of a battering ram, she curled up in the dark, switching off the flashlight when she worked up the courage.

Pure darkness. It was freezing in here, but Tamsyn held her boy close, and waited for her body heat to warm them up. She'd forgotten just how cold the English spring was, and she missed the Caymans then, that warmth that trickled down to your bones.

Her father had been an atheist, her mother undecided, and Tamsyn had never prayed before, didn't know how to. She put her silent pleas out to the universe, for some way to keep her boy safe, to keep her friends alive and free from monsters.

After hours of soul-searching in the silence, Tamsyn came to a realisation. She was the one drawing the attention from the monsters who invaded dreams, who stole minds and lives. For whatever twisted reason, they wanted *her*.

"I need to leave," she realised aloud, and then held her sleeping boy tightly, tears spilling on them both. "I need to leave everyone."

It might have been the ancient holiness steeped into every brick, or perhaps her tormentor could not find her here. She cried herself to sleep, and did not dream at all.

13

All thirty six survivors were crammed into the big kitchen, sharing oatmeal and jars of marmalade, eaten straight from the jar. This morning Reynolds had found a loose cow in the meadow, and everyone was enjoying the miracle of fresh milk with their morning tea.

Tamsyn shivered by the hearth, soaking up every scrap of warmth. In exchange for the best night's sleep she'd ever had, the Abbey had leached all the warmth out of her. Huddled up with her sniffling boy, she tried to weigh up her options.

Gather together some gear. Find someone she could trust to raise her son. Get the hell out of here, before anyone noticed. Fade into zombie England, and never come back. Now she'd made her decision, she was ready to go, as soon as she could slip away. It was the only way to keep these people safe, to keep Malcolm safe.

She'd been vanishing her whole life, ever since her mother died, and she was secretly glad to go out this way, the last voyage of the mysterious weirdo that was Tamsyn Webb.

"Everyone, a bit of shush please," Harry said, tapping on an enamel mug with a spoon. The happy chatter fell down to silence, and the survivors looked on their Prince, who climbed up onto a chair.

"Ladies and gents, we are bloody lucky," Harry said. "If it wasn't for this place, we'd be goners. So we need to make good use of this luck, and come up with a plan."

"I've been chatting with the RSM here, and the way we see it, we've got two options. We kit up, get down to Liverpool, and we head upriver to Manchester. We go in and we rescue our people from the zombies."

"Option Two. We stay here. We've got everything we need to rebuild civilisation. I can release all of you from your enlistment period, if that still matters to anyone. We start a village here, get our strength and numbers back, and slowly rebuild the world."

Half of the survivors looked confused. Why was Harry taking the cowards way? Their duty was clear. The other half looked guilty - after the terrors of their journey, all they wanted was the safety of this place.

"I'm just messing with you," Harry said, face splitting with a sudden grin. "Of course, we're going to do both of these things. RSM, you have the floor."

"Here is the plan," Leyland said. "I'm picking a crew to come up river with me. A small crew. We will sneak in and scout out this other group, see what we're up against. Get these people out if we can."

"But there is no point rescuing them if we have nowhere to go. That's where the rest of you come in. On the radio, this group said they had three hundred survivors. We are going to need shelters, walls, the grain harvested, more crops planted. That will keep all of you busy."

Leyland put an old folding road map on the kitchen table, and the group crowded around. He put a yellowed thumb nail at one point on the map.

"We are here. Pretty empty spot on the coast. There are a handful of villages within 10 miles, and Morecambe and Lancaster up the river a ways. Thousands of zombies within a day's walk of us. So here is the answer - as far as this district is concerned, we are not here. We do not look for supplies in the towns. We do not give any of these monsters an excuse to follow us back here."

"A fresh start," Harry enthused. "We can live out a generation, right on this farm. An old style village, where we crop, fish, build up our livestock. Give the monsters a chance to rot away, and then our kids and their kids can take England back."

Reynolds eyes locked onto Tamsyn's for a split second. Tamsyn felt her face flush, and tried to look at the fireplace.

Well, that's just a stupid dream, she thought. *I've gotta get out of here before you're all dead, and here you are planning our kids. Not gonna happen, buddy.*

"Tamsyn," Leyland said, jerking her out of her embarrassment. "Reynolds, Sushma, Watkins, Trevally, Chaudhari, Deacon and Tscharke. You are the Manchester team. We kit up today, and leave on dusk. Those people are waiting on us."

Tamsyn gave a start. How was she meant to slip away now? Then she had her answer. Somewhere between here and Manchester, she would make a run for it, and draw away as many zombies as she could from the mission. Two birds with one stone.

"I won't let you down," she said to Leyland, and meant it.

"I WANT you to do my hair," Sushma said to Tamsyn, halfway through sharpening up a hatchet for her.

"What? Like brush it."

"I want it to look like nice hair."

"Okay, you weirdo," she said. "Do you want to have a make-up party too?"

"Can you show me how?" the Gurkha said, deadly serious. Tamsyn was taken aback.

"You know you are already pretty, right? Don't feel like you need to tart yourself up for the gronks around here."

"I am not a tart. I need your help with this. Please."

They poked through the dead farmer's bedroom, pillaging the wife's dressing table. Being far from a girly girl herself, Tamsyn did her best to makeover the Gurkha. Rather than hide her scars she lightly dabbed over them with foundation - they were part of her and not worth hiding for anyone.

"You are the most drop-dead gorgeous killing machine I ever met," she told Sushma, and planted a kiss on her forehead. The Gurkha smiled, and gave her a warm hug.

Later, Tamsyn was with the new quartermaster, counting out jars of beetroot and mop rolls, when Prince Harry strolled past, beckoning to Tamsyn with a beaming smile.

"Well, come on then," he said. "It's all about to start."

Mystified, Tamsyn followed the group across the grounds, and back to the Abbey where she'd spent the night. A big group was gathered around the door, pushing to get inside.

"Come on everyone, let me through," Harry laughed. "I am the head of the Church of England now. I think."

Tamsyn entered into a scene of surreal beauty. Candles

and burning tapers were set in the ancient niches and along the old aisle, causing shadows to leap across the vaulted ceiling. A couple of the submariners were strewing flower petals along the aisle, to the empty spot where the altar had once stood.

There stood Regimental Sergeant Major Leyland, wearing an old suit of the farmer's, his big frame stretching it to the seams, and the sleeves were an inch or two on the short side. Still, he looked very handsome. He also looked very nervous.

"What the shit is this?" Tamsyn whispered to Harry.

"What does it look like?" he said. He took a little bunch of posies from one of the marines, and handed it to Tamsyn.

"Oh, no no no. What kind of arranged marriage bullshit is this?"

"Just for once, Tamsyn Webb, this isn't about you," Harry scoffed. Clicking his fingers, he summoned Reynolds, who had found a neat white shirt and trousers somewhere.

"Tamsyn," the Trooper said solemnly. Tamsyn's eyes opened even wider.

"Someone tell me what the hell is going on?"

"Alright, we've had our fun," Harry said. "Reynolds is best man. You're maid of honour."

"To who?"

A gasp, and they all turned around to see a vision framed by the door. A woman wearing a beautiful floral dress, tied in with a wide silk sash. Clutching a big bunch of roses and grinning nervously was Sushma Thapa, the blushing bride. Tamsyn dashed to her side.

"What the hell, Sushma?"

"We have been having it off for years," Sushma said, smiling across the Abbey to Leyland. "I thought you knew. Everyone knows."

Everyone in the Abbey started whistling and humming, a mangled tune barely recognised as Here Comes the Bride. Shaken and grinning goofily, Tamsyn took her spot.

THE RECEPTION WAS morning tea by the barn, and the honeymoon was a quick visit upstairs by the smiling pair. Within the hour they were back with the others preparing for their mission of doom, but this time as husband and wife.

"Just wanted to make things official," Leyland said. "We might not get this chance again."

"Weirdest wedding I've ever been to," Tamsyn said. "You loveable pair of idiots."

"Just so you know, I don't think it's a legal wedding," Prince Harry called out from underneath the tractor. "I'm not a registered celebrant."

"Good enough for us, Your Highness," Leyland said.

Tamsyn found her boy crouched up on the back steps, munching on a handful of stale biscuits. Reynolds had found an old box of toys, relics from the farmer's grandkids, and little Malcolm was surrounded by a phalanx of robots, action men, toy cars and knights in armour. It was the single happiest she'd seen her boy in a very long time, but the toddler still had the hint of something dark in his eyes. She wished she could have shielded him from all of the trauma of this rotten new world, but she'd dragged him through the worst of it.

Have I broken my sweet little boy forever? she thought.

"Do you like your new toys?" she asked, and he nodded, chewing away. Steeling herself, Tamsyn tried to remember everything about this scene. The way the sun was playing across the sea, how the wind ruffled the overgrown fields, even as it tickled at the rough mop that was Malcolm Webb's haircut.

I'm never going to see him again, she realised. *I'm abandoning my son.* Tamsyn had never been a good mum to Malcolm, but this was a new low to her lacklustre parenting style. Even telling herself that she was drawing danger away from her child did nothing to stifle the painful ache in her chest.

"Mummy has to go away for work," she finally said. "I want you to be a good boy while I'm gone."

The boy nodded numbly, a sole tear trickling down his face to join the mess of biscuits and slobber. Tamsyn felt buckets of tears running down her own face. *He knows*, she thought. *Two years old and he knows I'm not coming back.*

"I'm sorry that there are monsters in the world," she told him, eyes level with his. "You won't get to do normal kid things. That's not fair, mate. So you're going to need to be strong. Whatever happens, you must survive."

She saw the hatred in his young eyes, hatred for her, and it was a knife lodged deep in her chest, worse than the moments she'd seen her loved ones die. She deserved that look of venom, and she hoped this hatred would sustain him over the years, drive him, keep him alive. It was her final gift for her son, a bitter little present that he could open over and over again.

"Go away," he screamed, spraying out crumbs. "I hate you!"

"I know," she said. "But I will always love you."

Bursting into heaving sobs, little Malcolm batted away her reaching hands. He leapt up and ran into the house, and the slapping of his feet on the floorboards was a tattoo that

Tamsyn Webb branded into her heart, the sound of his life, the vitality of his pumping legs.

"I love you so much," Tamsyn told the empty steps, and then she cried out all of the hurt until she was empty. It wasn't enough.

THE DEAD FARMER had been a canny old soul, and kept his farm well-stocked. He had a big tank of diesel set out by the barn, and Reynolds stuck his head in the inspection port.

"He's put fuel preservative in this," he said. "It's still good."

It took the submarine engineers less than an hour to get the tractor up and running, and soon they had the boat motor turning over nicely. There was a big cooler in the centre of the boat for the daily catch, and they filled it full of water containers and food - there was no telling how many mouths they'd need to feed at the other end of the trip. If they made it.

Then came the serious end of preparation. They had five guns to share between nine people, and various farm implements such as axes and shovels. It was barely enough for self-defence, let alone a frontal assault through thousands of the undead. At Tamsyn's urging they wrapped strips of canvas around their forearms and throats, and made sure they had a plentiful supply of cloth to soak in vinegar and wear as bandanas.

"It's gonna really, really stink. No street sweepers left to pick up the guts and rotten meat. Wear these if you don't want to projectile vomit everywhere."

As the weak northern sun fell towards the ocean, Tamsyn

and the others piled into the back of the fishing boat, the trailer bouncing across the fields as a marine drove the belching tractor towards the marsh. There was a type of boat-ramp down by the water's edge, marked with stacks of stone, and their driver backed the boat out into deeper water.

Tamsyn had a minor panic attack when she remembered that first boat-ride up the Thames, when a crew just like this left Gravesend, only to be butchered by bandits in uniform. It seemed that every time she stepped onto a boat, it ended in disaster and death. As she looked across the faces of her shipmates, she saw their determination, a thick plate of bravery fastened over the terror they all felt.

These people are heroes, she thought. *Giving their lives to save those poor trapped bastards. I hope they remember this shining moment when the monsters are pulling out their intestines.*

Leyland thumbed the ignition switch, and the big outboard motor roared into life. It ran as smooth as pudding, and the boat wasn't leaking, wasn't in any sort of trouble. The fishing boat was a dependable old workhorse, and she felt the panic ease a little bit. Apart from the *Petty Cash*, every boat she'd ever boarded was a leaky death-trap. Even so, she strapped on a life-vest, earning a smirk from Reynolds.

"What? You can't wade 5 metres to the shore?"

"It's called expecting the worst, nimrod. That's how you survive now."

"You need some water-wings too?"

Sushma slapped Reynolds with a hand that could snatch a striking cobra, just a light pat on the cheek but enough to shock him into silence.

"She will never sleep with you if you behave like that,"

she said, earning protests from both Tamsyn and Reynolds. Leyland gave a whistle through his teeth.

"Enough! We are on a mission. From here-on out you will act like professionals."

"Yes sir," Sushma said to her husband, and meant it. Tamsyn wondered what kind of weird dynamic these two would carry into their marriage. She supposed the authority went in a far different direction behind closed doors.

"Look," said Tscharke, one of the other marines. He pointed to the foreshore, where Prince Harry stood watching them, little Malcolm standing by his side. The Prince saluted the boat, and Leyland led the group in a return salute.

Goodbye, my little mate, Tamsyn thought, watching her son until the fishing boat rounded the coast and left the little pocket of humanity in its wake.

14

As the Irish Sea gobbled up the weak sun, Leyland charted a course south, keeping the fishing boat a respectable distance from the land. Tamsyn had explained that engine noise drew the undead, and they weren't game to draw a super-pack out of Blackpool.

The moon was full and bright, and they could see the old seaside town clearly. Tamsyn felt a little sad as she looked upon the Blackpool Tower and the ferris wheel, the pier smashed apart in some long forgotten storm. The undead were here in force, beachgoers forced into an eternity near the arcades and the ice-cream parlours, dark little shapes moving across the silver sands.

YOU!

She sat forward with a gasp, head reeling. He was near, the Black Crown Boy, trying to get a grasp on her, to peer into her head. Her vision swam, and she could see the black threads forming across the drifting clouds, even over the yellow disc of the moon itself.

In panic she slashed out with her mind blade, parting those distant threads, and she ached for that peaceful moment in the abbey, that one time where holiness and thick stone walls kept her safe. She pictured herself and Malcolm there, curled up safely, the door held fast...

Just like that, the assault on her mind stopped. The black threads fell down from the sky, and the agitated shapes on the beach returned to their aimless strolling, well-clear of the painful salt water.

"Well, that was weird," Reynolds said at her side. He was scanning the shore through a pair of night-vision binoculars, lips pursed tight.

"Report, Trooper," Leyland commanded.

"At least two hundred Zulu Charlies looking directly at us. They were tensed up, ready to run into the water...and then they just changed their minds. Went back to making sandcastles and shit."

"Stick to the facts," Leyland said.

"I'm serious. Some of them are trying to make sandcastles."

In moments Leyland's pack of fierce hunters were crowding the side of the boat, fighting over Reynolds' binoculars as they looked on the beach. When it was her turn, Tamsyn saw some of the undead fumbling with bucket and spade, their best efforts a shambles of loose sand trodden flat by their neighbours.

"I saw this once," Tamsyn said. "Back in Gravesend. Poor old chap trying to mow his lawn. Grass was as dead as he was."

She surrendered the binoculars to Sushma, who found a sandcastle builder and laughed fit to burst. Leyland tapped Tamsyn on the shoulder, and leaned in close.

"You did that, didn't you?" he said, tapping his temple. "Found a way to turn those things around."

Tamsyn nodded.

"Do you think you can do that again? If a whole bunch comes at us?"

"I just don't know," she admitted. "I'm kind of making this up as I go."

It felt good to know that Leyland was accepting her strange new gift with no hesitation. She wanted to tell him the whole story, about that demonic schoolboy, of the danger they were all in just by being near her. She hoped and prayed that her mental defences extended beyond her own skull. What if a boatful of friends were to suddenly turn on her, tear her apart with bare hands?

Stop it, ya gloomy cow, she thought in Eddie's voice. *Get 'em to Manchester and then run like buggery.*

"Please don't rely on - on whatever this is," she whispered to Leyland. "We're about to go through thousands of them. One mistake and we are all dead."

"If whatever you have is not a reliable weapon, I'd rather not use it," Leyland said simply. "So we'll just have to sneak past all of those things."

"Good idea. The moment one of them sniffs us, we are in the deepest of deep shit."

THEY COASTED into Liverpool at about 2 am. The dour brick of the warehouses and heritage buildings, the rusting cranes and gantries of the docks, the sharp cut of the modern office buildings, all of it passed them by in a moon-washed sepulchre. Tamsyn saw tens of thousands of the undead, a pointless crowd that milled and jostled, climbing in and out of the broken shopfronts, staring at their boat as the engine reverberated against the buildings.

They lined the piers and the wharves ten deep, arms

outstretched, their hungry moan louder than the chattering engine, four or more football stadiums worth of rotten throats calling out for murder.

Around Tamsyn, Leyland's crew were completely spooked. They'd never been amongst this, never had to face the sheer world-killing power of the zombie apocalypse. Tamsyn felt alert and had that sweet tickle of adrenaline to fight off her tiredness, but no real fear. Not yet anyway.

Just another day in the office.

"Watch out for any wrecks," Tamsyn told Leyland. "People went stupid at the beginning, got onto anything that floated. It was like Benny Hill, but with murder in it."

Leyland took them slowly through the mouth of the Mersey, with Reynolds leaning over the prow with a flashlight. Long-wrecked boats and ferries were still tangled up and half-submerged, the undead passengers moaning, huddled up on the highest point from the water. It was almost tragic - all of eternity and they could only crowd around on their deck, unable to reach their friends on the shore.

"The river has some salt in it still," Tamsyn said. "That's very good. I don't think fresh water will scare them off. They can smell it."

"How could you possibly know that?" Reynolds called back.

"One of my best mates was a coffin-dodger. I saw the salt bring him back, and I saw some arseholes stomp him into paste right in front of me."

"Jesus, you're grim."

BANG!

Reynolds was so busy giving Tamsyn a hard time that he failed to spot the mostly submerged hull just ahead of them, and the fishing boat bumped against it, sending everyone reeling. It was a glancing blow without any damage to boat or crew, and everyone jeered Leyland good-naturedly. Tamsyn remembered how much the British psyche loved a good pratfall, and saw less worry and fear in the faces of her shipmates. Tscharke lit up a smoke and shared it around the boat, and to Tamsyn's surprise she had a puff, nearly coughing herself stupid.

This was important. The bonding of warriors. Camaraderie in the face of endless horrors. Tamsyn saw Sushma leaning against the gunwale, smiling cheerfully as she had since they'd left the farm.

"You're enjoying this, you crazy bitch," Tamsyn laughed. "Does nothing scare you?"

"My husband's boat piloting skills?"

"What about the thousands of cannibals just over there?"

"My life may measure in years. Maybe in moments. Waste of time to worry."

"You should write Hallmark cards. Or graffiti."

"I have always wanted to write my name on things," Sushma said. "Promise me we will do that."

In the distance, a splash, and then an awful scream that went on and on. One of their undead observers had missing its footing and taken a tumble into the Mersey, and the salt was wracking it with agony. The other zombies closest to the edge fought against the press behind them to get back, and Tamsyn marvelled at their animal cunning. Thousands of hungry eyes stared, pushing and jostling as they slowly followed the boat upriver, a slow and relentless pursuit.

If the Black Crown Boy could get a fix upon her, wrap those monsters in black string and drive them at her in the thousands, these hungry idiots would be able to drag the boat under by hand alone.

"It is over there," Sushma said, painting a section of the wharf with the flashlight. For a split second Tamsyn saw a great big pair of steel gates, built into a cement frame, and then the Gurkha pointed the light back down to the water. Easing the throttle back, Leyland pointed the boat towards the fixture, and then he finally cut the engine altogether, letting it drift towards the shore.

"What are you doing?" Tamsyn said. "We've got to keep following the river to Manchester. Don't go near the bloody zombies!"

"The Mersey turns into sandbanks just up past that bend," Leyland said. "Even this old flat-bottom won't be able to get through that mess."

"Oh. Oh shit."

"We've got to take the canal system. Which means we've got to open that bloody big gate just there."

On this side of the river, the city had given way to a sprawling parkland, but the undead had followed them out of the suburbs, hundreds shuffling through the trees. There were perhaps a dozen rotters lurking around the lonely canal lock, shuffling up and down the cement steps, moaning excitedly as their meal drifted closer.

"Listen up," Leyland said quickly. "There's no power to open up the lock. We'll need to look for the manual controls: one to drain the water out, one to open the paddles. It's probably a wheel on this big one, but you might need a windlass."

"Um, not all of us are sailors, Popeye," Tamsyn said.

"This thing," he said, holding up a metal rod. Seemed that the dead owner of the fishing boat had braved a canal or two in his time. "It's a big spanner that opens that."

As they pulled alongside the wharf, Sushma and Reynolds were already out and moving, blades flashing as they met the welcoming committee. Leyland gave the signal for the rest of his squad to follow, but clamped a hand onto Tamsyn's shoulder when she made to leap over the gunwale.

"I'll need you here with me," Leyland said. She scowled at the sound of popping guns, the hoots and whooping as the others fought their way to the top of the canal lock.

"You don't have to coddle me," Tamsyn said. "I've got more experience at this than any of you."

"Let them have this one," Leyland said. "They need to know they can do this without you breathing down their necks."

"What? Are you saying I'm *intimidating* to these people? You've got to be bloody kidding me."

"Even a good drill sergeant knows when to stop barking and when to let his people do what they've been trained to do. These people are experts at coastal assault."

"I don't like sitting out of the action," Tamsyn sulked. A triumphant cry that could only be Sushma. The booming of one of the shotguns.

"I need you watching the rest of those things closing in. If they start to do any of the weird stuff, do what you can."

"You and your bloody common sense. Okay, okay."

Tamsyn heard the squealing of metal, and the deep clunk of a hidden mechanism. The enormous gates before them were opening, inch by screeching inch. She could hear the excited groaning from all around them as hundreds of undead homed in on them.

"They need to do this faster!" Tamsyn said.

"Are you serious? My people are opening those great ruddy things by hand! It takes as long as it takes."

Tamsyn paced around in the boat, fretting as she heard the yells in the lock above them, the winding of the wheel, the splatter of blades, the cracking of guns.

"This is bullshit. We're all about to get killed."

"Control yourself. You knew this was going to be dangerous."

"We're sitting ducks here!" she said, a bubble of panic rising in her chest. She tried to reach for that peaceful feeling, the image of the stone ceiling in the abbey, but she was starting to lose her grip on this defence. Any minute now the Black Crown Boy was going to break through, get a fix on their location...

"Alright, gently does it," Leyland said, putting the boat through the gates as soon as he could. There was barely three inches of clearance on either side of the boat, and to the old Marine's credit he got them through without a scrape. The gate stopped, and after some clanking and cursing from above it slowly started to close.

"You have got to be kidding me," Tamsyn said. It was the longest five minutes of her life, hearing the screeching of the steel, watching the gates slowly seal back up. Above, she could see Sushma hacking a rotter into small pieces, and the crack of the farmer's shotgun, the shots patient, rhythmic, telling.

"Now, can you accept that my highly trained people have got this?" Leyland said, drumming his fingers on the steering wheel.

"Well, yes, they're doing okay, but there's a whole lot more of those things coming. From all directions."

"Noted. Now get ready, they're about to crack the other door. It'll move quickly after that."

The gate behind them closed with a dull boom, and then seconds later the far gate seemed to bleed water from dozens of points. Valves, and then slowly the fishing boat began to rise, one agonising foot after the other. Water and gravity were lifting them up to the level of the river on the far side, and it was like filling the world's stupidest bath full of foul water.

"Quickly? You've got to be kidding me. You realise we're dying here today."

"Hmm," Leyland said, watching the speed of the rising water. Leaning out of the cabin, he twirled his fingers, *go faster*, and his people fought to crank open the far gate, even though the water level wasn't high enough yet.

"Put your backs into it!" he called out. The zombies were close now, and she heard the horrified cries of Leyland's crew, felt their frenzy as the turkey shoot became a landslide of monsters.

Tamsyn laughed until she cried.

Sure, they were about to die in a stupid way. But at least she was far away from the others, from Prince Harry. From Malcolm. They were finally safe from whatever twisted demon was stalking her across the face of the earth.

All fear washed from her. They were stupid lost things, these undead, and they could only hurt her body briefly. Her whole awful saga was about to come to an end, and part of her was glad. The last few years had been exhausting, but knowing what was coming was freeing in a macabre way. Tamsyn could see the Abbey again, and she felt that holiness shiver up her back, sink deep into her bones. She closed her eyes and waited for the end, determined to spend her final moments in calmness, remembering all of the people who'd made her smile, the ones she'd be reunited with soon. She pictured them all in the peaceful abbey with her, and the abbey was growing until it was a cathedral, then it was the Vatican, then a shopping centre-sized structure, where she was completely safe and nothing could even see her.

Then above, the puzzled cries of the others. There was no more combat, and the guns were finally silent.

"Report!" she heard Leyland say from some distant place.

"They stopped and turned around!" Tsharck said. "It's like they lost interest in us."

"Did you do that?" Leyland said, and Tamsyn nodded beatifically.

"Then for heaven's sake, don't stop."

THIRTY MINUTES LATER, Tamsyn stirred from her trance with a cluster head-ache. Her mental defences fell away until she was back in the tiny abbey, the stone roof pressed in so close that it was a tomb now, and she held onto that image, fought to keep that last crumb of defence from the creature that even now was sniffing for her.

"Are you okay?" Sushma said gently. Tamsyn answered by rushing to the gunwale and projectile vomiting out into the canal.

"C'mon!" Reynolds teased. "The boat's barely moving."

"Shut up," she groaned, unable to muster anything more biting.

Once they left Liverpool, the canal cut a straight path through a waste-land of industry and marshland, the moon illuminating acres of empty space. There was the occasional undead wanderer in the distance, but it was peaceful out here, felt safe. Tamsyn couldn't appreciate it properly through the blinder of a migraine, and started rifling through the supplies.

"Oy! They're meant for those poor trapped bastards!" Reynolds laughed. Tamsyn found a packet of ibuprofen and dry swallowed a handful, and immediately sat still, willing the drugs to kick in. Leyland handed over the wheel to his new wife and sat down in the middle of the crew, who were dozing or smoking in the darkness.

"Alright people, listen up," he said. "I'm going to tell you about a boring place called Afghanistan. Lots of moments like this, with nothing in sight and nothing to do. And we could not stop watching for the Taliban, not for one bleeding moment."

That got their attention. Tscharke stubbed out his cigarette on his boot sole, and Watkins nudged Trevally in the ribs, the heavy-set woman waking up with a loud snort.

"We've got another twenty miles to go till we get to the end of the canal. Best as I can reckon, we'll hit the place near dawn. So we watch in shifts till I say so. Two people on lookout at all times. The rest of you, keep quiet. Can they smell cigarettes?" This he asked of Tamsyn, who nodded her head and prayed for death with the movement.

"No more smoking," he said, and was met with a muttered protest. He silenced this with a baleful stare. "This might all be Wuthering Heights out here, but we're about to sail into more monsters than we can deal with. We get in, we help these people, and we all get out in one piece. This is the only acceptable outcome."

Tamsyn reached for something inspirational, some final words to keep these idiots alive, but then she was over the gunwale, vomiting up the painkillers, to laughter and good-natured patting on her back.

I hope we all die, she thought, and meant it.

15

False dawn washed over the fields and the black thread of the canal. Tamsyn's migraine was finally easing off, and she took a turn on watch with Sushma. Trevally was hunched over the steering wheel, and Tamsyn couldn't remember even hearing the big woman ever speak. She decided that she liked her for that reason alone.

Of course, all the men slumbered away. Not one of them stirred as a lone zombie appeared from nowhere and fell into the canal, bobbing and splashing in their wake. The water was fresh here, and the rotter simply sank without further protest.

"He is a mockery of Samsara," Sushma said quietly. "All of these dead monsters are. Whatever is happening to you, you have some sort of power with Moksha."

"Samsara? Moksha? What?"

"It means freedom from the endless cycle of death and re-birth," Sushma said. "Buddhists call it Nirvana."

"Top band, that."

"I have heard old stories about holy warriors. The

Guides who turn some back into Samsara and rebirth, and who help some break free from that eternal river."

At the word 'Guide', the skin crawled on the back of Tamsyn's neck. She remembered the words of the Black Crown Boy, his threats. He called her Guide, and the last of her kind.

"There were stories in my village about a woman who died, but would not burn on the pyre. For five nights she wandered through the village, up and down the high paths, letting goats go loose, tipping rubbish into the well. She bit a child and gave it a terrible sickness."

"Well, that sounds familiar."

"So this holy man, he went to meet with the dead woman. He would not take a pistol or a sword, and many feared for him. A witness said that he spoke with her, and then she fell down dead at his feet. Finally, she burnt on the pyre, and was never reborn."

"What's that got to do with me?"

"I don't think you are the first to speak with the dead," Sushma said. "You are a holy warrior too."

"Ha! Not bloody likely. My dad never went in for church and stuff."

"I saw you turn those monsters aside. Released the others on the submarine. If death dogs your every step, don't fight it. Accept it. Less headaches that way."

"*You're* a headache, wrapped in an enigma, wrapped in bullshit," Tamsyn scoffed.

"Do you have better? What science explains the world now?"

Tamsyn was tempted to tell her everything then. The Black Crown Boy, her dreams, all of it. As she thought of Malcolm though, she knew she couldn't. She needed to walk away from these people, keep them safe from her curse.

Knowing Sushma, she was just as likely to follow her out into the great undead wilderness. Leyland too. Reynolds would probably follow until he wore her down or he lost interest. *I'm so sick of attracting bad boys and douche-bags!*

Soon she could see the outline of Manchester, a forest of tall buildings that was black against the pre-dawn sky, the canal like a path burnt straight into its ancient heart. Tamsyn had trouble remembering how many ruined cities she'd seen now, and it was always the same feeling, like she was an adventurer in some dangerous jungle, hacking into ruins with a machete and a death-wish.

Oh, how she missed her bow.

Oh, how she missed her *boy*.

"Sushma, I want to ask you something," she said. "If I don't come home from this - please, please look after Malcolm."

"You will come home from this," Sushma said. "Unless you do something stupid. If you are stupid, I will watch your boy. Give him lots of baby brothers and sisters too."

Tamsyn gripped Sushma in a bear hug, squeezing that sweet ball of murder and philosophy with all of her strength. They touched foreheads, and even the Gurkha let loose a solitary tear.

"I would rather you come back," Sushma said. "Make those baby brothers and sisters with Reynolds there."

"You have wildly misread that situation," Tamsyn said with a dull glare, and then she gasped, her headache back with a vengeance. She fell to one knee, clutching at her temples, and that was when she felt her mental defences finally crumble down around her. She frantically tried to imagine the abbey, but the Black Crown Boy was there, knocking aside her feeble attempts to keep him out.

That was when Trevally opened the throttle right up, the

boat bucking, careening from one canal wall to the other. The big woman was coughing, babbling, and then finally laughing her head off. Dawn came then, creeping over the skyline, and as Tamsyn got to her feet she could see the big bridge over the canal, a horde of zombies already falling over the sides and into the canal.

They were coming forward in a flat run, diving into the water. They were *swimming*.

Big clusters of the black threads filled the sky. The Black Crown Boy had been playing her for hours, had always known exactly where she was.

"We are Vanguard!" Trevally cried, one moment before Sushma lopped her head clean off.

"Wake up!" Tamsyn screamed at Reynolds and Leyland, but they were unresponsive, flinching in some private nightmare that they could not wake from. In the cabin, Sushma tipped the dead woman out of the driver's chair, and hauled back on the throttle. The old fishing boat had too much momentum though, and still they coasted towards that waterfall of flailing arms and snapping teeth.

"No!" Tamsyn yelled out. "We need to hit that bullshit as fast as we possibly can."

Sushma jammed the throttle to full, and quickly lashed a length of rope to the steering wheel, trying to keep the boat on a straight path. Tamsyn prised the combat shotgun out of Reynold's sleeping grip, and tried to remember his brief lesson. She steadied herself against the front railing, gun up and tracking.

"Hey, stupid girl!" Sushma yelled. "Do you want the dead men to squish you?"

Tamsyn blinked, amazed at her own stupidity, and in her mind she felt the amusement of the Boy, at an enchantment that had almost worked. Pushing through the pain, she rebuilt her mental defences, pushing that monster away. She fell back to the cabin, gripping the shotgun, shouting at every sleeping man she could see.

"Wake up," she kept saying, but this time it had the weight of command, the severing of an enchantment, and Leyland and the others came to their feet in confusion, shortly followed by terror.

"In the cabin. Now!" Tamsyn shouted, sending Tscharke forward with a swift kick to the backside. Everyone crammed into the pokey little cabin, clutching at their weapons, staring upwards through the windows as they passed under the bridge.

An avalanche of rotten flesh hit them, body after body crashing onto the prow, the deck, the roof of the cabin, and then they were bouncing across the cages and nets. Even as these corpses began to rise, more fell from the other side of the bridge, grabbing at the gunwales, and then the rest fell into the canal behind them, staring hungrily at the boat as the water swallowed them whole.

"Tamsyn! Do something!" Leyland yelled, and she swept out with her mind-blade, severing the black threads, but it was too little too late. They were close enough now that it didn't matter whether the Boy was pulling their puppet strings. Their endless hunger took over, classic undead style.

She tried to recapture the trick she'd learnt at the locks, imagining her mental castle pushing them away, but all she earned for her troubles was a sharp stab of pain behind her eyeballs, and every single zombie coming at her, and her alone.

She'd somehow made the things even hungrier.

"Keep them back!" Leyland shouted. "Don't let a single one through that door!"

Her whole universe became gunfire and fear, and she

sent shell after shell into that pressing wall of rot. Sushma kept low, allowing the bullets to pass over her head even as she severed knees and ankles, finishing off everything the bullets did not.

CRASH!

Glass shattered behind her, and Tamsyn felt a rotten hand snag at her braid, yanking her towards the broken window. She fought to free herself, but the dead thing reeled her in with freakish strength, grey teeth slavering and snapping...

Reynolds stepped in and very calmly severed the dead man's arm at the elbow, before punching his combat knife through its eye. Tamsyn joined him at the breach, shooting dead things until the gun stopped working. Then she was staving in zombie faces with the butt of the shotgun, until her arms finally gave way, muscle gone to rubber, the gore-streaked shotgun an impossible weight.

Reynolds gently plucked the shotgun from her hands, and patted her on the shoulder. Just like that, it was all done, and they were through.

With a shudder she removed the severed arm from her braid, prising loose the grip of those dead fingers. A wall of bodies surrounded the cabin, at least forty corpses sent on to their final rest. Some of them had dragged Watkins out through a window, nearly tearing his head off as they ripped open his throat, and Tamsyn saw Leyland carefully shoot the corpse between the eyes.

Chaudhari had a close scare, when one of them caught him by the arm and worried away at the canvas sleeve Tamsyn had insisted on. He was bruised and shaken, but the dead thing hadn't broken through his flesh.

Tscharke was not so lucky. He had two bites, one on his right bicep, another to the cheek. He paced around the deck, wide-eyed with terror, with the certainty of what he had to do now. What his comrades had to do *to* him.

"Well, can I have a bloody smoke now?" he cried, until tears and snot ran down his face. His comrades kept around him, stony faced, and someone fetched his pack of smokes, trampled on during the vicious melee.

When Tscharke's hands shook too much to light the crumpled cigarette, Leyland took his lighter and held it calmly by the dying man's lips, and let the smoke catch flame.

"Could you fellas just let me off here?" he said, half joking and half in earnest. "I could walk to the nearest pub and go out in style."

His eyes were glazing over. Tamsyn knew he had minutes at best.

"It's okay, mate," Leyland said. "You did a bloody good job just then. I saw you save Chaudhari there. Ministry of Defence would slap a medal on you if they were still a thing."

"You can shove your medals up your arse, Sergeant," Tscharke sobbed.

"Do you remember that bar back on Grand Cayman? I remember when you and Chaudhari and Watkins climbed up on the roof, with a bottle of vodka and a box full of Cuban cigars."

"Best night ever," Tscharke whispered.

"Was a shame to have you boys arrested. I just wanted to climb up there with you. Hey Chaudhari, what was that girl's name? The barmaid who worked there."

"Wendy," the sailor said, stoney-faced. "Her name was Wendy."

"She was an absolute freak," Tscharke said, a grin

fighting its way onto his face. "I'm pretty sure what that girl did to me was illegal."

That was the moment that Leyland put the pistol to the back of Tscharke's head and pulled the trigger. One sharp *crack!* and then Tscharke fell onto the bloody deck, just one more body to add to the pile.

EVEN AS TAMSYN held the Black Crown Boy at bay, shielding her mind with the last of her strength, he could guess at her location, the dawn sky filled with so many black threads that it was almost like night to her. He threw the undead into the canal, hundreds of them at a time, and they scrabbled against the sides of the hull, slapping against it with their rotting palms.

When they left the industrial outskirts and sailed past the first of the suburbs, the monsters came in thick and fast, thousands of them leaping into the canal at a run, thrashing through the water and climbing over each other, pushing others underwater and then themselves serving as a step for the zombies behind them.

"Save your bloody bullets!" Leyland shouted as his shooters opened up on the floating advance. "We'll get past this lot."

Chaudhari was behind the wheel, and tried to slalom the boat through the bodies, avoiding the larger clusters. The prow pushed most of them aside, but sometimes the boat pushed the dead things underneath the hull, where they beat a rapid tattoo against the bottom until they passed out the back of the boat.

Directly into the propeller, which churned and whined as it disintegrated body after body. Tamsyn had a horrible flashback to that time in the Thames, where she had to untangle an old friend from the blades of a stalled motor. If this motor seized up in the same way, they would die in this canal.

"Why do we keep thinking that boats are the best way?" she grunted, driving back some dead things with a big gaff-pole. One rotter actually made it above the wriggling mass of bodies, clamping a hand down on the gunwale, and Sushma smashed down her kukri so hard that it severed the wriggling fingers, lodging deeply into the wood.

"I'll have blunted it," the Gurkha swore, and had to grip it with both hands, pushing against the gunwale with her boot. That was when another hand reached up and over the side, gripping her ankle in a vice-grip. With one heave a dead woman lifted herself out of the water, lank hair running, mouth spread open as it lunged for her calf.

Tamsyn moved quicker than thought, making a kind of motion towards the creature.

"STOP," Tamsyn cried out, throwing out her hand towards the creature. The word was more of a command than a cry. The zombie stopped in mid-bite, but struggled against this bond, teeth inching closer and closer. The effort to keep the creature still felt like a vice around Tamsyn's temples, until she snagged the beast through the temple with the gaff-hook, dragging it away from her friend, the dead woman sinking back into the arms of its friends.

"Thank you," Sushma said, finally freeing her blade. "That one was hungry."

"They're all hungry!" Tamsyn said. She did not think she had it in her to use the Force or whatever it was on any more of the undead. As it was, the visualisation of her defences was bowing at the centre, the Black Crown Boy beating a way in with sheer force.

"Just breathe," Sushma said calmly, placing a hand on her shoulder. Tamsyn drew in a shuddering breath, and then another. The headache eased. Her defences held. Sushma smiled, not even turning to look as she split another boarder through the forehead with her sharp blade.

"Don't overuse that," she said, gesturing towards Tamsyn's head with her gore-streaked kukri. "You are like me, when I was lifting big rocks to get strong. Start with the small rocks."

There was no time for anything else but bursts of gunfire, and then everyone took to their hatchets and shovels, beating back the freaks as they tried to climb into the boat. The motor whined as it churned through another dead body, and it was starting to run rough.

Tamsyn wanted to use her mind-knife to sever the Boy's puppet-strings, but she didn't think she had it in her to break through so many. Dragging away another dead man with a gaff through the neck, she turned away to see Reynolds, shirtless now, an axe in either hand.

Damn.

"We need to clear the motor!" she called over to him. "Their guts are starting to jam the thing up."

"Righto then. Give us a hand."

"What! We can't just jump in there. We'll get eaten."

"Why - why would we jump in?" he said, genuinely puzzled. He called out to Chaudhari in the cabin, who cut the engine. The boat continued to coast forward, the dead things swarming all around them. They had to be ten, twenty deep in the water, and more were pouring into the canal by the second.

"Here we go," he said, leaning back on the motor. It was set on a hinge, and he began to pull it out of the water. Groaning, he struggled with the weight, and Tamsyn helped him to lift it clear. It was just like in the Thames all those years ago, with a dead body dangling from the propeller blades, ropes of intestine gumming up the rotor.

God, if only I'd realised the motor could come out of the water! Tamsyn consoled herself with the memory that a sniper had been firing upon her when she'd done her own underwater maintenance.

"Keep those things away," Reynolds said, climbing up onto the wet motor. He spent a long moment sawing away at the ropey guts, while the dead climbed up on their underwater human pyramid, falling over themselves as they tried to grab him.

Tamsyn tried to do her best Sushma impression, sweeping the gaff-hook back and forth, until she snagged one zombie under the collarbone, and it fell back into the water, taking the pole and almost taking her too.

With a cry of triumph, Reynolds cut loose the last of the intestines. Chaudhari started up the motor at his signal, and Tamsyn helped him tip the outboard back into the slavering pack of ghouls, the propeller acting like the world's biggest food processor. The boat surged forward again, still bumping over the freaks it pushed underneath the flat hull. Every now and then the motor chewed up another body with a worrying whine.

"That farmer will be rolling in his grave," Leyland grunted, staving in a zombie's head with a cricket bat. "Kept this boat in good nick for years, until we came along."

"Sergeant, there's just too many!" Deacon cried out, the Marine barely able to sweep the boarding zombies loose with the edge of an oar. Tamsyn was hard-pressed to keep her edge of the boat clear, hatchet rising and falling. It was so tempting to dip into her weird gift then, to turn them aside or stop them in their tracks.

One zombie, maybe. This many? Instant migraine, pass out, zombies eat your face off. Bad idea.

"Don't worry everyone," Reynolds said. "I've got this."

He snatched up a jerry-can of diesel, shaking the fuel over the sides of the boat, all over the gnashing faces emerging from the water.

"Reynolds, no!" Tamsyn cried out, a moment before he dropped a lit match over the side.

16

Everything was black smoke, thick and choking, the stink of burning meat fighting past Tamsyn's bandana. Even worse, the zombies continued their assault, climbing up into the boat, except now they were on fire too.

"Burning them doesn't work, you idiot!" Tamsyn shouted. "Didn't you listen to a single thing I said?"

"What the hell else were we meant to do?" Reynolds said huffily.

"Great. Now the engine is on fire. Bravo, genius," she said, clapping sarcastically. Sushma was squirting at it with an old powder fire extinguisher, but after a puff or two it completely gave out. She shrugged and used it as a new weapon, bludgeoning the boarders with the rusty canister.

"Get up on the cabin," Leyland shouted, and Tamsyn and the others scrambled up onto the roof of the cabin. At the end of this mad retreat, they were down to Tamsyn, Leyland, Sushma, Reynolds, Chaudhari and Deacon. They were down to gore-streaked hand weapons, Leyland had his pistol, and they were all about to die.

That was when the fire reached the fuel lines, and with a world shaking WHUMPF the diesel tanks on the boat exploded. Flaming zombies flew in all directions, and Tamsyn felt a razor-sharp sliver of metal kiss her cheek on its way into the sky. Those on the cabin roof were spared from the worst of the fireball, but the boat shuddered, simultaneously sinking and burning, the flames licking up towards them.

"Goddamnit Reynolds," Tamsyn shouted. "You took our pointless last stand and turned it into a Viking funeral!"

Leyland and Sushma held each other through the flames and the smoke, sharing a lingering kiss in their final moments. Reynolds looked at her hopefully and she rolled her eyes.

The pressure on her mental defences was immense, and it felt amazing to release it, to let that stupid Black Crown Boy through, for all the damage he could do now. That imagined abbey crumbled to the ground, and now she was simply an open book, a tired woman at the end of her tether.

"I'll see you in hell!" she shouted at the sky.

Then with the last of its momentum, the doomed fishing boat crashed into the side of the canal. Tamsyn went flying, arms pinwheeling, and then she caught the upper lip of the canal wall. She looked up, face to face with a thousand hungry corpses.

Now she was pissed off.

"BACK!" she shouted, and they staggered away from her. She shouted it again, and the undead turned away, clutching at their heads, attempting to flee from her.

"Quick!" she shouted to the others. One by one they made a running leap at the canal wall, slipping and sliding and fighting to climb up the lip. Finally it was only

Deacon and Leyland on the cabin roof, the boat sinking rapidly.

"Hurry!" Sushma shouted. Leyland urged the other Marine forward, even as he took to the wall in a flat sprint. In the old world, Tamsyn had seen a few episodes of American Ninja Warrior, and it was like that segment that was a mad run up a wall, all pumping legs and flailing arms, fingers scrabbling for a grip.

Leyland found his grip in the hand of his new wife, who clutched at the big man with all of her strength, fought to pull him clear. Deacon missed by barely two inches, and he fell screaming back towards the burning boat, the fiery undead falling all over him.

BANG! Tamsyn looked to see Leyland leaning over the edge, pistol smoking, and the last that she saw of poor Deacon was his face still in death, a smoking bullet hole in his forehead.

The undead she'd sent reeling were coming back now, shaking their heads as if groggy, and this time they had reinforcements. Perhaps two hundred zombies closing in around them, puppet strings dragging them forward at a quick trot, and then a flat run.

Slice. With their guide strings flapping, the zombies lost some of their momentum, but still they came forward at the sight of fresh meat.

Now that she wasn't wasting so much energy concentrating on a mental shield, she could feel an angry little pulse building up in her brain, an almost electrical hum just begging to be unleashed. The more she thought about that bastard Boy, and the closer his puppets got, the stronger it got.

It was power. Intoxicating. Irresistible. She let it all out, and it fell out of her mind in a bitter flood.

"BACK! ALL OF YOU BACK!" Tamsyn shouted, and the cordon of zombies fell away, screeching in agony, as if they'd been splashed with buckets of salt water. She said it again, and six of the closest zombies fell to the floor, and did not move again.

"This way!" Sushma shouted, running through the weak spot in the circle of undead. Tamsyn and the others followed her across the embankment, running flat out for the nearest housing estate, to the solid back row of fences facing the canal. The horde was hot on their heels, and Tamsyn only paused once to scream at the zombies right behind them, dropping some of them as if they were pole-axed.

Each time she struck out with her invisible weapons like this, she felt dizzier, and the last time she felt something *pop* behind her eyes, and then it felt like someone slowly scrunching cellophane in the middle of her brain.

Crying out with the sudden pain, she felt the tears fall, hot and sticky. There was no time to worry about what damage she was doing to herself as they hit the back fence of the nearest terrace house, Leyland waiting to give her a boost. Then she was over the palings and tumbling into an overgrown back yard, falling through the rotten remains of a rabbit hutch.

Leyland almost fell onto her, and then they were up and running towards the house, Reynolds already trying to kick in the door. The fence palings shuddered as hundreds of bodies hit it at once, and soon the posts were leaning with the weight, shuddering, and one gave an ominous crack.

Reynolds finally booted the door in, and they were running through some dead stranger's house, stepping over the skeleton of a cat in the hallway. The house stank in all of the wrong ways. A zombie lurched out of the toilet, rotting pants still around its ankles, and it fell flat on its face, reaching up for them, and there was no time to despatch it, because the fence had finally fallen, and a steady stream of monsters was filing in through the back door, coming at them in an awkward trot.

"Quick, open it!" Tamsyn shouted at Reynolds, who was struggling with the heavy front door. The owners had been security conscious, and there were chains, deadbolts, and a door handle that just wouldn't seem to turn.

"Try jiggling it!" Leyland said impatiently. Finally Reynolds lost all patience, and brought down his axe on the handle, snapping it clean off. Yanking on the chains he hauled the door open, and then they were out in the front yard. Sushma decapitated a dead postman who was lurking near the gate.

Beyond the twitching corpse of Her Majesty's postal servant, the street was completely empty.

"He drew them all towards the canal, come on!" Tamsyn shouted.

"Tamsyn, your face," Sushma said. "You are bleeding."

She touched her cheeks, and realised the tears were splatters of blood, and her nose was going too, a real gusher. The crackling feeling in her brain was easing up, but her headache was less of a sharp pain, more of a worrying pulse that she could feel in every neurone.

I can't do anymore of the funky stuff, she thought. *I'm likely to blow my brain up.*

"Keep moving," Leyland barked. By some miracle he still had the fold map of Manchester in his pocket, and he puzzled over it on the move, trying to figure out exactly where they were.

"None of this is on here!" he shouted. "This map must be fifteen years old."

"Just head towards the tall buildings," Tamsyn managed, and then her legs went into a wobble like a newborn foal. Chaudhari grabbed her by the upper arm, the lean Indian man hustling her along until the moment passed.

Oh god, I hope I'm not having a stroke, she thought.

The noise of the rabid zombie horde was getting closer, the Boy smashing thousands of his puppets against the row of houses. He'd emptied this suburb to attack the canal, and now he needed to redirect his entire force to capture them.

They'd broken through enemy lines. Now they just had to stay ahead of the super-pack, long enough to find the group hiding in Manchester, at One Angel Square.

KNEEL, came the command in her mind, and she staggered again in Chaudhari's grip, but this time she fought to free herself, every fibre of her being desiring to obey the Black Crown Boy. She went down hard onto the bitumen, cracking her head forward violently as she abased herself.

"Tamsyn, what the hell are you doing?" Leyland yelled.

"This isn't me!" she protested. Reynolds and Chaudhari picked her up, one under each elbow, and she remained frozen in that kneeling pose, limbs locked into place. Somehow she found one final reserve, and blocked out the Black Crown Boy, who even then was rifling through her memories and thoughts, mocking her in a thousand creepy ways, until the last brick fell into place and he was finally silent.

"I'm okay now, put me down," Tamsyn said, her limbs once more under her control. "Thanks."

"Try eating a salad now and then," Reynolds teased.

"We are Vanguard," Chaudhari said, suddenly clamping his hands around her face.

Chaos and swearing, and a perfect smile closing in on her throat, mouth spreading wide. Reynolds snatched

Chaudhari in a chokehold, but it took all his strength to hold the man back. Tamsyn severed Chaudhari's connection to the Vanguard, a move that made specks float across her eyes and gave her an odd heart spasm. Tamsyn signalled for Reynolds to let the man go.

"I'm sorry!" Chaudhari gasped, and spat out a wad of grey foam onto the ground, and again until his spittle was clear. "Something - someone - took control of me."

"It's not your fault mate," Tamsyn said, but then there was no time for anything but running, as more undead broke through the fences, smashed through the houses, and then they were all in a deadly marathon through suburbia.

As the mob came howling after them, individual zombies fell to the road, their bodies burnt out and broken from running, but there were still hundreds on their trail. Tamsyn was grateful for the exercise regime she'd pushed herself through, but she felt exhausted to the core, her link to the supernatural damaging her in ways she couldn't even guess at.

But even through all that, Tamsyn realised one thing - the attacks on her threadbare mental defences were lessening, almost as if the Black Crown Boy was losing strength. Eyes swimming, she could see the forest of black threads over the pursuing zombies snapping, shrinking, till only a cluster of maybe a few hundred zombies ran after them.

He's got limits. We can outlast him!

Leyland set a new pace, turning their panicked escape into something resembling an orderly jog, snapping at Reynolds when he turned up the speed, knocking over bins and otherwise trying to deny their pursuit.

"Conserve your energy, Trooper!"

"Yes, Sergeant," he huffed.

The closest of the running undead was barely fifty feet

behind them, and the distance was closing. The Boy was burning through the last of his puppets at a rapid rate, hoping to simply swamp them with numbers. Tamsyn was not game to try and slice those threads with her mental sword - it was down to the endurance of their living flesh versus the pack of rotting meat-puppets snapping at their heels.

The housing estate was a rabbit warren of streets and cul-de-sacs, and it took several frightening laps to get them out on the main highway into Manchester. They'd been one wrong turn away from oblivion, and the pack was close enough that Tamsyn could hear the bellows wheeze of their dried out lungs, could hear every creak of their ligaments as they stretched to the point of breaking.

There were perhaps fifty dead things still running after them, weaving through the logjam of abandoned vehicles on the A56. It was the same sad story here as all over the world - first the outbreak, then the panic in the population centres, then traffic jams that went for miles. Abandoned bags. Abandoned prams. Then the bodies, some of them still moving.

Every now and then, a black thread would flicker into life, and Tamsyn would warn the others before a fresh runner came lurching out of a car or from the culvert. They were ready with axes and bats, and Tamsyn smiled - her invisible adversary was running out of steam.

"Don't get cocky," she warned them. "The slow ones can still murder you if you're not paying attention. Keep well clear of the car doors and windows. More than one person has been pounced on in places like this."

Perhaps twenty-five of the undead left, careening into the cars, snapping off rear-view mirrors as they ran to the point of destruction. The ones still in pursuit were definitely starting to slow down, their tendons and muscles wearing down, but the living weren't in much better shape. At Tamsyn's best guess they'd been running for almost five miles now, broken up with bursts of terrified hand-to-hand combat.

They were getting closer to the city centre now, the highway bisecting packed terrace housing and the first of the office buildings. The static zombie population was climbing, and they were forced to run low, crouching between the vehicles. Some of the zombies noticed the commotion of the running zombies, and came out shambling, their pack instincts kicking in at the prospect of a hunt.

Tamsyn had a sudden pang of heartache when they passed a sign pointing towards Old Trafford. If Eddie had been with her, he'd have taken them to the home grounds of Manchester United, zombies or not.

"We've got a clear run into the city," Leyland said, slowing down to look over the map. "When we hit the outskirts, we're taking the ring road around to One Angel Square."

"Look at that," Reynolds huffed. "It's the Forest tour bus. Poor buggers."

An enormous bus marked with the logo for Nottingham Forest Football Club was still trapped in the traffic jam, but even worse, dozens of shapes moved around behind the filthy windows. An entire football team, damned to sit on their bus for eternity. Tamsyn caught a flicker of an old image when she looked at the trapped undead, of the driver sneaking back on board the trapped bus with a bite he tried to hide.

The rest was nothing she hadn't seen before.

"Keep to a slow jog," Leyland said, an eye to the pack of runners closing in on them. "We've still got a long way to-"

Tamsyn saw the flick of black threads fall on the bus, and a second later the windows were smashing outwards, with the entire Nottingham Forest team leaping out. Three undead players fell on Leyland, grabbing at his limbs and tugging him to and fro. A heavyset coach narrowly missed Tamsyn, striking the ground in a splatter of guts and putrid fat, but still he snatched at her ankles, mouth spread wide in rotten ecstasy.

Then all of the black threads winked out of existence - the Black Crown Boy had finally hit his limit. The running zombies slowed to their usual shuffle, slowly closing in on the carnage around the bus.

It didn't make any difference now. The standard slow zombies falling onto them were enough to murder anyone at this point.

"Get off me, you stupid bloody thing!" Tamsyn said. She'd lost her hatchet back on the boat, and all she could do was strike down with her free boot, snapping in teeth, breaking cheekbones, trying desperately to free herself while Leyland fought for his very life, barely feet away from her. His pistol fired uselessly into the air as the zombies jerked his arms around.

"Tamsyn, I'm coming!" Reynolds said, lumberjacking his way through the assistant coaches and support staff of the undead football team.

"Don't help me, help him!" she shouted, pointing to Leyland. She finally caved in the coach's skull and fought free of his grip, and whistled, clapped, did everything she could to draw the other zombies in her direction.

Chaudhari finally panicked and ran for his life, leaving them all to their fates. He got twenty feet and crashed into an open car door, flying over the top and cracking his head on the tarmac. A pair of zombies knelt down on him, slowly picking him apart like a cheese platter, and the poor bastard screamed and cursed and begged for what seemed like eternity.

"Go! Get the hell out of here!" Leyland shouted at them all. "I'm ordering you to go!"

Sushma screamed out in her native tongue, her kukri cleaving through arms, heads, anything she could reach, but as she reached Leyland one of the zombies sank its teeth deep into his throat, tearing out his vital workings with one sickening jerk of its head. The Regimental Sergeant Major gaped and worked his mouth in horror as his lifeblood spurted out in a great fountain.

Sushma hit the group in a murder frenzy, and she took out most of the football team before she sank to the ground by her dying husband, cradling him to her chest and sobbing.

"Sushma, you've got to leave him!" Tamsyn begged her.

"I don't care!" she howled.

"Let go of him. He's about to turn. Please, please listen to me."

"I will die here. With my husband."

Tamsyn slapped her, hard. The Gurkha glared at her like a tiger about to pounce, and for a moment Tamsyn feared she was about to lose her head. Finally, with an awful low moan, Sushma buried her kukri in Leyland's skull.

She left the blade lodged there, and staggered off towards the city, screaming her rage to the heavens. Try as she might, Tamsyn could not free the blade from the bone, and decided that Sushma had earned the right to abandon that useful weapon with such a poetic gesture.

She considered the pistol still clutched in Leyland's

hand, the one that did nothing to save him, so she folded hand and gun across his broad chest, as close to a warrior's grave as she could manage in the moments that she had.

The slow beat of leathery old footsteps against tarmac, off-rhythm, the scrape where bones were poking through the worn soles of feet that could not heal, that would wear away with every pointless step. Even without the guidance of some distant master, these broken old shells were deadly enough.

Time to go.

The three survivors regrouped past the turnoff, following the highway into the dead heart of Manchester. Reynolds handed Tamsyn one of his axes, slick with gore. Neither of them were game to approach the grieving Sushma, who was still beating a fist against her chest, and howling herself hoarse in wordless loss.

For all your mystical bullshit, you're just as human as the rest of us, Tamsyn thought.

17

In all the chaos, they'd forgotten the map. Behind them, the A56 was filled with hundreds of the slow undead, relentlessly tailing the three survivors as they headed towards the city centre.

"Leyland said to take the ring road around the CBD," Tamsyn said quietly.

"Yeah, but what's it called?" Reynolds said.

"I don't bloody know, do I? Just look for a sign or something."

Sushma was just a murder marionette at this point, stalking forward, destroying the undead with her bare hands. When a coffin-dodger emerged from the wreckage, she would snap off its head, slam it into a car door, or break off a side mirror and stab it through the temple. Reynolds and Tamsyn held their axes to the ready, and did not even get the chance to use them.

Tamsyn recognised this mental state, and had been there once or twice. Sushma would fall apart the moment she allowed herself a moment to breathe or think, and to her subconscious, the threat to her own life was so great that it wasn't allowing her out of that adrenaline state. This wasn't grief, not yet. It was a cousin to anger, but so far beyond rage that it wasn't even a human emotion.

Corporal Sushma Thapa was officially in beast mode.

"Watch out for lurkers," Tamsyn said, warily watching each vehicle they squeezed through.

"You said that already."

"So I'm saying it again. They will wait there for years to bite idiots like us."

A dead man lay trapped underneath a turned-over van, no thread with its flailing hands and mournful groaning, but Sushma went out of her way to stomp in the zombie's skull. She lashed out against the panels of the van, a one-two punch that left deep dents and blood smears from her busted-up knuckles.

A long, shuddering breath, as though she was about to snap out of her fury, but then she darted forward to a car complete with undead driver. One elbow broke the driver's side window, and then she snatched the zombie by the hair, deftly severing its head on a sharp jag of glass.

She threw the head at a big undead baker, and ducked under its flailing arms, pushing it forward like a rugby player, bending its spine backwards over a railing with a sharp CRACK! With a triumphant cry she flipped the dead thing over the edge, watching for a second as it fell down onto the underpass below.

"Does she want to die?" Reynolds said.

"In my experience, yes."

Suddenly a knot of the creatures pushed through the logjam of cars, coming at Sushma from all sides. With her kukri she would have been able to cut her way free, but she was fighting the things barehanded. With a reluctant groan Reynolds got in there, breaking in faces and chopping them down into the asphalt. Tamsyn knew she didn't have his raw muscle power but she took strategic blows, a knee here, an elbow there. They freed their friend from the scrum, but she shook them off, staring half-crazed, mouth working in fury.

"Go away!" Sushma finally shouted. "I don't need you."

"Do you want another slap?" Tamsyn said, getting in her face. "You were talking a lot about not being stupid, and now look at you. Do you think you're the first person to lose someone? Get a grip, sister, or so help me I will slap you silly."

That moment then, when the anger cracked a little and the grief rushed in, and Sushma pushed it down, madly smearing at the tears on her face.

"Give me that," she said, taking the axe from Tamsyn. "You have weak spaghetti arms."

"Did - did you just quote *Dirty Dancing* at me?"

"I am from Nepal. Not the moon."

"Ladies, step it up," Reynolds said, hip and shouldering another undead killer over the railing.

It was all Tamsyn could do to keep up the relentless pace, her deadly friends carving a path through that walking forest. These zombies had several years of weather damage, and fell easier than the fresh ones back in the Gravesend days, but the sheer numbers coming at them were terrifying. Soon they were up onto the roofs of the cars, playing a deadly game of the-floor-is-lava, leaping from island to island. Without the Black Crown Boy to rev them up, the zombies were back to their stupid lazy selves, barely able to clamber up after them.

They were still deadly.

"Do not stop," Tamsyn huffed. She leapt to the back of an oil-tanker, climbing the steel rungs with shaking arms.

When she got up onto the walkway, what she saw terrified her.

Thousands of zombies slowly converging on their location, choking up both ends of the overpass. Beyond that, the outskirts of the city, and tens of thousands of coffin-dodgers there, wandering aimlessly through the office buildings. She could make out the curve of the ring-road, and it was more wall-to-wall zombies.

The plan worked on paper - follow the canal straight through, and you only have a two block gauntlet to run to get to the building and back again. In a perfect world, where there weren't supernatural puppet masters and kamikaze undead, and a panicked escape from the only "safe" route. Now they had a whole city to get through.

Before her, the truck had crunched into an overturned hatch-back, pulverising it, and there was a large gap all around to the next safe "island" of vehicles. The truck was already fully surrounded by the undead. If she'd leapt to one of the other cars back there, they might have made it through safely, but she'd picked wrong, and just like that she'd made the last stupid decision of her life.

"Game over," she said to the wind, and felt better for it. They had done their best on a risky mission, and didn't make it. But Malcolm, Prince Harry, the other survivors from the *Vengeance*, they would farm and keep to their empty lands, hidden from prying eyes. She wouldn't be there to bring a big target down on their community.

They would survive. It made this bleak ending almost okay.

"So, is it the wrong time to ask for a threesome?" he said. Tamsyn laughed despite herself. It was right that there was some irreverent dickhead with her in these final moments, even if he was a poor imitation of her Eddie. Sushma pushed by with a grunt, clattering along the gantry until she stood above the truck cab with her axe across her shoulders.

"I am ready to kill more," she called back over her shoulder. "We lure them up the ladder, up the side of the truck. We should be able to kill five hundred more before we die of thirst."

"That's the spirit," Tamsyn said, a second before the explosions.

BANG! BANG! BANG!

She flinched, falling to her knees on the grating, instinctively reaching for a bow she'd lost years ago. The lessons learnt in the American war went deep into her muscle memory, and every fibre of her body screamed out *We're under attack!*

More explosions. Rising to her feet, Tamsyn realised that at either end of the bridge, random cars were simply exploding. Wherever there was a knot of monsters, a car would go up in a concussive fireball, sending the undead scattering.

"They're going up in a pattern," Reynolds said. "Someone's clearing a path for us."

"We are sitting on top of a goddamn *fuel tanker!*" Tamsyn cried. "We need to get off this thing, right now."

The loud WHOOMPH of each car exploding attracted the undead, who stepped over the writhing bodies of their fallen comrades, circling the flames hungrily. The crowd around the tanker parted, just a little, but there was their window, a gap where only a handful of zombies impeded their escape.

Sushma looked to Tamsyn, a mad grin touching her lips, and then she launched herself from the roof of the truck cab, feet first into the chest of a rotting train-driver. She hit the zombies around her like a dervish, axe spinning in a beautiful dance.

"Move it!" Reynolds huffed, sliding down the windshield on his backside. Tamsyn slid after him, arms flailing out in space. Her left ankle lit up with a burst of pain as she landed on the asphalt. A memory then of poor Ali with his busted-up ankle, and how he couldn't out-hobble the horde that devoured him.

It's just a sprain, she thought, testing her leg gingerly. She could still trot forward, but it hurt like a bitch. It was all she could do to wince and jog along behind the axe-warriors up ahead.

BANG! BANG! Two more cars went up in ball of flame, raining bits of metal and glass. A burning tyre rolled past Tamsyn, knocking a zombie over and setting it on fire. Tamsyn took a moment to drive her elbow into the windows of two cars, opening all of the doors to create a type of bottleneck.

"Stop messing around and keep up!" Reynolds ordered.

"Screw you! It's a good idea."

Tamsyn first noticed the devices as she threw open more car doors - a weird electronic gizmo, all chunky plastic and duct tape, stuck into the open fuel cap of each car. They each had a little radio antennae, an arming switch, and wires running down into the fuel tanks.

Some clever person had turned every car on this bridge into a remote bomb.

Which immediately told her that they were being watched. For now this person or persons seemed to be helping them, but they were still in the middle of more explosions than a Hollywood car chase.

Back when she had a Texan flag sewn on her sleeve, Tamsyn had learnt how to weaponise abandoned cars, amongst other things. Even with just a lick of decaying fuel in the belly of a vehicle, there was still enough in the way of fumes and go-juice to cause a decent explosion.

She looked back at the fuel tanker they'd been standing on, saw how at least a thousand undead were pushing around it, heading towards the explosions on the far side of the bridge. Then she saw the radio antennae strapped to the valves on the side of the tanker.

Tamsyn remembered the raid on the oil refinery back in America, and how the sheer force of that explosion nearly wiped out the whole facility and half of the forest around it. Take a tanker of that size, turn it into a bomb, and it was going to knock everything sideways, themselves included, with the added bonus of shrapnel for perhaps a mile in each direction.

"Those idiots are going to set off the tanker!" Tamsyn shouted. "Run!"

If only she had her bow, the old one, there was a good chance she'd be able to take out the radio transmitter from here. One shot, two-hundred and seventy feet per second, and the sheer force would be enough to wreck anything.

At this point, she didn't even have a nail file. It was ridiculous to be so vulnerable here. In frustration, she took a second to visualise the shot, groaning with the ease that she could have made it.

Then she saw it. A white line, a string from her hand, arching out towards the tanker. It was the same as the black strings from the sky, but opposite in intent. Instinctively, she knew she could only make one of these strings, and even then it felt wrong. Invasive. She felt her invisible line brush around the temples of a zombie who was right next to the radio switch.

Instantly she was *inside* of the zombie. She looked out through its blasted eyes, could see the three humans up ahead in a weird spectrum of heat, smell, movement, everything that shouted *prey* to this beast. Her borrowed limbs creaked with every jerky movement, and she felt how this broken body had been pushed through several hard winters, frozen, thawed and rethawed, subject to the endless wind, sun, rain.

More than that, she could feel the undercurrent of the creature's thoughts, down to the dim memories of a man still trapped in that rotting brain, a man who could be brought back with the salt treatment.

He was called Hayden back in life. A university student. He'd worked in a lab. Had a pretty girlfriend. These thoughts fell back into that darkness, overridden by the hunger, the need to hunt. Tamsyn pushed down on these urges, and the dead man stood still, puzzled as his comrades groaned and pushed past him.

Just reach out, please, she told the dead man. *Turn off that switch there.*

The zombie nodded once, a jerky affirmation, and clumsily he fumbled at the transmitter, throwing it to a label drawn in marker: OFF. Tamsyn withdrew her little white cord from the depths of that dead mind, and then she was back in her own body, sagging over a car door and violently heaving out the contents of her stomach.

"Get up," Sushma shouted at her, dragging her to her feet. Tamsyn wiped away the sick, and the back of her hand came away smeared with blood. Peering into the dusty car window, she saw that her eyes, her nose, even her ears were leaking blood.

That scrunching feeling in her brain was back, and it was bigger this time, each thought followed by an ominous crackle. Whatever she just did, it was cooking her brain big time.

How can the Boy control thousands of those things at once? What is he?

Sushma hustled her forward, despite her protests. There were gaps in the pack of zombies ahead, but a solid phalanx advancing on them from behind, the tanker-bomb that should have wiped them out now dormant.

A small window of space around them, but the zombies climbing up the overpass were regrouping, drawn to the living people, and Tamsyn understood a little now how these distractions would only work for moments. They were gifted, these undead, their senses enhanced until they were like owls spotting a mouse in a field of grass.

Tamsyn decided she would never underestimate a coffin-dodger, ever again.

"God, we'll never get through all that," Reynolds groaned. Up ahead, the zombies flattened by the car bombs were still crawling towards them on shattered limbs, and hundreds more of the undead were swarming towards the overpass, crowding in on each other as they came for the noise, and stayed for the *prey*.

Underneath them, the road was almost completely empty, but it was a good thirty feet from the railing down to the tarmac. The zombies that Sushma and Reynolds had thrown over lay broken and twitching, the splatter of guts and gore an indicator of how well they would go if they made that desperate leap.

"Hey, I think that's the ring road," Tamsyn said, following the curve of the road as it went around the city. It led to safety, to the other group of survivors, but it might as well have been on the moon.

She hit the railing in frustration, and stepped back into a fire-truck, long since abandoned in the break-down lane. Her bruised mind took a moment to process the sight, and then she was fumbling over the wheels and levers, looking for the right control.

"What are you doing? Do you want to spray the zombies with firefighting foam?" Reynolds scoffed, trying to deny the light of terror that was in his eyes. Sushma was already up and investigating the ladder on the truck, and she shook her head.

"We cannot point this ladder to the ground," she said. "It is no good."

Finally, Tamsyn found what she was looking for. Underneath the ladders were piles of flattened rubber and canvas, looped back and forth. She'd been looking for a reel or something, and only just realised these were the hoses. When Reynolds saw her tugging them loose, he lent his efforts to hers, pulling the hose clear of the truck.

"Over the side! Sushma, keep it coming!" Tamsyn shouted. All three of them fed the hose out and over the railing, until the weight of the hose took it from their hands, jerking out length after length of hose until the metal hose fitting struck the ring road with a distant clang.

"You go first," Tamsyn huffed to Reynolds. "You probably climb ropes for fun."

He opened his mouth to protest, but the nearest zombies were within thirty feet. Sliding the axe handle through his belt, the Special Forces trooper was over the railing and shimmying down. Sushma arched an eyebrow at Tamsyn, who was panting like a knackered race-horse.

"Be quick about it," she said to Tamsyn, and this echo of her mother's final words felt like a punch to the gut. The Gurkha was over the railing, gripping the hose with her knees and sliding down it one-handed.

Gritting her teeth, Tamsyn climbed up onto the railing, and she fought back against the vertigo, trying not to focus on the distant ground. Easing her shaky arms and legs around the hose, she slowly leaned off against the edge, ready to rappel down like the terrified amateur she really was.

A circle of the undead was closing in on the firetruck, dead fingers already reaching for the tense hose, wriggling under her weight. Ten feet away. Five. She knew they would simply launch themselves over the railing, grabbing her on the way through to their bug-splat ending.

One-handed, she undid her belt, fastening it around the hose until it held her tight. She reached out again, white line arcing from her mind, and she found Hayden, still standing by the fuel truck, looking at his fingers with confusion, and then she was back behind his eyes.

Hayden, I just need you to do one last thing, she told the zombie, and he reacted at his name, his sense of self emerging from the murk of his undead mind. The labels read OFF, RADIO, and BOOM.

Make it go boom.

"Boom," the zombie said through his rotten throat, and flicked the switch over to the label of the same name.

It went boom.

Tamsyn awoke on the ground, still fastened to the hose. Looking up, she could see the railing of the overpass, and enormous clouds of black smoke wafting over the edge. If there were any zombies left after that, they wouldn't be in any shape to chase after them.

"She wakes," Sushma said, roughly thumbing back her eyelids. "No concussion."

"Smart move, that belt slider," Reynolds said. "Only

thing that saved your life when you fell." She was still wrapped in his arms from when he'd caught her at the other end of the hose, stretched out by her friends to a taut 45-degree angle.

Our batshit crazy plan worked!

She felt like she was viewing the world through a rosy fog, and could feel every pulse as it rattled through her head. *Not good.* Unclipping herself from the fire-hose, she stood up on shaky feet. Apart from one or two lost zombies, the ring road was completely clear.

"We gotta move," she slurred, feeling slightly drunk. *A stroke?*

It felt like she was sleepwalking. One numb foot after the other, watching from some distant place as Sushma felled a zombie with one swift blow to the temple. Reynolds turned and was saying something to her, but the words weren't quite connecting between her ears and her brain.

"-don't you dare stop walking, Tamsyn. You're going into shock."

When she saw the remote control car zipping across the tarmac, she thought it was one more symptom of her overcooked brain-meat. It did a rapid lap of the three survivors, and finally stopped in front of them.

"You have to follow me!" the car said in a tinny voice.

Tamsyn cracked up laughing. She was officially headed to the funny farm. The moment passed, and she took another look at the little RC car. She remembered all the remote-control toys her friend Ali had enjoyed, and knew that this was a top of the line rig, worth thousands of pounds. Someone had added an extra big antennae, an additional battery pack, and a webcam strapped to the front. The voice was coming out of a speaker on the car's roof.

"The ring road's safe, but we've spotted a big herd coming your way. Follow me!"

With that, the car spun around in a tight donut and took off in the opposite direction, whizzing and whining as the unseen operator pushed it to its limit. Wide-eyed, Reynolds gestured for them to follow.

At one point the remote-control car took a turn-off ramp into the city centre. Spinning the car 180 degrees, the operator faced them with the camera, driving in reverse. Tamsyn looked at the dead milling around the city, and the streets and sidewalks looked as crowded as they must have before the undead.

"I know it looks bad, but we've got a short cut," came the tinny voice. *"We've blocked off most of the ring road, but past here they've gotten over our barricades."*

"Where are you taking us?" Tamsyn said to the car.

"No microphone. I can't hear you. Please, we've got to move."

BANG! An explosion from up ahead, in the city itself, echoing against the canyons formed by the tall buildings. A few blocks into the concrete and glass jungle, Tamsyn could see the zombies drawn towards the noise, thinning out the crowd on the road on the city streets.

"That will buy us some time. Quick!"

Her vision squeezed into a tight tube, part panic, part brain destruction, and all she could focus on was that stupid little car, her tired legs pumping left-right-left, some lizard part of her hindbrain moving her forward. In the past few years she had seen this shit over and over. London. Corpus Christi. All stops through to Washington DC and back again. And Cuba, God help her, in Cuba too. Cities had a measure of life to them, and they'd died when the people did.

It was the dirt on the streets that she noticed the most.

Give a smooth surface a few years unattended, and the dust would kick across, build little islands of silt and muck, and they'd catch up blowing paper and rubbish, and soon the neat black asphalt started to vanish. Tamsyn guessed in thirty or forty years' time there'd be weeds, grass, even trees growing on these streets.

Suddenly a dead pair of hands, gripping her around the forearm, teeth closing in, and Tamsyn was too far done to even be scared. An axe from nowhere, and Sushma was knocking seven shades of shit from the thing that had almost ended her life.

Focus, you idiot, Tamsyn thought, slapping herself in the cheeks to wake up.

It didn't work, not really. She was in that dreamy state where sleep was just a cozy moment away. *Just curl up in that doorway, Tam. You deserve a good rest.*

Her world was a fuzzy tube that showed only a dirty road, some people she thought she knew, and a remote control car slaloming through car wreck and walking corpses, and she trotted along almost happily, as if they were running through a carnival and an awesome new ride was just up ahead. She found herself humming a merry little tune, and even broke into a skip at one point.

BANG! Another car-bomb went up, closer this time, their unseen saviour clearing the intersection up ahead. Tamsyn smiled at the little flower of fire and ruptured steel, at the dead things drawn to it like bees to pollen. Then there was a gap in the dead crowd, and Sushma hauling her along by her collar, and Tamsyn running and laughing like an idiot.

Tamsyn stirred from this marathon through molasses to realise they were through the centre of the city. Ahead, the curve of the ring road, and just past that was the strangest building she'd ever seen. It looked like a sliced egg realised in glass and steel, embedded in the middle of the city. The top of the futuristic skyscraper was only partially finished, but someone had erected an epic patchwork of tin and plywood, marring the shiny finish with a weird Mad Max look at the top. Tamsyn saw ants crawling up and down the outside of the building, and then she realised they were people, abseiling down from the roof.

ANGEL SQUARE, someone had painted across the top of the building, and others had hand-painted angels on the patchwork panels, from renaissance cherubs through to post-modern winged insanity. What had started off as an ambitious office building had ended up as an imposing fortress, a Sistine Chapel painted on the outside.

"*Home sweet home*," the voice from the remote-control car crackled.

The ground level of the building was a clever barricade, a fusion of buses and welded steel plates, without so much as an inch for a dead thing to wriggle through. Old signs pointed towards the lobby entrance, but there was no way past the solid ring of steel. Tamsyn saw Reynolds take a run at the metal wall, hoping to scale above the buses, but every bolt had been shaved down, every weld and finger-hold sanded back. The wall was as smooth as a baby's backside, and not even a super trooper like Reynolds had a prayer of climbing over it.

"*Step back*," the voice from the toy car instructed, and Tamsyn blinked as the shadow fell across her face. A long shape, descending from above, blocking out the dazzling dawn light reflecting from the spit-shined windows. A window-washer's scaffold, slowly winding down from the heavens.

It was a genius idea. Doors and gates were weak points,

so why not eliminate them altogether? As their salvation slowly winched downwards, Tamsyn watched with some detachment as a few hundred of the undead turned from the distractions, slowly wandering over towards them. They were trapped against an impenetrable curtain of steel, with no retreat possible.

"Hurry up!" Reynolds yelled upwards, making a circling motion with his hand. "Winch that thing faster!"

"It's only got the one speed," came the faint reply from above.

"*Relax. You're going to be okay,*" came the tinny voice from the toy car.

KA-KRUNCH. A set of steel spears shot up from the pavers just in from the main road, punching up through the first rank of the undead. They were the automatic traffic bollards, converted into a rapid-fire weapon. For a second the zombies stood there twitching, steel protruding up through the top of their skulls, and then the spears retracted into the ground with a loud KA-CHUNK. A second later, they went up again, butchering more and more of the advancing undead.

There were still plenty of holes in the net. The undead that got past the bollard trap were picking up the pace now, arms outstretched as they got closer to the living trio. Sushma watched them impassively, taking the moment to rest against her axe, while Reynolds was psyching himself up, preparing to sell his life dearly.

That was when the water sprinklers started. Dozens of pop-up spray heads emerged from the long-dead lawns of the building, but some bright spark had increased the water pressure, turning them into great geysers of spray that washed in all directions. Tamsyn caught the mist of the closest one, and smelt the tang of salt water. The horde dispersed with screams of agony, pushing against each other to escape the pain.

Behind them, the clank of the scaffold as it settled on the pavers. Someone threw the little gates open, and half a dozen people came running towards them, some with guns, one with a first aid kit. Everyone was shouting.

"It's okay!" Tamsyn shouted. "We're from the government. We've come to rescue you."

Then her body finally failed her, and she fell face first into the pavers.

18

Tamsyn awoke to a tousled head, smiling down at her. A girl, perhaps ten years old, all crooked teeth, curls and freckles.

She sat up with a start. She was in a bed, and wearing pyjamas. A very nice bed. Curtains and canvas sheets served as walls around her, but they were open above to reveal the glass roof of One Angel Square, the patchwork of gleaming glass and plywood squares instantly recognisable.

"Where are my friends?" she asked the girl, who gave her a sympathetic look, but no answer. She looked away a little as she spoke, but made no move to leave. She had a complicated Lego structure in his hands, and she built and rebuilt it, over and over.

Tamsyn recognised it almost straight away. It was the exact shape she'd seen the Vanguard building on the Isle of Sheppey, an eye-twisting structure full of hollows, topped with reaching finger shapes curling up and outwards.

"Vanguard!" Tamsyn yelled. She was up and rolling out of her bed, trying her best to get away from the girl, before she got tangled up in her own sheets. She fell through a curtain and into someone else's bedroom, and when she felt herself collapse on top of another person, she started yelping and thrashing around.

"Help! Get me out of here! Vanguard!"

A pair of hands calmly untangled the cocoon of sheet and curtain trapping her head, and she realised she was on top of Reynolds. The Trooper looked up at her with a sly smile.

"Not how I hoped this would play out, but I'll take it."

"Gross. Quick, we've got to get out of here, it's –"

"Shh. Hush now," Reynolds soothed, patting her like she was a baby. "You are perfectly safe in my arms."

"Let go of me, you idiot! We're in danger!" Tamsyn yelled, losing all patience. She cracked her forehead down, head-butting Reynolds square in the nose. Rolling onto the floor, she fought herself free of the sheets and stood panting, hands in fists, reaching inwards for a weapon to fight off this newest monster.

The girl was still stood there in the wreckage of her cubicle. She put her Lego bricks down on the small bedside table, and sat down on the edge of Tamsyn's bed, watching her calmly. She smiled again, but it was a shy smile, not the mad grin of the Vanguard.

Her eyes swam, and she saw the girl's aura – white, peaceful, nourishing. But there was something else to the girl. When she looked at her, she got the same feeling she got from the old Abbey, the sense of shelter and safety from the Black Crown Boy. Reaching out tentatively, Tamsyn realised that her unseen enemy wasn't even watching her at the moment.

For now, Tamsyn knew she was completely safe. And it was something to do with this young girl.

"Tilly's a nice kid," Reynolds said, wiping away a bloody nose. "You, on the other hand, are a right bitch.."

"You deserved that," Tamsyn mumbled.

"Probably," Reynolds sniffed.

She sat down next to Tilly, who looked up at her with that same vague smile. Tamsyn picked up the Lego construction, and held it gingerly.

"Have you seen these?" she asked Tilly. The girl would not make eye contact with Tamsyn, and squirmed uncomfortably. For a long moment the girl looked down at her bare feet, swinging on the edge of the bed.

"Listen, Tilly, this is really important. How did you know how to make this?"

Tilly suddenly snatched the Lego from Tamsyn's hand and cast it across the ground, breaking it into pieces, and then she darted out through the flap of the door, running as fast as her little legs could carry her.

"I am just not good with kids," Tamsyn finally managed.

"Well she likes you," Reynolds said. "Tilly has barely left your side since we got here."

"How long was I out?"

"Almost two days."

"God, I really need to pee."

REYNOLDS GAVE her the tour of One Angel Square, which started with a trip to the toilet block. Tamsyn followed him through a shanty town of bed-rooms, partitioned with fabric, and rows of expensive looking tents, erected on the carpet of an office floor.

They were beginning to build more permanent structures here, and crews were erecting panels with power tools.

Men with tool belts and mugs of coffee swapped jokes and banter, while others hustled in insulation and lengths of timber. A pack of teenagers were attempting to move a dining setting and a lounge suite through the shanty-town, and one lad dropped the end of a settee on his friend's foot, to the laughter and eye-rolling of his mates.

Tamsyn looked around wide-eyed, as hundreds of people went about their day, smiling and offering her welcome whenever she passed by. These were clean, happy people, well-dressed and relaxed. Despite the utter carnage and terror surrounding their building, there was no thousand-yard stare. Just – peace.

I have got to get out of here! She thought in terror. *I'll bring the Black Crown Boy inside. These people are going to go crazy and kill each other.*

But as her vision washed over and she took in auras of deep green and peaceful blue, she wasn't so sure of that. There was something about this place, the feel of sanctuary and enduring shelter.

"Here are the facilities," Reynolds said, steering her towards the rear of the floor. There was a small break room, an office kitchen, and the toilets were here. At the thought of indoor plumbing she rushed forward, only to encounter a small line-up outside the ladies. She hopped from foot to foot, wondering if she dared slip into the men's or disabled toilets.

"Hey, you're that new girl," the lady in front of her said, a matronly type wearing a dressing gown and carrying about three towels. "Tammy."

"Tamsyn," she corrected her, and hated herself for doing it. "Sorry, I'm about to leak all over the floor here."

"Oh, where are our manners?" the woman exclaimed, and then pressed a towel and a bar of soap into her hands.

"Everyone, please let Tamsyn through, she really needs to go."

"I'm Tamsyn," she muttered. At first those in front protested at her cutting into the cue, but when they saw her muck spattered clothes and matted hair, she was ferried in on a sea of sympathetic looks and tut-tutting. At every step she collected another piece of toiletry, and by the time she was inside she had a set of clean clothes and enough moisturiser for a leper colony.

It was heaven. Clean facilities. Toilet paper. A shower that pumped out steaming hot water. Her time on the submarine had taught her to shower fast, but she lingered in the hot spray for a moment or two, the drain swallowing up the filth as she sluiced it from her body.

The sleepy feeling gave way to her usual jagged alertness, and with a thrill of panic she remembered the damage she'd been doing to her brain, and wondered if she was about to have a stroke, right here and now. But her headache was gone, with no more of the crinkly cellophane feeling behind her eyes. Even her sprained ankle felt fine.

Guess I just needed a good night's sleep? she thought, even knowing this wasn't quite true. She'd as good as cooked her brain using her freaky mind powers out there. By all rights she should be a vegetable now.

Still, Tamsyn couldn't remember the last time she'd felt so good. She left the bathroom feeling like a new woman, and high-fived some of her new friends on the way back out.

"Took your time," was all Reynolds said. "Hurry up, I don't want to miss breakfast."

"Are you seeing this?" Tamsyn muttered as they wound their way back through the sleeping quarters, and into a living area. A big TV with surround sound was pumping out cartoons for the kids, a trio of old men were dominating a snooker table, and something that looked suspiciously like a book-club was taking place by an honest-to-God café.

"It's a pretty sweet set-up," Reynolds said.

"Not that, the people. They have perhaps a million undead just outside the doors. Everyone here has seen the bad shit, every one of them, but this feels like a – like a summer camp or something."

"They do karaoke night on Wednesdays. They've got a genius wall of steel blocking all the doors. Of course they can relax now."

"Bullshit," Tamsyn said. "I spent a year in Corpus Christi, a whole city kept safe from the dead. They had every amenity you could think of. They also had eleven suicides a week."

She looked at the happy neighbourhood of survivors, merrily tinkering away or relaxing like champions. She found the whole situation slightly creepy. Being a PTSD veteran before the first dead thing even walked around, Tamsyn liked to think she could spot the signs. Just about every survivor she'd met since 2012 had the thousand-yard stare, or the nervous tic and shiftiness of survivor's guilt.

Here, there was a Tai Chi session going on next to a poker tournament.

"They're either on a shitload of meds, or something very weird is going on here," Tamsyn decided. "Be on your bloody guard, Reynolds."

"That book club looks especially vicious."

"Don't make me give you another blood nose."

At Tamsyn's urging, they took a detour on the way to meeting whoever was in charge. Reynolds led her up the stairs to another level of the office tower, this one stripped down to the cement and given over to industry. Welders were making more of the steel plates, others were taking apart motorbikes and four-wheelers, and there was a healthy weapons workshop here, with racks of spears and axes, crossbows and even a locker full of firearms. For some reason an old man was teaching two teenagers how to make birdhouses, and they were surrounded by dozens of finished examples.

Other levels were dedicated to agriculture. The outer shell of the building was a brilliant wall of double glazing with walkways between the inner and outer shells. Here the floors were all sealed in with plastic sheeting and a three-foot deep layer of soil across each office floor, and banks of UV lights. The effect was of an enormous stack of greenhouses, and Tamsyn saw crops of wheat, oats, fruit and vegetables, and even a small rice paddy that had the smack of an experiment about it.

When she heard the clucking of chickens, she hip-and-shouldered Reynolds out of her way in her excitement. Half of one floor was given over to an animal farm, with more ramshackle pens and cages under construction. They had chickens, goats, sheep, pigs, even a pony. There was already a queue of excited small children, waiting to go for a ride.

"How in the holy hell did they manage all of this?" Tamsyn said, awestruck.

The centre of One Angel Square was a deep well, from the sealed-in atrium up to the unfinished roof. Tamsyn had never been great with heights, and she approached the edge of the rail cautiously. It felt like looking at a cross section of a bee-hive, with the movement of workers and farmers on their levels, and acres of drying laundry hanging from the rails on the residential levels. A rudimentary flying fox system was in use, and she watched as a worker zip-lined from the workshop level back down to one of the farms.

"Why not use the lifts?" Tamsyn said.

"Apparently it takes up too much power. For us, it's more bloody stairs. Come on."

Tamsyn took one more dizzying look over the rail, all the way down to the atrium on the ground. It was the largest open space in the building, and so these survivors had etched out a miniature football field with white paint. More steel panels lined the whole of the ground floor, blocking out all of the windows and doors, and Tamsyn wasn't even sure that a team armed with explosives and arc-welders would be able to bust through all of that, let alone the undead.

This building was as secure as secure could get.

Plastic chairs and trestle tables were stacked all along the outer walls, and she supposed that the atrium doubled as a public meeting space. While she was mentally calculating the number of chairs, she saw a figure move out onto the pitch, looking directly up at her.

It was a woman in a bright yellow dress, waving. Feeling slightly foolish, she waved back, and then she had to hustle to catch up with Reynolds, who was approaching a set of big double-doors.

"Hurry up. I don't want to miss breakfast," he said, and threw open the doors onto the outside world. Tamsyn followed him out onto a broad balcony, a good thirty or forty feet wide, running the whole length of the building. Looking up, she had the feeling she was on a cruise ship, with receding terraces of glass rising up to the top of the building. Above them, the unfinished dome of the glass roof looked like an oyster. Tamsyn supposed that the entire roof could open like a louvre window in summer.

Here at the end of spring, it was still a little fresh, but hundreds of people were crowding this roof-space, rugged up against the cold. The residents of One Angel Square had set up an open-aired cafeteria, with rows of tables, a servery, and even a bar complete with tiki torches.

Quite a few people were leaning against the outer railing, nursing cups of coffee as they looked over the devastation of Manchester, but they were loose, relaxed. Even in the safest parts of Corpus Christi, normal people had quickly gone about their business, all but looking over their shoulders. Everyone had operated under a siege mentality, with the weight of survival in every movement.

Here, in a building literally under siege, the survivors had the air of a group on a charter holiday. One lady pointed out at the moving carpet of the undead, as if indicating an interesting piece of scenery.

"Shame that's not open yet," she muttered, looking to the bar. "I could do with a stiff drink."

"It's only eight in the morning," Reynolds scoffed. "Look, there she is."

Tamsyn scanned the people lining up in the queue, but to her surprise Sushma was behind the servery, cheerfully dishing out ladles of food. She saw her chatting to the people she served, and once she even broke out into raucous laughter.

"Wow," she said. "After what happened to Leyland, she should be weeping in her bed, or standing on the edge of the roof. That's just weird."

"She's a Gurkha," Reynolds said. "Most resilient bastards on the planet."

"I'm not buying it."

Taking up a plate each, they joined the merry queue of survivors, and made their way towards breakfast. Every five seconds someone was saying hello and welcome to her, and pretty soon Tamsyn was sick of it. It reminded her of a church camp, or that group that tried to sell her parents a time-share. By the time she got to the front of the queue, all she could muster in response to these well-wishers was a strained smile and a nod.

"You are awake," Sushma said, slapping a spoon-full of mush on Tamsyn's plate. She had her hair back in a ponytail, and wore a nice shirt and jeans, with an apron that said KISS THE COOK.

"Yeah, yeah, slept like a daisy. Sushma, are you going okay?"

"I am well. It is good here."

"I mean," and here she paused, lowering her voice. "Your husband just had his throat ripped out in front of you. I don't mean to be a bitch, but you've got to grieve and stuff. You'll go bonkers if you don't."

"I am okay," Sushma laughed. "It was sad, but it happened. I will miss him, but this life must go on."

Tamsyn let her eyes unfocus, and saw Sushma's aura. Green, deep and calming, where she'd expected a jagged red, shades of black, something to show the trauma she'd just experienced.

This was deeply wrong. As she searched her friend's face, she felt a tickle of fear run up her back. She was still there, the brave and funny woman she'd befriended, but there was something else missing. It felt a little bit like talking to someone on drugs, or someone wanting to con you into a pyramid scheme.

"You are not off the hook," Tamsyn said. "Give me some of that mashed potato there."

Sushma splattered more muck onto Tamsyn's plate, and smiled warmly.

∼

TAMSYN TUGGED off her filthy Doc Martins back at her bed cubicle, deciding she'd rather go barefoot than wear those gore-soaked feet coffins for one moment longer. Reynolds stretched out on his own bed, humming as he worked fruitlessly on a Rubik's cube.

"Don't go native," she warned him. "These people are not right."

"It's great here," he said, spinning the cube back and forth. "Safe. Safe and good."

She let her eyes unfocus, and saw that he was surrounded in waves of blue and green, a soothing blanket wrapped around his cynical little soul.

"Don't forget, we left the others back at the farm. We need to go back, warn them to stay away from here."

"Are you mad?" he said absently. "We need to bring them all here. Your little man would love it. All the other kids to play with, the pony rides and such."

Mother guilt racked her, like a sharp spike to the chest. All along she'd been assuming there was no safe place left, that the hidden master of the undead would get to her and anyone near her. But for some reason, this place was safe. It was good. Malcolm could have a proper childhood here, something she'd never been able to give him.

But is it a real childhood? she mused. *Do I want him tripping on whatever has got these people blissed out? He might be better off at the farm.*

"So, who's the boss here?" she asked Reynolds, who was completely absorbed by his cube. She'd seen him lose patience with things quite quickly, so to see this dedication to a pointless task was damn weird.

"Emma. Usually down in the atrium. Yellow dress."

Click. Click. Clickety click.

Shaking her head as she left the hypnotised man,

Tamsyn went barefoot down through the levels of One Angel Square, avoiding as many conversations as she could. At this point she'd give anything to chat to someone having a bad day, or to see a disagreement of some sort. All of this Brady Bunch saccharine bullshit was starting to get to her.

Get it together, she thought. *Don't you think you deserve to be this happy?*

When she reached the bottom of the tower, she walked out onto the football pitch, to see the woman in the yellow dress struggling with a trestle table. She was setting up some sort of gathering in the middle of the atrium, but no-one was down there but her.

"Little help?" she called out to Tamsyn, who dutifully trotted over and grabbed the other end of the table. A few minutes later they had a horseshoe of tables set up, and Tamsyn helped cart over plastic chairs.

"Thank you dear," the woman said. "It's good to see you up and about."

Tamsyn nodded, not knowing what to say. The woman sat on a chair, and pulled one directly in front of her, patting it with her hand. Tamsyn sank down in the chair cautiously, noting that her knees were now almost touching the other woman's.

"You can relax now, Tamsyn," she said. "You're amongst friends."

"I'm not so sure about that."

The woman gave a heavy sigh, and then patted Tamsyn on the knee.

"Let's start again. My name is Emma, Emma Menteuse."

She extended her hand. Tamsyn took it gingerly, and gave three quick pumps before letting it go.

"Look, I get it," Emma said. "You've been through hell

out there, and you're a bit twitchy. Just give this place a chance. Give *us* a chance."

"Emma, I have seen a lot of things since the dead did – did all of this. Weird things. And I know that something about this place isn't right." She paused. "I think I want to leave."

"Well, that's a fine thank you," Emma said, a little miffed. "Do you really want to go back out there? You'll get yourself killed."

"I'll take my chances."

Emma stood up, and stood behind her chair, hands resting on its back. She tapped her fingers, neatly manicured and painted. Tamsyn noticed a whopping great wedding ring on one finger, and a stack of fancy bangles dancing around each wrist.

"If that's what you want, that's okay. We can kit you out. Try and open a passage through the undead for you to escape."

"Cool," Tamsyn mumbled.

"No-one's stuck in here that doesn't want to be here."

"Don't give me that. You're putting something in the water or something. People just are not that happy and calm. I don't think they ever were."

"It's not the water," Emma said. Tamsyn was instantly on her feet, and she snatched up her chair, ready to use it as a weapon. Adrenaline turned her nervous system into a sour electric light show, and she was ready to fight her way out, instantly falling into that dark place.

Everything's FUCKED. Suspicions confirmed. Fight or die.

"Settle down. Now," the woman continued, staring at Tamsyn levelly. "We're not even sure what it is."

"Oh." She lowered the folding chair, feeling like a bad amateur wrestler.

"It's something about this building," Emma continued. "We try to keep our people busy and happy, but I'm not sure we even need to. When they get here from – from out there, people who were miserable and afraid, they find peace. Happiness."

"Bliss," Tamsyn said.

"Well, yes. That's what we call it, unofficially. The Bliss."

"Is everyone here a Bliss-head? Are you?"

Tamsyn tried to let her vision slip, to see the woman's aura, but she was still agitated from her near punch up with the Mayor of Freak Tower. She did not have the clarity of mind to make the mystic bullshit happen.

"Yes," Emma said. "Not as much as some, but I can feel it. Like taking a Xanax with a glass of wine."

Tamsyn felt the fight drain out of her. She wrestled the chair back into shape and slumped down into it.

"Believe it or not, this isn't the first time I've had this conversation," Emma said.

"I'm still concerned you've got a gas leak or something in here."

"The building is fine," Emma laughed. "Sure, it's weird here. Deal with it. Or don't. In a day or two you'll start feeling good."

"Yeah, well if it's so great here why did you send out the distress call?"

"That wasn't a distress call. That was us reaching out, looking for survivors."

"You – you didn't want to be rescued."

"No, Tamsyn," Emma said, reaching out and patting her hand. "We've got everything we need here. Room enough for people looking for safety. We wanted to rescue you."

∽

TAMSYN HUNG around for their council meeting, sitting in the "public gallery". Here they called it the Angel Square Subcommittee, and it was the weirdest meeting she'd ever sat through since the end of the world, including her time on the Privy Council.

No-one argued. There wasn't any politicking or squabbles between neighbours. It was like watching a group of moderately stoned conveyancers agree on almost everything that was on the agenda.

They talked about their supplies, and they were using tonnage as a measurement. *Tonnes* of food. The Activities Sub-Subcommittee were proposing a social rugby competition, and the coaches had already agreed on equal use of the football pitch. There and then they worked out a sports roster without a single disagreement.

That is strange. They should be bitching about sharing this area for HOURS.

Everything else on the agenda was saccharine sweet. The school was reporting exceptional grades from nearly all of the students. The pony was universally popular. There'd been one minor injury on the vegetable farm, and a builder had nailed his hand to a wall-frame, but everyone else was in perfect health, and the Sub-Subcommittee for Complaints had nothing to report.

"Onto our final point," the wounded builder said, hand still in bandages. Everyone had neatly lettered namebadges, and Tamsyn discovered that the resident idiot-with-a-nailgun was named Darren.

"Can we strike this from the standing agenda?" Emma said, feigning a groan. Everyone chuckled.

"I think it's time you promoted yourself, Deputy Mayor. You've been doing an amazing job, and this should be recognised."

"My answer is no, Darren. Same as it is every week. I cannot legally be recognised as the new Mayor of Manchester without a quorum from the standing Councillors. It wouldn't be legal."

"But they're all dead, Ma'am."

"I didn't make the rules. The Manchester Corporation did, back in 1838."

More polite laughter. Tamsyn rolled her eyes.

"Well, we just have another election. Vote in those Councillors."

"The Mayor didn't officially close off the last session of Council. Technically it is still in session. We cannot participate in the national election timetable until he dissolves the old Council."

"They were eaten by the living dead," Darren said. "Hey, I suppose they might still be able to lift up their hands and vote, right? If they're out there, walking around?"

More laughter.

"Sorry, the best I can do is run this place as a Special Subcommittee," Emma said. "It's just a name, right? I say we forget about the silly titles, and focus on looking after our people. Keeping them happy and healthy."

"Hey," Tamsyn heard someone whisper, a hand nervously patting at her arm. She looked to see a young person next to her, an androgynous teen with a fringe, baggy clothes and a baseball cap.

"You're Tamsyn." A statement. She nodded.

"I'm Elijah. We've spoken. Well, I spoke to you. Through the toy car."

"Hey, nice to meet you," she said, smiling. Elijah looked a little nervous, and this gave Tamsyn hope. *Finally. Someone who isn't part of the Happy Clappy Circus.*

She let her eyes unfocus, and fell back into the world of

head-ache inducing aura reading. Sure enough, Elijah was a confusion of colour. A bruised purple, a wiggling grey line, and a halo of fuzz around that. This was a troubled young teen, completely unaffected by the Bliss.

Looking up, Tamsyn took in the useless Subcommittee, and saw an almost uniform sea of deep green and blue. Pacified and docile, willing to agree to almost anything.

Then she looked towards Emma Menteuse, the Deputy Mayor of Manchester City Council, and to her shock she realised that the woman had no visible aura at all.

19

"We were here on a school trip," Elijah said as they huffed back up the stairs. "World's most ecologically sustainable building. The Deputy Mayor was here to cut the ribbon, all sorts of important people out the front. Some of the building's engineers, the architect, a whole crowd of folks."

Before Tamsyn could ask the awkward question, Elijah referred to *himself*, and that was good enough for her. Poor kid had enough to worry about these days without bigotry added to the mix.

"That was where I was on that day. You know, the last day."

On the day the world died, Tamsyn had been in the car with her Dad, driving back from her therapy session at Folkestone. She remembered clearly just how fast that madness spread. It seemed like a riot at first, people running, struggling, fighting tooth and nail, but it wasn't just in one spot, suddenly it was everywhere, and then her Dad was driving on the footpath, on the wrong side of the road, and then none of those rules seemed to matter anymore, not even the ones that said *"perhaps don't hit people with your car."*

Being on a school trip to a stupid ribbon cutting seemed about a thousand percent better than her own baptism of blood and guts. If she'd been brave enough to catch the bus on her own that day, she'd never have made it back to Gravesend.

"Do you go to the school here?"

Elijah shook his head.

"School is stupid. I prefer to figure things out for myself."

"My dad was a school teacher."

"Oh. Sorry."

"Don't be. He always admired autodidacts. At the end of the day, you're your own best teacher."

Elijah nodded, clearly struggling with a response. He led them through the workshop level, and Tamsyn cast a critical eye over the weapon racks. There were some crossbows here, but no bows. Stranger still, everything was under lock and key, even down to the knives and hatchets.

I'll have to lift some construction equipment, she thought to herself, thinking back to Emma, the freak without an aura. She was damned if she would trust this village of the damned, and desperately wanted a weapon of some sort as an insurance policy.

"I've got a studio back here," Elijah said. "Emma lets me make almost anything I want."

"What did she stop you from making?"

"Landmines," Elijah said. "She was worried about other survivors stepping on one. I'm kinda glad she said no."

He threw open a plastic curtain, and Tamsyn was looking upon tech-nerd paradise. A wall of CCTV screens, showing views of the city and of the interior of One Angel

Square. Benches covered in gizmos and gadgets, most of them disassembled or Frankenstein blends of items that didn't normally go together.

"Look," Elijah said, sliding into an office chair. He manipulated keyboard and mouse, and the CCTV screens above changed. These folks had fixed cameras on many tall buildings through Manchester, and nearly every square inch of the city was visible from Elijah's workstation.

"Did you want to blow up a Ferrari?" he asked shyly. He had another laptop open, and was scrawling through screens of gibberish that looked like something from the Matrix. On another screen he was zooming the camera in on a sports car, just one more abandoned vehicle in the city centre.

He pulled open a drawer, one filled with dozens of different car-key fobs. Tamsyn watched, fascinated as Elijah snapped open the plastic casing, plugging the fob into a tangle of wires and leads running back to the laptop.

Flashing a smile to Tamsyn, he pressed a button on the Ferrari fob. On the screen, the lights and indicators on the sports-car started flashing, and every zombie within a three-block radius was drawn towards it. No sound on the feed, but it was very obvious that this mad genius had set off a car alarm on an abandoned car halfway across the city.

"Now, hang on a minute," Tamsyn said. "That car is sitting on deflated tyres, and hasn't moved an inch since 2012. The battery has to be flat."

"No, the battery *was* flat," Elijah said. "That Ferrari is over a man-hole. There's twenty-two miles worth of cable running through the sewers, hooked up to a drip-feed solar charger on the roof of a Starbucks. There are forty-seven cars with working alarms throughout the city."

"Kid – you're an actual evil genius. I mean that in a good way."

They watched on the screen as hundreds of the undead converged around the Ferrari, pushing at it in their confusion. Tamsyn could see the device in the fuel tank, and watched as Elijah opened up a cheerful looking program called CAR BOMB MAYHEM! There were hundreds, *hundreds* of car bombs through Manchester, and this teenage kid had them all at his disposal.

"Just click on that icon there and the car will blow up," Elijah said proudly. Sorely tempted, Tamsyn reached for the mouse, but she withdrew her hand at the last moment.

"Don't set off the bomb. One day you might really need to use it."

"Are you kidding me? Just...just click on it. Please."

"You don't have to explode a fancy car to impress me."

Elijah looked genuinely distraught as he considered the explosive car on the screen.

"This is physically painful for me."

"If it's any consolation, you definitely don't need to go to school."

WHEN THE ANGEL SQUARE school broke for lunch, Elijah took Tamsyn to meet a few of his friends. They'd all been in fourth and fifth grade, and the ones who'd stuck with school were now in years 10 and 11.

"Not that they even have a proper high-school teacher here," he scoffed. "They've put together some ramshackle nonsense with our old teachers and whatever text books they could loot out there. Have old Mrs Sutton teach me physics? No thanks."

The school was tucked into the back of a residential level, a neat square of desks and chairs framed with hospital draw-curtains for privacy. Peeking past the emerging students, Tamsyn saw interactive touch-screens, laptops, every bell and whistle a teacher could ever ask for. When she remembered how hard her dad had to fight for paper and pens back in Gravesend, she felt a little angry.

You should have been here Dad, she thought. *It should be you teaching here, not this old battle-axe.*

Then she noticed the strangest thing. Straining her eyes into the world of auras, she saw that Mrs Sutton was grinning at nothing, dosed to the gills with an aquamarine halo of peace. Some of the students bouncing past to their hour of freedom gave off hues of deep green and blue, but Tamsyn spotted reds, yellows, even the same bruised colour that Elijah wore hugged to him like a shawl.

Nearly half of these kids were unaffected by the Bliss.

"Hey Quinn!" Elijah called out. A young woman with a bob haircut came running, and gave Elijah a big bearhug.

"This is Tamsyn, one of the new arrivals," Elijah said, and Quinn immediately attacked her with another fierce bearhug. Expecting more Bliss, Tamsyn gave the girl a quick scan, only to find Elijah's friend was surrounded by a rainbow, wriggling and pointed like an optical migraine.

"Were you the ones from the submarine?" Quinn said. "I was the one that spoke to you on the radio! How many of you got through?"

"Three of us," Tamsyn said drily. "Few dozen more of Her Majesty's Navy waiting at the other end of the river. Both the submarines went down in a suicide pact, and our rescue party got chewed apart getting here. I can honestly say that everything following that radio transmission has been an absolute shit-show."

Quinn snorted with laughter at the gallows humour, and Tamsyn found herself grinning back.

"May I be the first to welcome you to Manchester," Quinn said. "We have one tower full of happy idiots, a few million monsters outside, and all the pony rides you can stomach."

Tamsyn followed Elijah and his friends out to the balcony cafeteria for lunch. Over a tray of warm slop she met Sara, a heavily bespectacled girl who was driving the group crazy with a harmonica she'd found somewhere, mangling *When the Saints Go Marching In*. Louis was a young man full of dry wisecracks, and he spent most of lunch needling his mate Seb over a group assignment they'd screwed up.

"So this twit had one job. Translate an Elvis song into Latin, for Ancient Rome day. He picks 'Hound Dog'. He ended up talking about hot bitches and chlamydia."

"At least I didn't call Mrs Sutton a prostitute."

"It was an accident. Elijah's computer translator thingy gave me the wrong word."

"Wait. How do you know about his secret Latin translator?"

Elijah sat there, grinning at his friends like a Cheshire cat. When the penny dropped, they bombarded him with bread and swear words.

"I was trying to teach you a lesson!" he said, holding up his hands in mock defence. "There are no short cuts to an education. Crack open a book for God's sake."

"That was a dick move *par excellence*," Quinn said, fist-bumping Elijah.

Tamsyn thought back to her own school days, the endless banter, the days of no responsibility and boredom.

Then, the days of zombies against the wall, and boredom mixed with terror, and being the teacher's daughter.

God, these kids have it so good here!

"Look, I need to know something," she blurted out, and the teens stopped flicking food at each other, looking at her as if she was a unicorn.

"It's just, none of you have the Bliss. This whole place is full of happy-clappy whackos, and then there's the Scooby Gang here, yucking it up. Normal. Disgustingly normal."

"How do you know who has the Bliss?" Louis said, raising an eyebrow.

"I'm good at reading people," Tamsyn admitted reluctantly.

"Sure thing, Yoda," Louis laughed, but there was a bitter edge to the laugh. Tamsyn could see a tinge of thick yellow around him, almost a bile colour. *This kid is fighting to keep his shit together,* she realised.

"Things are really bad out there," Tamsyn said. "And I'm happy that people have found some sort of happiness in this fucked up world. But it's weirding me the hell out. I need some answers about the Bliss."

"None of us know anything," Sara said. "The Bliss is just a thing that happens here. All the adults have it. Some of the kids."

"We're the freaks," Seb said. "The only ones left with proper feelings. We argue with each other, cry, and have a proper laugh."

"Not that washed up fake happiness these poor sods have," Louis said.

"I mean, who doesn't like a good cry?" Quinn said.

Sara let out a mangled rendition of *Rudolph the Red-Nosed Reindeer* on her harmonica, and the table groaned.

"You'll make me cry if you play that again," Elijah said.

"You are just jealous," Sara said.

"We might still get the Bliss," Louis said glumly. "When we're adults."

Tamsyn looked at the crew, and even though she was a twenty-something hanging out with teenagers, she felt a sense of belonging, that she was among kindred spirits. These kids were normal mixed-up rowdy teenagers, who were instantly accepting of the paranoid outsider sitting in their midst.

"Did you know that I'm close personal friends with Prince Harry?" she shared conspiratorially. "And that he's still alive?"

"You're shitting me!" Quinn shouted gleefully. They all crowded around her with a thousand questions, and laughing, Tamsyn did her best to answer them all.

"THIS IS THE RADIO ROOM," Quinn said, proudly ushering Tamsyn through the very top level of One Angel Square. It was an elaborate set up, with every kind of communication device known to man. Fat black cables wriggled skywards, and Tamsyn craned her neck to see a bristle of antennae through the glass canopy, scratching at the clear blue sky.

"It can get pretty boring these days. Not many people out there to answer," Quinn said. "I nearly shat my pants when your submarine got on the radio. First positive contact in months."

"What other settlements are up in the north?" Tamsyn asked.

"Nothing now. We rescued some of the folks from Luton when the zombies overran their barricades, but that was months ago. It's just dead air and endless coffee up here most days."

The operators on shift were speaking listlessly into the microphones, while others were working with computers that appeared to be attached to a military mainframe. An old man was watching a bank of monitors, all of which were feeding back patchy satellite footage. Tamsyn was sure that if it proved worthwhile, Emma Menteuse would send someone up on the roof with a pair of semaphore flags, or perhaps a smoke signal.

She really wants to get people here, she mused. Remembering the xenophobic approach that places like Sheppey had taken to other survivors, she knew that this was a good thing the Deputy Mayor was doing. On paper she was great. But deep in her gut, she knew something sinister was going on here. She wanted to drag Sushma and Reynolds and these kids out of One Angel Square by the ears, and then run like hell.

"This is a lot of gear, must draw down a stack of power," Tamsyn said. "Do you have to ration your use of all this stuff?"

"No way," Quinn said. "It's all on 24/7. Proper rescue centre, this place."

"Weird that the elevators are off then."

"Ah, that's just to save power," Quinn said. "Better for us anyway, walking up and down the stairs. Did you know that exercise releases endorphins? It makes you feel good."

Even as Quinn rattled along with her own external monologue, Tamsyn saw one of the radio operators get up to stretch her back. The woman was perhaps six months pregnant, and from bitter experience Tamsyn knew the baby in her would be pressing on her bladder and most of her internal organs.

"I hope the toilets aren't too far from here," Tamsyn joked, and the pregnant woman offered up a pained smile. For one awful moment Tamsyn remembered her Millie, that poor starving baby stuck on a stranded boat, and how mad they thought the Gundersons were for trying for a baby.

Malcolm crept into her thoughts then, and she thought her heart was straight up going to burst into her chest. *I am the worst mother on the face of the earth!*

"They never finished building the loos on this floor" the woman said. "We've asked the Subcommittee to fix them up, but it's alright. They've given us a bucket and a curtain, right ladies!"

This was met with a chorus of groans from two other women up in the control panel. One of them wheeled to flip her friend the finger, and Tamsyn saw that this other woman was also heavily pregnant.

"Hardly seems fair they make the pregnant women go all the way up the stairs," Tamsyn offered.

"What? And leave the best job in the place to some man? It's a plum gig, this!"

"The secret is to take your time with the stairs. Rest a minute or so and then keep going."

"The sooner they ban pregnant women from here, the better," the old man by the CCTVs grumbled good-naturedly. "The farts these heifers give off are bloody criminal."

"Ooh, shut up Alan!"

"How would you like some little bastard pushing on your guts from the inside?"

"No-one made you open your legs, Yvette."

The jovial insults flew back and forth, while Tamsyn quickly scanned for auras. Green, blue, aquamarine, and even the bellies of the two pregnant women gave off their own mini-auras, the life within the deepest of green. That alone made her skin crawl – whatever was going on in this strange place was affecting the innocent lives growing inside the womb.

Not cool, freaky tower.

"So I do a shift on the radios, I work in the kitchen and I help with the pony rides," Quinn rattled off. "I'm a line umpire for the kid's football league, and I manage the wardrobe for the Theatrical Society. Grease was fun, but the Subcommittee wants us to do Cats next. Which idiot volunteered to glue fur onto dozens of leotards?"

"Um, you?"

"You betcha!"

Tamsyn had been a high-achiever in school, with her art and then competitive archery, and she'd been surrounded by Quinn-types – people cramming as much as possible into their days, every volunteer role and extracurricular activity that was going begging. She'd seen some do this for the love of helping others, and just as many as a coping mechanism against their own demons. Tamsyn wasn't quite sure where on the fence this cheerful whirlwind sat.

"What other jobs are there to do here?" Tamsyn asked. She was feigning interest in the employment market, when really it was the ideal cover to sneak around One Angel Square. She was looking for hiding places, weapons, the typical movements of the people who lived here.

"Well, there's farming, cleaning, all the boring stuff. If you've got any free time, you'll end up with a shovel or a broom in your hands. Even if you've got homework due."

"Ah, good. I thought you might be one of those people who enjoys having a schedule a little bit too much."

"Bitch, I rock my schedule. Plus I don't want to be knee-deep in shit, planting cabbages."

Quinn led Tamsyn back through the farming levels, and Tamsyn was disappointed to see that the farming implements were treated just like the weapons – itemised and kept under lock and key.

Volunteer to farm and get a pitchfork? she pondered. She'd already asked to join the patrols and scavenger groups, hoping to get her hands on a gun or even a knife, but an actual policeman muttered something about "probation" and "a full roster already".

Those who'd pointed him out only referred to him as the Constable, and if he had a name he didn't offer it. He still wore his uniform from the old world, complete with bobby helmet, equipment belt and radio. The Constable wore a radio handset clipped underneath his epaulette, and it squawked occasionally, the radio room calling in zombie movements from near the building. Tamsyn noted the pistol on his belt, an unusual sight in a disarmed police force.

Worst of all, the man had no visible aura whatsoever. Tamsyn didn't know what that meant, and didn't care to hang around to find out. The man had a dead-eyed lizard stare that she supposed went with his role, that base-level suspicion she'd seen in every cop--military or civilian.

"So what are you good at?" Quinn asked, snapping Tamsyn out of her reverie. Tamsyn thought for a moment, discounting her supernatural skills.

"I'm good at art," she said. "Got a scholarship the week before the world went to shit. Pretty good archer too. Um, I can drink most blokes under the table? That – that's about it."

"Maybe you could teach some of us to draw?" Quinn asked hopefully. "That would be a fun change from Mrs Sutton and Ancient Latin?"

"Yeah, maybe we could do that," Tamsyn said weakly. It

was the last thing she felt like doing. Quinn frowned a little at this, the first sign she wasn't eternally cheerful.

"Look, maybe just a few of you," Tamsyn offered. "I don't want to babysit fifty hormone monsters."

"Yes! I bet I can paint like a pro. Will we sketch any naked people?"

"No! That's not going to happen!"

"Prude."

As they passed back into the residential levels, Tamsyn finally noticed many more pregnant bellies were on display. She supposed she'd been too shocked by this place to register it at first, but after her trip to the radio room, she kept spotting big bellies, their cargo growing in serenity, in the green aura of the Bliss.

There'd been pregnant women in other places she'd been. Corpus Christi. Cuba. Even the Caymans had a healthy growing population. But as she did a quick stock-take, trying not to stare, she realised that fully half of the women of child-bearing age were visibly pregnant.

What is the Bliss doing to these people? she thought. *They're getting fat and docile here, and now they're breeding like rabbits.*

"I gotta get back to class," Quinn said. "See ya later, masturbator."

"I'm not even going to dignify that," Tamsyn said drily, and tried not to laugh as the zany youngster skipped back to the classroom. Suddenly at a loss, Tamsyn put her hands in her pockets, considering the bustle all around her.

The skin crawled on the back of her neck, and she turned just in time to see Tilly staring at her from behind a stack of lumber. Frowning, Tamsyn took one step towards the strange young girl, only to see her bolt away through the tents and ramshackle structures like a terrified rabbit.

"Wait!" Tamsyn called out, but the girl had already

vanished. Remembering her white aura and her construction of a Vanguard building in Lego, Tamsyn decided she very much wanted to talk to her tiny stalker.

"Are you avoiding us?" Sushma asked. Sushma, Reynolds and Tamsyn were at the bar out on the balcony, sipping cocktails by the light of the tiki torches. Tamsyn wore her new anorak, gifted to her by a woman too pregnant to fit into it anymore. Even then she shivered in the chill of the spring evening, the ice cubes rattling in her glass.

God, I miss the Caribbean.

"Yep, she's definitely avoiding us. I've seen her chumming around with bloody high-school kids. It's a bit unsavoury, Tamsyn."

"Look, I'm just weirded about by your Kumbaya bullshit," Tamsyn said. "I'm here now, aren't I?"

"You need to relax more," Sushma said, working her way through a huge margarita. "Sleep with Reynolds here, or a pretty girl if you want to."

"Give it a bloody rest," Tamsyn said, knocking back her drink. She called for another, and a grinning waiter hustled over with another rum and lime juice. She missed Coke more than ever at that point, but every bottle left on the face of the earth had gone flat and stale.

She thought about Malcolm again, and tipped that drink back in one long swallow, signalling for yet another. That familiar darkness was pressing in on her thoughts, and she decided that tonight was worthy of a grand hangover.

"Did you still want to go?" Reynolds asked. "Go back through all that mess outside to get the others?"

"She will never make it," Sushma said. "Dead within one hour."

"I'm not bringing *anyone* back here," Tamsyn said. "This place is creepy and wrong."

"Only you could go to a place where everyone is happy and the booze is free, and still find something to complain about," Reynolds said.

"Something about this building has infected your minds," Tamsyn said. "With everything you've seen since we left the island, how can you sit back and accept this?"

"Being happy is good?" Sushma said.

"That is the logic of a drug addict," Tamsyn said.

"That's good coming from you, you bloody lush," Reynolds said suddenly. "I've seen people eye off their drinks like you before. If there's still an AA left in the world, you belong there."

Tamsyn wanted to give him hell for his pointed remark, but these were the first sarcastic words he'd said in a while. Drawing back into the world of auras, she noticed that his deep green had given way to a jangled twist of red and black, just for a moment, but then normal Bliss service had resumed. He sipped at his drink with a relaxed smile and an invisible blanket of green around his very being.

Interesting, she thought. *Perhaps the Bliss isn't as strong as everyone thinks.*

Time for a little science experiment.

'Perhaps I belong in AA," Tamsyn said. "You on the other hand belong in a zoo, you fucking animal."

She tossed what was left of her drink in Reynold's face, and then he came across the table at her, face twisted into an angry snarl, all of that false green and blue falling away as he fell into redness and primal rage.

A definite overreaction, even from this pompous dickhead. Tamsyn fought for her very life, using her rudimentary hand combat skills from Basic to try and fend off a Special Forces Trooper. He landed a fist to her gut, and swept her legs from underneath her, pouncing on top of her. Hands around her throat, choking the life from her.

Then Sushma arrived, all chokeholds and applied strength, and she flipped Reynolds onto his back, pressing her forearm into his throat. She had the same rage in her too, but she fought it back, looking down with Reynolds with the same puzzlement that he returned from his own eyes.

"Do you still think this place is alright?" Tamsyn said, coughing her lungs out. Then the Constable arrived at the bar with a posse in tow, and gentle but insistent hands were placing the three of them in handcuffs.

TAMSYN WATCHED as the Constable fetched out a large set of keys, unlocking the elevators. Crowded into with her friends and the impromptu security force, the car rumbled into life, descending into the bowels of One Angel Square.

"Guess the elevator works fine if you're a bloody pig," she slurred.

"Be quiet," the Constable said. Tamsyn was having trouble reading auras, but she could still get the wash of green from the other tower dwellers, and a confused muddy brown from Sushma and Reynolds. This Constable was just like a blank space in the universe, empty somehow. Tamsyn twisted at the handcuffs behind her back, hoping to slip an arm loose, but it was no good.

Tamsyn realised it had been years since she'd ridden a working elevator. What they had here was a miracle of the post-zombie age, and for some reason the management of One Angel Square were keeping it under lock and key.

Saving power my arse, she thought.

After a long moment spent shuddering into the earth, the doors opened onto the old carpark of the building, now given over to a series of wire cages fastened into the cement. The cages were full of people, sitting glumly on the floor, or wrapped up in blankets, do their best to kip on the cold cement.

Looking at auras was starting to give her a headache, but she could see enough to know that she was in a room full of ordinary, non-Blissed people. They were scared and angry, and there wasn't a green or blue aura in sight.

"In," the Constable barked, removing their handcuffs and herding the three of them into a cage. He locked the door with an enormous padlock, the sort a hacksaw had no hope of defeating.

Two scratchy blankets, a bucket for the toilet, and the deep gloom of a carpark that never saw use. Construction lights were set up near the elevator doors, but this far back in the prison it was near to pitch black.

Tamsyn had done a night or two in pokey during the war in Texas, mostly for fighting and drinking, but even she was nervous. What was this place full of normal people? Were they ever going to get out of here, or shiver in the dark for the rest of their lives?

Her musing was interrupting by the sounds of Reynolds straining over the bucket, moving out his last meal with a series of heavy grunts.

"Oh my god Reynolds! We've only been in here for thirty seconds!"

"I've been holding this in for hours."

"Oh sweet baby Jesus, just kill me now!"

They spent hours in that endless night, and Tamsyn dozed when it was her turn for a blanket, trying to time-travel to either her release, her death, even insanity. Tamsyn heard the distant murmur of an argument, and even then the prisoners traded their sharp words quietly, hoping not to attract attention. Elsewhere, a man was crying, long loud howls that echoed and bounced around between the cement floor and roof.

It might have been a day or more. Tamsyn had dozed off twice when the elevator doors opened, admitting a handful of figures. Staring towards the bank of lighting, she couldn't make out much at first, but soon she saw the Constable, walking just behind the Deputy Mayor.

Emma Menteuse had her hand on Tilly's shoulder, herding the girl forward, into the rows of cages.

"You bloody animals!" Tamsyn shouted. "You let her go!"

"This way," she heard Emma say cheerfully to the girl. "Come along, my pet. We're almost there."

Some of the prisoners jeered then, shouting insults at the Deputy Mayor, while others broke down into tears, absolutely terrified. With the cacophony echoing all around them, Tamsyn shook the mesh then, looking for a weak point, trying to untwist a tangle of wire with her bare fingers.

There was no point. Whoever had built this cage had known what they were doing. The loose twists of wire were taut, clipped close with a set of pliers. Without tools there was simply no escape.

The trio passed by Tamsyn's cell, and Emma smiled gracefully when Tamsyn shook the wire mesh and snarled. Placing Tilly on an arbitrary patch of floor as if she was on the exact correct spot, the Deputy Mayor and the Constable stepped back, expectant and waiting for something.

"Go on, my dear. Begin."

Tilly looked up then, meeting Tamsyn's gaze, and the girl seemed deeply sad. Tamsyn had only a moment to perceive Tilly's aura go from white, to white-hot, to the centre of a sun going super-nova, and then she knew a darkness more complete than any prison could ever give.

20

She awoke in her cot, and for one long moment she relished in the warmth, the coziness, the feeling that everything was right in the world.

Then she remembered. The cells in the secret prison. Emma and her goon, and then Tilly. What Tilly did. She sat bolt-upright in her bed, and felt the Bliss fall away from her as panic set in.

Tilly was sitting at the foot of her cot, terror all over her face. She held a finger up to her lips, insistent. Tamsyn slowly swept her blanket aside, noticing that she was dressed in a new set of pyjamas she didn't remember receiving, let alone ever wearing.

The girl still had a white aura around her, but it was subdued now, a cheerful outline rather than the supernova she'd seen in the carpark prison. Looking at her own arm, Tamsyn focused hard until she could see her own aura, a muddy brown thing riddled with black and red wavy lines. The effort left her feeling drained and staggered, like crossing your eyes when you have a migraine, and she blinked through the sudden pain, willing it back into the background.

A new set of clothes was neatly laundered and folded on the bedside table. Her rotten old Docs were gone now, replaced by a neat set of tennis shoes in her size. Nodding to the girl, Tamsyn slid out of bed, and quickly got dressed. Tilly got up to give her some privacy, and leaned outside of the canvas cubicle, keeping a watch for anyone approaching.

With the haste of a paranoid survivor, Tamsyn was fully dressed and ready in thirty seconds. Force of habit made her look for a weapon, any weapon, but there wasn't even a lamp on the bedside table. Then she realised she knew two living weapons, trained killers who could take down any guards with their bare hands.

Pushing past Tilly, she swept open the canvas sheet passing for Reynolds' door, and recoiled in shock. There in his bed, cuddled and dopey, were Reynolds and Sushma, all naked shoulders peering out from the sheets, giggling and green auras.

"Do you want to join us?" Reynolds drawled.

"What are you idiots doing?" Tamsyn whispered harshly.

"We are having it off," Sushma said goofily.

"Your husband is barely dead! And – and him? You hate him!"

"It's okay, Tamsyn," Sushma said. "It feels good. This is okay."

Tilly tapped on her arm, and Tamsyn let the canvas flap fall back into place. She didn't want the poor kid to see that particular bad decision. Tamsyn followed the girl through the shanty-town, past the building sites. A Pilates class full of pregnant women, and it didn't take much effort to imagine Sushma joining in, belly growing with Reynolds' baby.

Remembering those few moments the Bliss had her in its grip, Tamsyn didn't need much more imagination to see herself pregnant next to Sushma, cooking up her own kid for whatever horror the Deputy Mayor had planned. Tilly still wasn't saying anything, so Tamsyn swept along in her wake, doing her best to paint an *everything-is-normal* smile on her face whenever anyone waved or said hello.

Over by the café, a woman was going into labour, but she was serene, beaming through her contractions. Smiling men with stretchers were approaching to rapt applause from onlookers.

This isn't a sanctuary. It's a fucking hatchery! Tamsyn thought.

Tilly led her past the bathrooms, to a rear staircase. The old fire exits. They climbed up three flights of stairs before Tilly cracked open the next door, this one held open with a wedge. Immediately Tamsyn was struck by the stink of the piggery, and heard the sound of the workers joking in the distance.

Another tug on the arm. Tilly was beckoning her towards a stack of feed drums, still packed onto a pallet. Food for the livestock, but how on earth did these people scavenge this, let alone without a truck and a forklift?

More supplies here, lifted directly from a fodder store. Bales of hay and lucerne for the pony. Dog and cat food for the pets she'd seen strutting around like little Egyptian gods. Poison bait laid out for the inevitable pests. This was an impressive operation, and something that few of the communities Tamsyn had seen could manage, let alone one trapped in the middle of a huge zombie horde.

Tilly was struggling to shift aside some hay bales, and

Tamsyn helped her drag them away to reveal a hole in the stack. Wriggling after the girl through the scratchy hay, Tamsyn soon discovered an ingenious hiding spot, crafted by extracting hay bales to form a tunnel. In the very centre was an empty space, surrounded by towering pallets of fodder and supplies.

The girl had made this tiny gap into her own hiding place. Tamsyn saw a little tangle of blankets, opened packets of food, and a handful of stuffed toys. Pinned to the side of a barrel was a collage of magazine cutouts and newspaper clippings, all featuring one face from the old world. Tamsyn recognised Nicky Cross, England's answer to John Edward. A celebrity medium from Sussex, Nicky Cross had her own TV show, where she duped grieving audience members with messages from those beyond the grave. They would weep with gratitude as Nicky gave generic platitudes from their dearly departed.

Tamsyn remembered watching the show with her mum and dad, just as sceptical as Malcolm Webb had been when it came to the supernatural.

"They've got microphones hidden in the foyer and the bathrooms," Mal said. *"Plants in the audience. It's the oldest scam in showbiz, and these idiots are falling for it."*

"God knows I wouldn't want to speak to anyone if I was dead," Jenny Webb said.

Swallowing down the aching heart that came with the sudden memory, Tamsyn took a closure look at the cuttings. The nose, the eyes – she looked up to Tilly watching her, and the resemblance was there.

"Nicky Cross was your mum," Tamsyn said, and the girl nodded.

"Did she make it to this place?"

Tilly nodded.

"What happened to her?"

Tilly frowned, shook her head in sharp little jerks.

"This would go a lot easier if you would just talk to me, you know."

The girl slumped down on her rat's nest of blankets, clutching her knees to her chest. She rocked back and forwards a little, as if seeking comfort, jaw clenched tight, eyes unfocussed as she drew inward. In that moment, the penny dropped, and Tamsyn Webb felt like the world's biggest arsehole.

"Oh, you poor thing. You've got autism, selective mutism, something like that. Could you talk before?"

Tilly lifted out one hand, finger and thumb spread slightly. *A little.*

"And when your mum, er, left," and here, Tamsyn put a hand across her own mouth. Tilly nodded. Tamsyn scooched into the tiny hiding space, settling down next to the girl on her makeshift bed.

"Don't blame you for clamming up, love. I lost my mum, back before the rotters were walking. I didn't talk to anyone after that, for months and months."

The estate wagon, sliding around the corner. That awful moment that she saw Simon Dawes plough into the bus shelter, killing her mother and all those other people. How helpless she felt! A girl holding a stupid magazine, her mother's angry words still rattling around in her ears, and no chance to ever make things right.

Blood, pooling around the wheels of a drunkard's car, and the awful screams of her mother, going on and on...

Tamsyn felt a small hand rest on her forearm, and then her world pulsed with white, healing her broken heart, washing away that old grief. She looked at the girl with amazement.

"You have a very special gift," Tamsyn said, and paused. "Do you make the Bliss?"

Tilly shook her head.

"But you can nudge people back into that green place, right? And the Deputy Mayor makes you?"

Tilly nodded, a single tear running down her nose. She sniffled and made to retreat back into her foetal position. Tamsyn patted her gently on the shoulder.

"Hey, it's not your fault. You're only doing what the grownups are asking you to do."

That evil bitch, pushing this child to become a monster!

"Did you get your special gift from your mother?"

Tilly nodded, smiling up at the pictures.

"I knew she was the real deal. I wish I could tell my father that he was wrong. Can't blame the lady for making a living from it."

Tamsyn paused, gathering her courage.

"I have a gift too. A link to the dead. I'm still learning how to use it, but it's real, and it's very scary."

Tilly nodded, sympathy in her eyes. Digging around in a plastic shopping bag, the girl brushed her fingers through a fat stack of Lego bricks, the sound instantly recognisable. She fetched out several little models of the Vanguard structure, built laboriously. It was close to what Tamsyn had seen on the Isle of Sheppey, that weird alien hand, stretching up into the heavens...

Next, the girl was digging through a little pile of books and toys, finally extracting a huge atlas. "Property of One Angel Square Community Library!" a sticker read across the top of the cover.

"Sure hope they don't charge late fees," Tamsyn joked, but Tilly ignored her, flipping through the pages. Map after map of the old world, realised in cheerful green and blue, those nations and borders nothing but ink ideas now, wiped away by a few short years of an undead cannibal plague.

Turning to a map of the United Kingdom, Tilly placed one of the models down on the Isle of Sheppey, and Tamsyn felt her blood freeze. There was no possible way this girl could know of the Vanguard site. Looking to make sure Tamsyn understood, Tilly flicked through the other pages, placing down Vanguard models all over the world. Hong Kong. Los Angeles, New York, Rio De Janeiro, Sydney, Cape Town, Paris, Berlin, Tokyo. Even one in Havana, which gave Tamsyn a mixture of elation and guilt.

Sucked in, you murdering Communist motherfuckers.

The Vanguard was all over the world now, building eye-twisting shrines to who knew what. The Black Crown Boy?

Tilly finally flipped the pages back until they were both looking at the United Kingdom. She placed a model back on the Isle of Sheppey. Then she placed one in Leeds, and made a point of crushing that model in her little fist, until it was broken into many tiny pieces.

"They lost one? It broke? Someone broke it?" and Tilly nodded, pointing to the pictures on the wall.

"Your Mum went against the Vanguard?"

Enthusiastic nodding. Pride in her eyes.

"The balls on that woman!"

Next, she placed a Vanguard Lego model very carefully on the map, and it sat exactly on Manchester. Tamsyn felt her heart freeze in her chest.

"Listen to me Tilly. This is very important. I need to know where this – this structure is. Can you point a direction out to me? Is it near this building?"

Meeting Tamsyn's eyes, Tilly reached down, pointing to the floor, more pointing. Way, way down. Below.

"The Vanguard are in the bloody building? Underneath us?"

Rapid nodding. Tamsyn saw relief in the girl's face when Tamsyn understood her, but after a moment this gave way to a look of absolute terror, and then the girl returned to clutching her knees, rocking, and nothing Tamsyn said or did could bring the girl out of her protective cocoon.

FORAGE, Food and Fuel. The Three Fs, as drummed into her in Basic. Back in the war, this had meant keeping an army supplied and on the move, but the lesson was just as valuable here. She would need to cache enough supplies for her mission and her escape. She would need to locate weapons, and fast. And last of all, she was going to need a *lot* of fuel.

Knowing that even a cheery old quack like Tilly's mum could take on and destroy the Vanguard gave her all the more motivation to get this done.

Tamsyn almost felt relieved to know that she was at war with an enemy, one that was keeping her and everyone in One Angel Square in a gilded cage. With her paranoia confirmed, she could go about the business of surviving, just the same as she always had.

Thank God I left Malcolm back at the coast, Tamsyn thought. *That's the first solid parenting decision I've ever made.*

Reynolds and Sushma were as good as useless, and when they weren't all over each other they were right into the Tai-chi, book club and whatever else was going. Her allies in this place were few, and they were all kids, but that was what she had to work with.

Taking a leaf out of Tilly's book, Tamsyn searched for her own hiding place. It had to be close to the food stores, and near to an escape route. The only way in and out of the building appeared to be the window-washing scaffolds, up on the roof. This was near the servery, the kitchens, and several half-built offices that were now an enormous larder. Volunteering for a shift in the kitchens, she did her best to smile into every vacant pair of eyes, dishing out slop while she scoped out the busiest area in the building.

"Cup of tea, ladies?" she said to the radio operators, greeted by a chorus of eager women when she entered the operations centre with a tray of afternoon tea. While she chatted amiably, she discretely scoped out the patchwork construction.

"So, no Alan today?" she asked.

"Alan doesn't work here anymore."

"He got caught peeking through the toilet curtain at Yvette," one woman said. "Dirty old bastard. He gets to dig cabbages now."

"Yeah, they won't let him up here again," another laughed.

"So do you get to use both the men's and women's loo now?" Tamsyn asked.

"Ha! Not bloody likely. They've only given us one bucket, and that's that."

After some more forced banter, Tamsyn pretended to need the toilet herself. Sure enough, the penthouse offices were barely enclosed from the elements, and the toilets and kitchen were yet to be plumbed in. It was only one or two flights of stairs down to a working toilet, but of course that wasn't feasible for a pregnant woman.

Recoiling from the stink of the shared bucket, Tamsyn continued down the corridor to what should have been the men's toilet. The internal walls weren't even finished here, and she navigated through a maze of open framework, past plastic sheeting and stacks of drywall and lumber.

Considering the busy radio room down the hallway, she wondered how she could get in and out of the place. The further away she went from the centre of the building, the less finished things were, until there was an area roped off with caution signs, where there wasn't even a floor in place.

Fetching an aluminium ladder, she did her best to silently slide it over the edge, until it reached the floor below. The room below looked just as abandoned and half-finished as where she was, which promised privacy.

She quietly moved some drywall around, leaning it against the frames as if it had been abandoned that way by the builders. When she was finished, she'd enclosed an area that wasn't visible to a casual passers-by.

Doing her best to wipe off the plaster dust and muck from her apron, Tamsyn wandered past the radio operators with a smile.

"You were in there for a while," one of them said. "Hope you cracked open a window."

"Get some more fibre into your diet," the other said, and the room broke into good natured laughter. Tamsyn forced a smile, even as all that vibrant, fertile green pulsing around these women's souls made her skin crawl.

After her shift finished, she poked around the rear of the kitchen level, eventually finding a service door to the unfinished part of that level. It would take her two ladder climbs and some zig-zagging between the floors, but she had a secret route from the food stores to her hiding spot, directly bypassing the shift workers.

When she went back down to the kitchen level to start stealing some supplies, she marvelled at the vast array of food they'd stored. Again, there was food stacked on pallets, still in the shrink wrap, all of it non-perishable. Some of the loading labels indicated these had been looted from a Tesco's on the other side of Manchester City, a feat that was probably impossible without a truck and a forklift. A further impossibility was the fact that each pallet held about 2 tonnes worth of food. The motorised window-cleaning scaffold couldn't possibly hope to lift that much from the ground all the way up to the roof.

Also, each of these store rooms held many pallets, all marked with Tesco loading labels. Whoever had moved these here had looted the entire warehouse. In a city full of millions of the undead.

All of this stuff could only have arrived via the elevator.

Holy crap. There's another entrance into One Angel Square.

21

"The best way to learn art is just to do it," Tamsyn told the class. "You're gonna suck. So just keep drawing until you stop sucking."

"Great motivation, Miss Webb," Quinn heckled from behind her easel. Tamsyn flipped her the bird.

"Stop being a smart-arse and sketch the bloody bowl of fruit."

She paced around the group of students, eyeing their progress as they attempted the life-drawing. Some of the kids were Blissed-out, and they happily scratched away at their pads, putting a token effort into the drawing. They just didn't care enough to put in anything beyond the minimum effort, which spoke volumes to Tamsyn about what the Bliss was doing to their minds and souls.

Then there were the others. Louis, Sara, Seb, and Quinn were coming at the assignment seriously. Even Elijah was sitting in on today's class, drawing the fruit as a set of surreal machinery, complete with seams and rivets. Louis was drawing them as a sinister, foreboding structure, while Quinn was going for a bubble-gum cheerful cartoon style.

"You evil geniuses," she chuckled. When the art lesson was finished, Tamsyn handed the class back to Mrs Sutton, who smelled of gin and looked like a rough nap that had ended too soon. Tamsyn's little gang of Bliss-avoiding weirdos looked sad to see her go, and in that moment she didn't mind being dragooned into a teaching gig all that much.

Tamsyn had a little time left before her shift at the cabbage farm, enough time to pilfer some more supplies. Slipping into the kitchens, she took an apron from a peg, and made her way back to the store-rooms. There was a pallet of drinking chocolate she had her eye on, as well as a crate of Operational Ration Packs still stamped up with British Army labels. Portable, highly nutritious and easy to hide.

Just as she was reaching for the box-cutter hidden in her apron pocket, she heard the first footfall, and then the hand fell on her shoulder, fingers gripping a little too hard. Her first instinct was to fight back, dirty and hard, but then she realised that people pretending to be happy and Blissful didn't do that sort of thing.

Keeping as calm as she could, Tamsyn looked over her shoulder and smiled pleasantly at the creepy face of One Angel Square law.

"Good afternoon, Constable," she chirped pleasantly. "Is everything okay?"

"We've had thieves in here," the man said bluntly. "Hoarders."

"Oh. That's terrible."

"What are you doing in here? You're slated for farm-work in half an hour."

"Sushma couldn't come to work today for – uh – personal reasons. Thought I'd take her pick list and round up the ingredients for today's pasta bake. Everyone loves pasta bake Wednesday!" she said, forcing a jovial small-talk laugh.

The fingers slowly withdrew from her collar-bone. The man really had the most nondescript face, and she struggled to pull in any one memorable detail, her eyes sliding past his clean-shaven chin, blank eyes, and neatly parted brown hair. It was almost as if a computer spat out a picture of the most average looking human being.

No aura. Nothing at all, nothing she could read with her strange new senses. It was as if the man in front of her wasn't even real, even though her eyes told her that there was a petty functionary staring at her.

"If you see anyone back here who doesn't belong, you come and find me right away," the Constable said. "They're stealing the food from children's mouths."

Tamsyn nodded.

"Hurry this up. You're needed elsewhere."

"Right away, Constable."

TAMSYN MOANED with pleasure as the hot water sluiced all the dirt and muck from her body. Farm work was back breaking work, and she was covered in filth. To her dismay she'd recently learnt that most of the fertiliser was coming from human volunteers, who far outnumbered the animals in the building.

They even called them Hero Buckets, brown plastic pails that could be found on every floor. No doubt Reynold's present in the jail cell was turned into the dirt, helping the carrots and cabbages grow.

These idiots are going to end up with hepatitis, Tamsyn

thought, scrubbing deeply with the shared bar of soap. Just outside the door was the next woman in line, pregnant and holding a stopwatch and whistle.

Two minutes of watery heaven. Probably a minute thirty next week. The week after that, they might be down to baby wipes and nose pegs.

Rumour had it that the big water tanks underneath the building were starting to feel the pinch from the hundreds of residents. Last night an engineer had hit on Tamsyn at the bar, oblivious to the fact that Tamsyn was pumping him for information and nothing more.

Smiling and flirting, she learnt about the water tanks under the building, complete with filtration plant, collecting and treating anything up to 5 gigalitres of rainwater, as well as the greywater from the showers and toilets. Designed for a futuristic office building with toilets and kitchens, this was now cleaning and drinking water for 300 or so people, as well as irrigation for the farm levels.

Brushing her hand against his, she then learnt about the power plant, hundreds of solar panels, roof-mounted wind turbines, a bank of high-end batteries, and now a rudimentary methane generator making electricity out of pig-shit.

"We won awards for this building," the engineer slurred. "Completely self-sustainable. Bloody big louver windows for summer, off-grid water and power. It's the only place to see out the end of the world."

"So is there any other way into the building?" she purred.

"Old cooling vents I guess," the engineer said. "We hid the inlets in that sculpture down in the plaza. But's that all blocked off now. There's also the old loading dock down in the sub-basement, but the Deputy Mayor got us to lock that level off from the elevators."

"Wow, a loading dock! There must be a road leading to the outside from there!"

"Too dangerous down there now. We don't want the kiddies wandering around the building and getting all ate up by those monsters. No, everything is locked and triple locked now."

Grinning at how successful his "date" was going, the engineer excused himself to find a Hero Bucket, at which point Tamsyn scattered from the bar and left him to a solitary evening. Minus his elevator keys, of course, which she'd deftly pocketed.

SKREEE! The whistle startled her back into today. With extreme reluctance she turned off her shower, still half soapy, and she exited past a dozen pregnant bellies, doing her best to pretend she was radiant and peaceful.

"Tamsyn," Sushma called out to her as she crossed the residential level. "We are doing the crochet club. You should come to it."

"Hard pass, loser," she called back. She found Elijah up in his workroom, along with the rest of his mates, and they were playing what appeared to be a game of Dungeons and Dragons.

"Hey, you should roll up a character!" Quinn said.

"I think I'll just watch, thanks," Tamsyn said. "You guys are the ultimate nerds."

Louis was running the game, weaving the other characters into a long-running fantasy story, complete with in-jokes, villains, and derring-do. Grabbing a spare piece of paper and a pencil, Tamsyn quietly sketched out their characters, fighting off an evil horde of goblins. When she showed them the finished drawing, the kids nearly lost their minds with excitement.

"Wow, that is so cool!"

"Draw my familiar! It's a faery cat with wings."

"No, you gotta draw the Sword of Vengeance."

Complying with their requests, Tamsyn was then struck with an idea. She quickly drew the shape of Sushma's kukri, the Gurkha knife that she'd left buried in her husband's skull.

"Whoah, that looks bad-ass," Sara said.

"Elijah," Tamsyn said quietly. "Would you be able to make one of these?"

"You mean, for real?"

"Yep, about this long," and she held out her hands. "Sharp enough to shave a gorilla."

"Why do you need this?"

Because you're all in terrible danger. Because there are actual monsters in your basement.

"Because it's bad-ass?"

Elijah frowned.

"I'll have to be careful. Secret even. The Constable gets a bit weird about my projects when they're dangerous."

"Actually, can you make three of them?"

AFTER SUPPER, Tamsyn made for her bed, aching and exhausted. Checking in on the lusty idiots next door, she saw Reynolds and Sushma dozing away, pulsing with green, green, and more green. She felt like the friend at the party who could not convince her drunken bestie that the man she was pashing was horrendously bad for her.

Once more Tilly was sitting at the foot of her bed, swinging her legs and waiting patiently.

"You've gotta stop doing that, kid," Tamsyn said. "There's things next door you're too young to be hearing."

Tilly made an exaggerated kissing face, all puckered up.

"Yeah, it's pretty gross until it's not," Tamsyn said. She looked to her bed with a heavy sigh. "Did you want to go for a walk or something?"

Tilly nodded. Her eyes slid towards the doorway to Tamsyn's cubicle. The girl was nervous.

"Yeah, I wasn't tired anyway."

Tilly led her away from the shanty town as fast as she could, yanking on her hand whenever she slowed down. She was taking them on a circuitous route to the service stairs, as if in an old spy movie and trying to throw off a tail.

I've got to get this kid out of here, Tamsyn thought. *Not just her. Reynolds and Sushma, once I throw a bucket of water over them. Elijah, Louis, Quinn, Sara. Anyone who isn't firmly in the Bliss.*

I'm going to need a shitload of supplies.

Tamsyn followed Tilly through a funhouse of drying laundry, lifting damp sheets and navigating through dozens of dangling bras, when she felt a polite tap on the shoulder. She turned to see the Deputy Mayor, this time wearing a cheerful floral dress, broad politician's smile fixed in place.

Tilly had disappeared as only children could.

"Tamsyn, just the girl I wanted to see," Emma said. "How are you feeling, love?"

"Much better, thank you," she gushed, doing her best to throw a winning smile. "I'm very embarrassed about what happened in the cafeteria. It won't happen again."

"Think nothing of it," Emma said, her smile framed by a set of dripping socks on the line. "Most people feel amazing after a night in the drunk tank."

"I do feel good," Tamsyn lied. "Very good."

"That is so wonderful!" Emma said, eyeing her intently. A predator's stare. "You're hard to get a read on sometimes."

"Resting bitch face meets poker face, I guess."

"Hmm. Well, if you're feeling down or need a friendly ear, make sure you come and see me. It's my job to make sure you are safe and happy."

"Will do," Tamsyn said. The Deputy Mayor bowed her head briefly, and then disappeared back through the flap of sheets and towels. For one second Tamsyn saw the Constable waiting for the Deputy Mayor, and their eyes met before a sheet fell back into place.

Skin crawling, Tamsyn looked frantically for Tilly, kicking over a forgotten washing basket and scattering pegs everywhere. Then a hand slid into hers, and Tilly was back, dragging her forward as fast as she could.

"You're hiding from her?"

Tilly nodded.

"I don't blame you. At all."

They left the clotheslines to sneak through the laundry area, Tamsyn watching for pursuit, still freaking out that the Deputy Mayor and the Constable had found her so easily. Tilly yanked her suddenly through the community library, past Ikea shelves laden with thousands of new books. They were still covered with price labels from Waterstones, and there was everything here, from fiction through to medical textbooks, engineering, every bit of knowledge a community of mindless slaves could ever need.

Tilly dragged her into a small reading nook, complete with beanbags and someone's abandoned coffee mug. A shelf of magazines blocked it from casual sight, as good a hiding place as any.

She sat with the girl, heart racing, waiting for discovery. After a minute or so, Tilly stood up, gesturing Tamsyn onward. On their way out of the library, she grabbed books seemingly at random, piling them into Tamsyn's arms.

Her aura was a pulsing white and grey, dancing across her fingertips as she brushed over the spines that she didn't even look at. Something was guiding her to these particular books, and Tamsyn looked at the growing stack in her arms, puzzled at the titles.

The Visions of Hieronymous Bosch. The Art of William Blake. A *Where's Wally?* book. Another atlas. A book of Moon maps. Bizarre occult textbooks, complete with fanciful depictions of devils and demons, and an illustrated copy of Dante's *The Inferno*.

Then Tilly led her on a brisk walk to the service stairs, bounding down, only looking back to see if Tamsyn was still following her.

"There must be five kilograms of books here," Tamsyn huffed. "Weird bloody kid."

This time Tilly led her to another secret hideout, a half-constructed greenhouse with sagging plastic sheeting stapled to the walls, UV lighting kits still in the box. Going by the dust on the tools the construction had been abandoned months ago. Tilly had brought more treasures up here. Stuffed toys were lined against the wall, arranged in order from smallest to biggest. A big poster of Nicky Cross formed the centrepiece of a weird shrine, complete with clothes, shoes, an old handbag, a hairbrush and copies of her book *I Can See Your Dead Parents, They Said to Get a Haircut*.

Leaving Tamsyn at the door, Tilly turned to her with a grin, and then her white teeth were blinding, everything was white, and then Tamsyn could only see a blank stretch of wall, couldn't even remember why she'd come here...

...and then the wall was gone, and she could see the empty room, could see Tilly standing in the middle of her lair.

"You made people forget about this place?"

Tilly nodded enthusiastically.

"Does your weird Jedi mind trick work on the Deputy Mayor? On the Constable?"

Tilly frowned, shook her head.

"Okay, we'll need to be quick here. They found me before, they could find me again." She dumped the books on the floor, her arms throbbing in relief. Taking up a staple-gun, Tamsyn stretched out the plastic and fastened it across the doorway, sealing them inside.

A ripping sound, and Tamsyn turned to see Tilly tearing pages out of the new books.

"What the hell? Why are you wrecking those books?"

Tilly ignored her, working faster and faster. She was lining up the torn out pages on the floor, a weird tarot of vandalism. Without looking up, Tilly pointed across the room, and Tamsyn found a plastic bag full of art supplies, brought everything over to the intense young woman. Tilly became a flurry with a craft knife, sticky tape, glitter and markers.

"This would go a lot easier if you could talk. Or even just write," Tamsyn said, immediately feeling like a bitch. In minutes the girl had constructed a bizarre collage, and then she sat back with ink stained hands, satisfied with her effort.

It was fucking *odd*, to say the least. There was Earth and even the Moon, floating happily in space, but all around the two were the horrific scenes of hell and torment, the weird demons and monsters pressing in on the cheerful blue-green globe. There was a glittering path connecting the earth to the moon, and then it kept going past the moon and out into the darkness of space, thinner and thinner until she'd used up all the glitter. Perhaps this represented an incredible distance?

Next, the pages from the atlas, nations laid out side by side. Again, she'd put a stick-on star over each Vanguard site, only to scribble black markers across each one. *Black stars*.

Now, the scenes from Where's Wally. Tilly had found the Wally on each page in record time, only to scribble over him with the black marker. Over his head was a rough shape in her childish hand, a box with points, and then Tamsyn realised this was meant to be a crown.

The Black Crown Boy! He was in every scene, surrounded by the happy beach-goers, the people at the fun-fair, the crowd at the shopping mall. With each picture Tilly had cut out more and more of the Hieronymous Bosch demons, placing them around the edges of the scenes at first, and then finally laying them across the crowds, blotting out the people, until in the second to last scene there was only a tiny handful of cartoon people around the crowned figure, oblivious to the solid ring of monsters hemming them in.

In the last picture that small circle of remaining people were marked in black, and they all had crowns. Tamsyn thought of the dozens of babies growing in One Angel Square, and she shuddered.

Underneath this serial killer collage, Tilly had the same maps, but this time upside down, and furious marker scribbles covering every landmass, a mixture of red, yellow and grey. This time the stars on each Vanguard site were the cheerful yellow from the packet. Making sure that Tamsyn watched, she drew lines in marker connecting up all of the stars from one earth to the other. The upside-down red world, connected to the broken blue and green world that she knew.

It was a lot to take in, and only one conclusion to draw.

"Is this where the one with the crown is from?" she asked, pointing to the red map.

Tilly nodded, then shook her head, then waggled her hand left and right. *Yes and no. So-so. Close.*

"How about this?" she said, pointing to the silvery trail through moon and earth from an impossible distance. "Did it come from here?"

YES! Nodding fast. She touched the moon, and then the red mirror image of the earth, and then finally the earth itself.

"This here," and Tamsyn touched the red world, "what is this place?"

Frowning, Tilly pointed at it, again as if to say *are you stupid?*

"I don't understand. Is that night-time? Is it a dream place?"

Tilly shook her head, shaking with sheer frustration, one tear leaking down her nose. Finally she ran towards the shrine of her mother, and she placed various items of hers around the map. Finally she slammed the copy of her mother's book down in the middle of that upside down, wrongly coloured world.

"Is it the afterlife?" Tamsyn asked, the impossible falling from her mouth. "Is it Hell?"

Tilly looked up, wide-eyed, a moment before the plastic curtain ripped open, staples popping in all directions. The Constable forced his way into the hidden room, a dozen smiling goons hot on his heels. Tamsyn threw exactly one punch before they beat her bloody. Not once did they stop smiling, even as they stood above her, boots and fists rising and falling.

22

She didn't pass out, not even when one of her ribs broke, and she was aware the whole time, everything amplified by pain. When they hoisted her from the floor she felt it in every inch of her battered body, from her pummelled face to where the boots had landed in her back, her sides, her shins. If she lived through today, she would probably piss blood for a week.

She tried to swear at her captors, spit defiance, but all she could do was spray blood and spit. She felt a broken tooth fall out of her mouth, and a dim recess of her mind wondered if there were any dentists left alive in England.

As they frogmarched her through the building, fat splatters of blood ran out of her nose, and her shirt was soaked in red. Between her feet, a grim Hansel and Gretel trail back to the plastic room, and she wondered if it had ever been secret, at least from the chief villains in this place.

The Constable. The Deputy Mayor. Whatever monsters lay at the bottom of the building.

She hadn't seen Tilly since the fracas, and hoped she had escaped. These bastards had some kind of sick hold over her, forcing her to use her gifts to keep the lid on the Bliss. Why was she cooperating with them, knowing what she knew?

Because if she behaves, she gets to play with Lego. Sleep indoors. Watch TV shows with other kids. She knows the score.

Once more the elevator, the Constable fetching out his key ring to unlock the system. Tamsyn idly thought of her own pilfered set, stupidly hidden upstairs in her supply cache. *I need those to escape!*

Even beaten and groggy as she was, Tamsyn realised she would never leave the bowels of this evil place. They were going to break her body, then her mind, and then she would manufacture babies until she was dead.

The elevator doors opened onto the darkness of the prison level, and Tamsyn winced when the Constable turned on all of the floodlights. Floor, darkness, blazing light, all of it swayed as her head span. She tried to reach inward for her gift, for any little trick that might work. Could she separate these smiling thugs from the Bliss, much like she could sever someone enchanted by the Vanguard?

I've got nothing left in the tank, she realised, her brain responding with fuzziness and a sharp pain to match the rest of her body. She couldn't even see auras, and her whole world was the cement floor, the old painted lines for the carparks, spatters of her blood, and then the floor of the cell they tossed her into.

"Fuh," she tried to say, lips peeled away from her teeth like some feral thing, her eyes struggling to rise above the level of the Constable's boots. He stood there for a long moment before slamming the cage door shut. *Snikt* as the padlock clicked shut, and then the footsteps back to the elevator, the floodlights shut down, and absolute darkness.

Not even then did Tamsyn fall into the peace of unconsciousness. For time unknown she lay there in the dark, seeping blood and tears, her bladder eventually failing. Her nervous system fired pain signals into her brain, over and over, each agonising throb the beat of the new clock that marked time in her universe. If there was water in the cell, Tamsyn didn't know how to get to it, and her body wasn't obeying her in any case.

Eventually she put her mouth over a pool of her own blood, and she lapped it up, her dried out tongue scraping against the cement, the hard-won moisture barely worth this further indignity. At that moment came the ding of the elevator arriving, followed by instant blindness when someone threw on the banks of floodlights.

Tamsyn heard the merry *tap-tap-tap* of high heels against cement. Closer. Close. Inches away. A key twisted in a lock. The cage opened.

"You've lied to me, Tamsyn Lottie Webb," Emma Menteuse said. "I don't think you are happy here at all."

Tamsyn tried for a smart-arse comeback, but the machinery of her throat was at near total failure. Emma took her by the shoulder and the knee, the hipbone, and another burst of agony shot through Tamsyn as the woman tried to move her. Tamsyn tried to fight, but she was like a mortally wounded bird in the jaws of a cat, barely able to twitch, knowing that it was all over. She felt the woman gently shift her onto her side, and then onto her back, cradling her head so she didn't bang it on the cement until she was staring up at the cage mesh.

Then, the crack of a plastic seal, and sweet water was running all over her face, trickling into her mouth, giving life back to her tongue and throat. She gulped at it gratefully, even as she hated the woman.

"Remember this moment, when you are asked to serve,"

Emma said. "Defiance will bring you back here, or somewhere worse."

More water.

"Can you talk now?"

"A little," Tamsyn wheezed. "Hey, fuck you."

"Look at you. Listen to your vulgarity. Do you still wonder why this happened to your race?"

"What. The Fuck. Are you?"

"Now, you are asking the right questions," Emma said, kneeling down until she was level with her, the knee-length floral dress just brushing the cement floor.

"But first, Tamsyn Lottie Webb. I have a question for you. Where have you hidden Tilly Jade Cross?"

"Ha," Tamsyn laughed tonelessly. They'd been in the same room, her, the Constable, the Happy Beat-Down Posse, and the strange young girl. One exit. There was no human way she could have escaped from that room, sight unseen.

"She has been missing for days," Emma said, brushing Tamsyn's split eyebrow gently with the ridge of a thumb, as if soothing away the hurt. "You have been spotted lurking near her known hiding places, and then you found a place we did not know of. You were found going through her belongings. Where is she?"

"Up my arsehole, bitch."

Emma pressed down with her thumbnail then, right on a nerve point, and Tamsyn cried out, the pain digging right into her skull.

"First the mother served us, until she thought to resist. To make war against us, the saviours of your kind! So now, the daughter serves in place of the mother, and proves to be the strongest of all. Then you arrive, and all order is lost!"

Tamsyn fought against that pressing thumbnail, but it

felt like the tip of a mountain, driving down into her, pressing her into the cement floor. Her useless arms flopped and twitched as the abused nerves fired throughout her body.

"Our master wanted you dead, even up to our doorstep, but I saved you. Me! And you thank me by hiding the girl. You threaten every life in this building until she is found."

"Even the babies?" Tamsyn managed. With a sigh, Emma withdrew her thumb, and the pain fell back down to just the throb of her beating.

"Especially the babies," Emma said. "They will grow, and be born, and serve in turn, but only if they know the Bliss."

"Serve who?"

"You have spoken with him. Do not play dumb here."

"Black crown boy," Tamsyn whispered.

"Ha! He is hardly a boy. But yes, we serve the Crown of Countless Suns."

"Crown of...you're fucking loopy."

"Here are the simple facts," Emma said, leaning in close, perfect lips moving just inches away from her ears. "First the Mindless, to cleanse your broken world. Then the Vanguard, to make ready and open the way. Next, the Host. A grand plan, and one you may yet be part of."

Tamsyn's mind reeled at these words.

"Ah, this is the moment. I have seen it in the eyes of Nicky Olivia Cross, when she realised this truth. A fragment of your people we shall save from destruction. We shall even permit the memory of culture, even what pitiful knowledge and history you attained."

"What are you?"

"We are the conquerors of this world, and many others."

"You're not even a human," Tamsyn said. Emma looked

back at her with a flat, deadpan stare, and she might as well have been a lizard in that moment.

"Oh, Emma Fleur Menteuse is still in here. She shared, oh so willingly at first. But now I control this body. Her mind is a library to me."

Tamsyn cringed away from this weird creature, wearing a woman like a puppet. Emma smiled, an inhuman curving of the lips that did not change that unblinking stare.

"When she was twelve, she beat a dog with an extension cord," she said. "An abortion at age seventeen. She defecated on an ex-lover's doorstep. Accepted bribes from companies who polluted water freely. A man had photographs of her, and when they met to exchange money, she had another man murder him with a gun. It was very easy to convince Emma Fleur Menteuse to serve us."

"In the name of the Crown, I am the Monitor of this place. All of these lives, mine to nourish. So I need my Tilly, my Guide! She is keeping people out of these cells!"

Tamsyn blinked. In the face of these revelations she was all out of sass.

"We know you are a Guide, Tamsyn Lottie Webb. By rights you should be dead out there, but I saved you from the Crown. Remember that."

"I was never in the Guides. I did Duke of Ed for a year but got kicked out for drinking."

Emma smiled at the joke, again merely the flexing of the face muscles in the correct way. It was like watching one of those Japanese animatronic robots perform as a creepy faux human.

"If Tilly will not perform her service, then her task falls upon you. Watching for sadness, anger. Easing those people back into the Bliss. Drink, get fat, do whatever else you want."

"Will you put a monster in my head? Make me into a puppet?"

Emma looked into the distance for a moment, as if conferring with another. Then she looked back at Tamsyn and smiled.

"If you serve, the Crown will not join you to the Host."

"Generous."

"We want you all to be happy," Emma said. "Every comfort will be given to those who bear the Host. Our kind do not enjoy wearing the bodies of the Vanguard."

Emma stood up.

"We know about your child, Malcolm Dean Webb. We watch the Prince and the others on the farm. Cooperate, or they will be joined to the Host. Understand?"

Tamsyn could only stare, shocked and terrified. The creature wearing a human skin patted her once on the head, locked her cell, summoned the elevator, and left her in the pitch darkness to cry and bleed, alone.

MORE TIME. Tamsyn dozed off once or twice in that perfect darkness. Even though every movement brought a world of pain, she could eventually sit up, and fumbled around in the darkness for the water that Emma had left in her cell. Questing fingers found a scratchy blanket and the toilet bucket, and she used these crude comforts, all the while her mind racing.

Of course they knew about her boy. And Prince Harry. These monsters had the ultimate leverage over her. Sitting slumped against the wire mesh, Tamsyn realised they had won. She was going to spend her life in here, using her supernatural gift to nourish the auras of these people. She would tend their cattle, preparing them to be suits for hidden monsters to wear.

I will do it for you, my sweet boy, she thought, thinking of Malcolm. *Anything to keep you safe from these bastards.*

The clunk of the elevator. Tamsyn turned away just before the floodlights fired up, letting her vision adjust as the footsteps came towards her.

Many footsteps. Excited whispering. She looked up to see many shapes converging around her cage.

"Forget about the bloody lock," she heard one say. "It'll take too long to cut through that."

It was Sushma and Reynolds, surrounded by kids. Elijah, Seb, Quinn, Sara and Louis. Leaning against the wire, smiling at her, was Tilly.

"We'll get you out of there, Tammy," Reynolds said. "Quick, get the wire-cutters."

She slipped over into 'Aura-Vision', and could see the man was surrounded by his usual mess of grey and brown, with jagged squiggles of red. Sushma was back, orange and fierce. They were free of the Bliss.

"Did you free them?" she asked Tilly, who nodded. Tamsyn pushed her fingers through a gap in the wire, gripping the girl's hand as best she could. The mute little girl gave off a smile that could melt an Eskimo's igloo. In her other hand Tilly was gripping the elevator keys, the stolen set Tamsyn had left hidden up in her cache.

Everyone had a heavy looking bag or backpack, obviously loaded up with supplies. These people were about to make a run for it, through a gauntlet of walking death. Sushma and Reynolds both held newly forged kukri, shining and sharp, while the others had improvised weapons, such as cricket bats, kitchen knives, even a cleaver hanging from Louis's belt. Elijah had quickly welded a type of pike together, with a strong cross-bar to keep the dead at their distance.

"It was the longest game of charades I've ever played, but young Tilly got the point across to us," Reynolds said. "Let's get the ever-loving fuck out of here."

Elijah had out a pair of wire-cutters, and set them around the wire links, ready to snip her loose.

"No, no," Tamsyn said, holding up her hands. "You have to leave me in here. Reynolds, Sushma, get these kids out of here, get them as far away from Manchester as you can."

"What? We're not leaving you in here."

"Reynolds, I am deadly serious. They know about the farm. About Malcolm. If I don't cooperate..."

"No," Sushma said. "You do not surrender now. That is not right. You are leaving. Today."

"You don't understand! They're going to hurt my boy! I have to do this!"

"Tamsyn, we will go to Malcolm. Better to fight than cry in cage."

"She's right, Tamsyn," Reynolds said. "Blackmail doesn't end with you being happy. They will dangle that kid in front of you for years, and probably use him anyway. We have to tell the others."

"What they do here is not right," Sushma said vehemently. Tamsyn noticed she was keeping her distance from Reynolds, and her heart broke at the sight. This formidable warrior had been used, and been powerless to resist. Now that the veil had been torn from her eyes, the Gurkha was shimmering with rage, black spikes through her vital orange. By rights she should be grieving her husband, catatonic for weeks, but she'd been pushed into a false new relationship, urged by these evil geniuses to breed babies for them. Even Reynolds had the good grace to be ashamed of what they'd made him do here.

Sushma had been forced into a hormonal science experiment, and had entered into it with a willing smile. Of all the things Tamsyn had experienced since the dead came back, this was right up there in the top three most shit moments. And they would do the same to her boy, to the Prince, to every person with a pulse. It wasn't ever going to end.

"Quick, cut me out of here," Tamsyn told Elijah, who set to the links with relief all over his face. "We've got to go."

"We might have to fight our way up to the roof," Reynolds said. "If we take out the Constable, we can seize the window-washer scaffolds, get down to the ground."

"No, there's another entrance below us," Tamsyn said. "Old loading dock. Or through the air-inlets. That's how they get all the supplies in."

Snip, snip, snip. Tamsyn watched Elijah cut the wire links. He was going as quickly as he could, but still Tamsyn fretted, watching for the elevator. Soon it was just big enough for her to wriggle through, but the sharp jags of cut wire scratched her in a dozen places, even with everyone hauling back on the edges of the hole. She cried out in pain as her broken rib grated together, but finally she was out, clutching gratefully at Louis as the big kid lifted her up.

"They made one for you too," Reynolds said, handing Tamsyn a razor sharp kukri. "We broke into one of the weapons racks too, and guess what? All completely fake. Blunt edges, blank rounds, bloody stage props."

Tamsyn nodded, gripping the handle of the sharp blade. It was perfectly balanced, as good as the kukri Sushma had left in Leyland's skull.

"It all makes sense now," Elijah said. "I saw the Constable's patrols go out, but the zombies never bothered them.

And they never came back with anywhere near enough food to keep us all alive."

"Elijah, did your cameras ever see a truck out there?"

"Only abandoned ones. They make the best bombs."

"There has to be a truck down there, or something. Someway they get tonnes of supplies into this place. We need to find it and haul arse."

"That can't be right," Elijah said. "There's no clear way for a truck to navigate the streets. Unless they carried those pallets by hand through that maze of dead cars, there's just no way. And I'd have seen that kind of movement by now."

In Tamsyn's mind, the solution to the logic puzzle presented itself. All of the food in the pallets was long-life, neatly stacked in the innards of the half-finished building. No-one could ever remember it being brought in, because it had already been there.

"Oh my god," Tamsyn realised. "They stocked this building before the outbreak. Emma knew about it, she bloody knew!"

The implications of this fell on the group, who made for the elevators in grim silence. School kids, bussed in to be cattle. Hundreds of people invited to a boring ribbon cutting. The zombies leaving everything alone long enough for the "barricades" to go up.

The barricades were there to keep the survivors in.

Taking the elevator keys from Tilly, Tamsyn unlocked the lift, hammering the "Down" button. She hefted the kukri in her other hand, and looked to her unlikely crew. It was time to get the hell out of dodge.

"Be ready for anything," she told the others. "There are Vanguard in the building."

The elevator should have opened instantly, but it was whirring, moving down from one floor above. The atrium level. Tamsyn stepped back, looking for somewhere to hide, but there was nothing but wire cages, surrounded by a cement tomb.

The doors opened to reveal the Constable, who looked calmly on this escape attempt. Then he pulled his pistol out, a quickdraw worthy of the Wild West.

It happened fast. The Constable fired his pistol rapidly, deafening at such close range. *Blam! Blam! Blam! Blam!*

Sushma fell down, folding around a bullet.

Seb dropped with a scream, gut-shot and twitching, his cricket bat clattering across the floor.

Sara stood swaying for a second, blood streaming from her eye, thick glasses starred from the impact, and then she sat down with a surprised "oh," and was dead.

"We are Vanguard," Reynolds said, smiling at Tamsyn, lunging at her with his knife.

Tamsyn tried to break Reynolds loose from the Vanguard, but in that sudden panic her mind failed her. She darted around him, and felt the sting across her back as the knife kissed her flesh, a glancing blow. She madly swung her kukri at the Constable's gun hand, hoping to knock the gun away before he could shoot any more of her kids. She was still weak from her beating, and her downward swing could have had more force behind it, but it was the best she could do.

She felt the impact of the blade, but still the Constable came on, gun lining up with her chest, and in that moment she knew death was coming, from the gun or from the Vanguard spirit piloting Reynolds.

"You are too much trouble to keep," the Constable said, the moment before his hand peeled away from the near-severed wrist, blood spurting everywhere, gun falling from his twitching fingers. Tamsyn saw the blood on the edge of her blade, and knew it had been a telling blow.

The puppet in the man did not even flinch or cry out. With his left hand the Constable flicked out an extendable baton, and cracked Tamsyn across the face, hard enough to knock her down.

"We are Vanguard," Reynolds said cheerfully, slicing off Louis's arm clean through the elbow, forearm, hand and cleaver dropping to the floor with a sickening sound. The boy fell back with a wail, looking at the spurting stump in horror.

"Stop it!" Tamsyn cried out, trying to reach for her gift, to bring Reynolds back from the Vanguard, but the splitting pain in her skull was keeping her supernatural gift out of her grasp.

Tamsyn saw Elijah charge in, screaming out in fury. He pig-spit the Constable on his pike, sending him back into the elevator, pinning the man to the wall. Unable to wriggle free from the spear, the Constable very calmly plucked a tear-gas canister from his belt and lobbed it out into the garage, driving the survivors back, coughing and gasping.

"We are Vanguard!" Louis cried out joyfully, doing his best to restrain Elijah with one arm. With size and weight alone Louis dragged the other kid down to the ground, bloody stump spurting all over him, trying to close his teeth around Elijah's throat.

Tamsyn climbed to her wobbly feet, found her blade.

"We are Van-" Reynolds began, and ended with a gasp. Tamsyn saw him clutching to Sushma, as if in a lover's embrace, and then they fell apart. He had Sushma's blade deeply lodged in his chest, blade locked into his sternum. Falling away, he drew his own blade out of Sushma's stomach, a worrying mess of guts slithering out through a razor-sharp wound that stretched from hip to hip. Face set like stone, the Gurkha fell back onto her backside, clutching at her insides and trying to keep them in.

One more tear gas canister came out of the elevator, this one striking Tamsyn in the face, hard. She staggered away from it, coughing, eyes running. Fingers fumbling across the ground, she finally found the pistol, shook off the dead hand that was still gripping it, and blindly fired it into the elevator car, unable to see through her streaming eyes and the thick cloud of toxic gas.

Perhaps ten seconds had passed since the elevator doors opened. Coughing and wiping away at her eyes, Tamsyn kicked away the spewing gas canisters, and peered through the painful mist, trying to see who was still alive.

Elijah, crying over Louis's body, both of them surrounded by a deep pool of the dead boy's blood. The Constable, slumped against the pike, face destroyed by a lucky bullet. Seb screaming in pain, and Sara sprawled across the floor, surrounded by a deep pool of her own blood. Reynolds laying still, serenely staring at the ceiling, hands resting around the blade that ended his life.

Sushma was applying a roll of bandage to her wound, winding strip after strip around the wound there was no coming back from. There was still a dark purple loop of intestine showing, and the bandage was already a deep red, sopping wet with each pass. She had another wound, a bullet through the meat of her thigh, and without a word of complaint she fitted herself with a tourniquet.

"Tilly!" Tamsyn cried out. "Tilly, where are you?"

She found the girl curled up at the foot of the nearest cage, shaking with silent tears. Quinn stood guard in front of her, waving a kitchen knife in a shaking hand, which fell from her fingers when she saw the fight was over, ringing merrily against the cement.

Tamsyn made to help Tilly to her feet, and her hands came away wet with blood. One of the bullets had pierced Tilly's side, and a steady stream of blood was trickling out of the hole.

"Oh god! Someone, we need help!" she called out, cradling the girl in her arms.

23

They held a desperate triage in front of the floodlights, Tamsyn tipping out every bag until she found a handful of stolen medical supplies. She packed in the gunshot wounds on Tilly and Seb, leaning on what first aid she remembered from the Texan Army. Tilly's wound was clean, bullet in and out and no organs punctured that she could see. Seb was a different story altogether, and the boy moaned in pain, white-faced as Tamsyn dug around in his wound, trying to find the bullet.

"I'm sorry mate, this is the best I can do," she said, packing the entry hole, and wrapped gauze around and around. Without proper medical care, it didn't look good for the young man. She took a surreptitious sniff near the wound, but the bowel didn't seem to be perforated. That left internal bleeding, infection, any number of ways the wound could go bad.

Sushma knelt down by Reynold's body, closing his eyes, trying to set the ridiculous grin on his face to rights. She drew the kukri from his chest, Excalibur from a stony heart, and rose holding two blades, the life leaking out of her by the second.

"Hurry," she told Tamsyn. "More may come."

"We're safe for now. I've isolated the elevator," Elijah said in a small voice. Only Elijah and Quinn had escaped from that encounter without injury, and they looked on the misery with thousand-yard stares.

Tilly touched Tamsyn's back, and only then did she remember that she herself had a wound. Questing with her finger revealed that Reynolds had sliced open her shirt, lifting a flap of skin with the edge of his blade. Not a deep wound, but it would need stitches, and it hurt like hell.

True to form, Reynolds had a bottle of vodka in his bag, and Tamsyn used it liberally on everything that looked like a wound, crying out as she splashed it on herself. When she went to treat Sushma, the Gurkha shook her head.

"Do not waste it. Here, let me drink."

Tamsyn watched as the Gurkha took a long pull from the bottle, and didn't begrudge her the booze. The whole front of Sushma's shirt and her pants were soaked wet with blood, with only a few strips of gauze keeping her intestines and organs inside. She had a bullet hole just above this, a neat little hole revealing the cavern of her stomach. This close, Tamsyn could smell the shit from a perforated bowel, and knew that it was game over for her brave friend.

She had to be in incredible pain, but even in the face of an awful lingering death, the Gurkha did not make a sound. Only the drawn look around her eyes and the visible evidence of her savage wounds spoke to the trouble that woman was in.

"It's time to go," Elijah said, speaking with a weight well beyond his years. He withdrew the pike from the Constable's body, letting it fall to the floor of the elevator car with a heavy thump.

Sushma and Tamsyn hauled the body out, dumping it unceremoniously on the cement floor. For a long moment she looked on the corpses of Reynolds, Louis and Sara, and then she shut down the floodlights, leaving them in a mausoleum big enough to fit hundreds of cars.

Rest in peace, Reynolds, you beautiful scumbag.

They crowded into the elevator car, weighed down with their own kit and the bug-out bags of their dead friends. Quinn, Seb, Elijah, Tamsyn and Sushma, their little escape posse already decimated before they'd even started.

Elijah turned the key, unlocking the elevator, and Tamsyn punched the button for the bottom basement level. When the elevator lurched into motion, Seb clutched his stomach, groaning.

"It hurts," Seb said.

"You will live," Sushma said, lifting the boy's chin up with the tip of her blade. "Be tough, today and every day."

Seb nodded, clearly terrified of the mad warrior woman.

"When I die later today, you will take up these blades," Sushma said. "Use them till you are free or until you are dead too. Okay?"

Seb nodded again, licking dry lips.

"I am good with kids," Sushma said to Tamsyn. "Maybe I should teach the art class."

One long moment as they descended into the bowels of the building, tight-lipped and gripping at their weapons. This was the point in an action movie where Tamsyn should have said something inspirational, something bad-ass in the face of danger, but she was just too scared and weary to try.

Ding.

The elevator doors opened onto a gloomy level, the light

from the elevator doing little to drive it back. A twin row of columns stretched out before them, and Tamsyn remembered the dwarven mines from that Lord of the Rings film. Silence. Tamsyn dug around in one of the packs until she found an old Mmaglightaglight, blinking and yellow as it drew on old batteries. Next to her, a click and a much brighter light, and Tamsyn couldn't help but smile. Elijah, a warrior-prince wielding a bloody pike, except now he had an LED lamp strapped to his forehead.

"You are such a goober," she whispered. "Alright, we need to find the loading dock, and get far, far away from these freaks."

Even moving quietly, their every footfall echoed against unseen cement. Another parking level, but this one was filthy with junk, until soon they were stepping over car bumpers, street-signs, loose bricks and tree branches.

She thought back to the Isle of Sheppey, to the mad structure the Vanguard had been building there. She met eyes with Tilly, who stared around fearfully. There were monsters on this level, merrily carting in junk from the outside world.

"Everyone, listen up," Tamsyn whispered, drawing the others in close. "You saw what happened with Reynolds and Louis. These bastards can take your minds over. If they bite you, I think it's a done deal, forever."

Tilly shook her sleeve until Tamsyn looked down at her. Again, the warm white glow around the girl, only now it was spreading out from her, dancing around all of their heads, little lace doilies that settled down around her own head and felt warm. Good.

Tilly was giving them protection from the Vanguard. The effort clearly cost her, and Tamsyn felt her clutch tightly to her sleeve, almost as if she needed help to stand up.

"Kinda wish you'd done that back in the prison," she said. The look of shame on Tilly's face made Tamsyn wish she could cram the words back down her throat. Of course she could have saved Reynolds, if she'd had a few moments to weave him this protection, drawing from her aura or her spirit or whatever the thing was.

Instead of a peaceful moment to prepare, there had been bullets, and chaos, and even with her powerful gifts, Tilly Cross was just a ten-year old girl. *God, Tamsyn, you are a right bitch sometimes.*

"I'm sorry, mate," she said. Tilly shook her head sadly, and withdrew her hand.

CRASH. The sound of something metal striking the cement floor, and footsteps, stomping over the rubbish, not even trying to be stealthy. This from behind them, towards the elevator. Tamsyn sent her torch beam dancing through the slow settling dust, and when Elijah joined it with his better light, they could see dark shapes weaving through the columns, shadows advancing towards them.

"Move!" Sushma shouted, and then she was off through the growing rubbish pile, leading the way with blades at the ready, legs pumping. Wide-eyed, Tamsyn and the kids followed her, tripping and sliding and navigating the stacks of junk in the dark. At one point Tamsyn barked her knee against a jag of lumber protruding from the trash. Nails scratching into her skin. A distant part of her mind worried about tetanus.

You aren't going to live long enough to worry about that! Tamsyn thought. A babble of shouting closing in behind them, happy sounds, dozens of running people proclaiming their allegiance to the Vanguard.

She felt the tickle on her mind then, someone or something trying to get in, turned aside by Tilly's clever mind-shield. *God, they're trying to paralyse us again,* Tamsyn thought, remembering that awful moment back on the Isle of Sheppey. Tilly staggered at her side, and Tamsyn dropped her torch, grabbing the girl by the collar to keep her up and moving.

Behind them, the weak torch flickered and finally went out. Apart from the sweeping light of Elijah's head-lamp, they were in near darkness. The big cement pylons seemed to never end, and the rubbish was stacked in little hills here. Some attempt at order was happening near the centre, with piles of lumber, stacks of salvaged metal, but at some point the scavengers had lost interest, scattering material in all directions.

"Which way is the loading dock?" Sushma shouted over her shoulder.

"I don't bloody know!" Tamsyn replied. "Just keep running!"

"We are Vanguard!" a heavyset man shouted cheerfully, crashing through a stack of cooking ware to try and seize Sushma. She met the man in a flurry of blades and kicks, stepping neatly aside to let him fall in at least three separate pieces.

"Vanguard!" more yelled out, drawn by the clatter of pots and pans. It was the creepiest game of Marco Polo Tamsyn had ever played, running from psychos through an insane junkyard in the near dark. Tilly clutched fearfully at her arm, and Tamsyn struggled to keep up with Sushma, her own blade held in a trembling hand.

Then a green glow, incredibly faint, but enough now to navigate by.

"It's an exit light!" Tamsyn shouted. "Go that way!"

"No, get off me!"

Quinn was screaming, fighting to break free from a smiling woman's grip. By the bobbing light of his lamp, Elijah punched his pike through the Vanguard's throat, while Seb prised her loose from the maniac's hands.

"No-one stop!" Tamsyn screamed. "You should have left her!"

"Fuck you lady," Seb shouted. "She's our friend!"

"Fine, get yourselves killed!"

The greenish light was brighter now, but the Vanguard were blasting through the detritus in earnest, gleefully pouncing on them from all directions. From Tilly came a white blast that only Tamsyn could see, the girl using her strange gift to sever the connection from dozens of the Vanguard. All around Tamsyn she could hear confused people cry out in the near dark, struggling with the next wave of Vanguard to pour forward.

Tilly staggered and almost fell, dazed with the effort. Between that and maintaining their mental defences, the girl was stretched to breaking point.

A human shield, bought dearly, Tamsyn thought. She hefted the girl up and over one shoulder, beaten muscles and broken ribs letting her know what a dumb idea that was.

In front, Sushma was carving through a wall of grabbing hands, severing fingers, slashing at faces and throats, her every movement calculated to disable, wound, kill. When a hefty looking woman snatching at her, Tamsyn flailed out weakly with her own blade, catching her across the face.

"Ah," was all the woman said, her sliced open nose bubbling grotesquely. She tried to talk about the Vanguard, but it was a mess of air and spraying blood. But not once did she scream. None of them did.

Green light. Just get through these freaks and run for the green light. So close!

She followed Sushma around a teetering stack of kitchen sinks, a moment before she realised the green glow was much too strong to be an exit sign, her brain half a beat before her legs. They all skidded to a stop, ending up in a panicked tangle of knives and weapons, forming up into a rough defensive huddle, completely cornered by the grinning Vanguard force, dozens and dozens of grinning killers emerging from the junk piles.

There was no exit light. In the centre of the stacks of junk was a construction just like the one on Sheppey, a twisting tower of crap that reached all the way to the ceiling, spreading out like a demented hand. The same eye-twisting shape that Tilly had made with her Lego bricks, over and over.

At the centre of the "hand", framed by the claw-shape, was a green fog, glowing brightly, occasionally pulsing with lightning bolts that crackled within it. It twisted her eyes to look upon that unnatural shape, at once in the basement of this building, and at the same time impossibly far away, an entire world held up in a tower of mixed junk and leftovers.

At the foot of the tower stood Emma Menteuse, surrounded by a group of Blissed-out people who swayed on their feet, grinning goofily. They were virtually humming in their own green glow, fed by the bizarre structure towering above them.

When she saw Tamsyn's group, the Deputy Mayor raised her hand. Instantly, the advancing Vanguard froze into place, straining as if held against an invisible fence. Tamsyn saw Sushma snarl, scanning around for threats, her berserker brain unable to fathom an enemy suddenly disengaging.

Tamsyn knew that the Gurkha was about to sell her life in the dearest possible way. All that was left were the logistics, and she settled for holding herself at bay, bloodied kukri knives held forward like a praying mantis about to strike.

Would she kill five more? Ten? Twenty, before they pulled her apart?

A glorious ending for any warrior, but no-one to witness it except these monsters and freaks. Tamsyn held no illusions about her own hand-to-hand skills, and she wished for her old bow, knew that she could have done so much for her own last stand.

A rapid-fire shaft, straight through Emma's eye. Perhaps three or four of the Vanguard as they charged in. One final arrow into that stupid green fog, just to see what would happen.

Nope. All she had was a home-made knife and a silent wizard over her shoulder. One hundred percent screwed, in the stupidest possible way.

Panting and terrified, the kids stared wide-eyed at the bizarre scene, eyes drawn to the top of the alien structure. They could see the green glow, just the same as her. So, not an aura then. Something physical, real.

"Here they are," Emma said. "The Guide and her apprentice."

"Just shut up!" Tamsyn said, a faint tremor in her voice ruining the tough guy effect. "You're the worst!"

"We had an arrangement, Tamsyn Lottie Webb. You have reneged upon that arrangement."

Emma spread her arms wide, as if benediction, herding her Bliss-heads forward, into the glow of the tower. Tamsyn's heart fell. She saw submariners, marines, people she'd left back at the farm on the coast. Prince Harry was there too, grinning away like a loon. They were Blissed out, oblivious to the unnatural scene they stood in, uncaring that raving Vanguard maniacs were all around them.

"You bitch! You lied!" Tamsyn cried out. They'd been here all along, hidden in the basement of the building. How long had they been right under her feet? Captured, given false happiness, safely ferried across England through the middle of the zombie hordes. Worse, they'd been escorted here by the Vanguard and the Mindless, smiling the whole way.

Then a sudden, sickening realisation flooded Tamsyn to her core, and Emma confirmed it as she bent down, scooping up a child. Malcolm, her Malcolm, alive and in the arms of a monster. He beamed up at her, his little soul wrapped up in a blanket of the deepest green.

"Mummy!" he shrieked. "I so happy!"

"You. You let him go," Tamsyn said, her motherly instincts ramping up to a primeval level.

I will kill for this child, she realised. *If I need to, I will die right now, just to see him safe.*

She tensed up, ready to run forward, to go to her certain death. Then, she saw the beautiful face of her Sushma, leaning in close until they were touching forehead to forehead. The Gurkha smiled at her through a haze of sweat and pain.

"I will get your boy," she told Tamsyn. "Let me do this."

"Sushma - I'm so sorry this happened to you."

"It's just a life," she scoffed. "We all die."

And then the Gurkha was racing through the cordon of Vanguard, her twin blades flashing. Sushma used her feet, knees, elbows, even her forehead as a weapon. It was beautiful, fast, and in the space of two short breaths she'd destroyed three of her assailants. Now four. Now five.

She was howling some tuneless song as she carved her way through the mob, half cries, half words in her native tongue. In that screeching madness she was beautiful, unstoppable.

Even hidden behind a wall of grinning, gibbering killers, Emma stood back, holding her baby boy. Something washed over her face, and she took an involuntary step backwards.

Just for one second, the mad architect of One Angel Square had shown fear.

"Quick!" Tamsyn shouted, a second before the invisible fence around the Vanguard fell. Once more the smiling killers were coming at them from all directions. Elijah and the other kids were flailing around madly with their makeshift weapons, and the panicked troupe fell into Sushma's bloody wake, pushing their way towards the foot of that insane altar.

"Stop them!" Emma cried.

"STOP THEM," a deeper voice cried, into the core of Tamsyn's being, and her protective mind-shield wavered at that moment. Tilly shivered on Tamsyn's elbow, hot to the touch, and Tamsyn guessed that she was burning up, damaging herself, pushed to the limit from blocking the mental assault.

The voice, the overwhelming force, it was all coming from the green fog above the weird tower thing, and Tamsyn could feel the looming presence of the Black Crown Boy.

"I AM NO BOY!" the thing in the fog said, gleaning the very thought from her mind. "I AM THE CROWN OF THE COUNTLESS SUNS!"

"You can kiss my countless arseholes!" Tamsyn yelled, slicing a Vanguard man across the windpipe.

Ahead, Sushma had sliced her way through to the leftovers of the submarine crew, who huddled back, confused by the violence all around them. Prince Harry seemed befuddled, looking at Sushma with familiarity, unsure of what to do.

"Stay back!" Emma cried out, holding little Malcolm up like a human shield, closing the fingers of one hand around his little throat.

"Please! Don't you hurt him!"

"Hurt him? He will live forever!"

At this, Emma Menteuse gave a wry grin, and looked up to the green glow. Tamsyn felt the looming presence of Emma's master, the Crown of Countless Suns, and in that globe of crackling green, a dark shape floated forward, like a cataract in a blasted zombie's eye.

A simple shape, etched in deepest black, a square with jags above it, as if drawn in a blocky, child-like hand. A crown.

It was hungry for meat, this Tamsyn knew down to her marrow, but not like a predator looking to fill its belly. It wanted to use people, to borrow their limbs, muscle, bone and brains. At first, just to cleanse the world, then to prepare it, and finally to carry the conquerors around in new bodies, like rich people in carriages.

And now they wanted to put one of those things into her boy, into her *baby*.

More of the Vanguard put themselves between Emma and Sushma, and here she could see the same black lines yanking them around like puppets, but they were threads, barely visible, even this close to the weird structure. For a moment these new arrivals held Sushma back from Emma and Malcolm, who continued to smile despite the rough handling from the older woman.

Tamsyn tensed up, willing herself to rush into danger,

when Seb ran forward, lobbing something at the tower as hard as he could. A cylinder with a burning wick, and it bounced from the side of the ramshackle construction, straight towards Sushma's head.

A pipe bomb.

The Gurkha batted the bomb aside with the flat of a blade, and it fell into a cluster of the Vanguard. *BANG!* The crude explosive scattered men and women in all directions, gasping and crying, yet still smiling as the life leaked out of them.

Behind her, the kids were lobbing more bombs, with more enthusiasm than science. Elijah had a whole bag full of nasty little things, with everything from firecrackers to Molotov cocktails. The thoughtful kids from her art class had turned into a determined cadre of resistance fighters, Elijah frantically lighting the fuses for Quinn and Seb to throw.

The gloomy basement lit up with every explosion, junk flying in all directions. The horde of Vanguard were falling like flies, their living bodies damaged in ways that zombies could withstand. Bombs were next to useless against the true undead, but against these puppets, Elijah's wicked little toys were most effective.

Another head spinning moment as the Crown tried to enter her mind. Tilly was openly shaking in the crook of Tamsyn's left arm, her defences paper-thin, body and brain burning up from the stress.

Putting her knife in her teeth, Tamsyn took a bomb from Elijah, alarmed by the sparking fuse cord. Hesitate for one moment too long, and she would be mincemeat. Drop the bomb near the bag of bombs? Mincemeat party.

Tamsyn didn't have her bow anymore, but she'd always had a decent arm. Easing Tilly to the ground, she took a few lurching steps, and whipped her arm forward, a trebuchet of meat and sinew, and the pipe bomb flew up in a lovely arc, sparking fuse and cylinder turning end over end.

She landed the bomb right in the palm of the "hand", directly underneath the green fog, the earthly form of the Crown of Countless Suns.

The bomb exploded.

24

Flinching from the force of the explosion, Tamsyn watched with satisfaction as the fingers of that twisted metal hand buckled outwards. The green fog that held the Crown sagged downwards, melting and beginning to dissipate, while the dark shape within darted around, pushing at the boundary, still trying to enter their minds.

As one, the Vanguard fell about, clutching their temples, twisted grins now grimaces of pain. Sushma took the moment, forcing her way through the writhing figures to reach Emma, still holding Malcolm.

"I'll snap his neck!" she spat, shuffling until her back was against the blazing tower, wreckage falling all around her. She shrank behind little Malcolm, struggling now to hold the wriggling child. He was howling with fear, all signs of the Bliss gone from his face.

All around them was chaos. The Vanguard were broken, and Prince Harry and the submarine crew were crying out in confusion, suddenly talking all over each other. The Bliss was gone altogether.

Above, the green goop was unbound, sliding into the "hand" of the eye-twisting structure. It was like watching one of those old jars of novelty slime running through a kid's fingers, gross but harmless.

Within the green, flashing mass, the Crown wriggled around, bulging against the outer membrane, fighting for freedom, desperate.

"Don't kill her!" Tamsyn yelled out to Sushma. "Please, put my boy down."

"You don't know what you've done here," Emma snarled. "Years of work, destroyed!"

"Look, it's over," Tamsyn said. "Let's talk about this, human to whatever it is you are."

"You will suffer, as Nicky Cross continues to suffer," Emma said through gritted teeth, glancing up at the broken form of her master. "You cannot defy us."

"Put the boy down," Sushma said, stalking back and forth like a cat on the prowl. She was hunched over now, fighting through the pain of her mortal wound through sheer willpower alone. The Gurkha stepped over the agonised Vanguard, blades twitching as she contained her fury.

"No. I do not think I shall."

"Tamsyn, please let me murder this fool."

"Tamsyn, Sushma!" Prince Harry shouted. "What the hell is going on?"

"Mummy!" Malcolm shrieked.

"Sorry, Your Highness, you'll need to wait for your explanation. First, this monster hiding in a human skin is going to let my son go."

A moment of Mexican standoff, where the women looked at each other.

A tendril of green goop slid down the weird structure, like snot falling from the nose of a gross kid.

Emma looked up for one split second, drawn to the image of the Crown.

Sushma darted forward and in the same swift motion she jammed both of her blades into Emma Menteuse's temples. In, out and done. Sushma stood poised, a beautiful praying mantis, scanning for further threats.

Emma slumped back against the tower, a look of surprise frozen on her dead face. Just like that, all of her schemes were undone. Whatever she was, she'd died fast, too surprised to do anything. Whatever power this demon had, it had died with the host body she'd stolen.

Who even were you? Tamsyn mused.

Malcolm screamed, an awful sound without end, his face covered with the blood that had spurted out of Emma's head. Tamsyn ran to her baby boy. She prised Emma's dead fingers from around his throat and clutched him to her breast, soothing his fear. She turned her back on the dead woman and the unsettling structure.

"You're okay, my sweet baby boy," Tamsyn said. "We're getting out of this place."

"What the hell is that thing?" she heard Prince Harry yell. Looking up in shock, she saw the green goop *pulling* Emma's body up to the top of the tower, like a snake snatching something from a tree in the Amazon.

"We're leaving, right now!" she shouted. With Malcolm on one hip, she slid her kukri through her belt, and hoisted Tilly to her feet. The girl was icy cold to the touch, and shivering so much her teeth chattered.

"I don't understand why we're here," Harry said. "We just – we all just felt really happy, and knew we had to walk here."

"What about the zombies?" Tamsyn asked.

"They didn't even look at us. Is this to do with your-" and here Prince Harry pointed to his own temple.

"Something like that. Now come on, we have to get out of here!"

At that moment, the green goop had lifted Emma's body up and into the summit of the tower it squatted in. With a sickening crack it broke her spine, twisting her body into unnatural angles, breaking her limbs, and then setting her just so.

The broken corpse was now a replica of the destroyed spire of the tower, realised in meat and bone. The green goop flowed across her body, and once more was floating in the air, crackling with lightning. The image of the Crown rotated, and fixed her with a malevolent glare.

"Oh, shit," she said, a minute before the Vanguard rose to their feet, all their screeching and head-clutching gone. All smiles, and all directed straight at her. Once more the weight of the mental assault came from the Crown, and Tilly moaned at her side, eyes beginning to roll back in her head.

"Run!" she shouted to the kids and to the rescued submariners. The smiling killers came at them in unison, and Tamsyn felt like she was in the middle of a rugby scrum. Even bare-handed, Prince Harry and his people were managing to break through the gauntlet of psychopaths. Tamsyn hitched up both Malcolm and Tilly, her brutalised body barely able to handle the weight, but she ignored the pain, doing her best to follow Sushma.

"Follow the walls! There has to be a loading dock in here," she shouted.

Sushma began to stagger then, her blades slowing by a fraction of a second. Even the world's toughest woman couldn't shake off a disembowelment. Sheer will alone seemed to be keeping her upright and killing, but she was on the way out.

"You hold on," Tamsyn shouted. "Don't you die till these kids are safe. Do you hear me, woman?"

"I'm dying, not deaf," Sushma said, removing the head of a lurching freak with one even stroke of a kukri. "Look. There is your loading dock."

By the bobbing light of Elijah's head torch, she saw the welcome sight of a roller door, the pathway largely clear of junk. Daylight, seeping around the edges. Quinn and Seb were already yanking on the chains, and then with more urgency.

There was a bracket through the cement floor, pinning the chains in place with a fat brass padlock.

"Shit!" she swore, only then remembering her son was in her arms.

They were pressed up against the roller door, freaks closing in on all sides. One of the sailors was nabbed by the Vanguard, dragged off howling by his ankles. His cursing ended with an abrupt *crack!* when they snapped his neck.

"You bloody bastards!" Harry yelled out, pushing back the Vanguard with a metal pole.

"Listen, Your Highness. Did they bring you in this way?" Tamsyn asked.

"Yes," Harry said after a moment of thought, pushing the Bliss away from his memories. "We came in through here. That lady had the keys for this lock."

He nodded towards the Crown's eye-twisting structure, now capped with the grotesque corpse of Emma Menteuse, arms at unnatural angles.

"Oy! Evil genius!" she shouted to Elijah. "Bust open this lock!"

"I'm trying!" he said, trying to force it open with his home-made pike. A snap, and then he cursed when a big sliver of the spearhead snapped off.

"Stop pissing around! Use a bomb or something!"

Some of Harry's people were assaulting the roller door itself, trying to bust through the sheet metal with bricks and poles. They did little more than dent it, and the rolling mechanism was too high to reach and dislodge.

"We used them all!" Elijah said. He dumped his pike in a rush, tipping his satchel inside out.

Something fell out as he madly shook it, bouncing across the cement until it landed at Tamsyn's feet. It was barely a fire-cracker, a little fuse stuck in a cardboard tube.

"Hurry!" Tamsyn said. The Vanguard were throwing themselves at the little group in front of the door, even as the unholy creature looming over them all writhed, that wicked green eye darting left and right.

SUBMIT, came the command from the crown, and Tamsyn felt her defences crumble. It was all she could do not to place Malcolm and Tilly on the ground and bow to that thing. In her arms, Tilly was twitching, teeth-grinding. The warm flush of the girl's urine ran down Tamsyn's arm.

Our shield is failing, she thought. The girl was baking hot to the touch.

"Mummy, I scared!" Malcolm cried out.

"I know, mate," Tamsyn said, squeezing her boy tight. All around, the scream of men and women, fighting to the death with scraps of junk, bare hands, teeth.

Behind her, Elijah had jammed the little bomb into the hasp of the lock. He flicked the wheel of a cigarette lighter, summoning sparks, fuse held close.

No flame.

"Light the damn thing!" Harry shouted, pole-axing

another madman in the face. They were boxed in now, pushed together like a mosh-pit. Tamsyn couldn't put the kids down if she wanted too, packed in so tightly with the others.

The merry clatter of a cigarette lighter dropped to the floor, lost underfoot. Elijah swore long and loud, begged anyone to help, asked if anyone had a spare lighter.

"I've got one but I can't bloody reach down to get it," one submariner yelled out. "Give me some room!"

Another man snatched from the outer rank, dragged into the Vanguard and beaten to death. Another buried a street-sign in an enemy head, straight down to the smile, but he wouldn't let go of the weapon and was pulled down, other Vanguard stomping him into a screaming paste.

Then Sushma peeled away from the group, hacking into the Vanguard like a explorer parting a jungle with a machete. Jostled from all sides, all that Tamsyn could see of her friend was a flurry of blades, arcs of blood in all directions, and the screaming of the Vanguard as she dissected them expertly.

The crush lessened. With Sushma's assault drawing away the Vanguard, the submariners were able to push back against the press, forcing the freaks away one hard-fought step at a time.

"Kid, catch the lighter!" the woman yelled, and tossed her cigarette lighter back towards Elijah. A sea of hands reached up to catch it, and they passed it back towards the roller-door, handing it down to the terrified kid.

Then Sushma screamed, a long note of horror that grabbed Tamsyn's heart and *clenched*. The Gurkha stood in the middle of the group of Vanguard, but her arms were down by her sides, her head raised to the roof. All around her, the Vanguard were kneeling and grabbing at her, but she stood perfectly still.

Then one of the grinning loons stood, waving Sushma's makeshift bandages. Another hauled on a rope of intestine, a good ten feet away from Sushma, and others ran out that grisly rope, a tug of war, a magician hauling out a hundred slimy scarves. Others held up their own grisly trophies. A stomach. What might have been her kidneys. Then that awful howl fell to silence, and the warrior was dead on her feet, jostled around and held up by the freaks who were still emptying her torso like a Christmas stocking. Her terrified stare blazed into Tamsyn, dead eyes levelled at the people she'd saved.

It wasn't a warrior's death. It was a sick butchering.

"You bastard!" Tamsyn shouted at the Crown. She felt the hatred pouring out of the green orb, contempt for her, even as it pushed against her weak shield. She did her best to augment Tilly's failing defense, trying to picture the Abbey on the coast, but she just didn't have Tilly's raw psychic strength.

SUBMIT! the Crown demanded.

BANG! Elijah's last bomb went off. A heart stopping moment, and then the other kids were hauling on the chains, jerking the door up one foot, then two, then four, and then everyone was scrambling to get out and into that amazing daylight.

It was a ramp going up to street level, littered with leftover bits of junk the Vanguard had dragged inside. There were two rotters lurking around by the roller door, but they didn't stand a chance as the survivors swarmed over them, taking them out quickly. The dead were nothing compared to the living terror hot on their heels.

Tamsyn was out there too, limping, every muscle

groaning from holding the two kids. If they hadn't beaten her, she might have been able to carry both of them, but she was running on fumes now. She ascended the ramp in a painful half-jog, struggling for speed as the Vanguard started slipping out of the roller door.

"I can help!" Elijah said, taking Malcolm. Too tired to fight off the unexpected help, Tamsyn resettled Tilly in both her arms, still struggling to heft the girl.

"Mummy!" Malcolm wailed, wriggling in the arms of his new saviour.

"You're okay baby!" Tamsyn cried out. "Mummy's right behind you!"

Tamsyn felt like she was carrying a bag of cement, and everything from her shoulders down was on fire. She reached the top of the ramp, huffing like a racehorse, knowing that she had maybe a minute or two before her body packed it in altogether.

Hide the kids. Draw the monsters away.

"Let me help," Harry said, taking Tilly from Tamsyn. He lifted her up into his arms, and then met gave Tamsyn a slow, creepy smile.

With one swift move, Prince Harry drove the girl against his knee, snapping her spine like a thick branch.

"What the hell? What did you do?" Tamsyn heard herself screaming from a thousand miles away.

Harry dropped the girl like a sack of potatoes, taking a moment to crush her windpipe with his foot. He advanced on Tamsyn, staring at her, pure hatred written across his face.

"You stupid girl. We took you in. You could have been safe forever. All of these people. Now look at what you did!"

Suddenly Harry's people stopped, and as one they turned towards Tamsyn, faces lighting up in that same creepy smile. Up ahead, Elijah and the others realised the evil change that had come upon the adults, and then they were off and running for their lives, weaving through a tangle of actual rotting zombies. With Malcolm still on his shoulder, Elijah clicked on a remote control, and a distant car exploded, and then another.

Then the Vanguard turned as one. They slipped around Harry and Tamsyn's tableau, fully focused on chasing after the kids. Tamsyn shivered in their wake, knowing that at any moment they could turn on her, rip her limb from limb.

Tamsyn slipped over into the world of her auras, and saw that Prince Harry was a blank space on the universe. A nothing, not human. Desperately she attempted to sever the Vanguard from their source, to free them, but she was beaten, demoralised, weak. Her mind knife bounced away, not even freeing one submariner from the Vanguard.

"I am going to find your child, and he will be a Host, perhaps for the Crown itself. But you, you I will put back in a cage. You just got promoted," Harry said, nudging Tilly's dead body with her foot.

"Emma?" she finally said. "Have you got Emma in there with you?"

"I was never Emma," he scoffed. "You will call me the Final Knight, every day that you are suffered to live in your cage. I serve the Crown, and now so do you."

Run, kids, she thought, and saw the trio outstripping the Vanguard mob with the greyhound slipperiness of the young, with her baby boy still miraculously safe. Elijah set off a bomb in a van right as the Vanguard swarmed around it, sending dozens sprawling in all direction, some never to rise or smile again.

"We did it, you know," Tamsyn said, looking down sadly

at Tilly's body. "We came to this stupid building, and rescued some people. Mission accomplished."

"Those children will be dead within the hour," the thing inside Harry said, lip curling up into a sneer. "Even now, the Crown summons the Mindless to hunt them."

"Nah, you don't know these kids. No chance you'll catch them."

"Perhaps."

Tamsyn felt peace, real peace. *Malcolm is safe.* On a primal level, she was satisfied that she'd protected her offspring, sold her own life to save his. She turned to Harry with a relieved smile.

"Sense at last," the Final Knight said. "Return to your cage. Submit. Behave."

Tamsyn slowly drew the kukri from her belt, and held it in both hands, looking the monster dead in the eye. Harry's head shook left, and right.

"I do not think you will kill this one," the Final Knight said. "I can see your shared history in his memories. He was fond of you. You, of him."

Tamsyn said nothing, held herself tense, preparing to strike. The blade wobbled slightly in her grip. The Prince stood head and shoulders above her broken body, and had army training that the Final Knight was no doubt absorbing from his memories.

I lose, she realised. *Finally, today, I end.*

She'd gone so far from Gravesend, seen so much, and there'd been no point to any of it. Eddie and her, her Dad, all of that war and death, and she was about to spend her life in a cage, fattening the humans up.

Sushma would have fought now.

So would Eddie. Baxter. Clem and Dawes. Her dad. *The world goes on!* Mal Webb had said, and she'd seen the world end twice. Her own world when her mum died, and then the rest of the place when the rotters showed up.

Fight him!

"Put down that knife," the Final Knight spat. "I will not waste two Host bodies on you today. Quickly, or you shall suffer."

He shifted himself into a combat pose, ready to disarm her the moment she came into range with the knife. The stance was equal parts muscle memory and whatever The Final Knight had pilfered from Harry's mind. Tamsyn didn't have a hope.

"You have a job now. Do it."

You're a bad-ass bitch! Fight him!

She'd only get the one move. In the distance she could hear the whooping of Vanguard, returning to One Angel Square. The Final Knight was calling in allies, taking no chances with her.

Go, Elijah! Keep my boy safe!

She lifted the knife.

"It's all okay now."

Prince Harry moved, just as she placed the sharp blade to her own chest.

"Hey arsehole! I quit."

The Knight hiding in the Prince drew up short, thrown by this change of events.

"You will be wasting a great resource with this self-termination!"

He came in with arms spread wide, determined to wrap her in a bear-hug, and that was when Tamsyn followed through with her move. Instead of driving the knife into her own chest, she swept it down and back up, a great arc in between Harry's reaching hands. A deep cut just above his groin, and Tamsyn learnt that the royals had intestines just like everyone else. Pushing up as hard as she could, soon her hands were slick with blood and gore, and she fumbled the knife as it struck the bottom edge of his sternum.

Oh god. I'm killing him!

"You wasteful little bitch," Harry said, blood bubbling over his lips. The Final Knight hiding within him stared out with shock, confused that this girl had bested him. Still he drew her in, trying to crush her with his failing strength. This pushed the kukri deeper into Harry's liver, doing untold damage, but still he came at her, pushing her down onto the ground.

"If you will not serve the Crown, you will die!"

Harry fought to rise up, to pull the knife out of his chest, and now it was Tamsyn's turn to grapple the man who'd once been her champion. They thrashed around together, Tamsyn slick with his blood.

"Shh. I'm freeing you, you stupid man," Tamsyn said. The light in his eyes fading, Harry's hands fell away from the hilt of the blade.

"I'm sorry I did this to you," Tamsyn gasped. "You were good to me when I didn't deserve it. I'm so sorry."

A moment then, when a calmness fell across the dying man's face. Was that Harry still in there, looking down on her, forgiving her for this sad little ending?

Then that wicked smile, miles away from Harry's familiar lopsided grin, and the Final Knight threw his head forward, closing his teeth around Tamsyn's throat.

In one swift movement, Prince Harry clamped down on her windpipe, savaging her like a wild beast. With the last of his strength, he tore out her throat.

25

Tamsyn opened her eyes with a gasp, clutching at her throat.

No gaping hole, no missing windpipe. Smooth skin greeted her trembling hands.

She was laying in her bed back at Number 5 St. Francis Avenue, Gravesend. It was just as she'd left it, back when she'd jumped the wall at the Safe Zone for the family photos. Mess everywhere, drawers pulled out and tipped, boy-band posters peeling away from the walls.

The only difference was that everything seemed dull, sepia with hints of silver-nitrate. Blinking her eyes, the effect faded. Tamsyn lifted her hands to examine them, expecting blood, only to realise she was in the same kit she'd worn here, over three years earlier.

Leather jacket. Man U scarf. Gloves and bracers.

What the actual hell? How can I have imagined all of that?

She scrambled out of bed, chest heaving, and she felt like she couldn't draw a breath. Panic, like she hadn't felt in years.

I just died. Throat torn out. Bled out. An awful, painful, scary death.

Now she was back home, three years in the past.

I had a baby. Eddie. My Dad. How did NONE of that happen?

Leaning in the corner was her old compound bow, with a half-full quiver. She'd dropped the rest of the arrows when she crawled across that icy pipe like an idiot. Back when zombies were the biggest of her problems.

Is the Crown of Countless Suns even real? The Vanguard?

She snatched up her bow and nocked an arrow, marvelling at the tension, the perfectly balanced instrument that had cost her Dad a small fortune. Suspecting a trick, she checked the closet, peered out of the door, and then back to the window, looking for Prince Harry, for any Vanguard, for anything that could keep her from thinking too much about where she was.

She even reached within, searching for her supernatural gift. Nothing. No auras, no special connection to the dead, no weird Jedi powers.

I'm losing my goddamn mind. Weirdest dream ever.

Using the tip of her arrow, she lifted the curtains back an inch. Her windows were as filthy as always, but all she could see was the garden hedge below, the neighbour's wall, and then fog, a real pea-souper. Gravesend was completely shrouded.

Good. Easy to hide from the undead in that.

Standing completely still, she waited for footsteps, for the sound of anything moving on the stairs or the hallway outside her bedroom door. Nothing. Wincing as the floorboards creaked underneath her, she knelt down by the tipped-out papers, and it was as she'd left everything. On top of the stack were the court records of Simon Dawes, proof that he was now alive and on the Isle of Sheppey.

I take this back to Dad.
I accidentally let the zombies into Gravesend.
Everyone dies.
Dad and I go to Sheppey.
Dad dies.
Simon Dawes fixes the Paraclete.
More people die on the ocean.
I get to America, and everyone in Corpus Christi dies.

Shaking her head, Tamsyn backed away from the papers. She had the chance to do everything different now, and it all started with changing how today unfolded.

No Paraclete. No Simon Dawes. Right now that massive horde from London is closing in on the walls of the Safe Zone. I can't let them follow me inside again.

We all have to get over the river to the Tilbury Fort, with whatever supplies we've got. It's gonna suck wintering out in that joint, but at least we'll survive.

Tamsyn stalked down the stairs, and did not bother collecting mementos or any of the photos. She'd lost the lot anyway in the water, when they shot her Dad on the beach.

Once more she slipped out of the silent house, out to the shed. *This is where you get the bicycle, and pump up the tires.* The fog was thick, and she could barely see the back fence. *Weird. It wasn't a foggy day when this happened. It had been still, bitterly cold. Snowing a little.*

If anything, today felt colder, a bitter chill that went right through her leathers and down into her bone marrow. Once more she saw that sepia tinge overlaid on everything, and white silvery edges to the shapes in her peripheral vision. Blinking it away, she once more saw the overgrown garden, flowers and lawn growing out of control, the white dusting of snow that she remembered, starting to settle across everything.

She repeated her motions of the day, finding the bike, pumping up the bike tires, slinging her bow across her back. This time she kept the claw hammer in her belt, the one she'd left in a zombie's head. Today, she held her hatchet across the handlebars.

I won't destroy the fence this time. I won't let them in.

She pushed her bicycle down the side path, past the gnome that she didn't bother to hide the house key under. Out on the street, she was careful of the snow slush under her tires, and she pedalled slowly through the abandoned cars and rubbish bins, peering through the fog for any sign of zombies.

That phone box there, one leapt out at me, she remembered, steering her bike well clear of it. But this time there was no naked dead man lurching out at her, nothing but the slow drift of fog. The streets were completely empty. She waited a long moment for the pack of zombies she remembered that were about to come around the next corner. She'd left her hammer buried in a dead boy's skull and barely got away with her life.

Nothing. Not a single coffin-dodger shuffling through these streets.

"This place was crawling with rotters," Tamsyn mumbled. Still shaken by her vivid dream of a future that never happened, Tamsyn was driven by one thing, and one thing only.

Find Dad. Get him the hell out of Gravesend.

The whole sequence of the day had changed. She remembered the next part, burnt into her brain. Thousands of the London undead, a huge horde pushing up against the walls of the Gravesend Safe Zone, with her caught on the outside. When they saw her round the last corner, she would have to pedal like the devil, just to keep ahead of that mob.

Nothing. Empty streets. Through the fog she could just make out the outline of the Jubilee Clock Tower, the train station, and the shape of some buildings beyond that.

The walls of the Safe Zone, every manner of junk that could be piled up and nailed together, and it was completely unmanned.

"Dad. Dad!" Tamsyn screamed. She pedalled the bike as fast as she could, past the train station, over the bridge. The west wall, the strongest fortification. Most of the town guard was usually along here, smoking cigarettes and grumbling out in the cold. She banged the back of her hatchet against the sheet-iron and wrecked cars, hollering at the top of her lungs.

Nothing. It looked like Gravesend was completely empty.

The wall guards used to send patrols and scavengers out over the wall with rope ladders, careful to pull everything back up when they were gone. She'd always been rubbish at climbing up things, even in Basic, and she held no illusions about her ability to scale up the wall.

There weren't many options. Bust through the loose fence paling on the other side. Risk her neck shimmying across the pipeline or roll down the steep slope onto the train track.

That left one option.

She rode hell for leather towards the Thames, dropping her bike and running when the fog revealed the water's edge. Swinging out over the side of the sea wall, she saw the railing bolted into the wall, the one that Jake Hammond and her little tearaway mates had used to sneak out past the wall to look for sweets.

God, I hope this holds my weight, she thought, slipping down until her boots touched the rusty metal. It groaned a little, but held, enough for her to shuffle along the wall, inch by inch, fingertips just reaching the top of the wall. Turning her head to the right, she could see a rusty old ladder running up the side of the abandoned West Pier – so that was how five small children could climb back up.

Knees wobbling, she continued to inch left, trying not to look down at the murky water underneath. The river seemed wrong, and it took Tamsyn a long moment to figure it out.

She'd been fishing out here with her Dad, catching nothing they were game to eat, just a way to kill off the tedium and fear of the post-apocalypse. She'd spent hours dangling off this wall, sketching the buildings on the other side, the wrecked boats, the corpses floating out to sea.

The Thames was a tidal river. It was alive, moving, flowing. Underneath her feet, this water was completely, perfectly, deathly still, like a brown pane of glass.

Eyes wide, she moved faster, all finger-tips and careful shuffling. The brackets where the railing was fixed to the sea-wall must have been at least a hundred years old, rusted through from the constant damp and rain, and it creaked and groaned every time she shifted her weight.

Above, she saw the ramshackle wall, overhanging the sea-wall by a good foot. Someone had thought to wrap barbed wire and spikes around the hanging lengths of sheet-iron and old street-signs, a pointless measure against creatures that felt no pain. Tamsyn was forced to duck low to get underneath the wall's edge, wincing when a barb caught her and yanked out a hair.

Creak. The railing groaned ominously, and then it suddenly dropped a full inch. Crying out, Tamsyn snatched up at the tangle of wire to stop her fall, barely noticing as the jags scratched her hands. She did not fancy getting wet in the Thames on a normal winter's day, but something about the water was alien. Wrong.

Don't fall in, for heaven's sake! Every atom in her body cringed at the closeness of the water, and she knew it was vital not to slip off the railing.

There's something very bloody wrong about Gravesend.

Slowly, she eased her grip from the barbed wire. Lucky, the jags hadn't broken her skin. No blood, just some weird shiny silver muck from the wire itself. One foot to the left. Now the other. The railing creaked again, and she stopped for one heart-shuddering moment.

Then she was past the underneath of the wall, and inside Gravesend's Safe Zone. Slowly, gingerly, she reached up, ready to hook her fingers on the lip of the wall. One frantic scramble and she would hoist herself up.

"Damnit!" she said. Even on tip-toe, her fingers were just barely shy of the top of the wall. The railing had dropped further than she thought.

The railing was only five inches wide at most. Her knees were brushing up against the cement, too close for her to squat down for a vertical leap. The best she could manage would be a short bouncing hop from her toes, but even as she tensed up the railing groaned again.

"I've gotta get off this thing!" she said. It was either go back the way she came, and hope to climb up on the wrong side of the wall, or risk pressing on, hoping the railing wouldn't snap off altogether.

Up ahead, she saw it. The Gravesend Pier, a glorious mess of wrought iron and sheet roofing, stretching out towards Tilbury. The last time she'd laid eyes on this place, the entire village had been escaping to the ferry, thousands of zombies hot on their heels. Just shy of the ferry was where Eddie's dad met his grisly end, a Shakespearean hubris that her father-in-law had totally deserved.

Just over a hundred metres of dangerously creaking rail. Not a person in sight. And a river she did not want to touch, on a very primal level.

Every footstep a prayer, the ancient rail creaking, straining, threatening to shear loose from the wall. Fingertips brushing the smooth wall, with nothing to grip should the railing give way again. She cursed Jake Hammonds and his little crew, weakening this old rail whenever they'd ducked out for boiled sweets.

Soon she could make out an old ladder on the side of the Pier. It ran down below the completely still water, to wherever the low-tide mark was on a normal day. It was close enough for her to lean out and grab the rungs, hoist herself up and into safety.

She was twenty metres away from this when a bracket gave way underneath her feet with a SNAP! The railing held in one piece, but it pushed away from the wall, until Tamsyn was almost at a forty-five degree angle, feet and legs working overtime.

Tamsyn reached the next bracket, which held, and once more she was vertical, more feet than legs. To her right, the buckled railing gave away with a rotten sounding *crack*, and a ten metre section fell into the water.

The Thames swallowed the broken railing with barely a ripple. Once more the smooth, glassy surface. It was not even behaving like water should.

Calf-muscles aching with tension, Tamsyn was right up to the Pier now, less than five metres to the ladder and safety. That was the moment another bracket gave, and this time the railing was folding, buckling right underneath her.

She ran, pushing off against the sea-wall at the last minute, arms flailing as she reached for the old ladder. Girl met steel in a lung-emptying collision, and she clung to it for dear life, smiling gratefully as she heard the rail slide into the river.

"Well, that was a near thing," she said to the universe, just as the rusty rung beneath her right foot snapped, her boot heel grazing the water.

Cold. Impossible, bone-freezing cold, and the feeling that she should just let go, let this bizarre version of the Thames slurp her down, down to the muddy bed full of Roman coins and broken glass. *No.* She snatched her foot out, struggling for the next rung, climbing up as fast as she could.

Quick as thought, something flicked up and out of the river, snatching her by the ankle. She could only look down in horror at something like an octopus tentacle, already spiralling up her calf, touching the back of her knee.

Cold, cold, but completely dry, and it squeezed tight, drawing her down towards the glassy surface. Gripping the rung for dear life, she let her right hand fall to her belt, drawing out the wicked little hatchet her Dad found for her.

She hit the tentacle like a lumberjack, fear lending a strength to her that she didn't know she possessed. The sharp edge parted the silvery flesh of the tentacle, sending out an inky blood with every stroke.

"Take that, you creepy squid!" Tamsyn cried out joyously, when another tentacle shot out, grabbing the other leg. Then another, wrapped around her waist, gently but persistently peeling her away from the ladder. One more around her wrist, shaking the hatchet loose.

Tamsyn turned to see the Thames boiling with tentacles. Thousands of tentacles, lashing the entire length of the river, as far as she could see. Scraping the sea-walls, exploring the wrecked boats, reaching up and onto the land.

It wasn't thousands of octopi or squid. It was one creature, one organism, both river and animal, and that impossible beast was pulling Tamsyn down, sending up more tentacles to encircle her, until all that was free was her head, and that one arm, gripping for dear life onto a rung.

The questing tip of a tentacle reached towards her fingers, gently prying them loose. Her capture was almost a respectful thing, the grip of the beast firm but insistent. As if she was a drunk in the pub, being gently escorted out into the street, but in this instance down into the bosom of some river-beast.

In a world where the dead walked, and then the living could become puppets, and a weird mind-demon could live in a tower of junk, the Thames turning into a polite tentacle forest was definitely on track.

"I've had such a stupid day," Tamsyn moaned.

That was when the first flash appeared from above, slamming into the river-beast. It was like a lightning bolt, or a laser beam, and it left the creature sizzling, retreating. Another bolt, and another, and now the tentacles were loosening their grip, sliding back over her flesh, retreating into the water.

Still shaking, she climbed the last of the ladder. Only when she was safely on the pier did she look up to see who her saviour was.

Standing on top of the sea-wall was a woman with a bow in hand, scanning the river for further threat. The nocked arrow was like a line of sunlight, painful to look at. Satisfied that the beast was gone, the figure slid the weird arrow into her quiver, bow vanishing into thin air, and only then did Tamsyn recognise her.

Waiting patiently for her was Pocahontas. The statue of Pocahontas, the one she'd sketched a hundred times back in the church yard. Her skin was pockmarked and aged, features a little washed out by decades out in the weather. Her eyelids were mere ideas, her mouth a thin lipless line.

This *statue* had climbed down from its stone plinth, and despatched a monster. To save her. It moved with a surreal grace, the metal flowing like the skin and fabric it was carved to represent. Soon Pocahontas loomed over her, metallic features drawn into a scowl.

"FOOL GIRL," the statue-thing said, her voice a mechanical scratch of scraping steel, the bass boom of air pushing through metal tubes. "YOU SHOULD NOT BE HERE!"

"You're telling me," Tamsyn said, the tremor in her voice betraying her cocky wit.

"ALL THE HOPES WE PLACED IN YOU. YOU WERE THE LAST ONE. THE LAST!"

"The last of the Guides, right," Tamsyn said. "Look, I don't know what kind of bizarre dream this is. That river? You? No way this is happening. I'm probably back up at One Angel Square, having a stroke."

"YOU DO NOT LAY ILL. YOU THREW YOUR LIFE AWAY. NOW, YOU ARE LOST."

The last word came out in a sudden, booming breath, Pocahontas closing her mouth with a metallic clang. Turning away from Tamsyn, the statue walked back into Gravesend, slowly, the rhythm of her tread an inhuman slide that no living creature could hope to emulate.

"I SHOULD HAVE LET MY RIVER BEAST TAKE YOU."

"What the hell? That thing was *yours?*"

Pocahontas ignored her, walking past the silent Three Daws Pub, once the hang-out of Eddie's dad and his cronies. Around the corner was St George's Church, where her Dad ran his school during the post-apocalypse, and Tamsyn followed the statue into the yard to the rear of the church.

Sure enough, the statue of Pocahontas returned to her empty plinth, gripping the granite sides, flowing upwards and inside out until she was once more in place, shifting into the pose that Tamsyn had sketched over and over. Arms held out to the sides, palms forward. Mid-step. Head lifted, alert.

Wiping away the snow slush, Tamsyn slid into her favourite bench. She looked up at the image of the warrior's daughter. No wonder she'd loved Sushma so much – the two women had been cut from a very similar mold.

"Hey," Tamsyn said. The statue did not stir.

"Don't pretend that you didn't just climb down from there. Rude!"

Tamsyn spent a few desperate hours searching Gravesend. She kicked in doors, smashed windows, raised hell with the old hand-klaxons. Nothing. No-one. Everything was frozen as it was that day she'd snuck out, but the Safe Zone was completely empty of life.

Except for back at St George's church.

In desperation, Tamsyn unslung her bow, and then she launched an arrow at the statue, straight towards Pocahontas's midriff. *Clang.* Another shot, and this time her arrow straight up snapped when it met the bronze.

"I wish I had one of your stupid lightning arrows!" she said, nocking her next arrow, only now it was a shaft of pure light. Tamsyn dropped the arrow in surprise, and it melted a pile of slush into water, the muddy ground into baked clay, before the light faded away, leaving a normal arrow.

"You'd better start talking to me!" Tamsyn said. With little more than a thought she nocked another bright arrow, bow flexing with incredible tension. Tamsyn lined up the arrow between Pocahontas's eyes.

"Don't ignore me!" she said. She deliberately shot wide, and the arrow punched into the stone of the church, shivering the stone like a strike from a catapult. Tamsyn looked wide-eyed at the sheer destruction she'd just caused.

"Last chance, bitch."

The statue did not move.

"Goodbye."

She sent the luminous arrow straight at the statue's heart. Quicker than thought, the statue completed that forward step, clapping both her hands together. The arrow shivered in her grip, inches away from her heart, still writhing and inching forward, denied of its target.

With one swift movement, Pocahontas snapped the arrow, the glow instantly fading. She dropped the broken halves to the base of her plinth.

"STILL YOU FIGHT!" she mocked. "EVEN NOW, WHEN IT DOES NOT MATTER."

"What are you saying?" Tamsyn said warily. "That I shouldn't have gone to Manchester? We didn't know it was a trap."

"WHILE YOU DREW BREATH, THEY FEARED YOU. THE CROWN, THE KNIGHT, ALL OF THEM. NOW, YOU ARE JUST A DEAD GIRL."

"I'm dead," Tamsyn said, the statement making everything real. The fog, the empty streets, the impossible things she'd seen. The light arrows. The loss of her mind powers.

"Is this place the afterlife?"

"IS THIS PLACE THE AFTERLIFE?" Pocahontas mimicked, bronze lip curled up in a sneer.

"Is it Hell?"

"NO, IT IS NOT," Pocahontas said. "NOT ANYMORE."

26

"What is your problem?" Tamsyn said, following Pocahontas. Every time the statue tried to return to its pose, Tamsyn had shot another glowing arrow at it, until finally Pocahontas had had enough. She'd climbed down from her plinth, knocked Tamsyn onto her backside with a shove that could have toppled an elephant, and now she was stomping around the town, doing her best to ignore her.

Pocahontas was doing a kind of guard circuit of the town, following the inside of the walls. By the time she got the Jubilee Clock Tower, Tamsyn was on her second sing-through of 99 Bottles. She'd found that she could pick up a rock and repeat the glowing arrow-trick on these, on almost anything.

Every now and then, Tamsyn would throw an explosive pebble at the living statue, which she would deflect from a forearm, quicker than Wonder Woman stopping a bullet. Behind them lay a trail of carnage, with exploded shopfronts, shattered roads, and several breaches in the now-pointless wall.

"It's kinda fun blowing up Gravesend," Tamsyn said, lobbing another glowing rock at the statue. This time Pocahontas batted the missile aside and came straight for Tamsyn, snatching her by the jacket, fist raised.

"Yeah, whatever. I'm already dead," Tamsyn said. "It's not like you can kill me again."

"YOU STUPID GIRL," Pocahontas growled, right up in Tamsyn's face. Her breath smelt like rust and oil, huffed out from whatever passed for her lungs.

"Go on, take your shot," Tamsyn said. "I'm not going anywhere."

Pocahontas relaxed her grip, and then flowed backwards. Once more she held her own bow in hand, glowing arrow nocked.

"ARE YOU SO SURE? DO YOU THINK DEATH IS THE ONLY END?"

"I don't know anything! Because you won't tell me anything!"

"I DO NOT OWE YOU A SINGLE WORD."

"Fine. Hey, I bet John Smith was fun in the sack."

"DO NOT SPEAK OF HIM!" Pocahontas said, letting an arrow sizzle dangerously close to Tamsyn's head. Behind her, a car went up in flames, but she dared not turn away from the statue's fury. The statue fumbled the next arrow onto the string, bronze hands trembling with rage. The tip of the arrow was aimed at Tamsyn's centre mass.

"Did you ever see the Disney movie? They should have given you bigger boobs. They made you look like a total sissy."

"SPEAK AGAIN, I WILL END YOU.

"Do you think I'm scared of a Disney princess! You're a joke, lady!"

A long moment as Tamsyn stared down Pocahontas, and

then she broke into song. *Colors of the Wind*, Pocahontas's cheesy number from the Disney movie. Slowly, the scowl on Pocahontas's face turned up, and the bronze face relaxed, curving up into a smile, and then laughter, booming out across the empty streets.

"There she is," Tamsyn said with her own smile. "Knew you had it in you."

THEY SAT in the Three Daws Pub, Tamsyn nursing a bottle of rum from behind the bar. It didn't taste right, and she supposed it was ghost rum, or the memory of alcohol.

"Can I get drunk here? Like, don't you need a bloodstream to get drunk?"

"OBSERVE," Pocahontas said, and quick as a flash she snatched up a fork from the table, stabbing the tines into the tip of Tamsyn's thumb. It stung a little, but not as much as it should have.

"Um, ouch?" Tamsyn said. Pocahontas squeezed at her thumb gently, until a droplet appeared.

It wasn't blood. It was silver, like mercury, and it ran down her thumb like a melting ice cream. The same as what she'd seen when the barbed wire bit into her hands.

"LICK IT," Pocahontas said. "THAT WILL CLOSE THE WOUND FASTER."

Tamsyn did so, and her new blood tasted amazing. Like sherbet and honey, ice cream and the kiss of a lover, like everything good from the life she'd just lost. Just like that, the hole in her thumb was gone, and the "bleeding" stopped.

"What is that stuff?" Tamsyn wondered. She took to the

rum again, and it was even more disappointing after tasting the silver stuff from her own veins.

"AETHER," she said.

It was the first nice thing she'd encountered here, and she wanted to take a bath in it, drink it until her guts burst. Every addictive synapse in her ghost-brain was firing, aching, *craving*.

She was a walking case of PTSD, but this stuff alone was worth hanging on for. Tamsyn had found a new substance to abuse, and she knew she would chase this until it destroyed her.

A large part of her didn't mind this outcome.

"IF YOU ARE BLED ENOUGH, YOU WILL END UP AT THE BEACH."

"Um, what?"

"THE FINAL SHORE. BEYOND THAT, OBLIVION."

"I'm sorry, you're talking in Dungeons and Dragons. What the hell?"

Pocahontas sighed. She settled in, wearing the face of a person forced to explain something very simple to a person too dumb to get it. She used the salt shaker to draw out a circle of grains.

"HERE. THIS IS PURGATORY. HELL. THE MIRROR-LANDS. DEAD PEOPLE COME HERE."

She moved the salt shaker into the centre of the circle.

"YOU ARE DEAD. SO YOU ARE NOW HERE."

With an impossible stretching of her bronze limbs to the neighbouring tables, Pocahontas put two other salt shakers into the circle of salt, and mimicked them beating up "her" salt shaker. Unscrewing the caps, she shared out the salt from Tamsyn's containers into these new ones. Finally, the shaker representing Tamsyn was empty. Pocahontas slid the empty shaker through the far end of the circle, further, and then to the edge of the table, and then she pushed it forcefully, letting it shatter on the ground.

"DO YOU UNDERSTAND?"

"So, I'm dead...but I can die again. And it's like Super Death?"

A heavy, metallic sigh.

"YES."

"Are there others in here, ones that will take my, er, Aether from me?"

Pocahontas nodded.

"Well, it's bloody delicious. I'm not surprised there's ghost vampires down here in Hell. Are they the ones in charge?"

"NO," Pocahontas said loudly, slamming her palms against the table. "THEY ARE THE CRIMINALS AND THE VILE. NEVER."

"So....so are you in charge?"

"I WATCH. I GUIDE. I GUARD," Pocahontas said.

"Ah. So you're a Guide too. Lemme guess, you could see all those auras and things when you were alive? Special connection with the dead and the dying?"

Pocahontas nodded.

"Does that make you an angel now?"

Pocahontas stood, and as she stood there was the weight of something unseen behind her, rising, oppressive to the room, pushing down on Tamsyn.

"THE ROD TO CORRECT. ERRORS JUDGED AND FACED. THE SOUL PURIFIED."

"Jesus Christ, you're a devil."

"HE IS NOT HERE."

GETTING any information out of Pocahontas was painful. Tamsyn got the feeling that she'd been so still and silent for so long that talking no longer came naturally. So of course, Tamsyn overcompensated. She told the living statue all about her adventures, of the world before. Of Eddie, and her Dad, even the TV shows and culture that had faded from the world.

"Wait a minute. You knew the song from the Disney movie, the one about you."

"WHAT OF IT?"

"How did you get to watch movies down here? You're hundreds of years too dead to have seen it. What gives?"

They were walking down the High Street, past the ruined and abandoned storefronts. Pocahontas paused in front of a home furnishing shop with TVs in the window. Leaning in close, she breathed against the dust, a flow of air too long for human lungs to hold.

Then she swept the dust aside with the palm of one hand, and Tamsyn looked in wonder at the suddenly clean glass, the appliances behind it, now boxy televisions from the 1980s, showing the Goodies. Then a news broadcast, showing the date as November 24th, 1987.

In the back of the store, Tamsyn could see people moving around. A salesman. Customers. Yipping out in delight, Tamsyn threw the door open, calling out in hello.

Within, the store was in ruins, long looted of furniture and anything not electronic. The place was musty and stale, and completely silent.

Tamsyn stepped back outside to see Pocahontas watching the show, booming out with laughter at the Goodies' antics.

"THIS IS MY FAVOURITE ONE," the statue said.

"You can see back in time?"

Pocahontas shrugged, as if this was no big deal. She breathed again, this time against the street, and brushed away the fog with both hands.

Tamsyn was now looking upon a scene from long ago. Cobbled streets. Horses and carts. People tipping chamber-pots out into the street.

"WHERE DEATH HAS TOUCHED, WE MAY LOOK," Pocahontas said. Sure enough, a boy had been killed by a runaway horse on this street, back in the 1700s. Looking back into the shop, she could see 1980s paramedics trying to resuscitate an old man in the back corner.

"So, who died in front of the Pocahontas movie?" Tamsyn asked.

"THE OLD PRIEST BACK AT THE CHURCH. WAS PLEASURING HIMSELF WHILE WATCHING MY MOVIE. HEART ATTACK, FIVE MINUTES IN."

"Oh my god. That is the creepiest thing ever."

"YES. I DO NOT LOOK LIKE THE DRAWINGS IN THAT MOVIE."

Tamsyn attempted the time-breath trick herself. While her lungs still worked, she found she didn't actually need to breathe in this place, and she huffed and huffed until she would have normally hyperventilated.

"THINK OF DEATH," Pocahontas boomed at her elbow. "REACH FOR A MOMENT OF DYING."

"Gotcha," Tamsyn said. Roaming up and down the street, she finally had an inkling, and she stood in front of a park-bench. Another long breath, and this time a wisp of fog turned into something thicker. She visualised a pane of dirty glass hanging in mid-air, and sure enough it appeared.

She wiped away the solidified fog with her hand, and found herself looking into the past. A different bench in the same place, and on it a drunk who'd died in the cold. Old timey policemen and ambulance officers stood around the corpse, disgust on their faces.

Tamsyn found she could move the "window" and panned around, as if doing a Google Street View. Going by the classic old cars and the blackout curtains on all the windows, she guessed this was World War 2, right in the middle of the Blitz.

"So many people have died here," Tamsyn realised. Roaming the streets, she went back in time, watching people choke on fish bones, slip down icy steps, knife each other in dark alleys. She went back further still, until she was watching a muddy village alongside the old Roman road, Roman soldiers fighting Iron Age Britons, and then earlier people, hunting, killing each other, being eaten by wolves, and then no people at all, just wild beasts, and complete and utter wilderness all around them.

"How far back can this creepy death-cam thing go?" Tamsyn asked Pocahontas.

"AS FAR BACK AS DEATH," Pocahontas said. "I HAVE WATCHED THE FIRST SLIMY BEASTS CRAWL FORTH FROM THE SHORE AND EAT EACH OTHER. IT IS NOT POSSIBLE TO GO BACK ANY FURTHER THAN THAT."

"Eddie would have loved this. Never would have admitted it, but he was right into history," Tamsyn said. For one brief moment she considered going over to the bus-stop where she'd left her mum to buy a magazine, moments before Simon Dawes drunk-drove through the bus shelter.

No. Not even now. I cannot see that again.

There was one thing she desperately needed to see though. Struck with inspiration, she returned to the Gravesend Pier, blowing and huffing until she'd summoned up another time window.

She relived that dark moment, where death had sat

heaviest on the town. Dozens of awful deaths when the dead broke through the walls, and everyone ran in a panic for the boats.

Ali, her silly little mate, struggling on crutches and pulled into a feeding frenzy. Monica caught up in that knot of violence, and poor Naomi forced to leave her lover behind, to die in that horrible way.

My fault. My fault. All my fault. Death follows me, and these people paid the price.

Terry Jacobs beaten to death by his own people, right on the dock, and then everyone who couldn't get on a boat dead, or pushed into the filthy winter Thames and as good as dead.

Once more she got to look upon Clem Murray, the old vet still just a grumpy drunk and not yet resurrected into a Re-Human, fated to die in Cuba. Eddie, her sweet Eddie, and her heart broke to see him, scared, clutching to the side of the overloaded ferry, the moment he stopped being an arsehole and started becoming the man she would fall in love with.

"There!" she cried out. Her Dad, dragging her away from the massacre and further downstream, to the leaky boat he would die taking to the Isle of Sheppey. For that one moment she could see her beautiful, brave, stupid old man, still trying to do the right thing, right up to the pointless end.

If she stayed here, she would watch this moment, over and over again, even though it meant reliving one of the worst moments of her life. She would wallow in all that guilt, the knowledge she'd as good as killed every person in this scene before her. Just to see her Eddie, and just to see her Dad.

"God, I run like an awkward duck," Tamsyn mused. "Hey, Pocahontas, check out my wobbling duck-arse run."

She turned. The statue was nowhere to be seen.

Tamsyn spent what felt like hours poking around through the empty village, unable to find her bronze friend. She paced the wall tops, looking out, and that was when she noticed the old Milton Chantry, surrounded by an overgrown civic park, door left open.

Built in the 1300s! her Dad had enthused. *Oldest building left in Gravesend!*

Pocahontas had left a rope ladder dangling over the eastern wall, and Tamsyn wriggled awkwardly down it, walking through the wrecked houses her people had long picked over for supplies. The old Chantry was still decked out as a museum, but Tamsyn slipped past the displays and dioramas, drawn by a strange sound.

"HOO. HOO. HOO." A brassy boom, a weird owl imitation, and then finally Tamsyn realised what it was. Her new friend, the spirit of Pocahontas, trapped in a brass statue and crying.

Tamsyn peered around a doorjamb to see the statue kneeling on the flagstones, peering through a time-window. She was looking at an old bed-chamber, lit by the flicker of an oil-lamp. A woman lay in a bed, writhing and coughing, a man in Puritan-era clothes weeping by her bedside. An older woman with a wine-pitcher and a damp towel left them alone, shaking her head.

No more to be done here.

"What of young Thomas?" the man said, his accent and English mangled and hard to parse. He brushed back her dark hair, wiping away sweat with a damp cloth. The woman was covered in smallpox sores, but was immediately recognisable.

"All must die," Pocahontas said on her death-bed. "Tis enough that my child lives."

The older woman returned with a sleeping toddler in her arms, about young Malcolm's age. She brought her over for Pocahontas to see. The dying woman smiled, and then closed her eyes for the final time.

Pocahontas let the death-vision fade into nothing, and now she knelt in a storage room, surrounded by mops and boxes of tourism pamphlets. Without looking up she addressed Tamsyn.

"MY THOMAS LIVED WELL," she said. "WIFE, CHILD, AND THEN MANY GRANDCHILDREN. MY BLOODLINE FLOURISHED UNTIL THE WORLD'S END."

"Is this why you stay here?" Tamsyn asked. "So you can see this?"

Pocahontas nodded slowly.

"Where the hell is everyone anyway? All the other spirits. The Guides or whoever."

"THERE IS A WAR," Pocahontas said. "A WAR WE HAVE ALREADY LOST."

"The Crown of Countless Suns?"

"YES. HIS FOUL TRIBE WILL BE HERE SOON ENOUGH, HUNTING FOR OUR BROKEN MILITIA. TILL THEN, I WATCH MY CHILD. I REMEMBER."

"What has gone on here?"

"THEY HAVE INVADED YOUR WORLD THROUGH MINE. LIFE, DEATH, ALL OF IT WILL SOON END."

"YOU DON'T UNDERSTAND. WE CANNOT FIGHT THEM. WE HAVE LOST."

"Nah. That's a piss weak excuse."

"THESE INVADERS ARE BEYOND EVERYTHING WE KNOW. THEY HAIL FROM ANOTHER UNIVERSE – EVEN WE DO NOT KNOW HOW TO DEFEAT THEM!"

"Kick 'em in the metaphysical balls. God, do I have to solve all your problems?"

"THEY DO NOT HAVE TESTES OR OVARIES. NO WEAK POINTS TO EXPLOIT."

"It was a joke, dickhead."

They were riding bicycles to London. Pocahontas broke three bicycles with her weight before adjusting her mass somehow, and now she was as light as a feather. Everywhere that had been a no-go zone during the zombie apocalypse was now a sweet place to ride, zig-zagging through the abandoned cars and buses.

"Alright. So if there's a war, where is the front? How far away is the enemy?"

"SPACE. TIME. IT IS NOT AS IN THE LANDS OF LIFE."

"What do you mean?"

"WE ARE HERE BECAUSE WE ALL AGREE WE ARE HERE. A MIRROR IMAGE OF THE ROAD TO LONDON. YES?"

"Alright, weirdo. I can see the Thames and at least three McDonalds. We're really here."

"NO," Pocahontas said, her metal brow furrowed in thought. Suddenly they were hurtling past the Eiffel Tower. Tamsyn got the speed wobbles and fell off her bike, knocking over a stand of cheap souvenirs.

"Ow. Shit. And what the hell?"

"NOW I HAVE MADE US AGREE THAT WE ARE IN PARIS. YOUR MIND WAS UNGUARDED, AND I WAS ABLE TO CONVINCE YOU THAT WE ARE NOW HERE."

"Well, that beats a bus through the Chunnel," Tamsyn said. "Can I have a go?"

"YOU! YOU CANNOT KNOW HOW TO-"

The women and their bicycles were suddenly in an empty Times Square, everything scattered and broken just as the last of the news cameras had shown the world. No people still, just an empty city, the ghosts of skyscrapers looming all around them.

"That's a neat trick. Thanks for showing me."

"HOW DID YOU GET THROUGH MY GUARD?"

"Well, I just imagined John Smith's pantaloons from your movie, and then I imagined that *you* were imagining it. When you were distracted, I thought of Times Square."

"YOU ARE AS A CHILD WITH A RIFLE," Pocahontas said. "FINE. LET US BE DONE WITH THE MIRROR-LANDS THEN."

She waved her hand, concentrating, and then both women were standing on a flat, featureless landscape, stretching till infinity in all directions. Their bikes were gone, and Tamsyn realised she was naked, her body smooth and featureless.

"ALL OF THAT IS GONE. EVERYTHING IS AN ILLUSION BUT FOR OUR SOULS," Pocahontas said. She was a metallic woman shape, as featureless as Tamsyn.

"Argh, I don't like it!" Tamsyn cried out. "Gimme my clothes back. Gimme my *face* back!"

"DO IT YOURSELF," Pocahontas said. Tamsyn frowned and tried to picture herself as she was back on Cuba, the slightly older body that she realised she missed. Once more she stood in t-shirt, shorts and boots, a bottle of rum in her hands.

"Argh, ghost rum is just balls," Tamsyn said, tipping it out.

"IT IS NOT REAL."

Tamsyn briefly summoned forth visions of herself in a wedding dress, on stilts, with flaming hair and machine gun arms, before finally settling back to Classic Cuban Tamsyn. Pocahontas shook her head, shifting back into the statue form.

"Why not go back to being flesh and blood?" Tamsyn asked.

"I CANNOT IMAGINE BEING ELSEWISE," said Pocahontas. "MY FLESH WAS WEAK, SO I FORSAKE IT."

"Check this out," Tamsyn said. "I can make my boobs go really big."

27

"GEHENNA. PURGATORY. THE PLACE OF TRIALS," Pocahontas said. They were walking, though in this place it was more an effort of will than a movement of limbs. Tamsyn could feel the sheer vastness of this place – there didn't seem to be an actual end to it, any borders or geographical features.

Just flat nothing, and her and her new best buddy.

"I thought it was meant to have nine levels," Tamsyn said.

"FANTASY," Pocahontas laughed. "DANTE WAS A GUIDE. HE WAS ALSO A DRUNK AND A MADMAN."

"Well, what about the fire? I thought there was meant to be fire for the sinners and whatnot."

"DO YOU WANT FIRE?" Pocahontas said, looming over her again, arms outstretched in her old statue pose, her metal face truly terrifying. "I COULD BURN YOU FOR A THOUSAND YEARS, IF YOU WISH TO GIVE IT A TRY."

"Calm down, devil-face. Just an observation."

Tamsyn had convinced Pocahontas to show her the invaders in the afterlife, to guide her to the occupied "territory". It was a long, tedious journey, and her mind told her they'd been sliding across the blank landscape for days now.

"YOUR MIND UNDERSTANDS WALKING, SO WE WALK. BUT REALLY, WE ARE NAVIGATING THE UNIVERSE."

"What? Like spaceships or something?"

"NO, FOOL CHILD. WE MOVE BEHIND THE STARS AND PLANETS. TWIST THROUGH THE EMPTY SPACES IN BETWEEN. I MUST REMEMBER EACH STEP ON THE GREAT LADDER, AND THEY ARE HIDDEN WELL."

"The great ladder?"

"IT CAN GO TO THE HIGH PLACE AND THE LOW. TIS FAR EASIER TO DESCEND IT."

"Okay. So Heaven and Hell are real then?"

"IN A WAY."

"God?"

"ALSO IN A WAY. YOU SHALL NOT MEET GOD. EVER."

"Hold on. You seem pretty quick with that answer. I'm never going to get to Heaven?"

"YOUR PLACE IS TO GUIDE. YOU MUST WATCH THE GREAT STAIR. CORRECT AND PREPARE THE SOULS TO RISE UPON IT. TURN BACK THE UNWORTHY."

"Right, right. So I'm eternity's door-bitch. Great. Well, tell me this. Why doesn't God hustle down his big staircase and kick out the invaders?"

"THE MOST HIGH – THE MOST HIGH CANNOT KNOW ABOUT IT."

"What? Earth and Hell have fallen to an invasion from beyond, and you can't tell the boss? Get him on the phone or get some angels or whatever!"

"YOU DO NOT UNDERSTAND. WITH A FAILURE OF

THIS MAGNITUDE, THE MOST HIGH HAS ONE OPTION ONLY."

"Yep. Go Old Testament on their arses."

"NO. WITH ONE THOUGHT, THIS UNIVERSE WILL CEASE TO EXIST. OUR STORY, OUR LEGACY, UNDONE WITH A THOUGHT."

"So, because there are rats in the cellar, God's going to burn down his house?"

"CORRECT."

"Oh. We're on our own then?"

"BETTER TO LOSE THE WORLD OF LIFE AND THE LOW PLACE THAN TO LOSE THOSE WHO ARE PURIFIED TOO."

"What about Heaven? The Pearly Gates, God's big plasma-screen TV?"

"THE HIGH PLACE WILL STILL BE SAFE. THE CROWN OF COUNTLESS SUNS DOES NOT DARE ASSAULT IT."

"Office politics. You just can't escape it."

As they trudged across the featureless plain, Tamsyn started to discern what Pocahontas was doing. The Great Stair was a meandering path, across solar systems, through black holes and nebulae, while simultaneously behind all of the pretty space stuff. Each time they stepped forward, Pocahontas was carefully guiding them from place to place, "descending" a sequence of points.

It was an easy journey, barely taxing on her spirit body, but Tamsyn supposed that climbing would be harder yet. She hoped she wouldn't have to find her own way back up to the Mirrorlands – one wrong step and she'd wander this empty place forever, lost and alone.

"So if this is Limbo, where are all the souls?"

"ENDLESS QUESTIONS FROM A CHILD!" Pocahontas said, exasperated.

"Shut up. I bet whoever taught you how to do your job suffered through twice as many questions."

"THAT – THAT IS FAIR."

"I'm a bloody quick learner, thank you very much."

"THE CROWN EMPTIED THIS PLACE OUT. BILLIONS OF SOULS, ROUNDED UP, TAKEN DOWN THE GREAT STAIR. MANY GUIDES HAD DREAMT PURGATORY INTO A PLACE OF BEAUTY AND FEAR, BUT NOW?"

Pocahontas gestured around at the featureless plain, a wounded expression on her face.

Seized by inspiration, Tamsyn applied the same visualisation she'd used to change her own appearance, and applied it to the landscape. In moments there were rolling hills to either side, a lush rainforest, even a pretty Disney style castle on the side of a mountain. Pocahontas squashed these flat in a moment, her will clamping down on Tamsyn's, defeating it.

"FOOL GIRL! DO NOT ANNOUNCE US TO THE FOE!"

"This place is like Minecraft. For reals. And you expect me not to make things?"

"YOU DO NOT KNOW THE DANGER WE ARE IN," she replied. "YOU ARE STRONG FOR A GUIDE. EAGER. THIS WILL NOT SAVE YOU."

"How many Guides are left?"

"ONCE, ONE GUIDE WATCHED OVER ONE HUNDRED SOULS. NOW, OUR KIND ARE DECIMATED."

"One percent – there must have been millions of us!"

"INDEED. NOW WE ARE GUERRILLAS AT WAR. FEW ARE LEFT TO OPPOSE THE CROWN."

"Alright. It's time to help the devils defend Hell. Are we almost there?"

"MERELY THIRTY THOUSAND STEPS TO GO."

"You idiots really need an elevator."

Soon, certain features began to rise out of the gloom of Purgatory. The ground here was scarred in places, as if burnt or scratched heavily. A few steps later, and there were the outlines of ruins, the slow curve of a hill, and the broken feet of a huge statue, blasted Ozymandias style.

"WE NEAR THE EDGE OF THE NEUTRAL LANDS," Pocahontas said. "THE LOW PLACE IS JUST BEFORE US."

"Hmm. So they didn't completely wipe out Limbo."

"OVER THERE, THAT WAS ONCE THE PALACE OF THE BURNING QUESTION. THERE, THE RIVER OF WOE. THE INVADERS HAVE UNDONE CENTURIES OF DESIGN!"

"Well, kick them out and then built it again. It's not like you had to even touch a hammer."

"THAT IS NOT THE POINT. MUCH CULTURE WAS LOST."

"What? The culture of torturing souls?"

"WE WORK HARD TO CURATE THE FALLEN! YOU COULD NOT POSSIBLY UNDERSTAND THE GREAT WORK."

"One: I never asked for the job. Two: We studied Crime and Punishment in school. Torturing people does not rehabilitate them! What, have you stuffed Heaven full of people with PTSD?"

"NO. THEY ARE PURIFIED. CORRECTED," Pocahontas said defensively.

"Endless power, shit methods and no oversight. Well, that's just wonderful."

"YOUR SARCASM IS WASTED HERE."

"All I'm saying is you probably deserved to be invaded."

Three more steps, crossing light years and dimensions, and they passed through these outer ruins. Instantly, the bleak landscape was transformed into a burning war zone. Towers that once stretched up to a sky of purest night, but now they lay in wreckage, burnt and broken. Here and there, solitary figures lurked in the distance, hiding when they saw Pocahontas approaching.

"THE LOW PLACE," Pocahontas said, attempting a whisper. "WHERE THE BAD ONES GO. THE ONES WHO DO NOT RESPOND TO WHIPS AND FLAMES."

"What, so you give them more of both?"

"YES. CORRECTION BECOMES PUNISHMENT."

Lakes of fire, crossed by bridges forged from bone and black iron. Palaces both beautiful and terrifying, stoved in by some incredible force. Factories festooned with smokestacks, but the only smoke rising was from the burning ruins. Tamsyn felt like she was looking on photos from the Blitz, but on a mind-bending level. Hundreds and hundreds of miles of infernal structures, most of it a smoking ruin.

Below the streetscape, gallows and guillotines lined the streets, interspersed with horrific statues, tree-shapes grown out of black glass. Abandoned wagons and cars that were all spikes and dripping blood, and underneath this was a street where each cobblestone was a skull, and then further down the street itself was gone, clawed down into the dark earth beneath.

Everywhere, the wreckage of vehicles, abandoned by the

score, broken and burning. Tanks carved out of glistening stone, blimps that seemed to be draped in skin, a broken-backed ship slowly sinking into a fiery river.

Destruction on an industrial scale, real World War I stuff, but not a single dead body.

So Hell was real, and it was a Hieronymous Bosch wet dream, except it had been taken over by something worse than the devils. A force of pure destruction, capable of crushing Pocahontas and all of her cruel kind in a place where pure thought could create a castle.

It took much more effort here to do so, but Tamsyn dreamt forth her bow once more, resting a shining arrow on the string. It felt like pulling a kidney stone out through her brain – the Low Place was not as fluid as Purgatory. It would have taken a great effort to create this landscape. Her bow wasn't likely to do much against the Crown of Countless Suns, but she hoped to tickle him in the ribs before he destroyed her utterly.

"YOU WANTED TO SEE OUR WAR, OUR FAILURE. IT LIES BEFORE YOU."

"Yep, you guys got stomped alright."

Movement. A handful of figures lurking in the rubble, watching, drawn closer by the appearance of the two Guides. They were pathetic things, spirits that were paper-thin, scrabbling out of the ruins of the fallen towers and dark manors.

"Stay back!" Tamsyn called out. They came at her in jerky movements, like stop-motion footage that wasn't quite right. Then one was suddenly up in her face and grabbing for her. The spirit looked like a wild-haired woman with a mouth stretching literally from ear to ear, stretching outwards like a snake with a dislocated jaw, ready to swallow her whole.

She loosed the shining arrow, and the creature fell backwards with a howl like steel scraping on steel. Droplets of silver muck fell to spatter on the road, even as the spirit fell in on itself, the woman-shape turning into wisps of fog, drifting, gently floating away. More of the thin creatures burst out of hiding, drawn by the smell of the Aether on the ground.

"VAMPIRES!" Pocahontas cried. From thin air she'd produced a musket, glowing red like a coal. The statue let off a shot at the nearest scavenger spirit, sending it reeling and bleeding. In the same instant she was a blur of movement, fast-forward hands feeding in gunpowder, the bullet, the piston-fast slamming of a ramrod, and and then she was shooting again, impossibly fast.

Bang. Bang. Bang. Each shot the sound of breaking crockery, a mad church bell, a screaming horse, all of it scrambled together into one maddening concussive force.

Tamsyn let off a few more arrows before the spirits fled. Safety, for the moment. Despite herself, she knelt down in the street, licking the fallen Aether from the tops of skulls like a dog. It was fairy floss, it was an amazing kiss, it was seeing her favourite band, each drop dancing across her tongue.

"What?" she said to Pocahontas, who glared at her in bronze disapproval. "This shit is delicious."

Her tongue rasped against bone. How long before she too was a mindless hunter, stalking through Hell for her next fix?

She licked again, and again.

SOON SHE SAW the first one standing over the ruined factories, a tortured metal hand stretching up to the black sky. A Vanguard structure, but down here in Hell it was impressive, dominant, much more sophisticated than the patchwork constructions up on Earth.

In the palm of the hand, that familiar green glow.

"THERE ARE MORE," Pocahontas rumbled, trying to keep her voice low and failing. "LOOK."

Through the swirling of smoke and ash, she could see another tower, and another, straight as a ley line, as far as her eyes could focus.

"NO CLOSER," Pocahontas said. "THE CROWN WATCHES FOR OUR MILITIA. SABOTEURS CANNOT APPROACH NOW."

Tamsyn released her mental grip on the bow, and it vanished. Concentrating on her hand until she felt cross-eyed, she eventually summoned a pair of binoculars. Good ones, like she'd used in the Army.

Getting a boost from Pocahontas, Tamsyn climbed up the guttering of a ruined factory, until she was up on the curved barrel of the roof. The tiles were like slabs of human skin covered in welty lesions.

"Oh my god, they've roofed it with *shingles*. Some clever devil likes his puns."

"SHAKESPEARE ENJOYED PUNS," Pocahontas said, appearing beside her without a sound.

"No shit."

"I DO NOT SHIT. HE TOLD ME MANY FINE PUNS UPON OUR MEETING."

"You met Shakespeare! Fuck off! Now I know you are bullshitting me."

"HE WANTED TO WRITE MY STORY. HE DIED OF A FEVRE, AND HIS NOTES WERE LOST WHEN ANNE DROPPED THEM IN HER TUB."

"Anne *Shakespeare* wrecked your story? In a - a bath?"

"NO. IT WAS IN STRATFORD-UPON-AVON."

The statue grimaced strangely. Tamsyn realised Pocahontas was smiling.

"I can't believe you just made a joke. Good on you!"

The pair crept to the edge of the roof, high above the street. Fetching out her mystical binoculars, Tamsyn focused on the Vanguard tower, and the figures milling around its base.

Impossible creatures. Miniature suns like she'd seen in her dreams, darting around like fireflies. Something that looked like a crowd of angry people, but it was one organism, a kind of slug with a thousand fleshy mannequins flailing and gesturing on its back. A thorny bush as tall as a house, pulsing with a dark red inner light, gesturing with sharp spines as it rolled around the tower.

Another thing that resembled the insides of a typewriter, metallic legs striking and spinning and running around, and these mechanical things wrestled with a group of beasts on stilts, something between a spider and a hippo, with dozens of limbs, each one ending in a pinpoint of brilliant purple light.

More things, a sickening mass of life, and it swirled around the Vanguard tower like a twisted imitation of the pilgrims circuiting the Kaaba. Scanning upwards with her binoculars, Tamsyn could see more of the miniature stars, and other flying beasts, every mix of beak, feather, fang and scale. Mixed with these beasts were dozens of impossible engines, things that were sprouting bits of B52 bombers, bi-wings, blimps and passenger aircraft. Defying every kind of physical law, these machines bristled with missiles and guns, and they orbited the tower on a lazy loop.

"YOU WANT THE INVADERS? LOOK UPON THEIR FOOT SOLDIERS," Pocahontas said.

"So if you guys are the devils – are these aliens or something?"

"THESE ABOMINATIONS COME FROM – FROM BEYOND EVERYTHING THAT WE KNOW."

"Aliens." Tamsyn squinted at Pocahontas, gesturing with her hands. "C'mon, it was a meme. You know, with that guy."

"THIS IS NO LAUGHING MATTER. THE CROWN OF COUNTLESS SUNS HAS FORCED A BEACHHEAD IN HELL. EMPTIED PURGATORY. AND NOW, HE LAUNCHES HIS NEXT ASSAULT."

The creatures around the tower reached a fever pitch in their excitement. Above, the green globe in the fist began to glow, gaining in intensity.

"THEY SEND ANOTHER ONE THROUGH. A HOST, TO WALK IN FLESH IN THE LANDS OF LIFE."

It happened like a bolt of lightning, a green line that stretched from the edge of Hell and back the way Tamsyn had come. The image remained in her vision long after it was gone. As she tried to blink it away, she noticed that the globe was once more quiescent, the guardians of the tower less frantic.

"FROM THEIR UNIVERSE INTO OURS. THROUGH LIMBO, UP THE GREAT STAIR, AND INTO THE LANDS OF LIFE," Pocahontas said sadly.

"We have to stop those bastards! They're putting monsters into people up there!"

"DO YOU THINK WE DID NOT TRY? LOOK AROUND YOU! OUR ARMIES WERE SCATTERED. OUR FIERCEST WAR ENGINES TOSSED ASIDE!"

"Alright, so they are strong. They outnumber the Guides. So, look for a weakness!"

"HO, A TACTICIAN! SURE, WE CONSULTED WITH SUN TZU, AND WITH ROMMEL AND NAPOLEON. SO, ENLIGHTEN ME! WHAT GREAT PLAN DO YOU HAVE THAT HISTORY'S FINEST GENERALS COULD NOT FORMULATE?"

"Oh, die in a fire, you sarcastic bitch. What I'm saying is we can't touch the towers. So let's deny the supply."

Tamsyn pointed deeper into Hell, in the direction of the towers.

"These creatures have minds, plans, ambition. They've conquered this land, so it means they're complacent. Maybe not much, but there's bound to be something they've overlooked. Some weak spot we can exploit."

"WE? I AGREED TO SHOW YOU THE ENEMY. NOW, I SHALL RETURN TO THE MIRRORLANDS. I WANT TO SEE MY CHILD AGAIN BEFORE I AM DESTROYED."

"Cool. Take the coward's way out and have me fight all your battles."

"I AM NO COWARD!" Pocahontas rumbled. One of the flying machines took an interest in the distant sound, but settled back to circuiting the tower. The bronze statue shook her head fiercely.

"I WILL NOT DIE POINTLESSLY," she said. "I HAVE DONE THAT ONCE ALREADY."

Tamsyn thought about the scavengers she'd dispatched, how their bodies had faded into fog and Aether. They'd all drifted off in the same direction, presumably where the Final Shore was.

"Well, let's try really hard not to double-die," Tamsyn said.

∼

As they stole through Hell, Tamsyn saw thousands of the Guides' war machines, destroyed or even abandoned. What passed for critical infrastructure in the Low Place had been systematically wrecked. Shattered pipelines leaked blood onto the streets, and not where intended. The Guides had a public transit system down here, trolley cars that travelled on cables woven from intestines. Now the carriages were toppled, sides staved in, and the cables were severed, miles of gut tangled up in the snag-toothed ruins.

More Vanguard towers, in greater concentration here. The freaky guards were double and even triple in number, surrounded by circles of shattered Guide vehicles. The resistance to the invaders had been fierce, and utterly pointless.

No wonder you ran back to Gravesend, Tamsyn thought. She doubted these plucky soul-purifiers had even slowed down the Crown of Countless Suns.

"WE NEAR THE PRISON CAMP," Pocahontas said, attempting *sotto voce* and failing. With a twinge of pain between her eyes, Tamsyn dreamt up a Harry Potter-style invisibility cloak, and wrapped it around herself in a flourish. Her outline pulsed like the Predator, and she was impressed.

"WE TRIED THAT. THEY CAN STILL SEE YOU."

Dejected, Tamsyn bundled up the cloak and threw it across the street, only to see it fade into a wisp of fog. She followed Pocahontas through a field that was a slurry of ash and blood, keeping low. Here, the crazed little suns were patrolling the skies, portable searchlights that painted the streets randomly.

This had once been a sculpture park, but only of subjects so hideous that it made Tamsyn gag to even glance at them. Pocahontas pulled her behind a twisted version of Michelangelo's David, and pointed down the slope.

A prison camp, of all the souls captured by the Vanguard. Tamsyn saw a swirl of pale blue shapes, like a big school of fish caught in a gyre, but it was souls, millions and millions of people, slowly turning and shuffling in a yard that was almost the size of Wales. An open space surrounded by the blasted districts, fenced by wire at least a hundred feet high. She realised the invaders had razed one of Hell's megacities to the ground, and dumped all their prisoners here.

The captives had raised their own structures, here a cheery little house, there a row of barracks huts, but mostly they walked, a slow twisting cyclone of arms and legs, and they were just so damn noisy.

Arguments. Crying and moaning. Talk and sermons.

"THAT IS EVERYONE. MOST OF THE SOULS FROM PURGATORY AND THE LOW PLACE."

There were structures in the centre of the camp. A building that looked like it was designed by Salvador Dali, polyhedral and pulsing, smokestacks venting yellow fumes in a dozen different directions. Every now and then a machine that was equal parts crab and bulldozer emerged from it, scraping up souls by the score and pushing them inside the building.

Then, the yellow smoke would intensify. The line of Vanguard towers connecting Hell to Purgatory and back up into the real world started here in the camp. The metal hands lit up, sending brilliant beams of light arcing across Hell.

"THEY ARE SENDING THE HOST THROUGH IN EARNEST."

Whatever was happening to the souls in that factory, Tamsyn did not think it was a happy ending.

Eddie. Her Dad. Everyone in life she'd ever cared about,

somewhere in that multitude of souls, right in front of her. She shook her head – the moment she found anyone she cared about, she'd fall apart.

If everything goes wrong, I'll find you both, she thought. *Plenty of time to catch up as a bulldozer pushes us into a ghost-furnace.*

"NOW DO YOU SEE THAT WE CANNOT HOPE TO WIN?"

"Well, I see you've got a big problem. And that you're an even bigger pussy than I first thought. Those people in there, those souls, they need our help."

The bronze woman looked pensive for a moment, but shook her head.

"WE WERE BEATEN SO EASILY. SO QUICKLY. I AM – I AM SCARED."

"God, me too, love. I can't remember a morning I didn't wake up shit scared of something. The trick is to go at your problems like a gung-ho dickhead anyway."

Tamsyn looked over the impressive security for a long moment, and then started scratching a map in the dirt with a summoned stick.

"We can totally do this. This is going to be just like a heist movie. But in Hell!"

The drifting sun beasts. The huge fence. The chamber of smoky death, deep in enemy territory. Millions of innocent souls, fuel for an enemy invasion. She thought back to the war in America, and remembered the most important lesson war had taught her.

Deny the supply.

28

Vanguard beasts came and went from the prison camp, sometimes herding in stray souls found out in the wasteland. A crew of beasts ferried out a new Vanguard tower to boost the Host signal up to Earth, stilt-creatures and enormous slugs hefting it across the bleak landscape.

A rolling thorn monster and a low-flying sun came through the marshlands and back to the prison camp, attracting little notice as they made a circuit of the fence. There were other guards here and there, but they moved by rote, barely observant as the new arrivals changed the overall pattern.

"I told you they were complacent," Tamsyn said from the depths of the thorn beast. By her side, the sun crackled in warning, the disguised Pocahontas unhappy with her breaking character.

"I cannot believe that not one of you thought of trying this," Tamsyn said, muffled as she embraced her disguise.

It was weird, moving on thousands of thorns instead of the two legs she'd always known. This form changing took a lot more effort than it did in Purgatory, and Tamsyn hoped that she wouldn't slip up, her head poking out at a dumb moment.

"I FIND IT UNSEEMLY TO DRESS AS THESE ALIENS."

"You're in a war. You don't get to be comfortable when you're fighting to survive!"

The fence was something between a plant and a construct, a wire-thin material twining and climbing and twisting up to the sky. Tamsyn reached out a thorny limb to touch it, and withdrew in sudden pain.

It was riddled with jags, and they pierced her new body's "skin", pain instantly flooding her form. *Poison?* Fat droplets of her Aether fell on the ground. That was from one slight brush against the fence.

"I guess we're not climbing over it," Tamsyn said to the ball of fire crackling to one side. "Can you burn through it?"

"I AM NOT ACTUALLY A SMALL STAR. THIS IS A DISGUISE AND NOTHING MORE."

"And I guess you can't fly either. Hmm."

They travelled up and down the fence-line to avoid suspicion. Just through the wire were the forms of people uncounted, wan-faced spirits who were too scared to look at what seemed to be just two more guards. The ground underfoot was a shin-deep slurry of mud, and Tamsyn suddenly understood. With that many people on the move, none of them could ever stop. The sheer force of so many things moving would grind underfoot any who attempted rest. Every soul that she saw looked broken, paper-thin shells that held in what was left of their Aether.

Utter destruction by trampling, or whatever unknown death awaited in the big structure. She was reminded of the misery discovered in Nazi concentration camps, and felt helpless, unable to save a single soul.

"We need to get past this fence," Tamsyn said.

"NO, WE CANNOT! IT IS DANGEROUS!"

"Look," Tamsyn said, rustling and shaking her thorns for emphasis. "You've done me a solid. If you want to go back up to Purgatory, just go."

"WHAT OF YOU?"

"I think I've worked it out. It's like your trick with the Paris thing. You see, I'm really not here. I really believe I'm on the other side of that fence."

And just like that, she was standing on the other side of the fence, appearing as her 15 year-old self. The effort shook her to her very core, but she'd done it. Back on the other side, the suddenly lone sun wobbled, amazed at her trick.

"Look, Pocahontas dear, you've got to shit or get off the pot. Either come in or go back up to Gravesend. We've attracted attention."

Other guards were converging on their location, drawn by the sudden disappearance of one of their own.

"AH, DAMNATION AND PILLORY," Pocahontas said, suddenly across the wire and standing next to Tamsyn. The jostling Tamsyn had been receiving turned into a blank space, as the other spirits in the camp gave them a wide berth.

"Oh, for heaven's sake. Stop looking like a big bronze statue."

Frowning, Pocahontas shifted form, once more resembling the woman she'd been in life. She wore nondescript modern clothing and could have been anyone on the street.

"I DESPISE WEARING FLESH," she said, but still her voice boomed out of a bronze throat, metal lips and tongue smashing and grinding out her words.

"It's not even real," Tamsyn said, punching her lightly in the arm. "Come on, before those guards get here."

They headed deeper into the camp, almost immediately swallowed into the great moving circle of prisoners. These souls had been badly treated, and looked like old photographs, touched by fingers too many times. Worn, their colour washed out.

"Please. I need Aether," one man said, clutching at Tamsyn's arm. He was dressed as an old style monk, complete with tonsure, and he looked like the idea of a man drawn on tissue paper. The fact that he wasn't in Heaven probably spoke to some hypocrisy or sin that put him on the naughty list.

"HANDS OFF," Pocahontas growled, leaning in and giving the spirit a hard stare. Muttering, the monk stepped away, stepping across the pattern of the gyre, heading out to the fence.

"DO NOT OFFER CHARITY TO THEM. NOT EVEN A DROP," Pocahontas said.

"I get it. I help one, and thousands will swarm us, expecting a taste."

Thin-lipped, Pocahontas nodded. Even in disguise, the older Guide forced an easy path through the immense crowd. Perhaps it was instinct that gave most of these spirits pause, even if they weren't aware that one of their torturers was hidden in their midst.

If they know, will they turn on us? Tamsyn thought. Already there was a hubbub by the fence where they'd crossed over. Three bright suns were flashing around, searching the wire for breaches. One spirit pointed in their direction, and then one of the flaming spheres flew over the fence, slowing coasting towards them across that sea of misery.

"Shit, we look like us," Tamsyn said. "Duck down for a second and change into someone else."

Tamsyn rose up resembling a brunette Taylor Swift with a crooked nose and a snaggletooth, while next to her rose a gallant looking man, middle-aged with an impressive beard and set of moustaches. He wore a cuirass and looked like he'd stepped out of an old-timey portrait.

"JOHN SMITH WAS A MAN MOST FAIR TO LOOK UPON," Pocahontas said. "I WAS PLEASED TO WATCH HIM CLIMB UP THE GREAT STAIR."

"Look, keep it in your pants. We've gotta get out of here."

Tamsyn and Pocahontas switched direction, moving parallel to the fence. A trio of suns passed over the spot where they'd been, blazing light and heat across the crowd. Hundreds of souls fell to the ground in a panic, trampled by their neighbours. Tamsyn caught the smell of fresh Aether in the air, and realised the souls moving against them were caught up in a feeding frenzy. These ghosts were diving face first into the mud and muck, siphoning up a fragment of life from those who were crushed.

A large part of Tamsyn wanted to turn and join in. Aether was just so damn good.

Geez, I really do have an addictive personality, Tamsyn realised. *I've got a taste for ghost crack.*

"How far can we jump?" Tamsyn asked. Overhead, the shining guards were more interested in the brutal soul stampede, and were putting it down with bright solar flares, tongues of flame licking against the souls and driving them back.

"NOT FAR," Pocahontas said. "HELL IS SET IN PLACE, NOT LIKE PURGATORY."

Tamsyn knew she was right – even that short hop through the fence was taxing. Teleporting over to the big structure was not even an option – Tamsyn's eyes told her that it was at least twenty miles away, not even counting the distorted physics of this place.

"Alright, we need to get out of this crowd," Tamsyn said. "Time for you to do that thing you mentioned."

"STEP ASIDE," Pocahontas commanded. As she barked at the souls in their way, they obeyed instantly. No more begging for Aether, no fighting or crying. Instant obedience, from the dead to a Guide. Pocahontas charted a course through the waves and currents of that moving multitude, clearing their way, only letting the crowd press back in when a drifting blimp beast passed overhead. The base of the basket resembled a spider's face, with banks of eyeballs scanning the crowd. As it drifted towards the place in the fence where they'd entered, it unfurled dozens of dangling tentacles, which quested in all directions, testing the air for intruders.

"Our disguises aren't going to hold much longer," Tamsyn said. "Quick, towards those buildings there."

In all the chaos, some of the spirits had imagined a barracks in the prison camp. It was a mix of eras, with Nissen huts meeting Ancient Roman tents, but it was as neat as a pin, with avenues, a crude stockade, and a thick rank of guards keeping all the other spirits out of their patch of Hell.

Soon Tamsyn and Pocahontas were at the line of palisades, a simple barrier to keep out the press of souls. An English Tommy from the Great War blocked the narrow entry-way, and he stared at them, arms across his chest.

"STEP ASIDE," Pocahontas commanded. For a moment the man wavered, but then he glowered at her.

"No. Nick off. This is our spot."

"WHAT? I AM A GUIDE. I ORDER YOU TO MOVE."

"I can only take orders from my commanding officer. And you're not her."

Pocahontas looked flabbergasted.

"I SHOULD REND YOU WITH WHIP AND FLAME, SOUL!"

"I've got my orders. I don't care who you are."

A current of foot-traffic pushed against them, but strangely enough they weren't forced into the palisades. There was a barrier here, and not a physical one. It was an idea, this boundary, held in place by a very strong will.

A very *military* will. Tamsyn knew what to do.

"My name is Captain Tamsyn Webb, once the Commanding Officer of the 6th Company of the Texan Republic Army, now serving in a militia. I request permission to bivouac in your camp."

"Permission granted, Captain!" the Tommy said, snapping to a salute with a broad grin. "Good to find another fighter in this sorry lot! Come on in."

Tamsyn was allowed past the palisade, but the Tommy held up his hand. Pocahontas was drawn up short, unable to step inside. She was furious, and let slip her disguise, embracing the full bronze statue experience, growing until she loomed over the soldier.

"I WILL RAZE YOUR PITIFUL CAMP TO ITS FOUNDATIONS! YOU WILL CHOKE ON A NOOSE TIED FROM YOUR OWN GUTS! YOUR MARROW WILL BURN FOR TEN THOUSAND YEARS!"

The soldier smirked.

"Jerry didn't scare me, and neither do you."

Before Pocahontas could have an aneurysm, Tamsyn placed a hand on the man's shoulder.

"I need her with me. She's my civilian advisor."

"Oh. A harridan like that is Red Cross or something, no doubt. Go on in."

"Thank you, soldier."

The military camp was a sea of order, buffeted on all sides by the chaos of the wandering prisoners. Soldiers of every nation and era kept company, playing at dice, cooking imaginary meals. Not one of them was armed, but a sense of discipline prevailed over the group.

"Oh, I get it. They're operating like a P.O.W. group," Tamsyn said. "Okay, now listen, we've got to find the commanding officer. If The Great Escape is anything to go by, officers are duty bound to attempt a break-out."

She watched a Roman Legionnaire playing soccer with a German Paratrooper, saw all sorts of busywork, but above all she noticed how these prisoners were observing things. Watching the patterns of the guards. Whispering in corners.

"Yep. Someone's gonna jump a motorbike soon."

TAMSYN FOUND the tent of the commanding officer, a simple structure of braced tree logs, covered with layers of thick wool and furs. There were a pair of guards at the entrance, one a Prussian officer with a pickelhaube helmet, the other a Pict complete with blue body paint and a long rectangular shield.

No weapons, not even here.

This pair kept her and Pocahontas waiting for what seemed like hours. Tamsyn fretted, watching the sky for guards, but the hubbub had died down. Only a handful of floating suns coasted over the camp, and none of them anywhere near this weird fortification.

The tent flap opened, a bearded face peering out for a

whispered conference with the Prussian. The tent flap closed.

"The Warrior will see you," the Prussian said to Tamsyn, and permitted her entry. When Pocahontas went to follow, both the guards blocked her path.

"No civilians!" the Prussian barked. "Military only!"

Pocahontas bristled, but was held back by the same power that blocked her at the gates. Whoever this Warrior was, they held great power over even the Guides. Licking her lips nervously, Tamsyn entered the tent, alone.

The inside of the tent was enormous, the internal dimensions at odds with the simple exterior. Tapestries, flags and banners hung from the ceiling, and what seemed like kilometres of silk ran across every other surface. On the floor, acres of furs and cushions, where hundreds of warriors lazed about, smoking on pipes or drinking. An entire cow was roasting over a bed of coals, and sunken steps led to an enormous communal bath, the water steaming hot.

The centre of the tent was taken up by a dais, and on the tenth step was a throne, an imposing hunk of black wood, barely carved into a seat. It was primal, incredibly old, and it did not need any further flourishes.

On the throne sat a woman. Even seated on that monstrosity it was clear that she was tall. She was a fierce looking Celt, with a tawny braid falling below her waist, thick enough to strangle a man with. She wore a colourful tunic, a thick cloak fastened with a broach, and a gold torc fastened around her throat.

She stared at Tamsyn, eyes that had seen thousands of years pass, and to her it felt like those eyes had instantly measured her and found her wanting.

"You are the Warrior?" Tamsyn asked. The woman on

the throne ignored her. For a long beat, she continued to stare at Tamsyn, even as the faint arguments of Pocahontas drifted into the tent.

"Excuse me. Are you in charge here?"

The woman on the throne continued to stare. Utterly silent.

"Fine," Tamsyn said, resigned. "I've played this game before. You keep me waiting, playing mind games and staring me out until I flinch. Well, I've got news for you, sunshine. I am a veteran of this bullshit. I have been made to stand in front of a Prince and all of his assorted dickheads, mostly men mind you, and sat through hours of this stuff. And do you know what my secret to winning a staring contest was?"

The woman arched an eyebrow.

"I used to stare each and every one of them down, and in my mind I would think 'you've got a tiny dick.' Over and over. I won every single time. Obviously I'll change this game with you. Right now, I'm thinking 'this bitch needs a root'."

All around the cavernous tent, the lounging warriors were tense, waiting for the Warrior to explode in fury. She blinked her eyes once, twice, and her lips spread out into a thin line.

Curving upwards at each end.

The Warrior smiled, and then she laughed, and it was a guffaw that could be heard across battlefields. The other soldiers relaxed and offered smiles of their own. Tamsyn had passed some sort of test.

"Once a knight stood there for two days before he was brave enough to speak to me," the woman on the throne said.

"I'm Tamsyn," she offered.

"My name is Boudica."

"Oh, my god," Tamsyn said, mortified. This was Britain's greatest warrior woman, a legend. Tamsyn had mooned over her statue by the Westminster Palace more than once.

"I'm so sorry I said those things to you!"

"Don't be," the Warrior said. "The truth is better than flattery or fear. Just say what you mean and be done."

"STEP ASIDE!"

With a sound like ripping canvas, Pocahontas had forced herself past the invisible barrier of will keeping her out of the tent, scattering the guards like bowling pins hit by the spare. Stomping up to the throne, Pocahontas glared at Boudica, murder in her eyes.

"YOU DARE DEFY ME?"

"Trust a devil to appear where she is unwelcome." Boudica descended the steps from her throne, fixing the living bronze statue with her own unyielding gaze.

"YOU. YOU WERE SUPPOSED TO STOP THEM."

"No general can win every battle, Pocahontas."

"Wait a minute," Tamsyn said. "Boudica, er, Your Highness? Are you also a Guide?"

"SHE IS A SINNER MOST GRIEVOUS," Pocahontas said. "A KILLER OF INNOCENTS, BACK IN HER OLD WAR."

"I was no worse than the Roman invaders," Boudica said. "It was the way of war."

"SIN IS SIN."

"She likes to say that," Boudica said to Tamsyn directly. "When she is peeling away skin. Burning your flesh, over and over."

"SHE EARNT HER PLACE IN HELL," Pocahontas said. "REGARDLESS, SHE WAS FREED FROM BONDAGE TO

FIGHT THE CROWN OF COUNTLESS SUNS – AND SHE FAILED."

Tamsyn saw the tense set of the two women, and felt that ugly moment grow, knew that there were about to be a nasty afterlife punch-up. She pinched her fingers in her teeth and threw out a loud whistle.

"Alright, ladies. Enough with the pissing contest. Boudica, you are attempting escape from this prison camp. Am I correct?"

"Who is asking?"

"Someone who wants to take down this shitshow. Can I help?"

Boudica smiled, probably the same flat grimace she'd used when killing Roman babies. With a flat chop of her hand, the opulent tent interior fell away, revealing the true contents of her headquarters.

Map tables, with people shifting markers representing forces in the field. Field telephones, connected to who knew what, but warriors of every era were taking calls, and sending runners to and fro.

Tamsyn had seen Churchill's London bunker on a school trip, and it looked like that times a hundred. There were sketches on the wall, of the sun-beasts and other twisted things that guarded the Vanguard towers. She was pleased to see arrows and the words "WEAK POINT" more than once on these.

"The war still goes on, devil," Boudica said. "We weren't the ones hiding out in Purgatory."

Tamsyn held up a hand when Pocahontas bristled.

"Please, Your, er Highness. I need to know two things and we'll be out of your hair. Firstly, do you have weapons?"

Boudica blinked her eyes, and a sheet of canvas fell away. An armoury beyond compare, with everything from knives to Sherman tanks. It was genius really – the hidden headquarters of the resistance fighters was hidden in plain sight, in the middle of a scarily secure prison.

"Cool, glad you've still got your toys. Secondly, please tell me you have a network of tunnels underneath this camp?"

Boudica closed her fist. A brick bunker wall faded away, to reveal a nexus of tunnel mouths, built to an industrial scale. People were coming and going with picks and shovels, there was the beginning of a rail and rail cart system, the works. It felt like the beginnings of the Tube system, and she even spotted signs written in several languages.

"Great Stair. The Final Shore. Ah, Factory of Woe. That is where we need to be."

"EXCUSE ME?"

"Just ignore her, she's a Disney Princess."

29

The soul-scraping machine came out of the factory again, legs scrabbling, dropping a dozer blade as wide as the wing-span of a jumbo jet. It carved a great swathe through the unfortunate souls that had been pushed close to the factory, and they screamed, begged, fought each other to escape, but they were pushed into the dark mouth of a doorway.

The machine disappeared back into the alien facility, and the entryway closed up like an iris or a sphincter. Above, the chimneys belched out more yellow smoke, and then a few moments later a series of panels shifted near the roof, this one level with the tops of the Vanguard towers.

A brilliant green flash across the sky, and one more invader shot across Hell, making for earth and a vacant human body.

Only then did they open the hatches under the ground, shoving souls aside. Emerging from the ground like ants, Boudica's forces quickly surrounded the alien factory, with everything from Sherman tanks to battering rams.

"Quickly now, force an entry!" Boudica commanded

from the back of a chariot. The crowd of souls thinned out here as they fled in a panic, but many were too slow, crushed under tank treads or horse hooves. Tamsyn stared wide-eyed at the carnage, strapped to the chariot next to Boudica, bow in hand.

"You are utterly ruthless," she whispered, watching the innocents get mowed down under their charge. Nothing was left in their wake of these Twice-dead but puddles of Aether, and the drifting fog as each soul went on to the Final Shore.

"DESTROY THEM," Pocahontas boomed across the field. She'd grown to the size of a bronze giant, a Native American Colossus of Rhodes with a hatchet the size of a bus. She rained furious blows against the walls of the factory, cracking the panels with each strike. In moments Boudica's secret army had surrounded the structure, hitting it with burning pitch, trebuchet stones, and tank shells by the dozen.

"This had best work, girl," Boudica said. "We reveal ourselves for this plan of yours."

"What good is hiding your army forever? You're resistance fighters, and now you're resisting," Tamsyn said.

"It is good to fight again," Boudica admitted. "There, beware that foe sneaking up behind us."

More suns, floating blimp things, even the strange mismatched aircraft, all coming in from the fence-line towards the factory. Boudica sent runners, and soon her immortal army responded to this threat, with blaring trumpets, waved semaphore flags, and the crackle of radios.

The force neatly divided into two. One half continued besieging the factory, the other turned to defend them from the forces of the Crown of Countless Suns. Boudica herself whipped her ghost horses into a frenzy, and joined in a charge against the approaching foe.

"Shoot true, young Tamsyn!" Boudica said, lashing the reins to a rail with a practiced hand. She called forth her own bow, a magnificent weapon of bone and yew, each arrow a vision of straight willow, fletched with feathers that seemed plucked from an angel's wing. Each ended in an iron arrowhead, the point so sharp that it scratched the very air it touched.

Tamsyn raised the replica of her own long-lost bow, but she struggled to summon a shiny arrow this far into Hell. The best she could manage were barbed-tip hunting arrows, each one shivering with the need to slay an enemy.

Her first shot went wide, but then she adjusted to the rumbling chariot. She sent an arrow through the centre-mass of a sun-beast, and it fell in on itself like a popped water-balloon, the bright flame winking out.

"Ignore the flaming gnats!" Boudica said. "They are bright but burn little."

The ancient Celt sent her own arrows against one of the blimps, which was closing in on them rapidly. It was a big one, and it dropped dozens of tentacles from its underside, looking like a Portuguese Man-O-War drifting through the sky.

Boudica had lodged a dozen arrows in its side, and it changed course for their chariot, pulsing through the air like a swimming squid. Tamsyn sent her own arrows up into the eyes of its underbelly, trying to blind the creature, watching the deadly forest of tentacles reaching for them.

"Follow me, foul creature!" Boudica roared, her battle-field voice carrying far.

Snatching up the reins she hauled her horses to the left, the chariot nearly overbalancing on such a sharp turn. Tamsyn kept the arrows going, but every shot went wide as Boudica drove them through a knot of panicked souls, hooves and wheels grinding them into the mud. At one point the chariot bounced across the soul of an obese man, and Tamsyn nearly fell out of the back. Like a striking snake, Boudica snatched her by the collar, dragging her back on the footboards.

"Lash yourself to the rail!" Boudica shouted. "Stop bouncing around like a sow on heat!"

Dreaming up a length of rope, Tamsyn did just that. More of the aerial creatures were in hot pursuit, more blimp-beasts and suns, twisted machines defying the laws of physics, and on the ground were slugs and thorn-balls, stilt creatures and other horrors, wave after wave of the things pushing through the fence, riding rough-trod over the poor souls caught between them.

Looking over her shoulder, Tamsyn saw that other chariots were joining them, and then a trio of tanks, their turrets blasting blimps and stars from the sky. Mounted Mongolian archers kept pace with armoured knights and US Cavalry, all thundering hooves, trumpets and war-cries. It was an impressive sight, and it thrilled Tamsyn to be at the front of this charge from every age of history.

Ahead, the forces of the Crown of Countless Suns were coming at them, pushing hard to meet the changing curve of Boudica's charge.

"Not enough!" Boudica cried. Only half of the Crown's creatures were pursuing them, and just as many of the monstrosities were still on a course to the belching factory, drawn by the guns and siege weaponry. Pocahontas had grown again, the bronze giant peeling away the outer panels of the alien factory, taking it apart like a boiled egg.

Now that she was at war again, Pocahontas was anything but subtle.

"That idiot devil!" Boudica cried. "We had them fooled!"

"Don't blame her totally," Tamsyn said. "You're still shooting mortars and throwing tanks at it."

"Gah!" Boudica swung her chariot further still to the left, leading the charge in a slow loop back towards the factory. The crunching. The screaming. To distract herself from the sound of souls being broken underneath the chariot, Tamsyn thought back to Basic and the brief tactics courses they'd given the grunts. She found herself approving of Boudica's manoeuvre. Sure, they'd lost the element of surprise, but now they would be able to catch the enemy between two forces.

It would work great until the other half of the Crown's assault force arrived. Then everything would fall apart into a deadly melee.

"Your Highness, we'll only have a minute or two to destroy that building," she said, pointing to the factory. "Then you must order your people back down into the tunnels."

"Oh, so you are the general now?" Boudica said, arching one eyebrow.

"Look, just take good advice when it's offered," Tamsyn said. "Do you have another site to fall back to?"

"Of course. Our fallback camp is by the Final Shore."

The far edge of Hell, the end of death itself. The weird place where the Twice-Dead souls drifted, to complete oblivion. Going by what she'd gleaned from Pocahontas, it was dangerous for souls to linger there, and was the place where a two-thousand year old soul and her secret army was least likely to hang out.

Then came that frenzied minute where they trapped half of the Crown's army between Boudica and the besiegers. The chargers carved into the rear of the alien host, and Tamsyn's whole world was the sighting pegs on her bow. She sent arrows into spine-beasts, into the slugs, into stranger creatures still. If it moved and didn't look right, Tamsyn put an arrow through it.

The Crown's beasts fought back fearlessly, sending many of Boudica's brave souls into the Twice-Death. Everywhere the Aether soaked into the ground, and puffs of fog drifted towards the Final Shore.

No prisoners, no surrender, no negotiation from these alien beings. The resistance fighters had to kill every single thing, and it cost them dearly. Cavalry fell left and right, horses swallowed whole into the elastic maw of slugs, or bled of Aether by the spine-beasts. Tanks were flattened, soldiers disemboweled, and then there was nothing in the mud, just drifting fog, and a puddle of Aether where a brave soul had died a second time.

Oh god, I just want to drink it all, Tamsyn thought, salivating at the sight of the nearest blue puddle. Boudica had caught a sharp spike through the meat of her collarbone, and when she wriggled it loose from her ghost-flesh she caught the look on Tamsyn's face. The pure *thirst.*

"You're as much a devil as that one," she said, pointing to Pocahontas. "Craving what isn't yours."

"It's not like that. I've only ever drank my own Aether."

"As you say. Still, when I find a vampire in my ranks, I end it. It is not a good end."

With a troubled frown, Boudica turned her attention to the horses, bringing the chariot back around to the siege. They had perhaps a minute or two before the other half of the Crown's force made it through the camp to finish the job.

"I HAVE IT!" Pocahontas cried, finally kicking in the front wall with her great bronze moccasins. Foot soldiers from every era of human warfare poured into that dark breach, and even a tank driver or two drove inside, big guns hammering away.

"Be ready," Boudica said, urging the horses into a quick trot. Tamsyn held an arrow ready as they approached the breach. Pocahontas shrank down to her usual size, saluting Tamsyn with her hatchet as she joined the other foot soldiers running into the breach.

Then they hit that barrier between outside and inside, and Tamsyn felt like she was being stretched out over a thousand miles, every fibre of this new body pulled out to breaking point... and then everything snapped back into place, and they she was back on the chariot, inside the odd building.

Inside, it was more of the warped alien architecture, but cavernous, and with the inside being much larger than the already enormous outside, Tamsyn immediately thought of an evil TARDIS. Here was a furnace the size of a pyramid, topped with a curlicue of pipes and flues to channel the yellow smoke out of the building. There were windows in here, fractals of all sizes, but they did not open to the misery of Hell – they were windows into elsewhere, looking on nebulae and vacuum, into worlds of water, sand, sharp crystal, and then into dimensions too warped for her eyes to perceive.

If these are the Countless Suns, surely the Crown isn't too far away!

Above the great furnace was another twisted Vanguard claw, but this one was real flesh, muscles and veined, and it held aloft a crystal the size of a school-bus. That hideous machine flexed and pulsed, and it leant forwards, as if genuflecting.

It was facing a slab of black stone, a jagged monolith with an impossibly smooth face, and that surface was darkness impenetrable, the light from a black hole filtered through oil, coke, coal, the screen of an iPhone.

A shape came forward.

The faintest hint of a squid shape came out of the darkness, but there were hands, tentacles, fins and fangs; a face with galaxies for eyes.

Something leapt forward from the stone in a brilliant blaze of green light, arcing towards the crystal, and then out through a pulsing aperture, to cross Hell and take over a human body in the waking world.

"Draw in! Watch the rear!" Boudica ordered. In moments she'd set an enfilade on either side of the breach: tanks and musketeers, archers and machine-guns. Even as the weird Crown army poured into the breach to take back this structure, Boudica ordered the rest of her assault team to lay havoc. They broke apart the furnace, even as the steam destroyed every soul standing near it. A great Sherman tank took on the crab bulldozer and lost, and then a team of samurai bled it deeply, and then a crew on a battering ram finished the job.

All around, intelligences from across universes and dimensions watched this destruction, and they seethed. Tamsyn could feel their impotent anger, and she laughed.

Behind them, the Crown's freaks were forced to enter through a narrow chokepoint, and were instantly chewed apart by the enfilade. It was an act of accidental genius – lodged as they were in the structure, it seemed that the freaky aliens would never be able to remove them. The Crown forces made to move to force another entry or damage the structure, which meant Boudica's crew had dictated the rules of engagement.

"We've got all the high ground, baby!" Tamsyn exulted. Not only had they seized the structure, but if this was the beach-head that the Crown of Countless Suns had forced into this universe, Boudica's resistance had cut them off completely.

"Destroy it all!" Boudica cried. Pocahontas was wrestling the giant arm to the ground, hacking away with her hatchet, while a trio of landsknecht with two handed swords chopped away at the "fingers". Soon the great crystal fell out of that twisted grip, crushing a handful of redcoats as it struck the floor.

"We need to break the stone!" Tamsyn cried out, but no-one heard her in that frenzy. When Boudica drew up the chariot to confer with her lieutenants, Tamsyn stepped onto the buckling alien floor, nocking an arrow to her bow. She made for the black monolith, watching for signs of movement.

A shape lurked out of the darkness within the stone, and then another. Soon there was a feeding frenzy of figures dancing just below the surface of the stone, struggling to emerge, but the machine had been broken.

"Go back to where you came from," Tamsyn drawled, loosing off an arrow. It struck the surface of the rock with a deep resounding CRASH, like someone smashing bin lids together in a parking garage. The tip of her arrow continued to touch the rock face, the entire shaft shivering, and that awful sound went on, and on, and Tamsyn couldn't take it anymore. She walked up to the rock to take the arrow.

That was when a boy appeared in the surface of the stone, reaching out for the arrow at the same time. The Black Crown Boy, dressed in his school uniform, all blazer, neat hair and unnerving smile. He yanked at the arrow, almost drawing Tamsyn into the black stone itself.

She struggled, gasped. Her fingers locked tight around the shaft of the arrow, even though common sense told her to let go, to step back. Tamsyn struggled against that inhuman strength, losing a half-inch, an inch, two inches of floor.

"Tamsyn Lottie Webb," the boy whispered, his voice muted on the other side of the stone. "You plague me for the last time."

"Boudica! Pocahontas! Help me!" Tamsyn cried out, only to realise there was no more noise. The thunder of cannon and tank, of musket and machine gun, the clash of swords, all of it was gone.

Rotating her head as much as she dared, Tamsyn saw that everyone was frozen in place. Literally. Every spirit body she saw was caked in ice, and even Pocahontas was frozen to the giant arm, bloody hatchet still raised on high.

"You must understand," the Boy said. "I am protecting my family."

"F-Fuck you," Tamsyn said. "You've got enough of the universe. Piss off."

"I am saving this universe, and all others!" the Boy said. "We come to guard against a terrible enemy."

"More terrible than you lot?"

"Our occupation is just. We needed to have a beachhead here, to organise our defence."

"You're lying," Tamsyn said, meeting the boy's eyes.

Is he telling the truth? There's something even worse than the Crown of Countless Suns?

She slipped a little, dragged forward a few more inches. Now her knuckles were awfully close to that glassy surface. It felt incredibly cold, and waves of sluggishness flowed down her forearms. This close, she drank in every feature of the Boy. He was almost elfin in appearance, dark hair flat and lank across his forehead, in a school uniform he was yet to grow into. She took in the emblem stitched on the pocket, and the Latin slogan "PRAETERITIS ET FUTURIS"

"You cannot possibly understand," the Boy sighed. "A pity."

"Your school slogan. It translates to "For the Future and the Past."

The Boy looked at her, confused. At that moment Tamsyn gave a little, and then suddenly yanked on the arrow, pivoting on her hip. The Boy's fingers breached the surface of the stone. Scrambling and scrabbling, he fought for control over the arrow, and his fingers brushed against Tamsyn's, so cold that she felt her ghost flesh coming away.

She saw flashes in her mind. A school. This boy, in a room with Emma Menteuse and an older man. An art studio, with clay sculptures, each one more terrifying than the last. An airport, and another child in a school uniform, dead, and then rising, the first of the mindless undead. The beginning of the plague.

A name.

"I see you," she said with a smile. "Your name is Henri."

With a gasp, the Black Crown Boy released his grip on the arrow, and fell back into the depths of the stone. Others came forward, shapes less human, attempting to force another breach into Hell.

"What scares you about me so much, Henri?" Tamsyn mused. Looking at the frozen army around her, she then searched for the bodies of the enemy instead. Here was a wounded sun-beast, a miniature star half driving itself into walls like a moth, dazed and trapped in a corner.

She visualised a rope for her next arrow, and pierced the sun-beast along one edge. Dragging it along like an angry balloon, she reeled the sun in, blinking at the fierceness of the heat. Walking around Pocahontas a few times, the heat was soon enough to melt away the outer rime, and the bronze woman freed herself with her hatchet.

"HAVE WE WON?"

"Not unless we can crack that stone," Tamsyn said, pointing. Pocahontas went at it with enthusiasm, with everything from her shining arrows to a rocket launcher.

Tamsyn freed Boudica before the sun-beast finally died, extracting her from the iceberg that had once been a chariot and horses. Shivering, Boudica drew forth a sword, and stumbled towards the black stone.

"IT IS NO GOOD," Pocahontas admitted, stalking away from the rock and throwing her rocket launcher to the ground. "IT CANNOT BE BROKEN."

"Weakling," Boudica proclaimed, and came at the black stone with ferocity, with a blade that surely could slice an engine block clean in half. She broke that sword, and the next, and then stood before the monument for a long moment, as the lurking beasts called to her. She took one hesitant step before mastering her will.

"Ware of that evil rock. It seeks to draw you in."

Keeping their distance, the trio tried everything they could, without so much as scratching the black stone. Tamsyn reached within for her gift, trying to find an aura, a weakness, but the rock turned her away, leaving her head ringing with a blinding headache.

"Look, it rebuilds," Boudica declared. Slowly, the shattered metal of the furnace was pushing out, like crushing a coke can in reverse. The flues and chimneys were righting themselves, and the first tower was twitching, wounds slowly healing over.

Within the hour, it would be as if they'd never assaulted this place.

Boudica looked to her army with despair. Thousands of

her warriors, trapped, and no time to free any of them. Over at the breach, more of the Crown beasties were entering the structure, this time unopposed, and the breach itself was slowly sealing shut.

"Come," Boudica said, a bitter note falling from her mouth. "We are defeated."

"I'm so sorry," she said. "I thought this would stop them."

"Don't be sorry for me," Boudica said, gesturing to the warriors frozen in place. "Be sorry for them. Their ending, this *failure*, it is upon you."

The trio ran from the broken structure, even as the black stone warped and shook, calling to them, the shapes within pushing against the smooth surface.

"Where do we go now?" Tamsyn cried.

"Back to the tunnels," Boudica said. She struck at the wall with her sword in a fast-forward blur, cleaving through the warped structure. Even as the Crown foot-soldiers closed in on them, Boudica forced this new exit, back out into the camp.

"Come on!" Tamsyn called out to Pocahontas, who was bracing herself to block off their path, hatchet raised.

"GO. I WILL BUY YOU SOME TIME."

"God. Don't be such a dickhead," Tamsyn said, yanking on her arm. "How many bad movies have you watched?"

"ALL OF THEM. I HAVE WATCHED EVERY MOVIE EVER."

"They're still like two minutes away from us. Get bloody moving."

Back out in the prison yard, there were only destroyed machines and churned up mud to show that a pitched battle had been fought over this place. The soul prisoners had pushed away as far as they could from the building, leaving almost a mile of empty ground.

Boudica was pacing around with a shovel, trying to find a particular spot. Tamsyn watched frantically as the remaining Crown beasts came at them, and joined Pocahontas in sending as many arrows at them as they could.

"You've lost the bloody tunnels?"

"We disguised the exits too well!" the Celt said. Finally she thrust the shovel into the earth seemingly at random, and in a fast-forward blur she carved a perfectly square hole into the ground before suddenly dropping out of view.

"I am in the tunnel," Boudica said faintly. "Follow if you would survive this day."

"Too bloody right," Tamsyn said, and scrambled into the hole, bouncing down the shaft and landing painfully on her backside. Boudica loomed over her, grim and scowling.

"To think that I gambled everything on you. And lost."

"Hey. I said I'm sorry."

Pocahontas landed lightly in the tunnel.

"I AM SORRY TOO. SORRY I DID NOT DESTROY YOU IMMEDIATELY."

Tamsyn said nothing.

30

The tunnel was low, and even Tamsyn had to walk hunched over. Pocahontas shape-shifted until she was three feet in height, while Boudica merely suffered through the indignity of being a tall woman in a cramped space. Every hundred feet or so, Boudica attacked the support beams, collapsing the tunnel behind them as they went.

"Which tunnel are we in?" Tamsyn asked

"I do not know," Boudica said. "I pray for our sakes we are heading to The Final Shore."

"A BAD PLACE TO BE," the pipsqueak Pocahontas added, her voice still loud and booming. "THOSE WHO LINGER THERE ARE DESTROYED FOREVER."

"Only the weak of will need to fear those waters, devil," Boudica scoffed. "Do you think you will be tempted to take a splash?"

"Alright, ladies, knock it off. So Boudica, you've got a camp near the Final Shore? More soldiers?"

Boudica nodded.

"We know now that a direct fight against the Crown of Countless Suns won't work," Tamsyn said. "You'll need to move your people, and keep moving them."

"I do not take orders from an apprentice devil."

"Whatever. Get killed by spiky balls and weird shit. I am done-zo with your attitude."

"I should bleed you out in the dark," the Celt snarled. She seized Tamsyn, pushing her against the tunnel wall with her blade held across her throat. "You have the stink of death on you. You come here with your silver tongue and your ideas, and now my army is lost."

Suddenly grown as large as the tunnel would allow, Pocahontas snaked a bronze forearm around Boudica's throat, hauling her backwards. The Celt swung her sword behind her, landing glancing blows on Pocahontas's legs, and the floor was slick with Aether.

The two struggled ferociously, ignoring Tamsyn as she slid down the wall shakily. The moment she was free to do so, Tamsyn crawled across the floor of the tunnel, grinding her tongue against the blue spatters of Aether, moaning in ecstasy. Fairy floss. A sneaky little drink from Dad's liquor cabinet. Eddie kissing her passionately. Face grimy with dirt, she looked up to see the other two staring at her, combat forgotten.

"Do you see what she is now?" Boudica said.

"OH. OH, MY SWEET CHILD," Pocahontas said. "YOU HAVE FALLEN FAR."

"Please," Tamsyn said. "Let me lick your wounds. You said it will help heal them faster."

"Better I strike your head from your shoulders, vampire," Boudica said, keeping her back at sword point.

"I know this looks bad," Tamsyn said, shaking. "I have

what's called an addictive personality, amongst other things."

"Modern nonsense," Boudica said. "You cannot explain away this evil."

"Come on. You killed Roman babies. This is hardly equivalent to that."

Boudica scowled, wrestling with her thoughts. Finally she sheathed her sword in one furious motion.

"If we reach the Final Shore, you are not welcome in my camp."

"Fine. I'll find a way to destroy the Crown of Countless Suns myself."

"You! You are a disaster! If we make it to the Final Shore, you should walk out into that deadly ocean."

"We could both go for a paddle, you and I," Tamsyn said, her bluster breaking through both fear and common sense. "Better than hiding from your enemy and pretending you're a resistance."

Tamsyn stared unblinking into that face of pure rage, before a bronze arm chopped down to separate them. Pocahontas pulled Boudica away.

"I WILL DEAL WITH THE GIRL," Pocahontas told Boudica. "SHE IS MY RESPONSIBILITY NOW."

"As you will," Boudica said. "Follow me, or go your own way, your movements no longer concern me."

Tamsyn felt another smart comment dance just shy of her tongue, but Pocahontas gave her a stern look, as if reading her mind. She swallowed the retort down like the acid it was made of.

The world was that low tunnel, lit by the roughest-looking wiring Tamsyn had ever seen, the flickering lightbulbs all that kept a complete darkness at bay. Eyeing off the wire, Boudica stopped her cave-ins, and then it was nothing but a miserable trudge that seemed to go on for miles with no-one willing to talk.

Then the tunnel took a sharp left, ending abruptly in a brick wall. Boudica's tunnel diggers had cleared enough of the wall that the trio could stand side by side, examining the brick.

"This bodes ill," Boudica said with a frown.

"It's just a bloody wall. Break it down!"

"Still your fool tongue! You know absolutely nothing," Boudica told Tamsyn. Reaching out to a particular brick, the Celt pushed it forward, and the whole wall swung forward effortlessly, turning on a hidden hinge.

They left the tunnel to stand on an abandoned train platform. It looked like a standard Tube station, but the tiles were blood-red instead of grimy white. The seats were slabs of bloody meat and gristle, built into frames of bone and pig-iron.

The name of this station was called SUICIDE'S FOREST, fixed into the wall in a familiar Tube-esque style. Another poster showed a schematic transport map, built into the simplified grid of lines and stations familiar to Tamsyn. It hurt her eyes to look at it. It seemed to be three dimensional in places, the script shifting between various languages, occasionally drifting into strange, esoteric script.

"Enochian," Tamsyn muttered, remembering one of the stranger books in her dad's enormous book collection. Supposedly it was the tongue of angels, which made a perverse kind of sense.

Other points on the grid had names like LAVA GLEN, WEEPING HEIGHTS and the disturbing BABY PIT.

"Are you serious? Devils need to catch the Tube around Hell?"

"YES," Pocahontas said. "THE GEOGRAPHY IS FIXED. SOME PREFER CARS OR POSSESS WINGS. EVEN SO – THE TRAFFIC IS – WELL IT USED TO BE –"

"Hellish?"

"YES."

Monitors overhead blinked and shifted, glitching instead of showing the arrival time of the next train. Looking over the razor-sharp edge of the platform, she saw two rails running into the dark maw of a tunnel. They were glowing red-hot, in places white-hot with licks of flame.

"Well, they do tell kids not to play on the rails. Where's the exit?"

"We cannot go up. The Crown has destroyed most of the Tube. Sealed off the rest."

"IT WAS OUR FALLBACK POSITION," Pocahontas said. "WE FOUGHT DOWN HERE UNTIL WE WERE DRIVEN OUT."

"Some of us reorganised," Boudica said. "Others fled."

Shaking her head at the barb, Pocahontas stood near the platform's edge, finally leaping down to land in between the burning rails. She pointed to the darkness.

"THIS LINE LEADS TO THE FINAL SHORE. WE MUST FOLLOW IT."

"Are you nuts? What about the trains?"

"THE TRAINS HAVE BEEN STILL FOR MONTHS NOW. IT IS SAFE."

Boudica leapt down onto the rail. Grimacing, Tamsyn followed, keeping as close to the middle of the track as possible. The heat rising from the rails was incredible, but even as it baked her weird ghost-body, she realised she could not sweat.

Pocahontas summoned a brass lantern from thin air, which bathed the tunnel in a sickly sepia light. Yet more mindless trudging in the gloom, and Tamsyn followed the blocky shape of the living statue, leaping between the sleepers and scrabbling over ballast, swearing whenever she slipped and her ankles brushed against the burning rails.

"Goddamnit, if this was real I'd have third-degree burns by now."

"It is very real," Boudica said. "Mayhap I should pin you to that rail, and rejoice as you sizzle."

"You are such a bitch!"

"You have cost us everything. And now you expect manners?"

"HUSH," Pocahontas said suddenly. She doused the lantern, leaving them only the faint glow of the rails to see by.

"BEHIND," she explained further. There was a faint sound, far behind them. A scrabbling sound, like the shifting of masonry, and then a clang that vibrated along the rail.

"They hunt us," Boudica said, voice filled with a kind of feral glee. She swept the sword out of her scabbard, scraping it against the hot rail. She sent up a shower of sparks, and a sound like nails down a chalkboard.

"Oh my god, shut up," Tamsyn said. "We need to run."

A nightmare sprint, and Tamsyn hurt herself in a dozen stupid ways as they ran from their pursuit. Even Boudica had given up on her own posturing and paced along behind them, a warrior's even stride, not once straying onto a burning rail or slipping on the ballast. Even without the legendary warrior's anger towards her, Tamsyn decided there was enough about this woman to make her hateful.

She's a perfect warrior and she knows it, Tamsyn decided. *Sushma was too, but she was ten times better to be around than this bitch.*

"THERE IS A SIDING AHEAD," Pocahontas suddenly announced. "MAINTENANCE FACILITY."

"Did you design this place?"

"I WAS ON A COMMITTEE."

Before she could add a smart-arse comment, there was more clanging behind them, and the vibration on the rails grew to a shivering whine, a sound like a dentist's drill that set her teeth on edge.

"Some beast is upon us," Boudica declared. "I will fight if none of you will."

"You ancient British idiot, it's a bloody train," Tamsyn cried. The trio fell all over each other in their haste to escape, and at one point Tamsyn tripped over her own feet, falling hip first across the left-hand rail.

Absolute, searing agony, throughout her pale pretend body, the rail burning the spot where a bullet had passed through her in Gravesend, all those years ago. The fire was destroying her very soul, and part of her wanted to give up, wait for the train to strike her, to drift towards the Final Shore in pieces, fall into her final death in the easiest possible way.

"On your feet," Boudica growled in Tamsyn's ear, hauling her up and dragging her along bodily. Recovering her balance she found her own feet, gasping and shaking as a bright light fell upon them. The headlights of the train bearing down on them, and then the screech of the steam whistle when they were sighted.

One final curve in the tunnel, moments before the train would strike them down, and then Pocahontas was scaling a small platform, bronze hand reaching for hers, and she stood on the hot rail, feet burning as she tensed up before that one, frantic, final leap.

A hand closing around hers.

Hands around her waist, hoisting her up.

The shriek of the train whistle, drowning out her own cries.

Tumbling and rolling, pressed against the platform by the weight of a metal woman. She lay there, shuddering for a long moment, even as the brakes squealed on the train, carriages grinding to a halt.

Boudica was nowhere to be seen.

With visions of the warrior woman splattered beneath the wheels of the train, Tamsyn untangled herself from Pocahontas, sobbing. One more life snuffed out for her, *because of her*.

"QUICKLY," Pocahontas said. "THEY WILL FOLLOW."

The train was wood-grain with the shiny gloss of a coffin, the door-handles set in chrome. The train windows were black glass, reflecting their faces as the train came to a stop.

"They're coming!" Tamsyn shouted. Her bow appeared in her hands, arrow already nocked. Standing in front of a locked service door, Pocahontas wrestled with a key-ring that appeared to hold thousands of keys, shifting and shimmering in her hands as she fumbled to find the right one.

The train door opened to reveal one of the enormous slugs. It poured out onto the platform. On its back were hundreds of mannequins, warty growths that resembled people, but now they'd grown swords and axes, dripping with green venom.

She sent arrow after arrow into the growth, hands a blur as she channeled the small amount of power she had here. The people-growths burst like fluorescent green zits, but still the slug came pouring out of the carriage.

"Hurry!"

"I CANNOT FIND THE RIGHT KEY! THIS IS A DIFFERENT LOCK!"

Crying out in frustration, Tamsyn turned and sent an arrow past Pocahontas's head, full force into the wood of the door. Even a normal bow could send arrows out at 200 miles per hour, so surely this one was close to breaking the speed of sound.

The arrow struck the wood and shivered into splinters.

"THIS IS NOT ACTUALLY WOOD!" Pocahontas said. "THIS DOOR IS SET IN WILL AND THOUGHT, AND IT IS STRONGER THAN STEEL."

"Find a damn key! You were on the committee!"

"DESIGN COMMITTEE. I NEVER PATROLLED HERE."

The slug was not fast, moving at perhaps a metre every five seconds, but there was nowhere on the siding for Tamsyn and Pocahontas to run to. It had all the time in the world to push them into the wall, to hack them apart. Tamsyn's hands were a blur as she moved into the fast-forward state of mind, sending maybe five arrows a second into the beast, but still it came on, more mannequins appearing on its bulk, the acidic mass threatening to simply crush them both.

"I HAVE NO KEY," Pocahontas conceded, appearing at Tamsyn's side with her musket. Tamsyn felt surprised as she simply accepted this strange end to her existence, fighting next to her old metal hero. Pointless as it was, she found herself fighting on, from sheer defiance and pig-headedness. These final moments fell away as arrows and gunshots peppered the slug creature, the floor slick with slime and gore.

"I wish that stuff was Aether," Tamsyn moaned, and at

that moment the slug stopped. Tried to turn and stuff itself back into the carriage. Squealed in agony.

The beast shook in the train carriage so much that it threatened to derail the train. Sizzling smoke came out of the doors, a rancid stink that sent the two guides back to the wall, even Pocahontas coughing and gagging. Green muck ran out of the door and down onto the tracks, flowing like an overturned bathtub.

Then the slug stopped moving. There was nothing left but the drip of slug blood, and the sizzling of burnt meat. Tamsyn stared at the train, thoroughly confused.

Boudica emerged from the train doors, holding a flaming sword in either hand. She was covered from head to toe in green slime, plates of her armour torn loose or flapping, but she stood tall. Undefeated.

"I have existed for two thousand years," she said. "No train will end me. No slug will feast upon my bones. I will not allow it."

Pocahontas surreptitiously slid the keyring back into her form. Boudica smirked.

"So, not all doors are open to you?" she mocked. "Well, get on the train then."

"Walk all over that?" Tamsyn said. "That's a biohazard."

"I've seen worse," Boudica said. "Board if you will. This will take us to the Final Shore."

"Can I drive?" Tamsyn asked.

THE INSIDE of the train was in a dire state. Slug gore coated most of the walls, even dripping from the ceiling in places. The floor was a mess of slug guts, the outer skin like a deflated balloon resting across the seats and tables. Tamsyn summoned up a Paddington style plastic mac, hat and wellington boots, turning away the poisonous muck.

"Do you need to wash that off?" she asked Boudica, who was still dripping in the guts of the thing.

"You are soft," the Celt said "It hurts no worse than birthing a child, or a sword through the ribs."

Apart from a mucus trail to show where it had been, the first carriage on the train was remarkably slug free. Tamsyn could see that the seats were decked out in a velvet material with button indents, made to resemble the inside of a coffin. Racks of complimentary newspapers, printed on what seemed to be human skin. Vending machines, filled with bags of ears, intestine chewing gum, and soda cans full of blood.

"You bastards are sick," Tamsyn said to Pocahontas. "This how everyone rides to work?"

"Not anymore," Boudica gloated. "Devils, the tormented, this whole place is broken by the invaders. Good, I say."

"WE WORKED IN SERVICE TO THE MOST HIGH," Pocahontas protested. "PUNISH THE EVIL. REHABILITATE THE LOST. REWARD THE GOOD."

"If I could storm your Heaven, I would turn over their altars, slay the sanctimonious, and I would bleed your precious Most High."

"HOW DARE YOU BLASPHEME?"

"What, is the Most High going to answer to the invasion, to any of this?"

"THE MOST HIGH CANNOT KNOW. THEY WOULD UNDO EVERYTHING, ALL OF CREATION."

"Is that all? Best they do that and fix this whole wretched mess."

Tamsyn ignored the bickering, letting herself into the driver's cabin. More bone décor, up to and including the control levers. Slime ran all over the controls, where the slug beast had operated the train.

"What happened to the other trains?" she called out, interrupting the theological debate.

"WE LOADED THEM WITH EXPLOSIVES, SENT THEM OUT TO DESTROY THE ENEMY. THIS ONE MUST HAVE BEEN IN A DEPOT ABOVE GROUND."

Looking around for a started key or button, Tamsyn grimaced at the array of twitching muscle fibres that made up the control panel. A huge eyeball stared at her from one corner, and she poked at it, annoyed. It blinked shut at the injury, and beneath her feet an engine rumbled into life.

"Holy shit. I'm doing this." Reaching up, Tamsyn found a skeletal hand dangling from the roof, and yanked it down. The whistle shrieked, as if tormented souls were trapped in the train itself.

"Honk honk, bitches. We're off."

Looking for the equipment fouled by the slug, Tamsyn found a lever made from a mummified woman's leg. Throwing it forward, the train lurched into motion, roaring and moaning through the tunnels of the Hell Tube network.

"Next stop. The Final Shore," a cheerful automated voice said from the loudspeakers. "This line terminates at the Final Shore."

A long awkward moment where the trio considered each other, Boudica looking like a cat preparing to pounce.

"Can you please put the flaming swords away?" Tamsyn told Boudica. "You're making me nervous."

"Just drive the train, apprentice devil," she said, sliding the swords into their scabbards all the same.

"REMEMBER, SHE IS MINE TO REHABILITATE," Pocahontas said.

"Better that you rehabilitate her head from her neck, devil."

Boudica was scratched in dozens of places, leaking out Aether that was rich and treacly, like aged wine. Tamsyn salivated, head woozy with desire.

She bit her thumb, hard, breaking the skin. No. It wasn't enough.

31

For many long minutes, their whole world was a myopic charge down a tunnel, three women staring at the stretch of brick and rail the headlights could reach, and then they were out of the Hell Tube system, rocketing across a desolate landscape.

Gone was the city with its smoking ruins. Here the train line ran across a stony plain, interrupted only by thorny bushes and cracked clay. Lightning cracked against the loose stones and shale, and every now and then Tamsyn could see the fog of a broken soul flitting across the plain, drawn towards utter destruction.

"We near the Final Shore," Boudica said. "Prepare your anchor."

"They're called brakes," Tamsyn said. She rested her hand on the leg throttle and looked around for anything else slime-encrusted. A jawbone, a hinged ribcage containing a smoky lump of coal, and what might have been a fossilised thyroid gland.

I'll slow right down and then mash all the controls. If it works in Mortal Kombat, it can work on a hell train.

The plains gave way to a slight rise, and they came onto an endless bank of sand-dunes, as black as midnight. The dunes were held together with dead plant life, thorns and dead branches waving in the wind.

Then they crested the horizon, and Tamsyn gasped. In the distance was an ocean, ink-black, with wild waves battering a coast-line. There was no sand here, only acres of sharp stones.

"Next stop, the Final Shore," the cheerful automaton announced. "This line terminates."

"It sure does," Tamsyn muttered.

There was a station here, a lone siding that served as a simple place to disembark. A ticket office, the glass shattered, and no-one within it. Another vending machine, but someone had yanked the door off its hinges, stealing all of the vile snacks and drinks.

Tamsyn hauled back on the lever and yanked on all of the controls until the train slid to a sudden halt, throwing them all around the cabin.

"Fool girl!" Boudica said.

"I didn't see either of you volunteer to drive," Tamsyn said, picking herself off the floor.

When the doors opened, the trio stepped out onto the empty platform. The sky felt low here, a brooding weight of bruised cloud, and Tamsyn flinched each time a bolt of dry lightning struck at the dunes, or the plain down below.

"I go to my camp now," Boudica said. "If you follow, I will slay you both."

"Don't let the door hit you," Tamsyn muttered.

"YOU HAVE PROVEN WORTHY," Pocahontas said. "IF EVER THE INVASION IS THWARTED, I WOULD LESSEN YOUR PUNISHMENT."

She held out her bronze hand to the Celt, ready for a handshake, but Boudica regarded it like a dangerous dog.

"Would you send me to the blessed realms for my service?" Boudica said.

"YOU CANNOT ASCEND THE GREAT STAIR."

"Then we waged your war for nothing!" she shouted.

When Boudica drew a hand's length of flaming steel from her scabbard, Tamsyn quickly stood in front of Pocahontas, showing the palms of her hands.

"Stop. Please. Yes, it's a shitshow, we're all agreed on that. Please, just go to your camp and we'll be on our way."

Still snarling, Boudica slammed her sword back into her scabbard. Without another word she left the abandoned train station and struck out across the dunes.

"Well, one of my heroes sure turned out to be a bitch," Tamsyn said. "Alright, what do we do now?"

"THIS WAY," Pochontas said. "YOU MUST SEE IT."

There was a well-worn track through the sand dunes, and some devil had thought to rope off the dunes to either side, so the posts now sagged drunkenly across the black sand.

Tamsyn felt the draw then, the urge to dash headlong, to slog through the sand to the path's end. Joy, relief, a whole parade of emotions washed over her, and it was as strong as the shameful urge to feed on Aether.

Come this way, every instinct seemed to tell her. *Everything's going to be just fine.*

"YOU FEEL IT," Pochontas said, a statement. "IT CALLS TO ALL, EVEN US."

"The Final Shore," Tamsyn whispered.

It took all of her willpower not to run forward like a maniac, but even so she trembled as they went down the path.

"DO NOT QUIVER," Pochontas said. "YOU ARE A GUIDE, NOT SOME BROKEN SOUL. HOLD FAST."

Then she saw it. A shoreline of broken rocks, stretching out endlessly, battered by an ocean of the purest darkness. Wave after wave fell onto the sharp-looking stones, sending up spray, and when she caught its scent it was heady, seductive, the oblivion that booze had never quite managed to deliver.

"LOOK THERE," Pocahontas said. A person-shaped fog fell out of the dunes, drifting across the shale and into the waters. The ocean reached for the broken soul, erupting in an excited frenzy of waves and spray. Just beneath the surface of the water, there was a flash of brilliant light, and then stillness.

"Where do they go? The souls."

"NOBODY KNOWS. NOT EVEN US."

"God, I want to go into that water so badly."

A long moment of washing the waves crash against the shore. The water offered oblivion, absolute and undeniable.

"So you tortured the souls who end up down here, right?"

"CORRECTION AND GUIDANCE, AS THE MOST HIGH DESIGNED."

"So why don't all your, er, clients? Why don't they just catch the train here and walk out into that?"

"THEY ARE FREE TO DO SO. MANY DO."

"Why not all of them?"

"THE URGE TO SURVIVE IS STRONG, EVEN IN THE ONCE-DEAD."

"That makes sense. Even as screwed as we are, I don't want to top myself."

Another soul floated past them by the roped-off path, ignoring the two Guides as it went in for a reverse baptism.

Another brilliant flash, this one joined by a lightning strike against the surface of a rolling wave.

"So, what now?"

"I DO NOT KNOW. I FEAR WE CANNOT DEFEAT THE CROWN."

"Surely there's something no-one's tried yet?"

"LET US PONDER THAT. THIS IS A GOOD PLACE TO PONDER THINGS."

It was a delicious moment, standing near the edge of oblivion, with just enough willpower to resist its call.

"This place needs a kiosk. I always buy an ice cream at the beach."

She heard a footfall in the sand behind them, just a brush of grit, but it was enough warning for her to turn, fumbling for her bow and arrow. It was Boudica, Aether tears running down her face, an enormous burning sword held above her head.

Her camp is gone, Tamsyn realised.

Falling arse-backwards onto the sand, she narrowly avoided that first furious swing, meant to take off her head. Pocahontas crashed into Boudica with tremendous force, holding off her blows with an axe carved from ice.

Sword and axe came together in a blur, both Boudica and Pocahontas moving into a fast-forward duel. Holding back, Tamsyn waited for an opening, sending an arrow towards Boudica, which she batted away with a flick of her sword.

Then Boudica sent her fiery longsword down, once, twice, three times, and Pocahontas was down, the haft of her axe shattered, her right arm severed at the shoulder, and her bronze torso staved in. The statue fell to the black sand and did not move.

Boudica turned to face Tamsyn, fixing her with a predator's stare. She came on slowly, sword raised. Then the whiff of Pocahontas's spilt Aether came to Tamsyn, and she reeled, caught between the danger of Boudica and her newest addiction.

When Boudica noticed, she burst out into laughter. Standing to one side, she gestured for Tamsyn to come forward. Every fibre in her body ached with the need to rush forward, to close her lips around those grievous wounds and drink her fill.

"Stop toying with me, bitch," Tamsyn said. Hands shaking, she sent an arrow at the warrior, which Boudica batted aside almost contemptuously.

Angry now, Tamsyn found her focus, and moved faster, faster, arrows leaving her bow faster than the laws of physics should allow, and still the big Iceni woman stood there grinning, knocking them aside lazily like a kid playing backyard cricket.

"I'm going to have to fight you, aren't I?" Tamsyn said shakily. Boudica nodded. Letting her bow and quiver vanish into thought, Tamsyn called up her own sword and shield, exact replicas of the ones King Peter swung around in that Narnia movie.

Apart from a quick course in hand-to-hand combat during Basic Training, Tamsyn had next to no experience in this sort of scrap. Holding her ground as the warrior woman came in, Tamsyn tried to sell her second life well.

She swung her sword, one high and low stroke, both countered dizzyingly fast. Boudica rained blows down on her shield, deftly shattering Tamsyn's sword the moment she tried to parry with that. Hiding behind her shield, Tamsyn fell back before those mighty blows, the sheer force jarring the bones of her weird ghost-body.

Letting out a primal roar, Boudica struck Tamsyn's

shield so hard it splintered down the middle. Holding up the jag of her broken sword and trying to will the blade back into place, Tamsyn flinched before the fiery arc of the sword, and then she was staring in surprise at the stump of her hand, gushing out blue Aether in spurts.

"Just gimme a sec," Tamsyn gasped. "Got a little scratch here I need to deal with."

Once more Boudica laughed. Stepping back, she placed the burning sword point down in the black sand, leaning on the pommel and waiting.

Tamsyn was treated to the odd sight of her severed hand dissolving into fog, drifting down towards the water. Licking the Aether from her stump until the wound began to seal over, she supposed the rest of her spirit would soon follow into permanent oblivion. Piece by painful piece, going by the look on Boudica's face.

The wound wasn't sealing over, not completely. She was going to bleed out, here on this lonely beach. It wasn't terrible to die this way but Tamsyn decided it was kind of annoying.

What a stupid ending to my story, she thought. *Everything I've gone through, and this? It's like getting murdered by Hitler's ghost in a Tesco's.*

Concentrating on the stump, she tried to imagine her hand growing back, only to meet a significant resistance. This far into Hell, things were fixed into place beyond anything she could change. Looking over to Pocahontas's mangled corpse, she wondered if there had ever been any Guides powerful enough to tame this warrior into submission.

The Celt was finally free of her hellish chains, but now she'd been stripped of everything she'd ever scraped together down here. Two thousand years of torture was enough to piss anyone off, and now all that anger was aimed directly at her.

"You know, I didn't exactly choose to be a Guide."

"I did not choose the Romans to invade my home. I did not choose the Crown to invade Hell. It doesn't matter what we choose. You are my enemy. That matters."

"That's – well I guess it makes sense. In a brutal Iron Age way."

"You still have one hand. Get up."

"Guess I'm finished anyway."

Shaking off the broken remains of her shield, Tamsyn looked to her empty left hand. No more bows, no hope of even touching the insanely quick warrior with hand-to-hand combat.

A gun? But she was a rubbish shot, even with her good hand. She wouldn't hit the side of a barn in this state. Her mind flicked back to her time in Corpus Christi. Disappointing Deacon on the gun range. Being worse than useless when it came to anything but a bow.

She remembered Reynolds at that moment, that arrogant beautiful arsehole. As her enemy tensed up, ready to stomp over and murder her, she knew what to do.

"Go on," Boudica said impatiently. "Pick any weapon you like."

"Are you sure?"

"I faced the might of Rome! I faced the worst devils in Hell. You are nothing!"

That was the moment when Tamsyn raised the SPAS-12 riot control shotgun, stock fitting snugly inside her shoulder. At that range, she did not need to be a good shot. She didn't even need her good hand.

BLAM! BLAM! BLAM! She pulled the trigger, hammering the warrior with fire, and Boudica couldn't hope to block the shot with her sword. Boudica staggered backwards, shot punching into her breastplate, greaves, and one lucky shell to the face.

"Welcome to the future, bitch," Tamsyn said, and then something was wrong. The gun felt spongy in her grip, less *there*. Even as she worked the slide, hoping against hope for another shell, the whole shotgun fell apart in her hands, drifting away like cigarette smoke.

I've lost too much Aether, Tamsyn thought. Even her skin was starting to seem thin, like tissue paper wrapped around bones. She was literally fading away.

It took all of her strength, but she rolled to her side. Got to her hands and knees. Crawling through the sand, Tamsyn struggled to get to the shattered body of Pocahontas.

There are no bodies down here, Tamsyn realised. *Whenever souls die their Twice-Death, their ghost bodies vanish.*

Pocahontas is still alive!

Drawn by the dribble of Aether coming from Pocahontas's grievous wounds, Tamsyn felt like the cartoon figure crawling through the desert for water, but this would truly bring her back. But more than that, she craved that sweet liquid, would drain her friend to the marrow and go back for seconds.

"That shit is delicious," she slurred, and a shadow fell across her.

Boudica, wavering in a spatter of her own Aether, sword raised up for a no-nonsense finish-your-enemy deathblow.

The sword fell.

It met another blade with a ringing CLANG!

Standing between Tamsyn and Boudica was Sushma.

The ghost of her friend wore a sharply pressed Gurkha dress uniform, complete with lanyard and beret. Gripping a kukris in each hand, she came at the bigger woman like a wood-chipper on legs. Wherever Boudica's sword fell, Sushma simply wasn't there anymore.

Boudica grew more frustrated by the second, laying about with a fury.

Sushma sought the weak points in Boudica's armour, patiently nicking away at her sides, underarms, the backs of her legs and hands. It wasn't even a contest. Boudica began to have trouble concentrating on her sword, and the fire wreathing the blade went out, pieces of her armour dropping off and turning into smoke.

"This is not fair," Boudica said, shaking her now wobbly sword. "I was wounded."

"And now you are dead," Sushma said calmly. Suddenly darting forward, she lodged a blade in Boudica's heart and another one through her eye. Just like that, the two-thousand year old warrior faded into fog, drifting down to the shore. A series of enormous waves crashed down around her broken spirit, and a brilliant flare lit up the surface of the water, brighter than an arc welder, a supernova, and then nothing was left of Boudica.

"I have so many questions," Tamsyn slurred, before lapping at the puddle of Aether in the sand.

"So do I," Sushma said with a frown.

SUSHMA HELPED carry Tamsyn over to Pocahontas, placing her next to the savagely wounded statue. Face still gritty with black sand and Aether residue, Tamsyn slumped across her broken friend. It was almost intimate, the way she suckled the leaking life-fluid out of Pocahontas's shattered chest.

"Why are you doing that?" Sushma asked.

"I've lost too much of this stuff," Tamsyn said, looking up. "Plus, it's amazing. Give it a try!"

Fetching up her kukris, Sushma cautiously licked some of Boudica's Aether from the flat of her blade. She shivered all over, and then made a face.

"This is bad," she said. "You must stop."

"I need it!" Tamsyn cried out. "I'll fade away. I'll go down into that water."

Sushma pressed her lips into a thin line, choosing not to speak as she examined the stump of Tamsyn's hand. Using her lanyard as a tourniquet, Sushma slowed down the flow of Aether from the wound, and Tamsyn supposed it was more the idea of Sushma's first aid than any physical reality.

"PLEASE STOP LICKING ME," Pocahontas said weakly.

"Oh my lord. She's still here. She's not gone!"

Tamsyn joined in the fierce embrace of her dying friend, leaking her own Aethery tears back into those savage wounds. Pocahontas stared up at the storm-clouds, barely moving.

"I WATCHED YOU," she said. "WHEN YOU WOULD DRAW PICTURES OF ME."

Licking at her bronze lips, they were suddenly pale flesh, and then the bronze ideal was gone, the false outer skin fading away like smoke. It was Pocahontas as she looked in life, but tissue thin, barely there.

"I loved to see your drawings, how happy you were on that bench, sketching," Pocahontas said, robbed at the last of her booming voice. "You were very good."

"How could you watch me? Without someone dying nearby?"

"I do not know," Pocahontas said. "But I could always see you."

Sushma stood at a polite distance, giving them a chance

at this final goodbye. Tamsyn felt sad that the Gurkha would never get to know this woman, who was surely a kindred spirit.

"I am so, so glad I got to meet you," Tamsyn said. "I'm sorry you didn't get to go back. See your boy."

"It is fine to end this way," Pocahontas said. "It is right that Boudica saw some justice from this old devil."

She struggled to sit up, and fell back, too far gone even for that.

"Listen," she said. "You must learn about your sickness."

"I'm not sick."

"Do not argue. You are a vampire. The thirst will only grow."

"It's not my fault! None of this is."

"That does not matter. I have one last request from you."

"What? Anything."

"When I die, leave your friend and walk into the ocean."

"Excuse me?"

"Destroy yourself now, while you are still yourself. Do not follow the path of the monster."

"I was always a monster," Tamsyn cried, and clamped her face against her chest wound, sucking down Aether greedily.

"No! Enough!"

Tamsyn rose, mouth ringed with blue.

"I was a monster when I killed all my friends in Gravesend! When I killed my baby girl in Corpus Christi! Everyone at the Caymans! I kill, and I kill, and it is all I can do!"

She felt the strong arms of Sushma around her then, hauling her back, and she struggled as she snapped at the wounds of her dying friend. She saw fear in Pocahontas's eyes then, and felt shame, just underneath that all-consuming need.

"Strike her head from her shoulders!" Pocahontas cried weakly. "If you call yourself her friend, do it!"

Then she was nothing but fog on the sand, and Pocahontas died her Twice-Death, drawn to the Final Shore, moments after her pitiful and meaningless end.

"I'm sorry!" Tamsyn cried, but there was no forgiveness, only waves upon the black stones.

32

Tamsyn walked down onto the rocky beach, the stones slicing into her feet. Sushma walked cautiously next to her, blades held down and by her sides.

"I won't do that to you," Tamsyn said.

Sushma said nothing, simply looked at her, measuring her.

"She was dying anyway! Come on, surely you never wasted anything in Nepal? Would you leave a dying rabbit where you found it, without feeding your family?"

"When you saw the ghost rabbit by your father's grave, I should have struck you down," Sushma said firmly.

"No. No, don't."

"When you spoke to your ghosts, brought bad things to us, I should have cut your throat. Better that than this moment."

She gestured to the water with a kukri, the waves growing fiercer the closer they got. Greedy to lick at her phantom body, and dissolve everything that was left of her.

"Go on. Walk into it."

"Okay."

She stood for a long moment, facing the inevitable. Oblivion, sweet and immediate, and barely fifteen feet away. A faint spray washed across her, tingling and eating into her skin. It was painful, bracing.

"I'm scared," Tamsyn admitted.

"I came a long way to find you, to do a great battle alongside my friend," Sushma said. "But I was too late. I lost my friend. I do not know you."

"I'm still me," Tamsyn said weakly. "Please. I can't do this if you hate me. You're all I've got left."

Sushma paused for a long moment, and then finally shook her head.

"That is not true," she said.

The Final Shore felt endless, all shifting jagged stones, a dune on the right, and hungry washing oblivion to the left. Tamsyn struggled to keep pace with Sushma, her energy failing by the minute. She sucked from the seeping wound on her severed wrist whenever the Gurkha wasn't looking.

"There," Sushma cried out, voice drowned by the roar of the ocean. Tamsyn struggled to see it through the painful mist, but there was a line, and another, and soon they were passing a row of wooden sleepers, turned vertical and driven deep into the shale. The wood was ancient, washed and bleached by death's waters, each post bristling with dozens of rusty spikes facing the waves.

Then she saw it. A shape, clinging to one of the posts, and it turned to face her, and then she was gasping, crying, sliding across the loose stones, banging her knees and her stump painfully whenever she lost her footing, and still she ran onwards.

"Oh my god," she said, falling to her knees at the base of the post. Above her was the pale ghost of a man, fastened to the post with a dozen rusty spikes, piercing through ribs, stomach, under the collarbones, through the shoulders. His arms and legs had been removed, the wounds seared closed. His guts were dangling from a deep horizontal cut, just brushing against the beach below.

"Eddie," Tamsyn said.

"Hey Tam," he said weakly. "This is proper romantic. A day at the beach."

"Please, Sushma, help me get him down," she said, fumbling at the spikes with her one good hand. They'd been driven in deeply, fastening his spirit stuff to the post in a dozen painful ways.

"I have tried," Sushma said. "I then offered to ease his passing. He said he was waiting for his fiancé."

The ocean gave a vicious thumping to the shore then, more of that painful spray biting into them all. It seemed like an awful punishment to be crucified here, mere feet from the release of death, while the sea could only burn at you, killing you one layer of ghost-skin at a time.

"Who did this to you?" Tamsyn asked angrily. "Was it the devils?"

"No, my love," Eddie said. "They're alright, that lot. We fought together."

Tamsyn thought back to her dreams, to her loved ones communicating with her. Eddie trying to warn her about the Black Crown Boy.

"You were in the Resistance?" she asked.

"Yep! Fought those bloody Crown things. Followed Boudica and Napoleon, real crazy stuff. Then we lost."

Eddie attempted to shrug, pinned to the post as he was, with barely his shoulders and no arms.

"What are ya gonna do, eh? No point whingeing about things, am I right?"

"You stupid, beautiful man. I'm gonna rescue you."

Gritting her teeth, Tamsyn pushed against the post, feet scrabbling in the scree. However it was fastened, it was deep, perhaps into bedrock. There was no pushing this over.

"Help me!" Tamsyn insisted to Sushma. "Use those things to hack through the wood!"

"It does not work," Sushma said. Demonstrating, her sharp blades simply bounced away from the post, without even leaving a mark. Tamsyn understood then that the idea behind Sushma's imagined blades was not stronger than the belief of whoever had planted these posts here.

Some boss devil. Or worse, the Crown of Countless Suns.

She slumped against Eddie, face against his torso. Faded as he was, there was the faintest dribble of Aether coming from his many wounds. It took all of Tamsyn's strength not to feast upon Eddie, but her resolve was fading by the second.

"We all watched you, you know," Eddie said. "Your dad, Clem, Baxter. Even Dawes. In that foggy mirror place, up the stairs."

"Where are they?"

"All gone. I'm sorry, love. Some, we lost in the war. Others were put up on these posts with me, when the Crown caught us chatting to you. The sea got to them all, except me. Those piss-weak bastards."

Knowing they were gone was another knife to the heart. She'd hoped against hope to end the Crown, and only then would she find her loved ones, talk to everyone again. Even her mother, and the thought of speaking with her again chilled her to the bone.

Another spray of death, and Eddie faced it gamely, a smile on his face as the droplets ate into his essence.

"Come at me, ya soggy piece of shit!" he yelled at the ocean. "You call that a drenching?"

Tamsyn was astounded. Even here, robbed of all hope and utterly defeated, Eddie Jacobs simply would not give up.

"I'm sorry about Cuba," she said.

"Don't be bloody daft!" he said. "I'd be pissed if you didn't put an arrow through me!"

"Malcolm is safe. Our little Malcolm."

"Good girl. We're not really dead, not if our little man is up there running around. You hear that, you stupid fucking ocean! Our boy is still alive! Wahoo!"

Tamsyn smiled, and hugged him tight, as tight as she could.

"I've got so many things to tell you, Eddie. I met Prince Harry!"

"That ginger twat? Piss off."

"Well, I bloody well did. We escaped from a sinking nuclear sub, which blew up underneath us."

"Ooh er. Regular bloody James Bond now, aren't we? Too good for a northern boy now, I bet."

She laughed, hard and long, and all the poison fell from her heart. At the end of things, everything was just fine, as long as her bone-head fiancé was nearby.

"I kind of miss the old days, Tam. You know, when it was just the zombies and going hungry and stuff."

"I liked Corpus Christi. Our house. Little Millie."

"That sweet little girl. Yeah, that place in Texas was alright. I loved our place at Florida Keys better. Big-arse pretentious house."

They laughed again, and then fell into their first comfortable silence. They'd done those so well, even when they'd been running for their lives from zombies, in the war, everywhere they'd been together since the world went to shit.

"What now?" she said.

"Well, you could stay and keep me company," Eddie said. "I think they left all the important things attached."

"Sorry. It's gone."

"What? Oh well. Climb up here if you want a moustache ride."

"Eddie, I'm being serious. What happens now?"

"Those alien bastards have taken everything over, but nothing's changed. You can still hide down here, just like we did on Earth with the zombies. You keep going as long as you can, and you fight for as long as you can. That's what happens now."

"We can't beat them."

"So what? Do you hear me pissing and moaning? 'Oh no, I've been nailed to a post, it's shitting terrible down here'. Absolutely piss-weak, Tamsyn Webb. Pull yourself together."

She laughed until she cried. It took some effort with one hand, but Tamsyn managed to climb up to Eddie, using the spikes as steps. They kissed, passionately and deeply.

"You are the most amazing man," Tamsyn said. "It was worth it. All of this. Just to see you again."

"Well, off you go then. Come back and visit me if you're willing to talk dirty."

One more kiss, and Tamsyn climbed back down to the beach. She looked to Sushma.

"Well, let's go. We've got a resistance to continue."

"Are you mad? You have to go out into the water now."

"No. I'm not giving up. If Eddie can do this, I can fight my own urges."

"Ooh, you dirty girl!" Eddie crowed from above. Tamsyn flipped the bird.

"What if you get worse? What if you become like the vampires I saw out there?" she said, pointing inland with her blade. Tamsyn had no doubt that the vampires Sushma had encountered were no more.

"It's not going to happen," she said, tapping her forehead. "Mind over matter."

"Oi, stop flapping your gums and leg it," Eddie called out. "Those bloody aliens have come back."

Tamsyn turned to follow Eddie's eye-line, and she saw the dunes erupt with skittering Crown beasts, clambering down towards them. Above, the sky suddenly filled with flying sunbeasts, the blimp things, every other abomination the Crown could fly.

Their escape had definitely been noticed. It looked like the Black Crown Boy had sent every last beastie to chase her down.

I really shook that pasty little piece of shit, she mused. *Poor Henri!*

"Here you go," Sushma said, handing her one of her kukri blades. "Stab one of those things or I will feel great shame for you."

"Thank you," Tamsyn said. She touched foreheads with her friend. "It's good to go out like this."

Sushma charged up to the advancing horrors, instantly swallowed by a wall of tentacles and freaky limbs, already dicing and slicing and crying out in Nepalese. It was a glorious end for a bad-ass bitch.

Tamsyn took her place by Eddie's post, wanting to eke out every moment she could with her man.

"It's a shame we can't get up those steps again," Eddie said. "Up to that mirrorworld. Go look at Kate Middleton in the shower or whatever."

"Wish I could see my mum again," Tamsyn said, bracing herself as the horde of freaks came onto the beach itself.

"Well, just do it then!" Eddie said. "If I've learnt one thing stuck up here, it's that people are driven by excuses and bullshit. Either find the staircase or shut the fuck up."

His words bit into her, and she was angry that he was wasting their last moments on a nitpicking argument.

"Find the staircase? I-"

Squinting at Eddie in fury, she saw it then. The first step was a spike in the sleepers, just below Eddie, and as she clambered up she could see the next one, just above the water's edge. Another one just above that, and then the next step was on the moon, and the next one just behind a nebula cloud.

Of course she could see freaky shit with a bit of focus. She was a Guide, after all, but this was new. The Great Stair wasn't fixed in place, but was here, exactly where she needed it to be.

What am I?

"There's the look of success," Eddie said with a smile. "You just needed the right motivation."

"What about you?"

"I'll bite their balls off! Just go!"

Tamsyn ran then, straight toward the water, which gathered up to swallow her. She leapt into the air, the bottom of her feet both scalding hot and freezing where the tip of a wave brushed at her, and then she was above the ocean, leaping from step to step. Climbing the Great Stair.

"I love you!" she cried out to Eddie. Even pinned to the

post like a butterfly, he still managed to wiggle and thrust his pelvis at her, tongue out and grinning wildly.

The servants of the Crown swallowed him into their feeding frenzy, and then Tamsyn was leaping through the universe, slowly climbing out of Hell.

IT WAS INSTINCTIVE, this impossible climb, but each step took all of her concentration. If ascending any staircase was harder than the descent, she supposed the same held true for a metaphysical construction that crossed the universe.

She felt a rumble below her toes, and looked *down*, and instantly regretted it. *Worst motion sickness ever.*

A few steps below her, past an asteroid belt, a black hole and a weirdly pulsing galaxy, and she could see abominations that could only be Crown agents, ripping at the Great Staircase, pulling the very steps out of the universe. Wrecking everything, even as more unspeakable things climbed past them to pursue her, catch and destroy her.

"I've gotta see my mum again," she kept telling herself, climbing and willing herself back to Purgatory. Behind her, the cosmos itself shook, stars and planets breaking apart in her wake. Just more collateral damage as the Crown of Countless Suns conquered one more universe.

We come to protect against a terrible enemy, the Black Crown Boy had said. Tamsyn decided he was lying. *What conqueror doesn't claim a noble cause?*

It was a clambering, crashing, batshit crazy pursuit through the heavens, and then Tamsyn felt herself flagging. Whatever this spirit body was made of, it had simply taken too much abuse. She'd hit the wall, and was starting to slow down.

"Gah, keep going you silly bitch," she chided herself. With each soul-jarring step she kept picturing her mum, and understood then why Pocahontas had returned up here to hide from the war.

If they were from blood, were found or even just accidental, family was everything. The chance to see them again, even if it was a bad memory was absolutely worth this.

"Settle down. You can eat me in a minute," she called out to her pursuers, wondering if something like her voice was echoing around in the universe.

One more step, and then she was off the Great Staircase, sliding across the grey nothing of Purgatory. She'd made it! Above, the Great Staircase continued up to the High Place, to Heaven, but Tamsyn she did not have the strength to continue upwards.

Pocahontas said that the Guides can't go up there, Tamsyn thought. *What a shit arrangement!*

She felt the ease and malleability of Limbo around her, and willed her missing hand back into existence, threw a bunch of spikes and other traps behind her to slow down her pursuit. Then she jumped around the Mirrorworld, visiting every place she could think of to throw off the scent. New York. Sydney. Hong Kong. Euro Disneyland. Waiting for a long moment, none of the Crown's monsters appeared. She made her final leap.

Gravesend. Where it all started, and was now about to end.

She visited the church, sadly noting the empty pedestal, the bench she'd spent so many hours on. Where she'd spoken with her friends, faced off against Eddie, chatted with her Dad about all kinds of things.

A peaceful place to end, but she dared linger no further.

Shifting herself through the streets with the last of her willpower, she found that awful place, the bus-stop in town where her world had come crashing down.

Apart from one attempt that ended in a screaming panic attack on her 16th birthday, she'd never come back here, even though it had meant catching two extra buses to get home. The bus shelter was exactly as she remembered it, that moment her mother had screamed at her to buy her damn magazine.

Be quick about it.

She felt the tremor as an army of horrendous aliens entered this realm, heard the crumble as they destroyed the imagined buildings of Gravesend.

Still she paused.

Be quick about it!

"Oh mum. Oh, I can't. I can't do it."

"Be quick about it," someone whispered in her ear, and she jumped. It was her dad, Mal Webb, impossibly *here*, already fading into fog and mist and then nothing. He'd found a way here, just long enough to lend her some courage.

She opened the death-mirror, looking onto the worst day of her life.

The people crowding around the bus-stop, playing with their phones, looking up the road with annoyance. One bus simply hadn't come, and the next bus was late, which is why so many people had been waiting there that day.

I'd wanted a magazine to pass the time, she remembered. *It felt like such a long time to wait.*

There they were. Her fifteen-year old self, and now her mum, poor Jenny Webb, flustered and wearing her work uniform, distracted and thinking of a thousand other things, just like all the other mums and dads waiting for the bus.

"Be quick about it!" her mum snapped at her, handing her a five-pound note. She was angry and frustrated, but by god she was beautiful in that moment. Tamsyn wept for joy, and found closure in this final moment of her existence. Peace that she'd been able to confront her past, in a way no shrink would ever be able to manage.

Behind her, the buildings fell. The whirring and burning monstrosities were overhead and in the buildings and closing in.

Be quick about it, she thought.

The church fell. The old pub fell. The Tesco collapsed in on itself. These creatures were systematically destroying her town. The Crown of Countless Suns was toying with her. Those things could have chewed her to shreds by now, but they were keeping their distance.

Is it fear he is aiming for? she thought, but even as the beasts roared around her, chewing the place into matchsticks, they would not touch her.

In fact, none of them had touched her, the whole time she'd been in Hell. They'd chased her around, and terrorised her, but the only injuries her ghost-body had received were from other souls. The Crown had tried to draw her into the stone, but he'd hesitated.

That feeling of peace and calm evaporated from her mind, replaced by a vague annoyance. All of that, and they *weren't* pulling her limb from limb?

Then the monsters were hauling forth a black stone into the circle they'd formed around Tamsyn. Another smooth-faced conduit, and once more Tamsyn was looking upon the Crown of Countless Suns, garbed as a preppy school kid.

"Well, hello Henri," Tamsyn said.

The Crown blanched but then recovered.

"You have seen your mother once more. Come. We will

escort you back to the Final Shore. As the last of the Guides, I have decided that you will be permitted to have a dignified ending."

"Nope. No thanks. Fuck right off."

She walked towards the stone, and the creatures backed away. She laughed.

"I'm going to watch my mother die a few hundred times. Get some proper closure. And then I'm going to figure out a way to crack that stone open, and I'm going to kick your bony little arse."

The Crown looked at her with a mocking smile, but when Tamsyn ran at the stone with her fist raised, he flinched, taking a step backwards. She drew back at the last second, not quite touching the stone, and she raised her remaining middle finger.

"Don't you go anywhere, you poncy little snot-faced bully. I'll deal with you in a minute."

She returned to the scene of the accident, replaying the moment again and again. Watching the carnage on repeat, making sense of the bounce of bodies, the tangle of flesh, the physics of the car meeting the bus shelter.

Dawes, once the bogeyman she'd hated so much, was now just an extra in this sad but not unusual scene. She'd seen so much evil since this day, and this was mundane now.

Even looking at her horrified young self, staggering back to the bloody scene and trying to save her mother, she discovered it was cathartic. She felt kindness towards young Tamsyn, not anger.

"It gets better, mate," she told herself. "You grow boobs. You get a boyfriend. You go on adventures!"

Confused, young Tamsyn looked up from her dying mother.

"Shit. Did you just *hear* me?"

She waved away the death-window, and called it up again, right to the start of the scene. This time she called at herself and her mother, telling them *stay away from the bus shelter! Danger!*

They looked around, confused, puzzled as she screamed and railed, but the scene still played out in the same tragic way.

"Enough," the Crown said from his rock. "You tinker with the universe in ways you cannot hope to understand."

"Shut up, Henri. I'll figure this out eventually."

"I have another offer for you. A better one."

"What, better than me kicking your arse? Whatever."

"I will give you safe passage to a copy of your world," the Crown said. "A playground, identical in every way to the world that you knew."

"You can make places now? Why bother invading everywhere?"

"I told you, we do this to save you from a great enemy! We are protecting the multiverse."

"You are doing a bang-up job of protecting us. Go on, tell me what your enemy is like. I might go and join them."

"The enemy, the true enemy, it cannot be reasoned with! It only offers oblivion, absolute and endless!" the boy said. "Our ways are strict, but we're the only ones that can keep them at bay."

"Said every tyrant ever."

"Submit. We will give you anything you want in your own private world. Fame. Riches. Immortality. We will not invade or harm that world. You will experience a life that will unfold in any way you see fit."

"Are you seriously blue-pilling me right now?"

"You have been a worthy adversary," the Crown said.

"Let your struggle end. Seek out happiness, and know that we will not take it from you."

Tamsyn thought of her last sight of Eddie, and shook her head.

"Go to Hell," she said.

The Crown was furious, and he shifted them all around the Mirrorworld, bouncing them from Beijing to Antarctica, and a moment of confused darkness in the bottom of the Mariana Trench.

Each time, Tamsyn extended her own will, bringing them back to Gravesend, to the bus-stop, but she was beginning to falter now. Her body was burning through Aether, and she began to crave it with the junkie's intense need. But there was no-one around to give it to her, no-one to pin down and steal it from.

"I will give you the prison," the Crown finally said. "All of those souls. An eternity of Aether. Run it for me, and you can drink a river of Aether till the end of time."

Her head swayed with the mental image. She wanted the blue stuff so badly! A row of souls, spigots in their necks, and she could drink and drink, with no-one to stop her. Her only other option was to be a lost soul, a vampire roaming the unclaimed parts of Hell. She would get very thirsty, and then she would end up back at the Final Shore, broken, beaten, starved of Aether.

"No," she said through gritted teeth. So they were back to teleportation tug of war, and she was losing. She shivered on top of Everest. Fought for freedom from a swamp. Jumped back to Gravesend a moment before being trapped in the World Trade Centre on September 11.

Once last chance to work out the puzzle. She opened the death-window and looked upon her young self, clutching the five-pound note.

"Take my offer. Or you will end up on a post at the Shore!" the Crown screeched behind her. She blocked out the distraction, trying to see how to manipulate herself, her mother, even Dawes.

Shit. I reckon I can change how this turns out. THAT'S why the Crown is so scared of me.

I can stop this all from happening.

She shouted at herself. Tricked an old lady into tripping over, hoping to lure people away from the shelter, but everyone returned back to their assigned places in the vision. She felt the shift that meant the Crown was about to teleport her somewhere stupid, and focused her attention, tried to untangle it like a video game puzzle.

"You stupid bloody girl!" she shouted at her teen self. "You keep making dumb decisions! Why can't you do it the right way!"

She leaned into the vision, yelling, pushing her face as far forward as she could.

The dream-mirror stretched impossibly thin.

She was pushing through the flat image, sliding through that membrane, and for a long moment she was stuck between Purgatory and Earth, present and past, self and past-self, and felt herself pulled in twice as many directions.

Absolute agony. She was about to break apart. Her head was the big bang, a hangover never-ending, every nerve ending dipped into a star and left there to send a pain signal thousands of light years back to her.

Then, a great lurch. Everything stopped.

She opened her eyes to see Gravesend, but this wasn't a vision. She wasn't in the Mirrorworld. She really stood on the side of the road, holding a five-pound note, looking at her dead mother in the flesh. She was twelve years old again, wearing her school uniform.

"Holy shit," she said.

"Tamsyn Lottie Webb, you watch your tongue!" her mother said, giving her the stink-eye. She began to move over to the bus-shelter.

"No! You can't go there!" Tamsyn screamed. She hauled on her mum's hand, trying to stop her from moving, but she didn't have the muscle she'd earned from hauling on her bow, the bulk she'd grown into as a young woman. She was forty kilos of nothing much.

"What has gotten into you today?" Jenny Webb shouted. She snatched her hand away, and walked over to the bus shelter.

Tamsyn slid forward, tangling her schoolbag in between her mum's legs. Jenny Webb got caught up in the straps and fell forward, hitting the pavement hard.

"I should tan your bloody hide, girl!" she shouted, but Tamsyn was already running past her, screaming and waving her arms.

"You've got to get out of here!" she screamed at the grannies, the office workers, the other school kids, everyone who was about to become mush. They looked at her as if she was a crazy person, and went back to their phones.

"There's a bomb in the bus shelter!" she yelled, genuine fear in her voice. "You have to run!"

That did it. Everyone ran away, even the most skeptical looking caught up in the rush. The bus shelter was emptied in seconds, everyone keeping a clear distance.

"Just wait till I tell your father-" her mother began, and at that moment Simon Dawes came around the corner in his estate wagon, drunk out of his mind, and ploughed right through the bus shelter which had been packed with people moments earlier.

Tamsyn confidently stepped forward, and helped Simon out of the car. She then promptly kneed him in the balls.

Her mother looked at her in shock, as did everyone whose lives she'd just saved. She heard the questions, the cries of disbelief and confusion, and ignored all of it, seizing her mother in the fiercest of all embraces. Someone took out their phone and took a photo, the one that would end up on the news. The one that would soon take be pinned to the Webb's fridge, in their house in Gravesend.

The article was titled "THE GIRL WHO KNEW."

Tamsyn had travelled back through time.

She had just under four years to save the world.

THE END

COMING SOON

Tamsyn will return in
THE TAMSYN WEBB CHRONICLES #3
DEAD LAST

Read on for an excerpt from the sequel:

EXCERPT FROM THE TAMSYN WEBB CHRONICLES #3 - DEAD LAST

Tamsyn Webb sat in a dressing room at the BBC with her Mum and Dad. She looked through the mirror with a thousand-yard stare as her mother wrestled a hairbrush through her locks, unhappy with the job that the hair and makeup people had done.

Tamsyn Webb had lived a life before this.

She'd been in a war, had grown to live and love and lose and have a baby boy. She'd seen the world ground to extinction under millions of rotted feet.

She'd died once, throat crushed, blood gushing out of her.

She'd gone to hell. Literally to Hell.

Then she'd found a way back through time. To the point of her mother's death. She'd prevented it, changed the course of history.

There were many moments where she regretted this.

"You are a twelve-year-old girl," Jenny Webb said, now scrubbing her face with a wet cloth. "It is not appropriate to cake so much make-up across your face."

Tamsyn had seen the life pass from her mother once. Jenny bled out in the tangle of a bus shelter, pinned beneath a drunk's car, amongst grandmothers and kids and office workers scattered like the wreckage of a rough Monopoly game.

"It's because of the stage lights, love," Mal Webb said. "Without it the cameras will just see a blank face."

Tamsyn had seen her father die on a beach, his blood mingling with the surf. Now he was picking through a tray of sandwiches and being his usual droll self.

"I'll never know why you agreed to this, Tam," Mal said. "The woman's a con artist."

I have my reasons, Dad, Tamsyn thought. *I'm a twenty-one-year-old woman stuck in the body of a twelve-year-old girl. The world fucking ENDS in four years' time!*

"I really think she knows things," Tamsyn managed through gritted teeth.

"Please. They've got microphones hidden in the foyer and the bathrooms," Mal said. "Plants in the audience. It's the oldest scam in showbiz, and these idiots are falling for it."

"God knows I wouldn't want to speak to anyone if I was dead," Jenny Webb said.

The dressing room was decked out with publicity photos of the TV show's host, Nicky Cross. Medium, psychic, Sussex's answer to John Edwards. Here she was hugging a grieving audience member, and another shot of her holding up a crystal ball.

"If it wasn't for the appearance fee, I'd never have agreed to you doing this," Jenny said.

"Mum, I've checked, and it's going to be enough for the Dexter Pro X," Tamsyn said. "And the arrows, and the club membership."

"You are not spending this money on a bow and arrow set," Jenny said. "It's going in your university fund, and that is final."

"It's not – it's not a kid's bow and arrow set," Tamsyn said, wincing at the force of the hairbrush her mother was yanking through her hair. "It's a proper competition shooter."

"Are you hearing this, Malcolm?"

"I sure am. It's the drumming lessons all over again."

"More like when she took up ballet. Two lessons, and we paid the full term for it, and lost the deposit."

"Mum! I'm not pissing around! I'm getting the Dexter Pro X!"

In that moment she had an edge in her voice, and the girl in the mirror looked back at her with older eyes. It was a command, given by someone who was used to being obeyed or listened to. She'd been a Captain once. Sat on the Privy Council. Whenever she ran into an obstacle or a difficult person, she always made a point to push back twice as hard.

"Language," was all that Jenny said after an awkward moment, pulling Tamsyn's hair back into a severe pony-tail.

This is some bullshit, Tamsyn thought. *I've got the voice of a kid. And my arms are weak. I won't have a draw strength worth a damn if I don't start practising at the range.*

Tamsyn was punishing herself every day, running, doing push-ups and sit-ups until she was physically sick. She needed to be able to draw that bow, and put an arrow through the Black Crown Boy. Henri. And if that didn't work, she'd need to be able to put arrows through zombie skulls.

She wasn't lazing around in front of the TV anymore, and studied like a demon. Tamsyn suffered through each day of primary school in a kind of slick horror. All of it, the pre-pubescent dramas of her school friends, the people and events she could barely remember, and she had to relive every godawful moment.

Always, she had that date in her mind. October 23, 2012. She needed to do this, right now. It was time to escalate her plan to save the world.

A knock on the dressing room door, and a "five minutes!" from some production lackey.

"Are you sure you want to do this?" Mal asked Tamsyn. "It's live TV. Whatever you say, they can't edit it out."

"It's okay," Tamsyn said. "I'm not nervous."

A lie. She wasn't just nervous, she was shitting bricks.

"Make sure you watch that potty mouth of yours out there," Jenny said. "Your grandmother and the ladies from my work are watching this."

"Have you got your notes?" Mal asked. Tamsyn nodded.

"If you get lost, just look at the index card. Your topics are on there. Move onto the next one if you get stuck."

"Thanks, Dad," she said, and meant it. Having her father alive and next to her made the insanity of the time jump just a little bearable. Malcolm Webb was reliable, brilliant, warm and kind. In the months following the incident at the bus shelter, he'd been her rock.

Her mother, on the other hand, was doing her best to drive her nuts.

"Remember to sit up straight, and don't do that weird thing with your eyebrows," Jenny said. "You will use your pleases and thankyous, and you will answer all of Miss Cross's questions."

"Mum, I'm not an idiot."

"You will speak clearly and enunciate your words. We all remember the time you mumbled your way through the school play. Your grandmother couldn't understand a word of what you said."

"She's deaf as a post. I doubt her hearing aids even work properly."

"I agree," Malcolm said. "She stood there grinning like an idiot at your Dad's funeral. Fifty well-wishers standing in line, and she didn't hear a word."

"Malcolm! You're not helping!"

An eternity of fussing and her parents bickering, and then that blessed knock on the door that meant that it was time, that she could finally go on the air and say her piece. She'd been through too much to blow this moment, and resented her mother throwing her off her focus.

She followed some berk with a clipboard past the backs of the sound stages, following what felt like miles of cable through a twisting corridor. No windows this deep into the building, and Tamsyn's claustrophobia kicked in just a little. For a moment she felt like she was back on the submarine, her baby under her arm, fleeing destruction in the crushing depths of the ocean...

Tamsyn had to remind herself that the deadly submarine ride hadn't happened yet, would hopefully never happen. Young Mal might never be born. Going on a psychic's TV show was simply the latest strangeness in her strange life.

In fact, she didn't care much about the TV show itself. She'd agreed to the whole thing just so she could get close to Nicky Cross. Ask her questions.

Ever since Tamsyn had stepped back into her twelve-year old skin, her supernatural abilities had vanished. When she was the last Guide left, it felt like she could reach out to souls for miles, see the auras around the living, all sorts of superhero nonsense.

Tamsyn's goldfish died last week, and she hadn't felt a single thing.

"Excuse me," she said, tapping the production assistant on the shoulder. "Can I speak to Miss Cross before we go in front of the cameras?"

"Sorry, Nicky meditates in her dressing room until it's go-time," the frazzled looking man said. "Not worth my job to knock on that door."

She froze up then, frustration and stage-fright gripping her guts.

"No. I need to speak to her. I need to see Nicky Cross!"

"Sorry love, it's not going to happen," the man said, waving them on and into the green room. The look on his face told her that he'd had this conversation hundreds of times.

The old Tamsyn might have broken his nose and legged it. She'd have dodged around the security officers, kicked in Nicky's door, and forced her to have a tense conversation at bow-point. After years of brutal survival and daily terror, Tamsyn was probably the only person in history to have post-traumatic stress before the trauma.

She quivered, tense from head to toe, adrenaline jangling through her system. She was shifting over from fight to flight.

"You'll be okay, sweetheart," Jenny whispered in her ear. "Be my strong girl."

"Thanks mum," Tamsyn said. For all that her mum could be a manipulative and controlling bitch, she had these moments of love and kindness. Dad rested a hand on her shoulder and squeezed, and then the panic faded.

Despite everything, she had her mum and dad back.

Then someone said her name. Leaving her parents behind, she walked through a foggy tunnel of hyperhyperfocusfocus on legs that weren't her own, blinking up at the bright lights. She spotted one of the production monitors on the way through, complete with a big banner across the screen. This read "THE GIRL WHO KNEW!"

She stepped in front of the TV cameras, and just like that, Tamsyn Webb stood in front of an audience of millions.

She'd seen this TV stage before, many times. The kitschy furnishings, leather sofas, and a new-age explosion of crystals, dreamcatchers, banks of flickering candles, the works.

In the Webb house they had a love-hate relationship with watching *The Beyond with Nicky Cross*. Jenny Webb was fascinated with England's answer to John Edwards, and spent Tuesday evenings half-convinced that Nicky Cross was the real deal. Mal Webb, ever the sceptic, scoffed at every "revelation". Tamsyn's parents kept this rolling argument going every week, but they both enjoyed the friendly ribbing.

As always, the audience was sat in bleachers set upon the edge of the stage itself. Just like on *Crossing Over*, the audience was the actual show here.

Rising from an ornate gothic throne, Nicky Cross led the audience in a round of applause as Tamsyn squirmed in front of the cameras. *God, I really need to go to the loo,* Tamsyn thought. What with her mother badgering her over every damn thing, she'd forgotten to go.

Nicky Cross, clairvoyant, psychic to the stars, was a bookkeeper's daughter from Sussex who'd found TV fame, and she hammed it up to the hilt with crystal balls and smoke machines. The act was part of what made her so confusing – she looked like she was taking the mickey, but damn if she didn't get things right more often than not.

"Here she is, ladies and gents! Tamsyn Webb, The Girl Who Knew! Twelve years old, and she had a premonition of disaster! She cleared a packed bus-stop, moments before a drunk driver ploughed into it."

Tamsyn opened her mouth, but everything she'd practiced saying refused to fall out. She froze in place.

Oh god. Don't pee yourself in front of Britain.

"It's okay dearie, we're all friends here," Nicky cooed, swanning over and putting an arm around her. "It's just you, me, the audience, and a few dozen ghosts."

Laughter from the audience. The TV psychic steered her towards the interview corner, a pair of towering leather armchairs in front of a fake fire. Tamsyn had seen everyone sitting in this chair from David Icke to Lily Allen.

"Just relax, you're doing fine," Nicky whispered, and Tamsyn felt the wave of panic subside. This close she could see the same high cheekbones and angular jaw that Tilly would someday share. The same girl who would be murdered by a possessed Prince Harry.

God, this is so weird.

She felt a warm glow in the woman's presence, and just for a split second, she could see the colour green, deep and warm all around her. An aura! For the first time in months, Tamsyn had evidence of the supernatural, right in front of her.

Nicky Webb was performing the Bliss on her, just like those bastards were making Tilly do in Manchester. It was just a little taste, but enough to erase her stage fright.

Tamsyn wanted to ask her a thousand questions, away from the cameras. How could she wake up the powers she knew she would have one day? How many Guides were in Britain, right now? How could they get a head start on preventing the zombie apocalypse?

How on earth would they be able to stop the Crown of Countless Suns?

"I tell you what, Tamsyn, it's a real pleasure to meet another psychic. Oh yes, my friends, I can see The Sight all over this one. In fact," and here she raised a hand on high, eyes to the ceiling, "I predict you will have your own psychic TV show one day. I can see the day, when the network says to me 'oh Nicky, you wrinkly old git, we've replaced you with someone who's younger than a hundred.'"

More laughter.

"I'm fine with it, though I'm damned if I'm gonna show my legs to get more ratings. Now Tamsyn, let's talk about that fateful day. You were walking to the bus-stop with your Mum, right?"

Tamsyn nodded. She'd rehearsed a ridiculous story about having a premonition, though it was nothing of the sort. She'd simply been through the moment before, travelled back in time, and had something like thirty seconds to prevent the worst day of her life.

"I – I had a feeling–"

She paused, hating herself for spinning an airy lie in front of the nation. *All I want to do is talk to this woman. Alone.*

"I get that too darling, but it's mostly wind." Laughter. "Just joking love. So, the buses were running late that day. There were three busloads of passengers waiting at the stop. A light drizzle, so people were packed into the shelter."

Tamsyn nodded, working up the courage to tell her nonsense story. She was not making good television. Nicky gazed over at one of the producers off camera, who was making some sort of frantic gesture.

Once more, the Bliss fell upon her, washing away the edge of her nerves – but Nicky's secret gift wasn't doing all that it could. Perhaps Tamsyn was a little immune to the effect now?

"It's okay, ladies and gents. I remember being twelve once. She's probably daydreaming about Justin Timberlake or something. You know, Tamsyn, we had him on last year, lovely boy. Sat right in that chair. I should charge young girls to sit in it."

Laughter. The last of the supernatural effect fell away, and the Bliss gave way to Tamsyn's usual default. Hackles up. Feeling threatened. Fighting back. Even still, she'd learnt a bit more patience as an adult, a calm she could call upon when dealing with the bastards in the Privy Council. Tamsyn had one moment of control, but then she felt a distant twinge of frustration as her teenage mood seized the wheel.

Bugger it all. It was time to drop some truth bombs.

"I can tell you what Justin Timberlake does. In the future."

A little ripple of laughter from the audience. Nicky raised an eyebrow.

"He dies sometime after October 23rd, 2012."

"That's – that's a bit dark, love," Nicky said. "We're light entertainment, even when our visiting ghosts like to pass on their love from the Beyond. You know, fixing problems with inheritances, giving relief to loved ones. Now, let's get back to the bus stop, and-"

"Most of you will die in 2012. Or you won't, and you'll wish you had."

Tamsyn was on her feet now, stalking around the stage, looking up at the audience. Some of them were chuckling at her, but more than a few were looking concerned. One of the producers was making the *cut to commercial* gesture but Nicky waved him off.

"What – what are you talking about, dear?"

"Zombies."

That did it. The audience erupted into howls of laughter. Fists bunched, Tamsyn wheeled directly to the camera, trying to pass on as much information as possible before they cut her off. In the wings, she could see the thunderous look on her parent's faces, and pressed on regardless. She would definitely hear about this, at length.

"There is a zombie apocalypse coming," she pressed on, deadly earnest. "It starts in France, and 95% of the world's population gets murdered by the walking dead. In my hometown of Gravesend, we lasted a little bit longer. Big walls around the town to keep out the undead. Still, everyone died. And it was my fault."

"Tamsyn, I'm not sure you're seeing things how they will really be," Nicky said, a little concerned. "Might have just been a nightmare, love."

"The nightmare is that I have already lived through the whole thing," Tamsyn said. "The reason I knew about the bus-station? The last time I was there, I didn't warn everyone. They all died. My mum, the nice old ladies, school kids. I stood there and watched Simon Dawes murder my mum with a car."

"The – the last time you were there?"

"Look, you're not getting the message. None of you are. You need to prepare. If you're not ready, you will die and so will your families. You will need food. Water. Weapons. Fortifications, if you can make them."

Off-stage, the producer was no longer trying to wrap this up. On the contrary, he was beaming. No doubt the ratings were going through the roof as the crazy twelve-year-old girl shared her bat-shit story.

Nicky was looking at her now, eyes narrowed. Someone

was messing around with her show, and she was clearly losing patience.

"Love, we had David Icke on a while ago. He told us all about the lizard people running a secret world government. Zombies? Maybe next week we'll get vampires or something."

The audience were rolling in the aisles.

"Miss Cross, soon you will have a baby," Tamsyn said. "I've done the maths, you're probably pregnant right now."

Nicky's eyes flew wide open for a second. Tamsyn knew she'd hit the mark. The woman was pregnant, she knew it, and she hadn't told a soul yet.

Hooting, whistling from the audience. This was now at a Jerry Springer level of trash television, and they were loving it.

"That is ridiculous, I–"

"Her name will be Tilly, and she will share your gift. Your real gift, not this over-the-top nonsense. She will have autism, selective mutism, and amazing supernatural powers. I also saw her die, right in front of me."

Nicky was on her feet now, white in the face and shaking.

"Shut up. Just shut up. How dare you come on here and say things like this?"

"I don't mean to upset you. But you do need to listen."

"You need to leave. Terry? Terry, take her off my set."

Some commotion in Nicky's earpiece, and she scowled offstage. *We've got great ratings with this bit,* or something similar. Tamsyn would get to say her piece.

"I know I sound like a nutter. But this is real, and it's coming. The governments of the world need to get in front of this thing. Have a plan to contain the outbreak."

The audience were in hysterics at this point.

"Contain France, the moment the reports go out. Please. If you don't, the world ends. It's as simple as that."

"Tamsyn, I've heard a lot of bullshit in my time, but this takes the cake," Nicky said, furious. "You are mentally ill, and you're wasting our time today."

"I am," Tamsyn said. "I'm losing my fucking mind. But I am telling you God's honest truth. This needs to get out."

No doubt someone in the booth was scrambling for the censorship bleeper but the camera crew were rapt. This was ratings gold.

"Here's the truth, all of it. My hometown of Gravesend is overrun by the undead. My father is murdered on the beach at the Isle of Sheppey. We fix a boat, and my mother's murderer captains us across to Corpus Christi, on the strength of a radio signal."

"Right. And I suppose I die too?" Nicky scoffed.

"You don't. You live, and Tilly lives. You'll be invited to cut the ribbon at One Angel Square, Manchester. Fancy building. You live for a few years there, and then you get killed doing something stupid and brave. I didn't meet you, but I met Tilly."

"Righto. I've never heard such guff. So you run from Gravesend to Manchester, dodging zombies?"

"Nope. I go to America. I get caught up in a civil war between the Republic of Texas and what's left of the United States, hiding out in Hawaii. President Palin was killed in the early days, and Vice-President Wycliffe is in charge."

"Palin? That nutter of a woman? Now I know you're making this all up."

"I – I am trying to tell you the truth!" Tamsyn yelled, close to tears, all bravado washed away by sheer mental exhaustion. "I was a Captain in the army. I did something terrible. Many, many people died, and it was all my fault.

Then I went to Cuba. I had a baby there. Little Malcolm, named after my Dad."

Over in the wings, Mal was staring at her, transfixed. Jenny was hopping mad, and Tamsyn could make out her mum's screeching even over the audience.

"The baby's father was killed by the Communist party, who weaponised the undead. I escaped on a boat, and found the Royal Navy, hiding out in the Caymans. I served on the Privy Council. Then, the Americans found us, and bombed the island. We escaped in the subs, and headed back to England."

"You should write this book," Nicky said. "Great bit of fiction, this. You could be the next J.K. Rowling."

Everyone was laughing now, even the crew. Tamsyn was seething, and wanted to hurt someone. She was beyond all caution now, spilling truth like a Cassandra with a jittery cup of tea.

"This is going to happen! I don't care if you think I'm mad. I stopped my mum from dying, and I'm going to do my best to stop this too. But if I fail, please, please block the channel Tunnel. If one biter gets through, you arseholes are all going to die."

"Please, tell me what happens next in your little story," Nicky said. "Do you fly a plane in it? Is there a car chase? Do you meet any aliens?"

"Oh my god. You are the dumbest bitch alive," Tamsyn said. "Just slip into your Sight and check my aura. I am telling you the truth."

Nicky stopped at that, and she did seem to stare at Tamsyn intently.

"I am a Guide, just like you. But I lost my powers when I came back. I can't do the aura thing anymore. I need your help, to relearn my powers. Oh, shut the hell up!" Tamsyn yelled at the jeering from the audience.

This conversation would have gone much smoother in her dressing room. Goddamnit!

"Suppose you are telling the truth tonight," Nicky said cautiously. "The Girl Who Knew. Not just a prang at a bus-stop, but a vision of the end of the world. This is some real Sarah Connor stuff, so forgive me for taking it with a pinch of salt."

"Salt. That's the thing I need to say. Salt is a secret weapon against zombies. Seriously, keep a super soaker in your home, and fill it with salt water. It could save your life."

"Alright, I think we've had just enough of this nonsense. Your story just doesn't add up, love. You saw this stuff, all when you saved your Mum?"

"No. You're not listening to me. I didn't see this stuff. I lived it. I grew into a 21-year-old woman with a baby. I've come back in time."

Mal was shaking his head now. A security guard was physically preventing Jenny Webb from storming on stage and hauling her off by the ears.

"Ooh, Sarah Connor all right. So how did you do it? Time machine?"

"No. I died. I died, and went to Hell. There was a way to come back and save my mum, and I took it."

"Right," Nicky said drily. "I think I know a bit more about dead people than you do. You are just making a fool of yourself on live TV."

"I died!" Tamsyn screamed, now bawling her eyes out. "I really did! I know it sounds mad, but you've got to believe me!"

"Alright then, how did you die?" Nicky asked.

"Prince Harry tore my throat out! With his teeth!"

Tamsyn blurted out, regretting the words the moment they fell out of her mouth.

It was in that moment that a thousand memes were born.

THE ADVENTURE CONTINUES IN "THE TAMSYN WEBB CHRONICLES #3 – DEAD LAST".

ABOUT THE AUTHOR

Jason Fischer is a writer who lives near Adelaide, South Australia. He has won the Colin Thiele Literature Scholarship, an Aurealis Award and the Writers of the Future Contest. In Jason's jack-of-all-trades writing career he has worked on comics, apps, television, short stories, novellas and novels. Jason also facilitates writing workshops, is an enthusiastic mentor, and loves anything to do with the written or spoken word. He is also the founder and CEO of Spectrum Writing, a service that teaches professional writing skills to people on the Autism Spectrum.

Jason plays a LOT of Dungeons and Dragons, has a passion for godawful puns, and is known to sing karaoke until the small hours.

OTHER BOOKS BY JASON FISCHER

Everything is a Graveyard, Ticonderoga Publications
Quiver (Tamsyn Webb Chronicles #1), Argonautica Press

ACKNOWLEDGMENTS

It's a beautiful moment, resurrecting my zombie novel and now adding this long-overdue sequel. This time around, huge thanks go to my Argonautica co-captain, Jason Franks. This would not be here without you, and you're the true champion of all things Tamsyn. Your insights and eagle-eye for edits are the stuff of legend in our small venture, and as you typeset this I imagine you are in some epic room, smashing my manuscript on an anvil with a big molten hammer while screaming heavy metal vocals. You bloody legend.

Next up I have a special thanks to my writing students over the past few years, both in my work for Writers SA and now at Spectrum Writing, my new service that helps writers with autism. You all inspire me to do my best, and when I put my own lessons to work I often have you folks in mind. Several of my writing students have been Tuckerised (meaning their names have been stolen and tacked onto minor characters throughout this book), a meagre honour but the best I can do. I hope you enjoy your namesakes, especially the ones who died horrific deaths!

To Logan and Lottie, I see your love for stories and the fun in your eyes when you play your adventures and games together. The apple does not fall far from the tree! You kids are awesome and you make your Dad proud.

Finally, as always, a huge thanks to my wife Kate, who always backs me to the hilt when it comes to this crazy creative life. I love you to the moon and back, and I thank you for giving me simply everything there is to give a person.

Printed by Libri Plureos GmbH in Hamburg, Germany